YOUNG AMES

YOUNG AMES

WALTER D. EDMONDS

THE REPRINT SOCIETY
LONDON

FIRST PUBLISHED, SEPTEMBER 1942
THIS EDITION PUBLISHED BY THE REPRINT SOCIETY LTD.
BY ARRANGEMENT WITH WM. COLLINS SONS AND CO. LTD.
1943

TO

M. E. E. AND J. B. E.

PRINTED IN GREAT BRITAIN
BY COLLINS CLEAR-TYPE PRESS : LONDON AND GLASGOW

ACKNOWLEDGMENT

Young Ames lays no claim to historical value of any sort, and the following acknowledgment is not intended to convey that impression. But when the fictioneer picks the carefully gathered findings from the books of better scholars, he ought in my opinion to admit it. In this case I shall say at once that young Ames would not have continued his career without the fortunate contemporaneous publication of Robert Greenhalgh Albion's two books on New York City's maritime commerce : *Square Riggers on Schedule* and *The Rise of New York Port*. And I should like here to recommend any one who becomes interested in the youthful city through its young Ames to read both books forthwith. Not only are their pages packed with information invaluable to the professional scrivener, but the incidents are so colourfully set down that he must guard, in feeding on them, lest they reappear in his own fictional version. And when I had finished the books, I made thorough use of their bibliographies.

Almost equally enticing are the three volumes of *The Old Merchants of New York*, 1862, by " Walter Barrett, Clerk," whose real name was J. A. Scoville. Here is a fabulous grab bag of a book that seems to become accurate in its very inaccuracies and to turn the chicaneries of business into the proud devices of honest enterprise. Scoville's pages were the source of Chevalier's corner of the cotton market, of young Ames's deal in rice, and of various bits of lore and history whose authenticity I am entirely unprepared to defend.

For the other necessary books, like Hone's *Diary*, I shall return the reader to Mr. Albion's bibliography for information and comment. But of course the greatest and best contemporary sources are always and will always be (until they are able to bird's-eye the radio beams) the newspapers of the day and place, and these were made available to me in the Baker Memorial Library of the Harvard Business School through the kindness of Dr. Arthur H. Cole.

W. D. E.

CONTENTS

YOUNG AMES

YOUNG AMES was listed as a junior clerk on the payroll of the famous commercial house of Chevalier, Deming & Post. The first time Mr. McVitty, the chief clerk, had put down his name in the counting-room ledger was under November, 1833.

" Wanted—a boy."

On his first day in New York, young Ames had seen the card tacked to the door of Number 42 South Street, and read it, carpet-bag in hand, while the raw wind off the East River ruffled his sandy hair. He hailed the first passer-by.

" Mister, can you tell me what kind of a house this is ? "

" It's Chevalier, Deming & Post." The passer-by was a prosperous-looking man. " They're a well-known commercial house. In fact," he added, " they are probably the second most important in the city."

Young Ames thanked him and entered. He went up a long flight of stairs to the counting-room and, asking for the chief clerk, was directed to Mr. McVitty.

He looked up at the gaunt grey face and the dim black frock-coat of the old man on his high stool.

" I saw that card on the door," he explained.

"And what made you decide to come in ? " Mr. McVitty helped himself to snuff and inhaled cavernously, but no visible reaction took place in his big nose.

" A gentleman told me it was the second-best commercial house in the city," said young Ames. " The way he said it, I thought it might be the first."

" Did you ? " Mr. McVitty looked at the freckled face and blue eyes with sudden interest. " How old are you ? "

9

"Eighteen," said young Ames without a quiver.

"What's your name?"

"John Ames."

"Where's your home?"

"I came from Rensselaer County," said young Ames.

"Did you run away?"

"I came down on the boat, sir."

"Humph," said Mr. McVitty. He looked at the country tweed jacket, short in the sleeves, threadbare at the elbows. "You're no use to me if you're going to be taken up on apprentice papers."

"I won't be," said young Ames. He grinned impudently.

"Humph," said Mr. McVitty, for the second time. "Can you write and cipher?"

"Yes, sir."

"Get up at my desk and write me a line. Write me this: 'Seest thou a man that is hasty in his words? There is more hope of a fool than of him.'"

Young Ames went up on the stool like a monkey and wrote with a rapid hand.

"It's legible, at least," said Mr. McVitty, taking the paper. "I'll take you in to one of the partners. Mr. Post's not in but Mr. Deming will do. Come along."

He knocked on a door and entered as if he disbelieved in the formality of knocking. "This is young Ames," he announced. "He is looking for work with us."

Mr. Deming looked up from putting coal on the stove. "Let him see if he can make this damn' thing draw," he said and watched young Ames take a poker and lift a nest of clinkers from the grate. It was only a minute before the draught caught hold.

"Any letters?" asked Mr. Deming.

"No," said Mr. McVitty.

"Relations?"

"Have you?" said Mr. McVitty to young Ames.

"The fire's drawing, sir," said young Ames. He found the two men looking at him with disapproval.

"My people won't bother me," he conceded, after a moment, "if that's what you're driving at."

"Does he write?" asked Mr. Deming, and took the paper Mr. McVitty extended. An expression of impatience came over his face. "I wish you could think of another proverb once in a while, McVitty."

"'A servant will not be corrected by words : for though he understand, he will not answer,'" said Mr. McVitty.

Quick as lightning Mr. Deming turned on him.

"'He that, being often reproved, hardeneth his neck, shall suddenly be destroyed, and that without remedy,' McVitty."

Mr. Deming burst out laughing. Mr. McVitty looked disgusted. Young Ames moved his sharp blue eyes from one to the other and kept a blank face. He checked the draught on the stove a little and Mr. Deming moved close to the warmth and lifted his coat-tails with satisfaction.

"He's all right as far as I'm concerned, McVitty. Take him out and suit yourself."

Mr. McVitty took young Ames out of the office, shutting the door with a nice compromise between a firm closing and a defiant slam. He frowned down at young Ames.

"A junior partner must have his joke, supposedly. But a junior clerk does not enjoy the privilege, you'll understand, Ames."

"Yes, sir."

"Then you're hired. Seventy-five dollars a year and there's a room and bed in the top of this house. You'll feed yourself."

"Yes, sir."

2

He had to sweep and dust the counting-room every morning before five-thirty, when Mr. McVitty arrived on the minute of his bulging tortoise-shell watch. He had to have the fires drawing in the stoves of the partners' offices and see that the inkwells were full, sand was in the boxes, and water boiling in the kettle in the counting-room so Mr. McVitty could sip a cup of it as he made the rounds of his matutinal inspection. The rest of the day he made himself useful performing errands outside for Mr. McVitty, carrying letters for the partners, learning his way round the city, and running on and off boats until he knew every ship in the East River docks, the name of her master, and often of her mate. He was expected to pick up useful knowledge of shipments of other companies and to give no information about his own.

Mr. McVitty was a relentless taskmaster. What little copying young Ames was given to do, like insignificant notices of a private view of a new shipment before it was put up for public auction, had to be correct to the last comma. Mr. McVitty would permit no erasures, no blots. " As long as I'm chief clerk, no paper that isn't perfect goes out of this house—unless the clerk that's responsible goes with it," and he would crumple the offending sheet and hurl it at the nearest basket. Or he would jab his long finger at a sentence and cry out, " If there's one thing worse than not having a decent complement of commas in a sentence, it's having too many. Look there and there ! You've been sticking them in like flowers in a charwoman's hat ! "

Even the junior clerks who ranked him found chores for him in the few minutes a day when Mr. McVitty was not running the legs off him. But he was full of ambition and he seemed to have a wiry indestructible strength. His out-grown country tweeds soon became a familiar sight along the waterfront, in and out of shipping houses and dockside saloons. Men seeing him run past would say, " That's young Ames of Chevalier, Deming & Post. I wonder what's on *their* cards." The first time he overheard that remark, young Ames managed to put additional import-ance into his passage along the street.

He carried it even into the counting-room. They would hear his thick-soled brogues lolloping up the stairs and the whole force would stop and turn on their stools, and maybe even Mr. Post or Mr. Deming would stick a head through his door. Young Ames would come pounding in, breathing hard, run straight to Mr. McVitty's desk, and drop a ten-cent package of shot beside the ledger. " Here is the shot for your pens," he would say. And Mr. McVitty would publicly curse him with Scotch economical pro-fanity.

But then it was young Ames who noticed the telegraph working one windless afternoon when he was coming back through Hanover Square, and he saw another young man staring aloft at the black and white barrels sliding up and down on the semaphore and remembered that he had seen him before going in and out of the Exchange building.

Young Ames dropped into conversation with the young man and said : " What is that ? " like a country boy.

" The telegraph," said the young man with a glance at Ames's frayed tweed jacket. " It's a way of sending messages."

" You mean it makes words ? " said young Ames, letting his jaw hang and showing his gums.

" Of course it does."

" Oh, you're pulling my shirt," said Ames. " Nobody could read words out of them barrels. I'd bet any man a shilling."

The young man plopped like a peeled potato. " I'll bet you. Here's the message. But it won't do you any good," he added, with another scornful glance. " They're veri-fying a message from the Staten Island Station. The

Oxford's in off Staten Island and reports sighting the *Grosvenor* two days out with a broken mast."

" My God," said young Ames, making himself appear so awestruck that the other's breast swelled visibly, " what people are those ? "

" They're ships," said the young man, taking the shilling complacently. He didn't even bother to look after young Ames.

But young Ames knew that the *Grosvenor*, which was one of the Pruyn & Co. ships, was so long overdue from Belfast, that she was supposed to have been lost at sea ; and he went pounding down Old Slip and round the corner to Number 42 as if three dogs were chasing a cat in the seat of his breeches, and clashed up the stairs, and yelled the length of the counting-room to Mr. McVitty to take him to Mr. Post or Mr. Deming or even Mr. Chevalier.

" Are you crazy ? " Mr. McVitty shouted him down. " Making such bedlam. Besides, they're in conference."

" I've got to see them." Young Ames was panting and crimson with excitement. He went to Mr. McVitty's desk and snatched a pen and scribbled on a loose piece of paper the word *Grosvenor*. Mr. McVitty stared at it while intelligence slowly dawned in his eyes. Then he came down off his stool with a kind of hop that fluttered the skirts of his dim black coat, crumpled the paper, and put it in his pocket. " Aye," he said. " Come on."

That was the first time, though he had been working for the house for two months, nearly, that young Ames exchanged a word with the senior partner. He wasn't at all embarrassed.

Mr. Chevalier had staring, blue, imperious eyes and they examined young Ames with chilled distaste. His voice was short and hard as he demanded of Mr. McVitty the cause of this disgraceful disturbance.

" The lad's picked up something," said Mr. McVitty.
" Who is he ? "

Mr. Deming grinned. " It's young Ames," he said. " He's the most junior, junior clerk so to speak."

Mr. McVitty cleared his throat with unction. He had a dignified, deliberate manner of address that he reserved for Mr. Chevalier. But young Ames did not wait for him to retail the news. He told it himself in a few words. " It's that bid of Mr. Wandell's for our linen I was thinking about, sir," he finished. " The price will go down when the news is out, won't it ? "

" He's right," said Mr. McVitty, unnecessarily.

The partners exchanged glances and Mr. Post said : " If it's true, there's not a moment to lose or LeRoy's will undersell us."

Mr. Chevalier stared hard at young Ames, but he couldn't put him down.

" If it's true," he agreed.

Mr. Deming said : " We can't verify it. If we try, the whole thing will be over the city before it's posted."

" Yes," said Mr. Chevalier. " We've got to believe it." He looked at young Ames again for a moment. " Post," he said, " take a hackney coach. But get out at Madison and walk the rest of the way. If old Wandell saw you coming in a coach, he'd be wise in a minute."

Mr. Post went out at once. Mr. Deming said : " Well, I might as well get back to my desk." Mr. McVitty made a signal to young Ames, but Mr. Chevalier said : " Leave young Ames here, McVitty. Send someone up to the Exchange to wait for the bulletin."

3

After Mr. McVitty had noiselessly closed the door, Mr. Chevalier without saying a word stared for some time at young Ames. Then he asked : " How long have you been working here ? "

"Since the first week in November, sir." If young Ames felt nervous, he didn't show it.

"It's not very long," observed Mr. Chevalier. "But you seem to have made yourself pretty familiar with the business."

"Oh, everybody knows about that dicker with old Wandell," said young Ames. "I'd been wondering whether he'd close or hold off for the *Grosvenor*. If she was lost he'd lose money."

Mr. Chevalier made no comment for a moment. Then he said : "I suppose 'everybody' means you."

He tapped the Dominican mahogany of the table top. The polished surface reflected his fingers and the yellow of his madras waistcoat. He sat upright, his blue coat beautifully fitted, his black tie unmussed. Behind him, in the pale sky beyond the window, the tops of the masts of docked ships were like gleaming needles. Suddenly a flock of pigeons went by on a level, blue-and-white flutter of wings that was faintly audible through the glass. A moment after they had gone, a low-flying gull swung by so close that young Ames made out his round eyes staring in at Mr. Chevalier's back. He brought a sense of outer cold strikingly at variance with the warmth of the room.

Mr. Chevalier broke the silence.

"I suppose you realise that we stand to lose several hundred dollars if your information is incorrect."

"Yes, sir. But there's no mistake, so we'll save some, won't we ? "

Mr. Chevalier tapped again. "Have you considered the fact that this fellow may have been manufacturing information for your benefit ? "

Young Ames wasn't shaken. He even laughed. "Oh, no," he said. "That lad took me for a country cousin. He was so anxious to show off he didn't have time to think of anything but the truth."

"You seem pretty sure of yourself for a young man."

"Well, you have to be in this business, sir. You couldn't

live with old McVitty if you weren't. He's always barking
as it is."

"Mr. McVitty's been with this firm for forty years,"
Mr. Chevalier said bitingly. But he couldn't discourage
young Ames.

"Well, when you start at the bottom like me, you have
to be pretty sure of things if you're going to get ahead."

Mr. Chevalier gave a thin smile.

"Ah, you expect to continue in the business ? "

"Naturally," said young Ames. "I mean to make a
fortune."

"You won't find it too easy, perhaps," said Mr.
Chevalier.

"I'm not afraid of work," said young Ames, which was
true enough.

"There's more to it than being industrious," Mr.
Chevalier said dryly. "There's intelligence and integrity
and something you can only call instinct." He studied his
clerk's freckled face appraisingly, as if he hoped to find
one or more of the qualities he had named. "Where did
you live before you came to New York, Ames ? "

"Outside of Troy."

"We do some business with people in that city. Was
your father connected with any firm there ? "

"No, sir."

"What did he do ? " Mr. Chevalier asked quietly.

"My father was a minister. He wasn't interested in
money." The colour in young Ames's cheeks deepened
suddenly and his voice became defiant. "He didn't have
a church. Sometimes, when he had to, he got a job teaching
at Lansingburgh Academy ; but he was always in debt.
He wanted to write books, but nobody would publish them.
We lived with my aunt, who didn't have much money
either. My mother died when I was small. I don't remember her. My father died nearly two years ago. I quit
school and took a job long enough to pay his debts, and
then I got out of Troy. I haven't any brothers or sisters."

Mr. Chevalier seemed to ignore the manner in which young Ames delivered this information. His eyes remained cool and his voice was noncommittal as he said : " It doesn't offer much of a background for a mercantile career."

" Being poor sharpens your instinct for making money more than being rich, I guess," said young Ames. His cockiness seemed to have returned ; and Mr. Chevalier said shortly : " I hope your instinct hasn't misled you this time, or you'll have to begin your fortune somewhere else. We cannot afford people who make mistakes."

" That's just what I was driving at, sir." Young Ames cocked his head. " I think Cummings has come back."

" Cummings ? "

" The clerk McVitty sent to the Exchange, sir."

" How do you know ? "

" He wouldn't send Gibbs, and the others are working on the inventory," said young Ames. If he saw the hard look Mr. Chevalier gave him, he did not show any awareness of it.

Naturally it was Cummings. Mr. McVitty came in to report that young Ames's information was quite correct, and young Ames was sent back about his work. He was performing some unimportant chore for Mr. McVitty when Mr. Post returned three-quarters of an hour later with Mr. Wandell's signature to the bill of sale. He went into Mr. Chevalier's office and was instantly followed by Mr. Deming and Mr. McVitty. The latter poked out his head and gave a call for young Ames. Young Ames went in with a slight beating of the heart. He faced Mr. Chevalier with something that might have been modesty in his deportment.

Mr. Chevalier said : " Your information was correct, as you know. I had you called in to tell you that your information has saved the firm a very handsome sum of money. You have done very well. That is all, Ames."

Young Ames was red-faced when he returned to the counting-room. He didn't say anything but went to his desk and climbed up on his stool and threw his pen at the board wall. He didn't look round when one or two of the other clerks snickered. As Gibbs, who handled the translating for foreign correspondence, put it, he looked as if he had stopped almost long enough for two consecutive thoughts.

4

Gibbs was his best friend. A man of about forty, he had run through a small fortune and been forced to take what work he could get. Having a distant connection with Mr. Chevalier, he had secured a job as translator. He had a natural gift for languages and did his work competently, but he refused to do anything else, and if there was no translating sat on his stool and read novels. He seemed to have no ambition, unless it was to get a rise out of the chief clerk. " I've shot my bolt," he said, " the boss won't see me starve, so why kill myself working ? "

He had a deeply lined dark face, and he wore his hair rather long. His clothes were shabby, but their former elegance showed through. He roomed at the top of the house, the only other lodger besides young Ames. They had become friends. At least, Gibbs listened with amusement to young Ames's visions of his future greatness or his vehement opinions on the handling of the business, and to do him justice, Gibbs seldom made a thrust through the avenue-like openings in some of young Ames's most heated logic.

" I'll carry you along with me, Gibbs," young Ames would say. And Gibbs would answer : " As long as you carry me, I'm willing. How long do you think the process will take ? "

" Well, as I figure it," said young Ames, " I ought to be a junior partner in three years."

Leaning back on the jerky rockers, he would stare at the coal fire in the grate and listen to the wind off the East River whistling up the steep breast of the roof above them. Perhaps Gibbs, watching his freckled face and unruly sandy hair, had a dream or two of his own ; but if he did it lay in the past. That made them good companions, as if their trains of thought were always travelling towards each other.

" Here I put them in the way of saving four or five hundred dollars, and what do I get ? " young Ames demanded. " They tell me I've done well. ' That is all, Ames.' "

" Well, Johnny, you've got to remember you're a clerk to them. It's your business to work for the firm. Besides, what did you want ? "

" By God, he might have shaken hands with me," said young Ames. But he didn't stay down long. The next morning he was as bright as ever, as if he thought that with a night to think over what he had done for them, the partners might wake up to his actual worth. When Mr. Post sent for him, he went in cocky as a spring robin.

He found Mr. Post entertaining a staid gentleman of middle age. " This is Mr. Dickerman, a friend of Mr. Chevalier's, young Ames. He has a box to take on the Hoboken Ferry, and wants to get a porter for it. But naturally we couldn't hear of that, Mr. Dickerman. We'll have one of our clerks take it up. We can spare Ames easily for a couple of hours."

" You're very kind, Mr. Post."

" Not at all. Ames, take Mr. Dickerman's box to the Hoboken Ferry—Canal Street, I presume ?—at Canal Street, Ames. Mr. Dickerman will join you there at nine o'clock."

Young Ames felt savage as he lugged Mr. Dickerman's box. It didn't weigh much ; what irked him was the fact that they considered he could easily be spared. He felt even more savage an hour later as he stopped on the slip and watched the ferry pull away into the raw, grey-green water of the North River. The steam from its whistle hung like cotton wool in the cold December air. He was thinking of Mr. Dickerman's last words to him : " My thanks to Mr. Post, lad, and tell him I'm very much obliged for the trouble he has taken."

Walking back along Hudson Street he began to plan ways and means of getting rid of Mr. Post when he himself became a junior partner. He didn't suspect that he would always feel grateful to Mr. Post for sending him on this useless errand. For two blocks ahead, on the corner of Beach Street, young Ames fell in love.

He had chosen that route instead of following Canal Street to Broadway, because it would take him past one of the wealthiest neighbourhoods in the city, and more than once in the past he had come by St. John's Park to stare at the firm brick respectability of the house fronts on Laight Street, particularly that of Mr. Chevalier's house, which had become a symbol round which he hung his ambitions. But these, heretofore, had been connected entirely with business and money ; he had never included a girl in his self-portraiture. There had been no room for a second person, and he had no inkling of an idea that she was approaching him in the smart carriage behind the two greys.

He was passing under the high ornamental iron fence of St. John's Park that excluded all but the select possessors of keys, and the church clock was striking for half-past nine. A street musician unslung her hand organ on the corner ahead, and began to crank. The notes, emerging on the bright air, tentatively shaped a tune. It had a slight, sad little lilt that matched the grey ragged dress and threadbare shawl the woman wore. Two or three gentlemen on their way downtown passed her without a glance. Her eyes followed them under the shawl's fringe ; she did not beg ; but her hand, continuing its slow work of cranking, was more eloquent than any words she could have uttered.

It roused John's blood. He felt in his own pocket for a loose penny and let it clank in her cup. Only then did he observe that the carriage had stopped beside them. The door was opened and a young woman alighted to enter the corner house.

It might have been her quick step to the kerb that made young Ames pause, or the supple erect slender grace of her back, or the faint frosty perfume from her fur mantle. The brim of her cabriolet bonnet hid her face from him, but, thinking it must be young, he lingered a moment longer in the hope of seeing it. She put a piece of silver in the woman's cup and asked whether she had had any contributions that day. The woman made a motion towards the cup, where young Ames's penny lay beside the twenty-five-cent piece.

" I'm sorry." It was a girl's voice, fresh, inexperienced, impulsive. John's heart warmed at the sound of it.

As she turned away from the organ-grinder, a gentleman, crossing Beach Street, lifted his hat and started to pass. The girl looked after him. The colour rose in her cheeks, and young Ames saw that she was lovely.

Her face, framed in the flare of the bonnet brim, was oval. The beginning of a smooth part of black hair showed on her forehead, a good round forehead over strongly marked brows and dark eyes. She had a wide mouth, almost too wide, and her lips were parted slightly by a quick intake of her breath as she lifted her chin from its nest of blue ribbons. For the space of an instant the tune stopped and the street was still but for the retreating footsteps of the gentleman. Then the notes recommenced under the woman's mechanical cranking, and suddenly the girl joined her voice to the tune.

She sang, bright-faced, defiant, her fresh clear voice transforming the lilt to make it gay and tender. The unexpectedness of it, taking even young Ames, who had been watching her, by sharp surprise, brought the gentleman to a ringing halt. He turned, flushed as he met the girl's eyes, hesitated, and came back. A mole, young Ames thought, could not have misunderstood her expression. Certainly the gentleman did not, for he contributed generously to the woman's cup, and then he stopped to hear the tune through.

But the girl no longer looked at his chiselled cool face, on which he had already controlled the flush. She turned to young Ames, whether from coquetry to put the gentleman in his place, or because she read in young Ames's eager freckled face his violent partisanship, it never occurred to him to question. He stood there in his ragged country tweeds, hatless, ruddy with the cold, and drank in every line of her face and movement of her lips and shadow of her eyes. It was only when the gentleman—not to be cheated out of his money—moved over beside him that young Ames became aware of the faultless and opulent styling of the olive-green coat and saw the snuffy brown of his own shoulder against it. As he told Gibbs about it that night, he realised that to the girl he must have appeared shabby as a beggar himself. But just the same, he said, she went on singing to him. Not even the beautiful pale gentleman would deny that, he thought.

Several pedestrians had gathered at the novel sight of a fashionably dressed girl performing a street singer's part, and while she sang the gentleman passed around his pearl-grey beaver hat and took up a collection that overflowed the woman's cup. Then, almost before he was done, the tune stopped and the girl ran up the steps. The gentleman brandished the hat and called for three cheers and everybody joined but young Ames. The girl stopped on the threshold and turned for a moment to acknowledge the salute. She looked above the heads of the little knot of people till she met young Ames's eyes and she gave him a flashing smile. There was no doubt of it, he told Gibbs, none at all.

Did Gibbs suppose there was any possibility that she could have felt the same way about him that he did about her?

Gibbs thoughtfully wet his lip with his hot gin and lemon and said—his eye on young Ames's earnest face— that no man could ever be sure of what a woman felt. He could only be sure of what she meant him to feel she felt, and all he could do was to hope she was sincere.

" Not her," said young Ames. " She's sound as a straight ash." It seemed strange, he went on, to meet the girl you were going to marry and not even know her name.

Gibbs thought it was time he started to put the brakes on young Ames for his own sake, and he said : " I can tell you her name."

Young Ames was off-hand. He pointed out that it didn't matter what her name was since it was going to be Ames anyway, in the end. But it was obvious that his very insides were crawling with curiosity.

" Her name's Chevalier," said Gibbs.

That brought young Ames bolt upright.

" The boss's daughter ? " he asked. " I didn't know he had one."

" He hasn't. It's a complicated business. Her real name was Carter and she and her mother came from the South. If you really want to know the ins and outs, I can explain them to you."

Young Ames by that time had recovered his poise. He said : " Maybe I'd better know."

" Well," said Gibbs, " Ferdinand Chevalier founded this house. He died in 1793, leaving the business to George, who's our boss, and the cash to Louis. He didn't trust Louis with the business ; you see, Louis spent all his time playing round the city. But he's been all right with the money, he's not lost it ; and he's a kind of tobacco-store Indian trustee on half a dozen banks and insurance companies and all the beneficent societies in New York. He used to have a fine time standing off the fashionable mammas with daughters to marry. Then about five years ago he got sick and George sent him off on a tour of America." Gibbs refreshed himself with gin and lemon.

"In Charleston he met a young widow with a young daughter, named Carter. She showed him how to make juleps one day and by the time he had mastered the process he found he had promised to be her husband. He brought her back and set her up in fine style. It made quite a sensation, for she's good-looking as well as ambitious. George was building his house on Laight Street, so Louis built himself an even handsomer one on Beach, across the Park. I don't think old George thought much of Mrs. Louis, but the girl became a regular pet with him and he persuaded Louis to legally adopt her."

"I never saw Louis Chevalier," young Ames observed.

"No. But he used to be round all the time till he had his illness. He had kind of a stroke right in our counting-room one day about two months before you got here. I guess his Missus had kept him going too lively for a man of his age. Nobody sees him now. I've heard she won't even let George see him. He can't speak, they say."

Gibbs finished his glass and sighed. "I've always imagined the old buck, a good fifty-five or sixty, and the young widow—she wasn't yet thirty—pouring the juleps into him. Charleston is a nice place. Camellias blooming, magnolias—I guess I'll never see it again."

Young Ames listened to the last remarks with impatience. "You haven't told me the most important part," he complained.

"What's that, Johnny?"

"Her first name."

"Oh," said Gibbs. "Her name's Christine."

"Thanks," said young Ames. He was silent so long that Gibbs got alarmed.

"See here, Johnny," he said. "You aren't getting any damn-fool ideas, are you?"

"No," said young Ames. "I was only figuring what time I'd see her."

"See her? What are you talking about?"

"Day after to-morrow's New Year's. You said that

every lady in this city kept open house on New Year's, didn't you ? "

" I did," admitted Gibbs. " But do you think the butler would let you into the house ? "

" Why not ? "

" Look at your clothes. You'll see nothing but swells, at Chevalier's, coats from Bailey, or Dermott, Prentiss. How would you look ? "

" Something will turn up," young Ames said.

" And there's another thing you might as well face. Men, like George Chevalier may hire people like you and McVitty and me, for that matter, and they speak civil to us. But they don't like us mixing up in their families. Democracy isn't something social, Johnny. It's a way of doing business—even Andrew Jackson's democracy. Every time anybody spreads the eagle's wings, it's so he can pick up dollars in the shadow of them, boy."

" I don't deny it, do I ? " young Ames demanded. " But I'm going to be a partner and that makes it different."

" Of course," Gibbs said. " But you're not now and you better not try breaking into the Chevalier house if you expect to get to be."

He couldn't make a dent though.

" Want to bet on it ? " asked young Ames.

5

By eight o'clock the next morning, Mr. McVitty had worried himself and most of the counting-room force into a state of the jeebies. Three of the clerks had to be kept on at the inventory ; Gibbs for once was genuinely busy with a series of communications from Barbeault & Frères (Paris correspondents of Chevalier, Deming & Post) and the replies that must go out that night on the *Ariadne* ; so the rest of the preholiday business devolved upon Mr. McVitty himself, Cummings, and young Ames, who well before ten o'clock had become aware of the limits of even a youthful pair of legs.

Yet everybody took the rush in fairly good part, Mr. McVitty becoming almost abandoned in his use of the snuff as well as unusually responsive to a few of Mr. Deming's jokes. The junior partners were in and out three or four times before lunch and they always entered looking a little redder than the thermometer would have warranted at any other season. Even Mr. Chevalier shared a little of the holiday spirit and forgot to speak with Mr. McVitty about Mr. Jackson's vindictive (as he called it) removal of the deposits from the United States Bank ; and when he returned from his lunch at Delmonico's, he exhaled a faint aroma of unmistakably rare brandy. All the clerks took on a new lease of energy, it seemed, after that ; all, that is, except young Ames.

"What's the matter with you ? " cried Mr. McVitty. "Are you asleep on your feet ? Here's this letter to go to the supercargo of the *Ariadne*, and you say it's a house you don't know. It's a boat, it's a ship, it's a barque " ; and with a spasm of spontaneous lunacy, Mr. McVitty woofed like a dog. Young Ames shuddered, said " Yes, sir," and went out.

In spite of himself he could think of nothing beyond ways and means to manage calling on Miss Chevalier with credit. He had a natural vanity, and all morning he had been eyeing the clothes of passing gentlemen, becoming more and more aware of the shortcomings of his own. Once or twice he tried deliberately to put the idea from his mind ; but how could he reject her face, fresh in the cold air, with its framing bonnet and the nest of blue ribbons under her chin ? Or the chilled fragrance of her clothes as she stepped out of the carriage to stop beside him and the organ-grinder ? Or the way she had put the gentleman in his place by singing to John Ames himself? For she had, he told himself over and over, just as she had smiled to him later from the stoop.

He delivered the note to the *Ariadne's* supercargo, a man not much older than himself, who took it and said unhappily that John or any one else who did not have to sail on New Year's Eve was a lucky man. In a vaguely detached way, John could feel sorry for him. " To-morrow," said the supercargo, " I'll be wallowing in a damned dirty waste of waves, but you'll be marching the town and calling on your girls."

" Make it the singular number," said John.

" You're a good man," said the supercargo sadly, shaking his hand, and John returned to South Street, saying to himself that by God, clothes or no clothes, he would make good the supercargo's words. Ten minutes later he was at his desk catching a well-earned few minutes of rest. Then Mr. McVitty appeared in the senior partner's door and called : " Young Ames ! "

" He wants to talk to you alone," Mr. McVitty said, as young Ames desultorily approached the office. The announcement quickened young Ames. At last, he thought, they had decided to recognise the value of his services. He entered feeling a good yard higher.

6

" Ah, young Ames," Mr. Chevalier said affably. " I've an important commission for you."

" Yes, sir," said young Ames, squaring his shoulders and feeling his heart pounding him. It must be important, the way the boss was clearing his throat and looking thoughtful.

Mr. Chevalier fixed his blue stare on young Ames.

" Can you tell a good goose when you see it ? "

" Goose, sir ? "

" Yes," said Mr. Chevalier irritably. " Goose. You're from the country. You ought to pick a good goose. You like goose, don't you ? "

" Yes, sir." Young Ames looked flustered, and Mr. Chevalier began suddenly to look embarrassed.

" I'll trust you. It's confidential, you understand ? "

" Yes, sir."

" I want you to go to get me two geese at the Franklin Market. Mr. Burton, I believe, keeps the best poultry stall. The birds should not be old, but well fattened. A goose with a small liver—what is it ? "

" I couldn't say."

" You're polite, Ames. Here's some money. Never mind the expense. Now, Ames, I'm leaving for home early. I'll be going home by Gouverneur Lane. You can meet me at the corner of Water Street. You think you can select a satisfactory goose ? "

" Oh yes," said young Ames. He had never bought a goose in his life, but that didn't bother him. He thought he would be able to find a way of picking out a good one, and the business would be a diversion.

" Very well, I'll be waiting for you in twenty minutes," said Mr. Chevalier.

" How long will you be ? " demanded Mr. McVitty as young Ames issued from the senior partner's office.

" It will take half an hour," young Ames said, reaching for his hat and going out with a self-important swagger.

He found Mr. Burton's stall in the crowded market, but took his time in approaching it. Several customers were buying, and two or three of them were expressing interest in geese. Mr. Burton, in a fur cup and a white apron tied on over many clothes, was a lively little pouter pigeon of a man, strutting under his dead poultry. Young Ames watched him closely. One of the first things he noticed was that every time Mr. Burton reached down a goose, he took it from one end of the row. If the customer showed dissatisfaction, Mr. Burton took a bird from the far end. Consistently he passed by the middle three or four until a gentleman in a fur-lined coat and a very swell-looking hat came up to buy. For him, without question, Mr.

Burton took down one of the middle geese, and the gentleman accepted it also without question.

Young Ames made his move. " I want two geese," he
said. And as he had expected, Mr. Burton took down a
pair from the end.

" These won't do," said young Ames.

" Why not ? "

" Look at their feet."

" What's the matter with their feet, young rabbit ? "
demanded Mr. Burton.

" Old age," said young Ames. " Maybe they died
of it."

" Well, do you see any better ? "

" Yes, hand me those two right in the middle," said
young Ames, pointing to one white and one grey one.

" They don't match," said Mr. Burton.

" I'm not eating the feathers," said young Ames.

Mr. Burton looked at him with respect. " You know
poultry, young man. But they'll cost you more."

" That's all right," said young Ames, paying over.

He shouldered his way out, lugging the two birds, and
went down Water Street to Gouverneur Lane. He had to
wait there for only a few minutes before he saw Mr.
Chevalier approaching through the dusk. He came up
at a quick step, carrying his gold-headed cane under his
arm.

" Ah, Ames. You have the birds. They look very well."
He accepted the change, pursed it, and said : " You may
give me the geese."

" They're heavy, sir. Don't you want me to carry them
home for you ? "

" No," Mr. Chevalier said sharply. " I shall carry them
myself." He cleared his throat. " I have one more
message for you. Call at Bailey, the tailor's, at Cortlandt
and Broadway, about eight to-night. He has a coat for
me but I won't trust him to deliver it on time. He's always
late. Stay there till he gives it to you. If it's late you can

fetch it up to my house before noon to-morrow. That's all, Ames. Good-night."

Young Ames watched him walk away. He was swinging his cane now. He made a picturesque figure in his great-coat and neatly tilted grey hat.

Young Ames took his time returning to the counting-room. His mind was again occupied with what seemed to him, the more he thought of it, the almost insoluble problem of his call on Christine Chevalier. It was only when he was climbing the stairs into the gas-lit bustle of the counting-room that he stopped to wonder why Mr. Chevalier had sent him out to buy two geese.

7

Gibbs gave him the solution. He was sitting at his desk under the gas jet that always whistled like the stoppered nostril in Mr. McVitty's nose with a cold coming on.

"Hallo, Johnny," he said. "Been buying the governor's geese?"

Young Ames was surprised. "What do you mean?" he asked.

"Oh," said Gibbs, "the old boy has somebody buy him a couple of geese every New Year's Eve, so he can carry them home through the streets like a good old-fashioned Federalist merchant. He thinks it has a good effect on the populace. It's his idea of being democratic and anti-Jacksonian at the same time. But he hates going into the public market. Gibbs eased his long legs. "One of the warehouse men named Phinney used to pick them for him, but he died two years ago and last year old McVitty got two string-and-feather items thinking he'd be econo-mical. So the boss must have decided to try you. If you picked well, Johnny," he said with a grin, "I may be borrowing from you on pay-day."

John gave a high-pitched laugh.

" I'm serious," said Gibbs. " A couple of geese might
be the beginning of that fortune you're talking about.
Look at David Reynolds and his twenty-five cents in
apples, or Astor's cookies."

He got down off his stool and said he was through.
Even Mr. McVitty seemed to agree. The ledgers were
being locked up in the safe. " I'll leave you to turn out
the gas," he said to young Ames.

Young Ames turned out all the gas jets but the one with
the whistle, which acted as a sort of companionable coun-
terfeit of Mr. McVitty. He tightened the covers of the
inkwells, stuck loose pens upright in the shot, emptied the
sandboxes into a coal scuttle and the wastebuckets into a
huge hamper. Having finished with the counting-room he
performed the same duties in Mr. Deming's and Mr. Post's
office. But in Mr. Chevalier's he lingered a moment, then
suddenly moved over behind the table, pulled out the
leather-backed chair, and seated himself firmly.

The room was only dimly lit through the door by the
counting-room gas jet, but what light there was fell across
the desk in a fairly defined beam that marked shadows of
the inkwell and the little silver bell. Young Ames picked
up the bell and jingled it. Then he set it down and,
attracted by the whiteness of his hand in that light,
drummed on the table top with his fingers. After a moment
he stopped doing that. A great concentrating wave of
stillness, that seemed to have been collecting all over the
building, poured into the room ; and for a moment he
felt frightened and half rose. But then his ear picked up
the reassuring whistle of the gas jet and he leaned back
against the leather.

It was a quiet comfortable place to sit and think and he
sat there for quite a while. There was no wind, and no
snow, though the sky was overcast. The street outside was
quiet except for an occasional hail of a ship's watch, and
the yowling of a cat on the corner of Gouverneur Lane.
In the dim room, young Ames's face became as solemn as

a burgomaster's. He felt the premonitory fingerings of an idea in his mind. It took no definite shape, the geese he had bought, and Mr. Chevalier. It was not finally resolved till nine o'clock.

Then, on the stroke of the hour, returning from Bailey, the tailor's, he opened the door of Number 42, locked it behind him, climbed the stairs, and stepped into Gibbs's room.

Gibbs looked up from shaking out his good coat.

"Hallo, Johnny," he said, holding it up. "It's not what it used to be, perhaps, but the fit's still there. There was nobody in this city like old Prentiss to cut a sleeve." His eyes fell on the parcels young Ames carried, and he said : "Hallo, what have you got?"

"A coat," said young Ames.

"A coat?" echoed Gibbs.

"The boss wants it delivered by noon to-morrow. Want to see it?" young Ames said carelessly, and undid the twine of the larger parcel. "It's pretty good, don't you think? Bailey made it."

Gibbs said : "It's quite a coat." Deliberately, he studied young Ames's face. "What's on your mind, Johnny?"

Young Ames said : "I and the boss are about the same build." He had slipped out of his own jacket and now, before Gibbs could say a word, he had put on Mr. Chevalier's new coat. "It fits pretty well. You've probably got a tie you can lend me, I've one decent shirt myself. And I had enough money to buy a ready-made pair of trousers and a white waistcoat at Lamont's."

Gibbs said : "You've gone crazy."

"Look at me," cried young Ames. "Tell me if it fits. You ought to know."

"It fits too damned well. But so does a winding sheet."

Young Ames, however, had learned all he wanted to know. "You'll lend me the tie, sir?" he asked. "Who's to know? All I have to do is keep out of Mr. Chevalier's way."

Gibbs's voice softened in spite of himself.

"You're crazy," he said. "But I'll lend you the tie, and God help you, Johnny."

8

It was as if the fall of the knocker had opened the door. But the coloured butler appeared at once, polite and solemn, in an expensive livery of plum colour and yellow. He bowed his white head, stood to one side, and let young Ames pass.

There was a hushed air about him.

"Gentlemen please leave their hats upstairs on the left."

Young Ames's unaccustomed boots trod an Oriental carpet up the stairs. He went carefully, trying not to crackle the paper of the parcel under his arm. It was a lucky thing, their sending you upstairs like this to leave your hat, but he wondered why they did it. He found himself in a bedroom where greatcoats made a pile on the bed, and hats containing gloves stood bottom up on bureau and dressing-table and washstand.

He left his own scuffed beaver in a corner on top of the parcel. It would be simple enough to whip upstairs, undo the parcel, take off Mr. Chevalier's coat, slip on his own. All that would be left would be to find Mr. Chevalier's own room and lay the coat on the bed as though the butler had laid it there. He had figured it all out in five minutes. "Smart fellow," he said, smiling at himself in the glass and tightening Gibbs's black tie under his chin. It was astonishing how decent clothes changed a man's appearance.

Of course he did not see his freckled face and unruly sandy hair as others were going to look at them. Neither did he take notice of the tightness of his chin or the rather desperate stare his own eyes gave his image in the glass. But he did feel the slow hard pound of his heart and he went to the window, which was open a crack, and drew in the cold air as deep as his lungs would accommodate it.

The window fronted St. John's Park. Across the space, through the bare branches of the trees, black where the noon sun was melting the light coat of snow, he saw Mr. Louis's house. He had summoned up the nerve—after waiting three-quarters of an hour to see whether Mr. George would enter or leave it—at last to knock and been told that the house was not receiving that day owing to Mr. Louis's illness, but that Miss Christine had gone over to Mr. George's and would receive there with Mrs. George.

Young Ames had not waited a minute. But on his way over he had had the inspiration to pick up his package from its hiding-place behind the fence rails. The whole thing had solved itself. He had mounted the stoop and lifted the knocker before he had time to think further, and here he was. He took another deep breath ; then, hearing a new arrival mounting the stairs, stepped out on to the landing.

He stood aside for the gentleman to pass. The gentleman acknowledged the courtesy with a slight bow and John nodded his head, for there was no room for him to bow also, and started down.

It was on his passage down the stairs that some sense of his enormous effrontery was born in him. He now heard for the first time the subdued hum of modulated voices, and he realised that their accent was not his. His eyes took in the richness of the carpet, used on the stairway, too. He saw the heavy mahogany of the door and the white, hand-carved frame of it. He looked at the Italian marble top of the hallstand and the gold French mirror over it, things that he had never seen the like of, and he would have stopped and turned and sneaked downstairs to leave the coat and melt away like a licked puppy if the old butler had not looked up at him.

The butler was waiting with a grave, polite face. Likely, thought young Ames, he had seen scared people on that stair before this, and he stuck out his chin and forced him-self to smile.

The butler said :

" What name shall I announce, sir ? "

" John Ames."

" I thank you, sir."

The butler moved on hushed feet to the mahogany door, put his brown hand on the crystal knob, and said, " Mr. Ames."

Young Ames found himself confronting the drawing-room.

9

His eyes made one desperate circle of the room without finding her, then fixed themselves on the lady in the purple silk dress seated on her French sofa, flanked by three or four attentive, elderly gentlemen. Their conversation hushed and he forced his feet to approach her.

She had a pale, still, friendly face, and a comfortable figure. She held out her hand and smiled. She was used to scared young men, too, and her eyes were kind enough as she said he had honoured her by calling. He made his bow and replied that it was pleasant to have the sun shine on New Year's Day, conscious that his words were slurred ; but she agreed pleasantly and said that he must find his way into the dining-room and library where the younger gentlemen were being entertained by her niece.

He was thankful to take her suggestion. Now he knew that he had been crazy, exactly as Gibbs said ; but he couldn't have known it before. He kept telling himself that, desperately, as he slipped into the dining-room and sought cover from the protective group at the sideboard. Their conversation, quick with a light chatter of people and parties that called for understanding laughs, baffled him as completely as a foreign language. He saw the old butler casting his eye at him from the drawing-room door and quickly joined in a laugh.

The sound made a man, who leaned one elbow on the sideboard, turn quickly.

"Ah," he said. "You've no eggnog. May I offer you a cup?"

"Thanks," said young Ames, wondering whether he were a relative of the family.

The gentleman handed him a creaming cup and said, "Happy New Year."

"Thanks," said young Ames, helplessly, and sipped and thought the custardy richness would stick forever in his throat.

"My name is Seixas, sir."

"Mine is Ames," said young Ames.

"In the city?"

"With Chevalier, Deming & Post," stammered young Ames.

"You are fortunate," said Mr. Seixas. He smiled abstractedly, struck into the stream of conversation, so that young Ames, left again to his own devices, felt himself drowning.

He tried another sip of the eggnog and felt the first swallow go down. But the second took its place. "I'll be sick," he thought, and swallowed hard. He did not know whether it was polite to put down a scarcely tasted cup. He did not know where to put it, anyhow. Holding the thing in his hand, a blatant advertisement of his spuriousness, he sidled past the sideboard group towards the library, hoping against hope to find an open window.

But the library was warm from a fire snapping in a white marble fireplace; and the windows, which faced on a yard with a pear tree and a tiny arbour and a musing cat, were irremediably closed. Turning his thwarted eyes away, he encountered the eyes of Miss Chevalier; and he was positive that she must have witnessed the whole of his abject manœuvre.

She was standing at one side of the hearth, her fingers lightly dangling a small fan. The flat yoke of her dress, deep rose, set off the creamy bareness of her shoulders ; the spread of the heavy silk skirt, her slender waist. The moment young Ames saw her she turned her face and smiled at something the gentleman beside her was saying.

He was the same man whom she had recalled by her singing to the organ-grinder yesterday, and he was speaking to a third person who was hidden from John by the window curtains in the corner of the room. " I saw you crossing College Place last night," he was saying. " And they looked like devilish fine birds, too. I don't know where you get them, sir. Upon my word, I don't. But I suppose it's your secret."

Young Ames listened in a kind of paralysis.

The girl turned her eyes towards the man in the corner, but they met young Ames's in passing, and he was sure she had recognised him. She spoke solemnly. " Oh, it's a tremendous secret, isn't it ? "

Her eyes returned to young Ames. They were mischievous, a little puzzled too, and the corners of her mouth bent down and twitched as she controlled a smile.

Young Ames did not need to wait for the third person's voice. He knew the worst already, and he stood there with his cup of eggnog, helpless and forlorn, and feeling a green prickle start upon his forehead.

" Not at all," said Mr. Chevalier, with a trace of testiness. " It's no secret, I buy them in the open market. The Franklin Market, as a matter of fact. It's just a question of getting them yourself, Atwood. I used to buy all the poultry, but I haven't time nowadays except on New Year's."

" Everybody watches for you, sir," said Mr. Atwood, with his cool politeness.

Mr. Chevalier made a pleased sound in his upper throat, " tut-tut " or " pshaw, pshaw "—young Ames couldn't be

sure ; said, " Let me get you another eggnog, Atwood,"
and stepped out in front of the girl.

" Thank you, sir," said Mr. Atwood. He turned to
the girl. " Won't you have some more sherry, Miss
Kisty ? "

" No, thank you," she said. " I think I'll move from
the fire. It's a little stuffy."

" Shall I open a window ? " he asked, with rather per-
functory solicitude.

" Yes, do, please," she said. " That one, I think," and
passed it with a quick step, making a cool rustle of her
skirt, towards John.

" How nice of you to come," she said, and her eyes
looked into his, still amused, but sympathetic and with
some understanding.

He made his bow with a precarious manipulation of the
eggnog. She took it from him with a quick gesture and
set it on the window-sill behind the curtain. " Nasty, isn't
it ? " she whispered. " What's your name ? Quick."

" John Ames," he said, feeling his hands go wet.

She made a little curtsey and said to Mr. Atwood, who
was joining them, " May I introduce you gentlemen ?
Mr. Atwood, Mr. Ames."

Mr. Atwood surveyed young Ames coolly. He had a
good memory for faces. " I've seen you before, haven't
I ? " he said. He did not say they had met, young Ames
noticed, and hated him.

" Yes," he said. " On the corner of Beach and Hudson
Streets yesterday morning."

His chin came up a little, and he faced Mr. Atwood.

" Yes," Mr. Atwood said slowly. " I remember now."
Miss Chevalier quickly broke in.

" Will you fetch me a glass of water, Mr. Atwood ? "

" Yes, of course. Do you still feel faint ? "

" A little," said Miss Chevalier, giving young Ames a
blooming glance.

" Perhaps I'd better stay with you."

" Oh no, Mr. Ames can take care of me."

She put her fan against her lips as he moved away, and said to young Ames : " Good for you. Do you feel any better ? "

Young Ames was gulping the cooler air like a fish on the bank. " Not very much," he admitted.

He felt wholly ashamed of himself, of his using the boss's new coat, of his trying to pass himself off as a gentleman, and of the miserable mess he had made. It seemed to him that everything she had done for him served only to rub it in.

" I've no business here," he said.

She turned surprised eyes, but she did not say anything ; and he blundered it out.

" That coat I was wearing yesterday . . . maybe you didn't notice it." She nodded, and it made him feel worse to know she had noticed it. " That's the only coat I have," he went on. " I'm only a clerk in Mr. Chevalier's coat. I mean I am a clerk in his counting-room. This is his coat." He looked down at himself. " I haven't spilled on it anyway, thank heaven."

She giggled, and he raised his miserable eyes to find her nodding at him over her fan.

" I thought it must be. Uncle's been describing it for days. The lapel is very special." Her eyes roved. " I think Mr. Atwood had suspicions too."

" I've been a fool," said young Ames.

" Why did you come ? "

" I wanted to see you. I didn't know."

She gave him a quick level look.

" Didn't know what ? "

" What it would be like. I thought everybody was like everybody else and only the clothes were different. I thought if I had on a coat like this one I'd be just as good as him."

" Him ? Oh, Mr. Atwood. And now you find you aren't ? Doesn't it make you mad ? "

He shook his head. " I've just made a mess. I'll get even you laughed at, maybe. I'm sorry."

She said, " I think it was brave of you to try." And he listened for a hint of amusement in her voice. " I wonder what Mr. Atwood would look like if he had to go round in old clothes and earn his living."

Young Ames lifted his chin. That hadn't occurred to him. But then he saw it wasn't very logical.

" Will you offer me your arm ? " she asked, and took it. " Mr. Atwood would love to offer his, I assure you. That looks better. It will make you feel better too. I know. I felt the same way at Miss Barstow's wedding. I *said* eggnogs were horrible. Now, if anybody laughs at you they'll have to laugh at me too. Let's start for the dining-room."

He forced his feet ahead. He was very conscious of her nearness, of her curls just opposite his shoulder, of her bare neck, of the brooch flat against her breast suspended by a chain of tiny gold links, and of the perfume she wore. She was fanning herself with small rapid strokes.

" I'm still faint. Oh, dear." She spoke in a low voice with a hint of new laughter. Her fingers pressed lightly on his numb arm. " Here come Mr. Atwood and Uncle. You're escorting me to the stairs." She put a little more weight on his arm so that he had to bear up and stiffen his back. " That's fine," she whispered and lifted serious eyes to Mr. Atwood.

" Oh, thank you for fetching the water," she said. " I don't think I'll have any. I still feel quite faint, and I think I'd better go upstairs for a few minutes. Mr. Ames is kind enough to see me to the hall. Oh, Uncle. Have you met Mr. Ames ? "

Mr. Chevalier lifted his gaze from the two cups of eggnog, saw young Ames, and nearly dropped the drinks.

" Young Ames ! " he exclaimed. " What . . ." His face flushed and his staring blue eyes suddenly chilled.

But young Ames had finally caught up with himself

again. He had begun to realise how much the girl was taking on for his sake, and he determined to act his own part from then on.

" Happy New Year, Mr. Chevalier," he said. He saw Mr. Chevalier's impassioned eyes fix themselves on the coat, and sheer outrage sparkle in them. " I came to tell you that the business was satisfactorily completed, sir. But I didn't like to interrupt your conversation with Mr. Atwood about the geese."

For once Mr. Chevalier was puzzled. " Geese ? " he demanded in his cold voice.

But quick as a flash, the girl had caught on.

" You remember, Uncle. You and Mr. Atwood were saying how hard it was to find a good goose in the market. It was just before I was taken giddy."

Mr. Chevalier's blue eyes fixed themselves on young Ames's.

" Yes," he said. " Geese. They're hard to find."

He paused. The flush receded from his face, but his eyes remained stern. He looked at young Ames's white, frozen lips, and perhaps he saw his glistening brow.

" Let me offer you an eggnog," he said.

Young Ames, afterwards, said to Gibbs that he looked genuinely malicious. " I had better take Miss Chevalier to the stairs," he said.

" Yes," she said. " Please."

Mr. Atwood, however, smiled. " It's a shame to deprive Mr. Ames of his eggnog," he said. " Let me take Miss Chevalier," and he removed her from young Ames's arm with a practised smoothness.

She tossed young Ames a smile over her shoulder as she passed into the drawing-room. She didn't care whether her uncle saw it, and he did. He switched his blue eyes to young Ames and held out the eggnog.

Young Ames took it. He watched Mr. Chevalier now and he felt that he didn't care what Mr. Chevalier or the eggnog did to him.

" A Happy New Year to you, Ames," said Mr. Chevalier.

" Happy New Year, sir," said young Ames.

He took it down ; he took it down steadily, he told
Gibbs, all in one piece, so that it never had a chance to
stop, with Mr. Chevalier watching him over the rim of his
own cup every second.

When he had emptied the cup, he set it down with an
easy conscience.

" I'm afraid I must be on my way, Mr. Chevalier," he
said.

" Your coat's upstairs ? " asked Mr. Chevalier.

" Yes, sir."

Mr. Chevalier made a short bow.

" If there's anything you want, Amber can tell you."
He walked with his precise stride beside young Ames
through the drawing-room and handed him over to the
butler.

10

The very mystified coloured butler watched young
Ames take off his handsome coat and lay it in his hands.

" Will you put that in Mr. Chevalier's room ? " he said.

" Thank you."

" Thank *you*, sir."

Young Ames put on his own coat ; he marched down
the stairs, opened the front door for himself, and stepped
out on the stoop.

Mr. Chevalier was standing there.

" Ah, Ames," he said. " You're an unscrupulous rascal.
But these are unscrupulous times."

" Yes, sir," said young Ames, wondering whether he
was going to be discharged on the spot. But he didn't
care then, he told Gibbs.

" What is that pet proverb of Mr. McVitty ? " asked
Mr. Chevalier.

"'Seest thou a man that is hasty in his words? There is more hope of a fool than of him,'" said young Ames.

"Remember it, Ames. It's a good proverb."

Young Ames was shaken. He couldn't think of anything to say for a moment.

Then he said, "Happy New Year."

"Ah, yes," said Mr. Chevalier. "Thank you, Ames. The same to you."

I I

ARRIVAL OF THE "LILY DEAN"

SIPPING his matutinal cup of hot water before the counting-room stove, Mr. McVitty remarked irritably to young Ames: "The habits of ships are unaccountable, unjustifiable, irresponsible, and perverse, like women. It's a pity that nobody has thought of anything better."

Young Ames, who was busy filling the deskboxes with metallic sand, said mechanically, "Yes, sir."

"We've had no foreign advices in seventy-one days from Liverpool. Seventy-two from London. Seventy-five from Paris. It's immoral," said Mr. McVitty. "I've been here fifty years in this office, and I've never seen anything like it."

"No, sir," said young Ames.

"Trade's become as cautious as treacle on a frosty morning," said Mr. McVitty. "The city's going to pieces and the nation is no better. Nothing's healthy except that madman in Washington, and he's drunk, I don't doubt, the horse-racing wastrel." Mr. McVitty pulled out his bulging tortoise-shell watch. "And you're late, Ames. It's time you had the sidewalk swept off instead of lally-gagging and loafing in front of the fire."

He went over to the files where the inward and outward

ladings were hung alphabetically on their two wires. They were sparser than young Ames had ever seen them, and Mr. McVitty's long grey face became almost dyspeptic as he fingered them.

"The *Sheffield*'s in port, and the *Charles Carroll*. When do they sail?"

"Both sailing to-morrow," said young Ames.

"So they are," said Mr. McVitty in a displeased tone, as if he had hoped to catch young Ames out. He returned to his desk, climbed up on the stool, spread his coat-tails behind him, took snuff, and continued his jeremiad against the Atlantic service. "Forty-six packets between this place, Liverpool, London, and Havre. And to-night not one of them will be in this port. It's a monstrosity, Ames."

Young Ames was glad to take the sidewalk broom from its pegs. He had already run up to the Exchange to catch the northern mail at six o'clock with letters to Albany, and the telegraph bulletins had been as bare of news as they had for over a month. He clattered down the stairs and began lustily to sweep the sidewalk.

The docks had a half-deserted air which the overnight fall of snow intensified. There were only two Atlantic packets in sight. The air was cold and heavy; the sky like lead. The gulls, querulous, swung low across the housetops. The dockhands, coming out of cellar saloons, moved lethargically and breathed thick fog.

Young Ames, having completed the southern frontage of Number 42 South Street, paused for a moment to look at the sky. There was a big wind making up, he thought, and he lifted his thin freckled face and sniffed a deep-sea smell in the air. The small waves of the East River lapped the dock piles with an icy spiteful sound and the sparse shipping creaked as if the cold were in its oaken bones. The wheels of the first carts, coming down past Franklin Market, squaked tight on the new snow; the horses had their blankets rolled up behind the hames. New York, at the end of January, 1834, was not the thriving city of quick fortune it had seemed when he had arrived in November, but the body of a city with its bones bare for the wind to blow through. "Gibbeted," Mr. McVitty said, "by that madman, Andrew Jackson."

Gibbs said : "Never mind, Johnny. It's easy for a young man to get discouraged in January. There's been some tidy fortunes started in bad times, remember."

Young Ames leaned on the broom, shivering a little as the cold bit through his jacket and stiffened his sandy hair, and he thought for a moment that a fortune for someone without a penny or relation to his name might be a long way off.

But, anyway, he hadn't been fired for going to call on Miss Chevalier in the boss's brand-new coat. The blood rose in the back of his neck as it did whenever he thought of that episode or when Gibbs reminded him of it. Mr. Chevalier must realise that he was pretty useful to the firm to let him stay, he thought. It didn't occur to him that the niece might have put in a word for him, but if it had he would not have been completely displeased. He thought of her for a moment as she had stood beside him in her uncle's drawing-room, confronting the old gentleman, lovely in her deep rose dress, faintly perfumed, and suppressing her amusement heroically ; and he wondered how many thousand dollars he would have to make before he could get up his nerve to ask her, and then how many thousand more before he could get up his nerve to ask her mother, or Mr. Chevalier, he was not sure which. "One," he began counting the sweeps of his broom, "two," and he wished a thousand dollars was as easy to sweep up as dry frosted snow.

It was fifteen thousand dollars by the time he came to the corner of 43 and encountered Wentz, the junior clerk of Pruyn & Co., Chevalier's most active competitor, completing their walk.

"Hallo, Ames," said Wentz. "Didn't I see you turning up Gouverneur Lane this morning ? "

"It's possible," said young Ames, neatening the kerb. He knew what Wentz wanted, a report on the telegraph bulletins to save himself a trip to the Exchange. Wentz was a nosy man, nearing thirty, with a gangling body and eyes that ran in the cold. He had a fur cap on his head and a double muffler round his neck. "Cold morning," he observed.

"If you've nothing to do," agreed young Ames.

"Business is getting bad, Ames."

"When did you hear that?"

"You're a twig, you are," Wentz said with attempted bonhomie. "No, sir. The latest I hear is that Lamar & Phisterer are backed against the wall."

"I heard about that yesterday," said young Ames unguardedly.

Wentz whistled. "Then it's true. Did they try to do business with you?"

Young Ames was ready to kick himself. "No," he said, "we're not having any." God, he thought, if Mr. McVitty knew about this, I'd get a combing from him; for the fact of the matter was that Mr. Chevalier, to do old Mr. Lamar a favour, had bought one of his barques, the *Lily Dean*, out now on the Liverpool run, for thirty thousand dollars. It had caused Mr. McVitty a great deal of alarm, for it was the first ship Chevalier, Deming & Post had ever owned, and no doubt it contributed to his remarks of this morning on the habits of ships.

"Casting your money on the waters," Mr. McVitty had grumbled. "Just out of sentimentality. Even the insurance is run out."

Wentz now said : "No offence, Ames. I just heard the rumour. Naturally Chevalier wouldn't buy one of those tubs any more than we would. No special news on the bulletin?" he added casually.

Young Ames grinned inside.

"It's there for any one that wants to go up," he said. "Of course, more may have come in since."

" Good God ! " exclaimed Wentz. " A boat's in ? Which one ? I've been running up there so often this past week I've left tracks in the cobbles. The boss is getting edgy about this lack of foreign advices. I guess it's the same with you ? "

" Not particularly," said young Ames, though he could feel the cobbles in his own feet. " Everybody's in the same fix. So what's the difference ? "

Wentz immediately became off-hand.

" That's so," he agreed. " It's the *Crawford*, I expect. When did she come in ? "

Young Ames was beginning to enjoy himself thoroughly.

" They didn't say."

He hoped it would do and it did. Wentz pretended to linger a moment, and tried to remark on the heavy sky, and said something more about trade, and then gave it up and whipped back into his own door.

Young Ames watched him go with a wide grin on his freckled face.

" Ames," said a voice just behind him. " Was that Pruyn's clerk you were gossiping with ? "

His grin froze and he turned slowly to encounter Mr. Post, the junior partner. He said, " Yes, sir."

Mr. Post stood straight and square in his black great-coat with the false capes. He was a sober man with an uncompromising wooden face. He was neither easygoing like Mr. Deming nor an explosive, old-fashioned gentle-man like Mr. Chevalier. He looked down now at young Ames with opaque dark eyes, then glanced at the side-walk.

" Since you've finished the walk, come in with me."

" Yes, sir."

Young Ames followed the stiff figure up the long stair-way. Though he knew he was likely to get a lecture, he didn't lose his cockiness. He didn't see where he had done anything wrong except let out that news about Lamar, which Pruyn's knew already. As for the rest, anything

that he might do to harass and confuse Pruyn & Co.
seemed perfectly all right to him.

2

The clerks were all at their desks in the counting-room.
Gibbs cocking his eye at young Ames sardonically. "In
for it?" he whispered as Ames hung up his broom.
Young Ames winked back. "Caught talking to Wentz,"
he whispered back, and went after Mr. Post through the
door of his office.

"Close the door, Ames," said Mr. Post. He was already
seated at his desk, and his face was forbidding. "I overheard your conversation as I came round the corner," he
said. "I recognised the fact that you were talking to an
employee of a rival firm. It was my duty to listen. Do
you understand that?"

"Yes, sir. But I didn't give anything away, except
about Mr. Lamar's being here yesterday."

"What did you say about Mr. Lamar?"

"Only that he'd been here."

"Did you tell the clerk we'd bought the *Lily Dean*?"

"He asked, but I denied it, sir."

"He believed you?"

"I said nobody but a damn' fool would have bought
one of those Lamar boats, sir."

"He agreed, I suppose," Mr. Post said in his dry voice.

"Yes, sir."

Mr. Post cleared his throat.

"Why did you tell the clerk all that rigmarole about
the *Crawford*?"

"I didn't tell him anything. *He* did all the talking."
Young Ames could not help grinning; but Mr. Post did
not find it amusing.

"How long have you been with us, Ames?"

Young Ames gave a gulp.

" Since November, sir."

" How old are you ? "

" Eighteen, sir."

" You've a great deal to learn." He raised his eyes from young Ames's shabby waistcoat to his face. " You've too much imagination," he said. " I don't think you meant to say anything to injure the firm; let us hope that you haven't."

" But, sir, I only said I had been up to the bulletins. I didn't say anything. *He* thought the *Crawford* must have come in."

" Exactly," said Mr. Post, without even a glimmer of amusement in his wooden face. " That's the trouble. Pruyn will send the clerk up again for further bulletins. When he gets there he'll wonder just what our game is. He'll report to Pruyn and Pruyn will be on the stretch to find out what we have up our sleeve. We don't know yet whether we have anything up our sleeve, of course, but if we have, it's going to be the devil to keep them from finding out."

The freckles began to stand out in young Ames's face as his colour drained.

" God in heaven ! " said Mr. Post, looking hard at him. " I thought you'd been up there."

" There wasn't any news at all when I was there, sir."

" There is now. A Liverpool packet's reported off Sandy Hook. I don't understand it myself, but she happens to be the *Lily Dean*."

" Good God ! " said young Ames.

" Exactly," said Mr. Post. " She's our ship now."

" You mean she may have news from Liverpool bearing on the market ? "

" Exactly," repeated Mr. Post.

" Nobody's buying cotton," young Ames muttered. " It's been practically warehoused since the end of November."

For an instant the woodenness disappeared from Mr.

Post's face ; and young Ames, meeting his eyes, had a queer feeling that he and Mr. Post were pretty much alike in their determination to get on top. It was a strange idea, because young Ames had no liking for Mr. Post, any more than Mr. Post had for him. He rubbed his head irritably, leaving his sandy hair on end.

" We've got to get aboard her and find out," he said.

" That's obvious."

" I'll need the bill of sale, all the papers, sir, and a note to the captain telling him I'm in charge."

Mr. Post stared. " Have you gone crazy ? "

" No, sir, but I'm going down the bay and get aboard her before she comes in," said young Ames, and then caught himself. " If you'll give me permission, Mr. Post."

" What can that accomplish ? "

" Good God, don't you see ? " young Ames cried excitedly. " If she's got news of a jump in the market, we'll hold her out in the bay till nearly dark before bringing her in." His voice became heated. " To-morrow's Sunday, Mr. Post, and no banks open. If anything is up, Chevalier's will have a full day to beat the mails."

Mr. Post said slowly : " You've forgotten the tide."

" No, sir, I know it will be running out, but there's an offshore wind building up to carry her in."

" How will you get to the ship, Ames ? "

" I'll take the Wall Street Ferry and hire a cab in Brooklyn. I can get to New Utrecht in an hour. Then I'll get a boat and board the packet in the Narrows."

It was all as clear as day in young Ames's mind ; but Mr. Post rose and went to his window and looked at the river.

" You're right about the wind, anyway," he said, after a moment, " it's begun to blow up already."

" I'd better hurry," said young Ames.

" I ought to consult Mr. Chevalier."

" We can't lose time. Good Lord, sir ! Aren't you a partner ? "

Mr. Post said : " And I'll have to go with you."

" No ! " Young Ames lowered his voice hastily. " The whole of South Street would spot you, sir. You'd be known even in Brooklyn. But nobody'll notice me."

Young Ames held his breath. He was shivering like a terrier when Mr. Post finally turned and said : " You may drown, and there may be nothing in it anyway. But go get McVitty. Tell him to bring the papers and the seal of the firm."

3

Mr. Post had been right about the wind's freshening. The boat was pitching like a cork ; and young Ames, crouched in the bow, was eating spray at every dip.

It terrified him. He was sure that every downhill slide would take them under ; and against his narrow chest under the tight-buttoned jacket he could feel the packet of papers (thoughtfully wrapped in oiled silk by Mr. McVitty). But after a little he saw that the boat never did go down. The bows met the swell of the new wave with the precision of a well-danced minuet, carried him upward, and, when at last he gained enough nerve to take his eyes from the water, gave him a brief glimpse of the land.

The village itself looked low in its surrounding waters. Castle Garden showed little more than a rounded roof, like the shell of a turtle. He saw the buildings up Broadway clear enough, and the tops of the trees in Battery Park, but the docks along the East River were only visible from the top of a larger than ordinary wave. He was astonished to see how far behind they had fallen.

Whenever he looked at the two boatmen he had finally persuaded to set out with him from New Utrecht, he suffered spasms of impatience. They rowed with short, stiff, deliberate strokes, hunching over their laps. They never bothered to look round for their direction. They paid no attention to him either. They thought he was crazy, and only went on the promise of an extra five dollars to be paid on their return to the city.

Mr. McVitty had allotted young Ames ten dollars for the expense of the boat. " It's an extravagance," he had said, gloomily inhaling a monstrous dose of snuff. " I knew that damn' ship would bleed the firm white. Pay attention to me, Ames. It's an unconscionable amount of money for a junior clerk to have the spending of, especially on an enterprise any sane man would consider wildgoosical. But a chief clerk must take orders from a junior partner. Treat that money as if it was your own. Bargain, beat down, haggle, but don't give it up easy. ' He becometh· poor that spendeth with a slack hand.' And I hope you don't drown."

Though his face was stiffening with cold and spray, young Ames grinned. The boat had not cost the five dollars Mr. McVitty had deemed an extravagance, nor the ten he had set as the ultimate limit, but fifteen. He himself felt no compunctions. It gave him a sense of power to feel the resources of a great commercial house behind him : for a moment he had an instinct of his future so powerful that he felt it almost within his hand. Then a wave slapped half a bucketful over his knees and brought him back to the boat and the Narrows.

The action of the boat changed. The slide down the next wave was longer. There was a real swoop through the trough, and when she rose young Ames had the feeling that the boat was rearing backwards. He heard the boat-man nearest him grunt. They were out in the open now and the wind was strengthening. A snow squall, skirting the course of the wind, whipped over them, for a moment flattening the tops of the waves by what seemed to young Ames the simple process of cutting them off and blowing them in his face. At a breath the whole world was shut out and he and the boatmen were enclosed in a roaring white icy inferno.

He saw a wave materialising out of nothing, reaching towards them, taking them on its shoulder ; and he turned aft to see it slide out from under, rise behind them, and vanish into the white oblivion. Suddenly he felt small and mournful. Even suppose there was a chance for a corner in cotton, and he held the ship in the bay until the mails were closed so that Chevalier, Deming & Post did get the first whack at it, John Ames's moment would go by like the waves. On Monday he would be just young Ames to empty the scrapbaskets, sweep the walk, and run over to DeCamp's after ink, pens, and paper. Then he saw that the men were only paddling with their oars—at least that was how it looked to him.

" Hey," he yelled. " What have you stopped for ? "

The nearer one, who answered to the name of Bill Doaks, if he felt like it, turned a crimson face with a spray-crusted, stained moustache.

" Hey ? " he yelled back.

Young Ames scrambled perilously back to him.

" What are you stopping for ? " he roared. Even the hairs in the man's ear had ice on them.

Mr. Doaks got the attention of the second boatman by banging his heels on the bottom. He cocked his head towards young Ames, and repeated his question in a fog-horn bellow. Then both of them burst into laughter. Cold as his face was, young Ames flushed. It wasn't pleasant laughter either. He had the feeling that these men hated him. It occurred to him that he had taken his money out of the oiled-silk packet which to them might have looked like a wallet. Sheer panic overwhelmed him as he realised how simply they could pitch him overboard and nobody ever know.

Incredible as it would have seemed an instant before, he felt himself sweating. He who had had the whole idea and started out to get the firm a corner in cotton was sweating with fear. The thought enraged him.

" Why don't you go ahead ? " he shouted.

Mr. Doaks turned the red face back towards him again like a part of a machine.

" Hey ? "

" Why don't you keep on ahead ? "

" Where's ahead ? " He banged his feet on the bottom, and the second boatman listened to a report, and they both laughed uproariously and went back to their steady paddling strokes.

Young Ames realised he had been a fool. In this wet white blindness they could not see where they were going. Now as he watched them he saw that they were keeping the boat pointed steadily in the wind, to wait out the squall. He settled back with a deep breath and felt the cold strike in. Then another awful thought occurred to him. Suppose the snow should keep up ? Suppose the *Lily Dean* should pass them ? Suppose the snow didn't stop for the whole day, for a day and a night ? Suppose it was a blizzard. What would become of them ?

Once or twice in the past young Ames had toyed with the idea of getting a job as a supercargo. He realised now that that had been a mistake and that his real talents lay in trade.

" Hey, you ! "

The red face was back at him again.

" There's a bucket. You better do some bailing. "

" Bailing ? " yelled young Ames.

" Throwing the water overboard. Maybe it'll keep you from catching cold. "

The face disappeared, there was another banging of feet, and a new burst of laughter. Somehow it relieved young Ames. He found the bucket and with numbed hands took hold of it and started to bail. The action did nothing to warm him, but it kept his mind busy. He forgot to look at the waves, and forgot also a little speculation he had indulged in a few moments before which concerned his burial, suppose his body were ever recovered. Would the firm provide a headstone ? Would any one lay a flower at its foot ? He had almost wept at the idea. Now he nearly cried when a lurch of the boat threw him against the gunwale and caught his fingers between it and the filled pail.

He did not notice that the squall had stopped until he felt the boat move with a stronger heave of the oars. Then he looked up and outward.

New Utrecht Island had moved inexplicably to the left and the whole Long Island shore seemed to have been drowned entirely. Then, as the boat rose, an anæmic gleam of sunlight came down, turned the water an ugly olive green, arched the Narrows, and for a moment showed the shore, low and dun-coloured. Three gulls, like cuttings of white paper caught in an upward draught, swept out of a trough, and following their blown flight he saw another squall riding in from the bay.

The first boatman was eyeing it over his shoulder. Young Ames saw his round nose wiggle and his moustache blow out like the stiff bristles of a seal. " There's a bit of blow in that one," he yelled to his partner. " Head her up, Jarge."

Jarge, who had a brown lantern jaw and mild, grey, slitted eyes, had a look for himself. He shifted his tobacco cud, turned back, and took a quick stroke. " Hunh ! " he said. The first boatman said " Hunh ! " and they began to lean on their oars. They paid no more attention to young Ames.

He felt the boat taking life. It cut over the top of the next wave and went down diagonally, like a sidestepping, frisky horse, gathered itself in the trough and went over the next with a rush. He thought, " A bit of blow," with a cold contraction of his stomach.

He heard the rush of another squall on the water before it hit them, braced himself, and got a good grip on the bucket. If he ever got on that eternal barque, he thought he wouldn't care whether it sailed into New York head on, straight up Broadway to the Park, and distributed information from the deck in six-foot handbills, so long as he got ashore. The wind forced the breath back into his lungs and piled spray and snow upon it, and a piece of seaweed came off a wave and stuck itself on his face. He clawed at it frantically, grabbed hold of the gunwale, and held tight. The men, he saw, were really rowing to keep the boat headed up.

But she rode through suddenly into a clear grey clamour of pure wind, and Mr. Doaks glanced round again, a squeezed look on his red face, and yelped : " There she is."

Young Ames whirled and wedged himself into the bow. He couldn't see anything but the waves, the grey sky, the smear that was Staten Island, and another squall leaning over the end of it. He thought for a moment it was going to hit them but then he saw that from some freak of the wind it had switched almost south-westward, and suddenly he could see the whitecapped lacing of the waves along its edge as it swung towards Jersey and passed impartially inland.

His eyes turned back to the open sea and he saw the ship, bearing a little to the north of them. She was carrying almost no sail, and leaning a little, as if she remembered the squall ; and when a larger wave lifted the boat high he could see the foam pile up against her bow.

From the boat she looked lofty and unconcerned. It seemed impossible that she would ever condescend to notice an insignificant bobbing chip like themselves, let alone pick them up. It frightened young Ames to think of it. He leaned towards the boatman's bushy ear, and yelled : " Do you think she'll stop for us ? "

Mr. Doaks did not turn his head. But his heels banged the bottom and he roared at Jarge. Suddenly both heads turned towards young Ames. Mr. Doaks roared : " You said she'd pick us up, by God."

" I said I had to get on board her," yelled young Ames. " I've got to get on board her."

The lantern-jawed Jarge unexpectedly disgorged his

quid overside. He turned his face full on to young Ames
and his voice came out strong enough to beat down a
hurricane.

"You God-damned little lime-juiced hogbottom."

He turned back as suddenly and said : "Hunh !" and
the boat seemed to jump at the waves.

4

"Hail her," yelled the first boatman. "Stand up.
Wave to her. Wave your shirt."

The *Lily Dean* seemed to be rushing directly on them,
her bows leaning forward, running water like a hound's
slaver over a bone ; and the sound of her approach was
louder than destruction. Young Ames, white and numb,
made shift to stand and wave his arms.

"Hey !" His voice sounded feeble as a duckling's peep.
The *Lily Dean* loomed over him with a crashing of yards
and waves to smother all sound but her own.

Then Jarge let loose a bellow that would have stopped
a fleet. "Ahoy !" he roared. "Ahoy the *Lily Dean* !"
And young Ames realised they had been seen.

Some of the crew were leaning over the rail. He saw
ropes being let down to the water. A man in the stern
with a cap on his head and a long red muffler round his
neck roared through a speaking trumpet. It was like a
miracle in the crack of doom to see her come around.

Jarge and his partner waited for nothing. They were
already manœuvring the boat into the barque's lee. As
the black side reared over their heads, spilling cataracts,
young Ames felt sure they must slide down under her
belly. But the boatmen heaved lustily on their oars ; the
small boat rose as the side went down ; and the two came
together with a precise compression of time. Jarge had a
rope in his fist and Mr. Doaks was fending off from the
ship's side.

Just how he and the boat and the boatmen were taken aboard the *Lily Dean* was never clear in young Ames's mind. He had a vague impression of a voice bellowing from the stern ; of himself telling the man in the red muffler that he would talk to the master of the vessel and nobody else, and that he would talk to him right away ; of being haled down a steep companionway and finding himself at last in a reeking hot cabin, with the man in the red muffler, who in some fantastic manner turned out to be Captain Brown, asking him bitterly what in the name of several deities all this was about.

" What's the price of cotton in Liverpool ? " young Ames asked.

The captain, who had a heavy, studious sort of face, drew a painful breath.

" Who the hell are you ? " he asked.

" I forgot," stuttered young Ames, through chattering teeth. ". Here's the papers. Our firm's bought your boat from Lamar."

The captain took the papers and untied the oiled silk clumsily. Then he adjusted a pair of spectacles to his nose and squared his elbows. He read the bill of sale, apparently word for word, while young Ames fairly hissed with impatience. The captain rubbed his forehead. " Help yourself to the rum. It's in that locker behind you." While young Ames eagerly found a stone jug and a single, small, thumb-marked glass, Captain Brown bore down on the letter from Mr. Post. He ran a horny thumb over the seal. " Yes, sir," he said at last, " Chevalier, Deming & Post seem to be my new owners all right. But it's upsetting. I come across on the damnedest passage bar none this rotten old tub ever made, with a whole litter of gales chasing me all the way and the sticks saying in her God only knows how, and a young whip-snapper comes aboard me and tells me I've changed owners. For God's sake, how fast do I got to sail this damn' boat, anyway ? "

" Cotton ? " repeated young Ames.

The captain looked up at the faint voice.

" Up six cents when I left," he said. " What of it ? Ain't Smith brought in the *Napoleon* yet ? He cleared two days before me, and she's a crackajack."

" You're the first boat in in seventy-one days, Captain. Your news is going to give us a corner on cotton, if we play it right." The shakes began to get young Ames. They had been right.

Captain Brown took off his spectacles and rubbed his forehead with both hands.

" Smith ain't in ? You suppose he went down ? My God," he cried, lifting himself with his hands. " He promised to pay me forty dollars in New York ! "

" I don't know," said young Ames feebly.

Captain Brown looked at him again. He let out a yelp, grabbed young Ames in his huge fists, and rushed him to a port. " Let her reach bottom," he said. Young Ames looked down at the ocean. He felt like a letter being opened by the village blacksmith. Then he was hauled back and dumped in a chair. " Brandy," said Captain Brown. " I thought you were a sailor when you came aboard. My God."

He poured into the same dirty glass, and young Ames made a face. The captain saw it. " You needn't get critical," he said. " It's the only one left and I had to take it to bed with me to keep it from getting broke." He watched the colour come back into the pinched freckled face. " That's better," he said. He pointed to the letter. " I'm under your orders, apparently. What do I do ? "

" You keep out of New York till the mails close, that's all," said young Ames.

The captain's eyes bulged.

" I can't do that," he said.

" You've got to."

" We've been sighted by the telegraph. Do you know that ? Do you think I'm going to take a whole day sailing the harbour for the whole town to laugh at me ? "

"You're under my orders," young Ames said stoutly.

"We're at sea, my boy, and I'm the boss on this packet." Captain Brown struck the table with a hamlike fist and blew at young Ames like a walrus. "Don't you forget it either."

For a moment young Ames thought he was going to be sick again. He breathed hard and confronted the captain's stare as steadily as he could. Then he said slowly, feeling rather like a man making a statement on the gallows. "Maybe the firm could make it worth your while. How much would that be? Twenty-five dollars?"

He was right. An acquisitive gleam came into the captain's eyes.

"If you put it that way—*fifty*," he suggested. "For my feelings' sake, and another fifty for my reputation maybe."

"One hundred dollars," said young Ames. It was no time to haggle. But he thought of Mr. McVitty.

"Hold on a minute," said Captain Brown. "I've got to be insured in case that fool Smith don't make port."

"That's not our business, and you know it," young Ames said firmly. "We don't own the *Napoleon*."

Captain Brown sighed.

"All right," he said. "But you'll have to put it on paper."

"If you'll give me paper and ink I'll do it now."

"Yes, but will they honour your word?" asked Captain Brown, looking intelligent.

"I'm their agent," young Ames pointed out. "Doesn't it say so in that letter?"

Captain Brown let him have Mr. Post's note, and young Ames read it.

"ARMITAGE V. BROWN, *Master*.
"BARQUE *Lily Dean*.
"SIR,—By the enclosed bill of sale, you will observe that the ownership of the Lily Dean has changed from Lamar & Phisterer of this city to Chevalier, Deming & Post

of the same. This letter will be brought to you by John
Ames, a young man in the employ of Chevalier, Deming
& Post, and you will obey as closely as is consistent with
the safety of your ship any orders he may give you. In
this matter you may accept him as acting as the representative of this firm."

It was dated and signed " Henry F. Post, Partner."

" It will do legally, I guess," said young Ames, in a
slightly bitter tone. " A young man in the employ " ; not
" our Mr. Ames," not even " our representative." He
might as well have said " young Ames " and let it go at
that. Mr. Post was an unfeeling man. He drew a deep
breath and steadied his voice. " I'll make it out as an
agreement to pay a bonus of a hundred dollars in recog-
nition of your fast passage. Will that do ? "

" As long as the figures read one hundred dollars," said
Captain Brown affably. " People like you and me have
got to look out for ourselves, don't we ? " He tightened
his muffler carefully. " I ought to be getting on deck,"
he said.

Left alone, young Ames stared at the sheet of blank
paper. His hand shook a little as he reached for the pen.
He had an idea it might very well be the last bit of clerking
he would ever do for Chevalier, Deming & Post ; he
didn't need Mr. McVitty beside him to realise that a
hundred dollars was a lot of money for a clerk to throw
away.

Then he sucked in a small breath, ducked his head, and
wrote with a flourishing hand.

5

In Mr. Chevalier's office on the front of Number 42 South Street the three partners and Mr. McVitty were in conference. They had a quart of brandy from the oldest pipe in the cellar and glasses on the table.

"Do you suppose he made it?" Mr. Deming asked, breaking the silence.

"We'll know pretty soon."

Mr. Chevalier, immaculate, his white head brushed to the last hair, drummed his fingers on the table top.

"Send one of the other clerks up to the Exchange to relieve the man you have there, McVitty."

Mr. McVitty went out into the counting-room. They heard him tell Cummings to go up and relieve Gibbs, the translator. "Tell Gibbs to report to Mr. Chevalier immediate."

"It's blowing up, gentlemen," said Mr. Chevalier, who had gone to look out of the window. "It must be nasty outside the Narrows."

"He'll be aboard by now," said Mr. Post.

"Aye, if he's aboard at all," said Mr. McVitty gloomily.

"There wasn't any one else to send," Mr. Post said defensively. "It was mostly young Ames's idea, anyway, and he was dead set to go."

"There's one thing," said Mr. Deming. "Suppose the master don't agree to delay?"

Mr. Chevalier turned back into the room.

"I don't think we need worry about that. I fancy young Ames won't hesitate to bribe him."

"What makes you think so?"

"Any clerk that has the nerve to call on his employer's niece in his employer's new coat and wish his employer a Happy New Year in his employer's own house won't hesitate to spend his employer's money."

"Your coat?" asked Mr. Deming.

Mr. Chevalier sat down, helped himself to a little brandy, and briefly described young Ames's New Year's call. He had barely finished by the time Gibbs appeared at the office door.

"No bulletins," he said, his eye on the brandy.

"He must have got aboard her," said Mr. Deming.

Gibbs said : "I damn' well hope he did. Whoever sent him ought to be horsewhipped."

Mr. Post's face stiffened.

"I sent him," he said coldly. "He wanted to go."

"Of course he wanted to go. The whole thing must have been his idea. But no decent man would have sent a boy out on a day like this."

"That will do, Gibbs," Mr. Chevalier said.

"All right," said Gibbs. "I've said what I wanted to. I can borrow a horsewhip if Johnny doesn't get back."

"That's enough," said Mr. Chevalier. Then for a moment his eyes softened. "I know you're fond of the boy, Howard."

Gibbs looked at him stonily, turned on his heel, and banged the door after him. For a moment Mr. McVitty's outraged snorting breaths were the only sound in the room.

"Forget it, Post," Mr. Chevalier said abruptly. "And if you can't quiet yourself, Mr. McVitty, please go out." He drummed on the table. "We're not going to have time for sentimentality. Who's that?"

The man running up the stairs came direct to the office, knocked, and immediately entered. It was Cummings. "The boat's reported in the Narrows, sir."

"Yes."

"That's all, sir. The bulletin is unsatisfactory. The weather is thickening, and I understand they can get only parts of the message. The Exchange is very excited, sir."

Mr. Chevalier thanked and dismissed him.

"Do you think he made it?"

"He must have," said Mr. Deming.

Mr. McVitty blew his nose and went out to the counting-room. This wasn't his way of doing business. " I wonder did he have to pay the boatman ten dollars," he thought, and took snuff. He was getting as bad as the rest of them.

In the office he had left, Mr. Chevalier said : " Gentlemen, I've drawn up letters of credit in favour of Maitland & Henriquez in New Orleans for a million, with orders to buy while there's a bale left in first hands."

Mr. Deming looked at him with admiration. Chevalier had always seemed to him a staid sober old Federalist merchant. But Mr. Post only nodded coolly.

" All we need to go ahead is definite advice on the market," said Mr. Chevalier.

It was then that they heard young Ames galloping up the stairs to the counting-room.

6

It wasn't exactly a gallop, for the seasickness was still in his legs, and he was a little bit scared now he had the firm to face, with an expense account of something like a hundred and forty dollars. For it had been Captain Brown's idea to get him ashore at New Utrecht again, and Jarge and Mr. Doaks had required an additional fifteen dollars as a persuader.

Though the trip had been quick, with only a short way to go, the water was worse. It was something he knew he would dream about to his dying day. It had shaken his confidence ; and the drive to Brooklyn hadn't helped, for the hack driver, luckily still in town at the same saloon, had very nearly embalmed himself by the time young Ames found him, and after the first quarter mile had fallen off the box. Young Ames had had to do the rest of the driving himself.

He walked slowly into the counting-room to meet a stony silence. He could have counted fifteen before any one moved ; and then it was Gibbs, with a sudden wide smile on his dark face who said : " Good God ! It's Johnny."

" Amen." Mr. McVitty sounded like a man in church. He took a prodigious double helping of snuff and sneezed for the first time in any one's memory. In the midst of the explosion, they heard Mr. Chevalier's bell ringing imperatively.

Mr. McVitty got unsteadily off his stool. He stuck his head through the office door, sneezed, gasped, " It's the boy," and beckoned to young Ames. " They want you," he said. " I cannot go in myself." He closed his eyes tight and shut the door blindly at young Ames's back.

Young Ames stood still. He was still shivering, his damp clothes like graveyard garments sticking to his body, and he confronted the three partners like an errant puppy. For a moment they had nothing to say. Then Mr. Chevalier filled a glass with brandy.

" Here," he said, " you need it, Ames. It's the 1801."

His blue eyes speculatively watched young Ames's face. " You've had a rough time," he said.

Young Ames drank his glassful, laid it down empty, and nodded.

" Stout lad," said Mr. Deming.

Mr. Post said nothing. His wooden face was no more than attentive, as far as young Ames could see.

" Mr. Post was right about the cotton," he said, addressing Mr. Chevalier. " It's gone up six cents."

" Have you got definite assurance of that ? " asked Mr. Chevalier.

" Yes, sir. The captain said Liverpool was wild about it. He has advices for half the houses in this city, handed on at the last minute." He drew a deep breath. " I had to offer Captain Brown a hundred dollars, Mr. Chevalier. I wrote him out an agreement over the firm's name and signed myself as agent.

He waited.

Mr. Chevalier only nodded. " It's cheap," he said.

" There's forty dollars spent on boat and hacks. About forty, anyway. Some of it's still owing because Mr. McVitty only gave me twenty-five."

" Mr. Deming can take that up with Mr. McVitty."

Young Ames let out a long breath.

" Thank you, sir."

" Our thanks are to you," Mr. Chevalier said shortly. " When will the ship reach the city ? "

" Captain Brown said she'd be in about five. He daren't wait longer. He said the gales were catching up with him. It's been a miraculous passage for the *Lily Dean*; the *Napoleon* cleared two days ahead of her."

The partners exchanged glances.

" It's possible she might come in any time," said Mr. Deming.

Mr. Chevalier said : " Yes."

Mr. Post only nodded. He turned to young Ames.

" Did the *Lily Dean* have any advices for us ? "

" One from Constable & O'Hara. I saw it when Captain Brown opened the safe to put in my agreement for the hundred dollars. I've got it here."

" You've got it ? " exclaimed Mr. Deming.

" Give it to me," said Mr. Chevalier.

He opened it, read it, and glanced up.

" There's no mistake. Frank Constable says cotton shows no signs of stopping. He urges us to buy."

He turned to young Ames.

" How did you get hold of it ? "

" He left the safe open," said young Ames. " But it's all right, sir, I told him about it when we were pulling away from the ship."

Mr. Chevalier's blue eyes protruded slightly.

" Do you remember my saying you were an unscrupulous rascal, Ames ? "

" Yes, sir. You said the times were unscrupulous, too."

" I am confirmed in my opinion," said Mr. Chevalier. " That will do, Ames. You'd better get on dry clothes."

He turned to the partners. " We must get our man off at six to-morrow. The question is, who's to go ? " He caught sight of young Ames still in the doorway. " What is it ? " he asked irritably.

" I thought I'd better say that Wentz of Pruyn & Co. is keeping a watch on this place, sir."

" We know that," said Mr. Chevalier. " Ask Mr. McVitty to come in at once."

7

It was snowing again. Young Ames in his room at the top of the building looked out of his dormer window and saw the snow making snakes along the roof.

He was dressed in his ready-made clothes, the grey trousers and white waistcoat he had bought to wear with Mr. Chevalier's coat on New Year's, but he had no coat of his own to go with them. He felt tired and discouraged. The excitement was over as far as his own part in it was concerned. He had been sent up like a child to get dry. He looked at the tweed jacket he would have to put on, still sodden with salt water and smelling like a sheep in front of the fire.

Mr. Deming had called him a stout lad, but Mr. Deming was impulsive. Young Ames had long since come to realise that what Mr. Deming said did not mean very much in the firm's policies. Mr. Post had said nothing at all. Mr. Chevalier had given him brandy, which he would also have given a chilled horse, and said he was unscrupulous. He hadn't liked the packet from Constable's being removed from the safe. " I ought to have told him Captain Brown gave it to me," young Ames thought.

The river was darkening. There was no sign of the *Lily Dean*. He knew that she hadn't docked yet, for he could see Old Slip plain enough from the window. But he thought she must be in the river because a knot of people were huddling against the snow at the end of the pier. If Brown could hold her out for twenty minutes the game would be won. Chevalier, Deming & Post would have what amounted to exclusive and positive knowledge of the market to themselves for twenty-four hours.

In spite of himself he let the excitement of it creep into him again. When Gibbs entered with a bottle of Marseilles Madeira, and a pastry hot from the cheap store in Jones Lane, he found young Ames with his nose glued to the pane.

" She's not in yet," he said. " Come and eat."

" I can't eat till I see her get in. What time is it ? "

" Past five, Johnny. You've done a hell of a good job for the house." He put the pastry on the bureau that had an upended chamber pot for one leg, and pulled the cork from his bottle.

" Come on, Johnny. It's only Marseilles, and you deserve some of Laurie's old 1811 if any one ever did." Gibbs's dark face grew thoughtful as he stretched himself on the teetery chair and held a clouded glass to the light of the fire. " It's not like gin for the alcohol," he said, tasting it, " but it is more elegant. Come along and sit down."

" I can't. I ought to go down. "

" Nothing's doing. Only McVitty left. The partners all went out an hour ago. Cummings is out on Old Slip."

Young Ames hesitated. Then a shouting that the wind made thin and far came up to the window. He turned to look out again and saw the *Lily Dean* in the river. She was inching her way in, a dark shadow, her lights glistening through the wet points of flying snowflakes.

" She's coming ! " cried young Ames.

" It makes no difference now," said Gibbs. " We've got the corner in our hip pockets."

" By God," said young Ames. " I wish I had a thousand dollars ! "

" Why confine yourself to that ? Make it two, while you're wishing. Come and eat."

" Even five hundred," said young Ames. " I bet Mr. Post would let me put it in on the credits for myself."

" That stick ? " Gibbs snorted. " But I bet they'll give you a bonus anyway."

" Ten dollars ! " Young Ames's face fell. He took the glass from Gibbs. He'd as lief have had liquorice water. But he took it down, and then started the pastry.

" Kidneys," he said.

" It's not every day you get a corner in cotton," said Gibbs. " I recognise the fact even if Chevalier, Deming & Post don't."

They were comfortably at it when Cummings came into the counting-room. They could hear his feet on the stairs. The rattle came up through the stairwell and echoed under the roof outside the door of young Ames's room.

Then, a little while afterwards, they heard another step, much slower, ascending the two flights towards them, and in a moment Mr. McVitty had entered.

" Ah, Aloysius," said Gibbs. " The pastry's gone, but have some wine."

" I'll not join in wasting your substance," Mr. McVitty said disapprovingly. " Ames, Mr. Chevalier will be wanting the advices off the *Lily Dean*. He left instructions for you to fetch them to his house. They're ready." He blew his nose slowly, and relined it as deliberately with snuff.

" You're not sending him out again to-night ! " exclaimed Gibbs.

" It's orders," said McVitty.

" By God, I'll take them myself."

" He does not want you. He wants Ames," Mr. McVitty said so portentously that young Ames looked quickly into his gaunt grey face.

" He's been wet and cold, and it's courting a chill to send him out," said Gibbs.

"You need not worry. Mr. Chevalier's a thoughtful man," said Mr. McVitty. "Are you ready? Come along, Ames."

8

With the papers buttoned into his coat, young Ames emerged from the door of Number 42 and took the wind full on the face. He had a glimpse of a carriage waiting by the kerb, the coachman muffled up, and the horse restless in spite of their harness blankets. But he paid no attention to it, turning blindly uptown.

The voice came to him clear through the driving snow, and he wheeled with a quick shiver of premonition. For the first time he recognised the team. Then he saw that the window of the near door had been let down.

He went back and looked in. There was just light enough for him to see the red-lined interior, but he did not need to see the person who had called to recognise her. He remembered the chilled faint perfume as if it had been yesterday instead of a month ago.

"Yes, Miss Chevalier," he said stupidly.

"Won't you come in?" she said. "It's freezing cold. Uncle lent me the carriage to take a bottle of wine to Miss Verplanck and asked me to pick you up on the way home. He wants you to supper. Just us," she added. "Uncle and Aunt and me."

Young Ames climbed in dumbly, closed the door on his heel, and had to try again. The team immediately started off and darkness entered the carriage.

"Here's the robe," she said, and his hand touched her glove.

The carriage proceeded smoothly and silently through the snow. Young Ames sat in stiff silence. He knew he must seem like a fool. He had been thinking of her all through the month, and he hadn't a word to say to her.

As they passed a light he stole a glance at her. She was looking straight ahead, her lips composed, her hands hidden in her muff.

But at the next light her eyes encountered his and he looked so caught out that she laughed.

" I'm afraid you can't see me very well, Mr. Ames."

" No," he said unhappily.

" We'll soon be home," she said.

" Yes," he said.

No, yes ; didn't he know any other words ? All he could do was sit there and smell the sharp smell of his damp tweed jacket slowly engulfing them both. But she showed no sign of noticing it. She sat mercifully quiet the rest of the way, and when he looked at her again her eyes were lowered, and she seemed lost in her own thoughts.

They turned off Broadway at Chambers Street, entered Hudson, and kept up a spanking trot to the corner of St. John's Park. When they drew up at the house on Laight Street, young Ames got out quickly and held the door for her. She accepted his hand lightly, stepped quickly over the sidewalk and stood waiting on the stoop with the snow driving into the fur of her cloak. She had her hand on the knocker, but before she knocked she faced young Ames in the door light and smiled.

" It's not like your last visit, is it ? " she asked mischievously. " The impostor has turned into the conquering hero."

Young Ames gaped.

" I just wanted to say I feel very excited about it. I think it was wonderful. Uncle is very excited too." She let the knocker fall. " Now," she said, " we shall be very decorous and proper and speak only when we're spoken to."

The coachman, who had stayed waiting on the box, drove the carriage away as soon as the door was opened by the butler. They stepped out of the driving snow into the hall with its comfortable hush of warmth. Miss

Chevalier gave young Ames a slight nod and hurried up the stairs.

The butler, having discovered that young Ames had neither hat nor greatcoat, said : " Mr. Chevalier says for you please to come into the library till the ladies come down."

He led the way through the ladies' salon and the dining-room into the library at the back of the house where Miss Chevalier had rescued young Ames from his eggnog on New Year's.

Mr. Chevalier was alone in front of the fire.

" Come in, Ames," he said. " I hope you're free for to-night."

" Free ? Yes, sir. I've brought the advices."

" Oh, thank you." Mr. Chevalier put them on the table. " A glass of Madeira, Ames ? " He poured glasses for young Ames and himself. He stood a moment silently regarding his clerk, his glass half raised, and young Ames, feeling all at sea, imitated his posture.

He saw Mr. Chevalier's face slightly flushed from the warmth of the fire and the wine he had already taken. The blue eyes, usually so uncompromising, were specula-tive.

" Post and I talked it over," he said. " Post agreed with me." He raised his glass. " We've decided that it is better that none of the firm go. It would create comment."

" Yes, sir," said young Ames, raising his glass also.

" So, before we get down to business, let's drink to the success of your trip to New Orleans."

Young Ames drank automatically, and the wine was in his throat before the meaning of Mr. Chevalier's words took hold in his brain. He almost choked.

Mr. Chevalier said slowly : " I should prefer it if you spent the night here. My coachman will take you down to the Amboy boat to-morrow morning. He'll leave you on Washington Street and you can walk over to Pier 1. I have a thousand dollars cash for you and the letters

which you will deliver to Maitland & Henriquez. You'll
have a day's start on the mails and you mustn't lose the
distance. You'll have to use your own judgment about
bribing stage drivers and steamboat captains."

" Do I get the boat in Pittsburgh, sir ? " young Ames
asked. He had to ask something.

" Wheeling," said Mr. Chevalier. " It will save you a
day." He paused. " I take it you're willing to go."

" Yes, sir."

" Then I'll give you the money to-night. You've shown
to-day you know when to spend," he added dryly. " But
you'll have to make the thousand reach New Orleans."

" Will you pour me a glass to drink to Mr. Ames's
journey, Uncle ? "

Miss Chevalier was standing in the door. She was
wearing the same rose dress he remembered, and she
smiled when she saw that he did. Her colour rose a little,
but she regarded young Ames with level eyes.

" Might a lady make suggestions, Uncle ? "

Mr. Chevalier glanced at her indulgently.

" Yes, Kisty."

" I do not think Mr. Ames's coat is adapted to the
bribing of steamboat captains. It's no criticism of the coat
in itself, please understand, Mr. Ames."

But young Ames suddenly laughed.

" I agree, Miss Chevalier," he said. " But what can I
do ? I haven't any other."

She nodded.

" I remember that one of Uncle's fits you very well.
I've asked Amber to bring it down to the hall, with Uncle's
approval. Will you change now ? "

Young Ames glanced at Mr. Chevalier.

" She's quite right," said Mr. Chevalier. " I'd never
have thought of it." Suddenly he burst out laughing.
" Good Lord ! " he said, " I said these were unscrupulous
times. Even the ladies are infected by them."

III

DOWN THE RIVER

Boarding the Amboy boat at twenty to seven in the morning of February 2, 1834, young Ames found himself to be the first passenger. It was nearly half an hour before sunrise ; the Jersey shore was still invisible in the darkness beyond the dirty grey river. The air was biting cold. A light wind was blowing from the north-west, and the waves slapped the edge of ice that bound Pier 1.

In the steamboat cabin his stomach was suddenly constricted by the mingled reek of coal gas and dead tobacco. One of the hands was feeding the stoves from a liberal scuttle ; but though the draughts glowed red-hot, the fires had succeeded in creating only small islands of warmth. The hand eyed him, and went out, letting the door swing shut. He obviously was not a talkative man.

Young Ames sat on a side-wall bench ; but he did not feel well sitting down, and he got up again and went to one of the stoves. It, however, seemed to be still delivering more gas than heat, so he abandoned it. Standing all alone in the middle of the floor, he felt his confidence oozing out of him. New Orleans was over two thousand miles away, and he had only thirteen days to get there if he was to beat the Great Southern Mail that would start on Monday. That mail would be carrying advices to buy cotton from most of the commercial houses in the city ; if it got there before he did, Chevalier's letter of credit for a million dollars would be worth no more than the wax used to seal it with. He patted his chest to make sure that the packet was in place inside his waistcoat, in the pocket Miss Chevalier had sewn there for him.

" You'll want a safe place to carry it," Mr. Chevalier

said last night. " Have you got an inside pocket to your waistcoat, Ames ? "

" No, sir," he replied. But when Mr. Chevalier started to call for one of the maids, Christine Chevalier asked if she might not be allowed to sew Mr. Ames's pocket. " It will make me feel as if I had some share in the business, Uncle," she explained.

His mind recalled the picture she made sitting in her uncle's parlour, taking quick competent stitches and glancing upwards at his face as she bit the last thread. The waistcoat had been against her cheek and the thread had cut a line on her underlip.

He had not seen her in the morning. Though there was no reason why he should have expected her to come down at that hour, he was disappointed. Mr. Chevalier was not a good substitute. His dressing-gown made him look gaunt and he wore a stocking cap over his head, with a coloured silk tassel flicking his arrogant nose. " Always eat well for a journey, Ames," he said, compelling his junior clerk to have a second helping of boiled ham when the first had already felt like too much. " Here's the packet. And here's your thousand dollars. You'd better divide it up among your pockets. I'll ask no account of it if you get to New Orleans in time." He stared hard with his china-blue eyes. His voice dropped a note. " I'm depending on you, Ames," he said. " If we get this corner in cotton, we'll come through. Otherwise it will be bad times. Credit's gone to smash. Damn that ignoramus. The carriage is ready for you."

Young Ames stowed away the packet and the money, and wiped his mouth.

" Good-bye, boy," said Mr. Chevalier, holding out his hand unexpectedly. Young Ames realised when he took it that it was the first time he had ever shaken hands with the boss. Mr. Chevalier's nose twitched. Perhaps it was the sight of his own coat on his junior clerk. " Good-bye, sir," said young Ames.

The hoofs of the horses were muffled on the snow. St. John's Park was silent, and the houses all the way down Greenwich Street were dark. There was only the track of the first water-cart making loops along the kerb from door to door to show that any one else in New York was awake. . . .

He crossed the cabin to a window facing the pier. He could see quite a way along Battery Place towards Bowling Green. On the right, Castle Garden raised its turtle roof towards the sky. The horizon was beginning to pale. The mail cart came along Battery Place, and two men started lugging the mail sacks on board. Then the first carriage appeared from Washington Street. It was followed at irregular intervals by other carriages and hackney coaches. The boat came to life. A couple of men took stations on the foredeck to cast off the ropes. The pilot appeared with a seaman's cap on his head and a green muffler round his neck. Men started yelling back and forth, and steam burst from the safety valve in a harsh tearing sound.

Young Ames paid no attention to the passengers embarking. He did not turn from his window even when they entered the cabin. He had seen their faces as they came on to the pier and recognised none of them as belonging to Pruyn's or any other commercial house.

The warning bell in front of the smokestack began to ring. A carriage came spanking up to the pier ; and a man who had been loitering on the north corner of the pier stepped forward to look at the occupants. Young Ames recognised Wentz, Pruyn's clerk. He himself ducked back from the window before he realised that it would be impossible for Wentz to recognise his face at that distance with the cabin lights behind it.

The men by the ropes were getting ready to cast off. Beyond Wentz, at the corner of West Street, young Ames made out a second loiterer, whose tall figure seemed familiar. Suddenly the man reached out and grabbed a passing boy. They appeared to talk for a moment ; then the boy came rushing on to the boat. He burst into the cabin shouting : " Mr. John Ames, Mr. John Ames."

The warning bell stopped, and in the abrupt hush young Ames turned and said, " Here."

" Package for you," said the urchin. He thrust the package into young Ames's hands and bolted out.

Mechanically unwrapping the package, young Ames watched out of the window. The ropes were being cast off. There was a stir in the boat, and the sigh of steam going to work. The wheels groaned in the ice, broke free, and started churning it against the piles ; and the pier, carrying the whole of Manhattan Island with it, began slowly to back away from the boat.

A lump came into young Ames's throat. He did not want to go to New Orleans in that moment, at all ; and as he stood for one instant, slack-handed, watching the river come between the boat and the pier, he almost let the package drop.

Then he looked down at it and saw that the wrapping contained a flask. A slip of paper was tied to the flask by a white cord. He lifted it close to read the scrawled message.

" Good luck, Johnny," it said. " I thought you might need something so send this. I had it in my pocket the last time I went to Charleston. The brandy is the 1801, but old C. won't miss it. I've got two dollars on you to beat the mail. Old McVitty was the taker. Cross my heart. Howard."

Young Ames looked back at the city. The boat was already swinging to head downstream ; but he could make out the figure of Wentz walking slowly along Battery Place. The tall man had come away from the building on West Street. He was standing on the end of the pier now.

Young Ames felt the lump get very big, but he felt better, too. He jumped to the door, opened it, and stood on deck. Gibbs saw him, for he raised a long arm. Gibbs thought he could beat the mail, and Gibbs knew a lot.

He stayed on deck until Castle Garden was down in the bay and the boat was wearing away east of St. George's instead of for Amboy Creek. A deckhand, whom he asked about it, spat overside and said there were six inches of ice in the channel and they'd have to go round Staten Island. No, it wouldn't take too long. Maybe three hours if it wasn't rough outside.

2

At Amboy Landing, young Ames had his first sight of a brigade of cars, for the locomotives had been put in service last fall. He could see the engine even before the boat landed, a black contrivance with a naked smokestack, at the head of a line of oversized, coachlike cars resting on iron rails. The very look of them, he thought, was speed, and he wished they had a railroad built all the way to Pittsburg. It quickened his blood to see them waiting for him.

He wasn't the only passenger to be taking his first ride. Several others, he could see, looked excited, even apprehensive. Every one in New York had been shocked in November when the last car of a train bound to Border-town had come off the rails and overturned, killing one man and breaking the legs of two innocent children. A lady in a fur mantle took one look at the engineer putting a fresh log into the firebox, and demanded that her husband make the man promise not to drive too fast. Avoiding other people's eyes, her husband went up beside the engine and passed the engineer a cigar. From the man's face, young Ames judged he hadn't said anything about going slow. He looked excited. But he told his wife : " The engineman has promised to keep under fifteen miles an hour, dear." Several people smiled, in spite of the wind that made them shiver.

Before the lady's suspicions were aroused, the porters

came off the steamboat with the bags and parcels and mail and started stowing them in various of the cars, while the captain, a gentlemanly man with a drop on the end of his nose and a tin horn slung from his shoulder, assigned the passengers to the seats their bags were stowed under. In ten minutes more they were all aboard.

Young Ames thought he was lucky to have a seat facing forward. By leaning his cheek against the window he hoped to have a view of the engine on the curves. But now he watched the captain, who was glancing first back and then forward, to where the engineer stood beside the big driving wheel and tied his hat on with a strip of red cloth. The captain blew a long blast on his horn and shouted, " Go ahead, Harry," and swung himself through the door of the front car.

Every one could hear the hiss of the engine and the first scraping of the drive wheel on the iron rails. The car gave a violent jerk, and the lady in the mantle a slight scream. A succession of jerks followed, of gradually dimishing violence ; and suddenly they disappeared altogether, and the cars were rolling away from the river with a steady clacking over rail joints. The smoothness was incredible. The anxious lady's husband remarked on the fact in a loud voice. " By Jove," he ejaculated, " it's like flying."

The cars went off through a deep cut that shut off their view with snowbanks, but before long they were out in level country, and the captain said, " We're going pretty well now."

One of the passengers asked how fast they were going, at which the captain pulled out his watch and appeared to listen. In a moment he said they were travelling at about twenty miles an hour. The lady in the mantle immediately hoped that they would not have a concussion with another train, but was assured that that was impossible. " Harry is a first-rate engineer," the captain said. " He knows how to drive."

After the first excitement, however, most of them settled down. There was little to see, for the smoke and sparks from the engine stack, pouring past the windows and rattling against the sides of the cars, obscured any good view of the country.

At Bordentown, thirty-six miles on their way, the end of the railroad, they found that the Delaware was frozen tight, and instead of the steamboat, stagecoaches were waiting to take them as far as Camden. A slight drizzle had begun, and after the speed of the cars the slow lurching of the coaches seemed insupportable, but by four o'clock they reached the quay, and at five young Ames found himself in the Mansion House at Philadelphia.

The proprietor assured him of a room and a place on the Pittsburgh mail, starting at four o'clock the next morning. There was no earlier stagecoach leaving ; and the mail, he was told, would get him to Pittsburgh by noon of the third day. He had a hearty supper and a clean bed to himself. He had taken a whole day to come just under a hundred miles ; but by the time the Southern Mail left New York to-morrow morning, he would be three hours out on the road to Pittsburgh ; and in Pittsburgh he would hire a special to carry him to Wheeling.

As he put out the candle, he wondered for a moment whether Gibbs was eating supper alone in his room under the roof of Number 42 South Street. He reached out towards the chair on which he had left his waistcoat to make sure that the letter of credit was still in the pocket Miss Chevalier had sewn for him. " There, Mr. Ames," she had said. " I hope it will hold." She had known very well it would hold, he thought ; it seemed strange that a girl who would some day inherit a fortune should be able to sew with such competence. But before he could go on with the idea he had fallen asleep ; and it seemed less than a minute till the porter waked him for the Pittsburgh mail.

3

In the late afternoon of February 8, the Ohio steam
packet, *Express*, swung down the river into the Louisville
quay shortly after the rain stopped falling. In the pilothouse, the pilot, one foot on a spoke of the wheel, eased
her in with a feeling of satisfaction. They had made a
fast passage from Wheeling, riding a rise of the river.
Except to load wood, they hadn't made more than half a
dozen landings. It made him feel a little bit more like
one of the crackajack Mississippi pilots. While his cub
looked on admiringly, he hooked his finger elegantly on
the bell-pull and rang the engine-room. The thrash of the
paddles stopped. The boat slid in over the grey river, her
escape pipe suddenly plumed with steam and her gallows-
frame beam idling slowly to rest as she came into the
dock.

On the forecastle beside young Ames, the captain stood
by the landing plank and folded a hundred dollars in
bills.

". Maybe you'll find a Mississippi packet ready to go,"
he said. " But Saturday's a bad day, mister." He was
curious about the young man in the swell coat and creased
trousers. He had seen some pretty fancy gentlemen on his
packet, but this fellow with the freckled face and sandy
hair was not his idea of one. He had money, though, and
money made the wheels go round. " You'd· better go
straight to Allen's Hotel. They'll tell you there."

The plank thudded on the dock, and young Ames went
over it holding his carpetbag in his hand. There was a
hackney coach down the quay. " Allen's ! " he said to
the driver.

" Cost you a dollar," said the driver, unhurried. " You
better wait and share."

" Go ahead," said young Ames. " I'm in a hurry."

"This ain't France," said the driver. "But it's all right with me."

They lurched off at a smart trot, swung down Main Street, and pulled up in front of the hotel with a shower of muddy water off the wheels.

"Wait for me," young Ames said.

"A room, sir?" asked the desk clerk.

"I want to find out if a New Orleans packet is ready to go," said young Ames, putting a dollar on the desk.

The clerk glanced at young Ames, swung nonchalantly to a notice tacked on the board behind him, trailing his hand over the dollar bill and sliding it into his pocket, all in one motion.

"The *Independence*, Captain Stankard, is down to leave at five," he said.

"Is she a fast boat?"

"High pressure," said the clerk. "She's a seven-day boat. Stankard's got new boilers."

"Thanks." Young Ames was out on the street again. The hotel clock had said ten minutes to five.

"Can you reach Shippingport in ten minutes?" he asked the hack driver, and eyed the slat-ribbed team. "Two dollars," he suggested.

"They don't run good for two dollars," said the driver. "But they go pert for three. Contrary bastards, mister."

"Three," agreed young Ames.

He hardly had time to slam the door. The spray from the tyres came up like a mane, collapsed, and fell back into the ruts. The first pothole jerked his bag off the front seat.

He had done some fast coach travel coming over the Alleghenies. Those mail-line drivers could snake their coaches down the mountain roads on the dead run. But for sheer action this stiff and mildewed hackney coach and two slat-ribbed horses beat the cars. He put out both hands, right and left, to hold himself in place. Even over the muddy rush of the wheels he could hear the driver flailing his whip on the peaked rumps of his team.

The driver was enjoying himself. By God, if the gent wanted fast time, he could take the consequences.

" Come all ye young people, I'm going for to sing,
  Consarning Molly Edwards and her lovyer, Peter
      King . . ."

It was only a mile to Shippingport, but he'd show the little Yankee that Kentucky still had horses, and at least one man to drive them.

From time to time, young Ames risked a glance towards the river. He could see it, a pewter sheet, marked with the threads of eddies like long hairs. The grey and dun hills beyond careened against the watery sky. Six minutes after the hack left Louisville, the rain came down once more.

It slanted against the horses as they gathered themselves for the long slope down to Shippingport. A few small rain-soaked houses, a few warehouses back from the quay, a turn in the road and a wild juicy slewing of the hack's hind wheels, the driver jubilantly roaring a line from his song, " I'm done a-driving hossis and I've come a-courting you," and the team was floundering in the mud with the pole between their eyes.

" There's the God-damned boat," shouted the driver. " Boilers, beds, buck niggers, and bugs, she won't carry no faster, mister."

Taking the three damp dollars from young Ames, he put them inside the hatband of his hat and watched his ex-passenger run for the landing. He looked small enough to be the runt of a runt-bug breed when you saw him in front of the white mass of the steamboat.

They had already hauled up the gang-plank, the boat was fired-up and steam-high ; you could tell by the way the escape-pipe kept popping. By God, it would be a shame now if the young fool didn't make her. The pilot was craning his neck out of the window looking away from the landing.

"Put down that plank," roared the driver.

He jumped down after young Ames and went hollering in his wake. A little crawfish like his passenger wouldn't be heard when the wheels began to churn and the boat was already sliding back into the river. "Give me your bag," yelped the driver, and wresting it from young Ames's hand slung it beautifully on board the forecastle.

The big buck nigger beside the landing plank opened his mouth in a pink and ivory gape.

"You bring that bag back here," shouted the driver. "You on the roof! We'll put the law on you, by God. There's five hundred dollars in that bag. Don't you dast throw it, either, you fool nigger. If she sinks in the watter, they'll put you in jail and take you out to burn on Sundays."

The darkey, disturbed, picked up the bag and went shouting half-way up the larboard stairs for the captain. In a minute the captain himself came out on the pro-menade deck. He was a squat, immensely broad man with a full black moustache and a white stock like a Methodist preacher. His voice could be heard, when he chose, across the Mississippi in a snowstorm. He chose to use it now. "What do you mean throwing things on my boat?"

"You bring that bag back," yelped the driver. "A hell of a steamboat man you are. You let a passenger put his valuable on board, and then you back out before he can put his tobacco in the water. He's a nephew of Andrew Jackson." The driver could think fast when he had to. He turned a solemn face to his passenger. "Where do you want to go to? New Orleans?" he asked quietly.

"Yes." Young Ames had seen the captain's start. It amused him to think what Mr. Chevalier would say if he knew that his business representative was getting attention not for the sake of Chevalier, Deming & Post, but for Andrew Jackson. He grinned for the first time in five days, and said, "Bank business."

For an instant, even the driver looked impressed. But he recovered himself with a squirt of tobacco and shouted to the captain : "It's business with the Bank. Are you a Biddle man ? "

By this time the pilot, condescending to notice the exchange, had already rung down the engines. The boat was drifting.

The captain walked to the limit of the promenade deck and craned up.

"You'll have to put in again, Mr. Kitchel," he said. "We've a passenger on State business."

Young Ames turned to the driver. "Here," he said. "Here's a dollar extra, and it's not from me. Take it from General Jackson and drink his health."

"By God," said the driver. "I'll do it to the last cent. Say, mister, *are* you Old Hickory's nephew ? "

Young Ames winked.

The driver slapped his wet buttock. "By God," he said. "I can see it. It's the hair, and the white face. By God, there's a pitcher in Ellery's tap. He must have had freckles too, when he was your age. No offence."

4

The big buck nigger caught young Ames's arm and brought him on to the deck as if he were a baby. "Yes, *sah* ! " he said, showing his gums. "Sho' was close ! "

"All right, Nep." Captain Stankard had come down from the promenade deck. He was a great bear of a man, taller than young Ames by a good head, when they came face to face. It was only his immense breadth that made him seem short. "Amory Stankard, sir," he said, holding out his hand. It swallowed young Ames's fist and constricted it with fingers that had thickets of wiry black hair between the joints.

"My name is Ames, Captain Stankard." Young Ames watched a negro waiter take his bag away from the deck-hand. "I'm sorry I had to trouble you to come back for me. They told me at Allen's that the *Independence* was a flyer. I couldn't afford to miss her."

Captain Stankard rumbled in his thick chest.

"I'm proud to serve any man that claims kin with Andrew Jackson, Mr. Ames." He turned to shout after the waiter : "Put the gentleman in Louisiana, Henry."

The packet had been tenderly backing into the channel. Now she swung with the current. In the hidden spaces behind the boilers, the engine-room bell struck sharply. The paddles bit the river. The fire doors clanged shut and a roar shook the chimneys as the draught took hold. The wheels gained speed. The deck quivered underfoot like a live thing, laying hold of the soles of young Ames's shoes, till he felt the flow of power in his entire body.

He took one look at the grey river stretching out ahead ; he could see the smooth surface plucked with rain, but when it came in to the bows it was like glass ; he didn't need to be told that this was a fast boat. He turned to find the speculative eyes of Captain Stankard studying him with a cold grey light like that upon the water.

"I didn't think I'd make it, Captain."

"Well, you did, sir. You said you were making the full voyage to New Orleans ? "

"Yes," said young Ames. "As a matter of fact, my business isn't official, and I'd rather not have it get public."

"I understand, sir. When you deal with unscrupulous men, you've got to go Injun. By God, Old Hickory's the man to Injun when he needs to, sir."

"Yes," young Ames agreed. He was climbing the larboard stairs behind the captain. He paused on the pro-menade deck before the entrance to the saloon. "I've

heard this is a seven-day boat, Captain. Will it be worth
your while to guarantee me under seven days to New
Orleans for seven hundred dollars ? Half down, and half
when we reach New Orleans," he added.

A thousand dollars would have sounded more like
Andrew Jackson, he thought ; but seven hundred was all
he had left in round figures. Captain Stankard stopped
short.

" I'm proud to serve General Jackson, sir," he said. " I
don't believe in the United States Bank. I'd rather take
a loan from a bitch polecat in hell than I would from
Nicholas Biddle."

Captain Stankard let out a breath of fire and whisky,
and young Ames could not help admiring him. He'd have
to remember that estimation of Nicholas Biddle to tell
Mr. McVitty when he got home. But he said gravely :
" I believe Mr. Jackson would honour your opinion,
Captain Stankard. You know, though, he's not the man
to let his friends down. If he found out about it, he
wouldn't like it."

" Everybody knows that. Old Hickory likes his friends
and hates the British. If he wants to pay me seven hundred
dollars, I'm proud to take it. I'll get you there. I've got
two creation pilots on this packet and I've got the boilers
to give them what they ask for."

5

Henry, the black waiter, was assiduous. Every time
young Ames turned around he seemed to be handy, saying :
" Yes, *sir*, Mr. Ames." It made him feel important.
Washed, his unruly hair combed, and his clean shirt on
his back, young Ames circulated through the main cabin
and had a whisky at the bar.

He had been to the office, under Henry's guidance, and
there had paid over the three hundred and fifty dollars

he had promised. The captain had sealed it and locked it in his strongbox.

" She stays there, Mr. Ames, till you bring me the other half in New Orleans, or I pay this back to you if we're late. But we won't be. Mr. Kitchel's shoving her along right now and we'll do better when we hit the river."

" I guess you know how to handle her, Captain," young Ames said.

He made his voice off-hand. He wasn't going to show that three hundred and fifty dollars meant anything to him. He was a Jackson man, passing out the Federal money. You passed a law and filled your pockets and those of your friends.

" I'm not going to lose by it either," Captain Stankard said. " By lightning, no. It would be fun helping lick Nicholas Biddle, but the way Old Hickory does it, I find it a pleasure. We'll cut the small landings right down the river, sir."

Already the *Independence* had passed Clarksville and Portland. The pilot was holding her offshore now.

" Stankard's out for a lightning passage," said a quiet elderly gentleman in a high white hat down the bar from young Ames. He had a soft, cool voice. " Must be running on a wager."

" Mr. Kitchel's hunting swift water all right," agreed the bartender. " They say there's a Jackson man on board and Captain Stankard's trying to beat seven days down."

" Is that so ? " inquired the gentleman. " I'll have to circulate around a little and see if we can make a pool. Know who the man is, Jerry ? "

" Well, not exactly," said the bartender in a low voice. " But was you outside when we left Shippingport ? " He sent a glass down the bar towards his black helper. It might have been chance that made it stop close beside young Ames's hand. " I was inside myself, Mr. Willoughby, so I didn't get sight of him then."

Trying not to look self-conscious, young Ames leaned his elbow on the bar and met the kindly, intelligent eyes of Mr. Willoughby, and then looked beyond them. He could feel the vibration of the engines coming up through the boat and bar to his elbow, putting a tremor on the surface of his whisky.

" It's confidential business," said the bartender in his low voice. " One of Jackson's moves against the Bank, they say."

" I see," said Mr. Willoughby, raising his glass. " Good luck to it, I say, Jerry. I wonder if we'll beat the *Tecumseh's* time."

Young Ames thought he had better get away from the bar. He wasn't used to whisky anyway ; small beer at this time of day was more his style ; but a man couldn't be long on a packet like the *Independence* and not be influenced by the thick carpets, gilded woodwork, and the mirrors. As he made his way down the long saloon, he was aware of heads turning to look after him. The waiter, Henry, was moving here and there, offering newspapers or fetching drinks or a shawl for a gentleman with a cold, for there was a continual slight draught from bow to stern. " Dat gent'eman's from Mr. Jackson in Washington City," he whispered. " He's in a hurry to bust the bank in N'Orleans. Paying Cap'n mos' a thousand dollars, he is. Yes, sir ! "

Two gentlemen at a corner table, out of the way of traffic back and forth through the saloon, glanced after young Ames, then at each other, and nodded. He squared his shoulders and stiffened his back. Nobody had ever looked at him this way before. It was a brand-new experience. He wished Mr. McVitty could have been aboard to see it.

He went out on the promenade, standing back under the overhang of the hurricane deck. It was nearly dark. In the west there was only a liquid silvery sheen, but it served to mark the river ahead. Behind him, along the promenade, the windows of the saloon and staterooms made regular bright squares against the deck and rail.

When the furnace doors were open, the draught sucked up the towering stacks and a long trail of sparks was left behind them. For an instant he could see the red glare upon the water. Craning over the rail, heedless of the rain, he saw the bow wave folding into it, and beyond, the foam from the wheels a red-hot froth. Mr. Kitchel was driving her.

" Breath of air, sir, before supper ? "

A gentleman had come out of the saloon.

" Yes, sir," said young Ames.

" They're laying supper now, but I like to get a breath myself. Cold night, sir."

" Yes, it is," said young Ames.

" First trip down the river ? "

" Yes."

" We'll be opposite Salt River before very long. The *Independence* is a crackajack. No finer packet on the river. I use her whenever I can. You from the North, sir ? "

" I was born in York State."

" Fine state, York State, sir. Have a cigar ? Maybe now you'd like to have the towns pointed out to you. If you do, I'll be happy to oblige you. My name is Felton, sir. William Coffee Felton, of New Orleans."

Young Ames gave his name.

He was beginning to feel cold, so when Mr. Felton suggested that they have a drink before supper, he agreed. Mr. Felton was insistent that he be allowed to buy Mr. Ames his choice. Young Ames took whisky, and Mr. Felton, commending him on his preference for straight liquor instead of cocktails, had whisky himself. When young Ames asked him to name his second, he said that Mr. Ames was monstrous polite and he would be honoured. As Mr. Ames had already toasted their great mutual national hero, he suggested that they drink to any young

lady Mr. Ames might care to name. Young Ames said
he would but in a public place he preferred not to name
her and Mr. Felton said he honoured him for it. He was
a gentlemanly fellow, and young Ames was glad to have
a seat beside him at the long table.

He was hungry. The fried chicken and sliced ham and
oranges and the sweet potatoes that he selected from the
menu seemed to him the finest meal he had eaten in his
life. His neighbour on the other side from Mr. Felton
proved to be a Mr. Gratwick, also from New Orleans, and
he expressed the hope that Mr. Ames have a pleasant and
successful trip and asked whether he would not like to
while away the evening with a friendly game of cards. Did
he play poker, perhaps?

Young Ames said he had played brag a little, but not
enough to be much good, but he would be glad to try a
few hands. The whiskies were buzzing slightly in his head.
He felt fine, however, and he was anxious to make friends
of these two gentlemanly men.

They played for a couple of hours after supper. At first
young Ames experienced a slight shock to find that the
others expected to play for money, but when they saw his
hesitancy they said it would be for a small stake, say a
dollar limit, just so he could get his hand in.

The whole affair seemed very friendly to him, sitting in
the corner of the saloon. He could see the people playing
cards or backgammon all down the immense length of it,
reading or smoking by the windows. When he so much as
lifted a finger, Henry or another waiter would appear as
if by magic. It was his first experience of luxurious living.
It was a wonderful feeling. He, young Ames, the junior,
junior clerk of Chevalier, Deming & Post, was as good
a man as any one on the boat in actual fact.

It occurred to him once when he lost a dollar on two
pairs that he was playing with Chevalier's money; but
after all it was money he would not need to spend now.
Mr. Chevalier himself had said he need make no accounting

so long as he got to New Orleans ahead of the mails. And he was as good as there.

Besides, as he saw half an hour later, he was not risking it. He was playing too sharp for these fellows. He had rolled up twenty-five dollars. Quite a group of onlookers had gathered round to watch. Among them he noticed Mr. Willoughby following his play with intelligent eyes. Mr. Willoughby did not look as if he approved.

By the time the game broke up for the night, young Ames was fifty dollars to the good. It was the most money he had made in his life. As he lay down in his comfortable clean bed, he thought that at last he was beginning to get on in the world. Then he realised that he had had a little too much to drink and he made up his mind to be careful.

6

As Mr. Felton said, packet travelling was a pleasant way to travel, but when you got on board a Mississippi packet like the *Independence* it made a man feel downright national. As he watched the river unfold a continent, day by day, young Ames began to realise that there were people to whom New York was just the name of another town, a little bigger than Louisville, perhaps, maybe like Memphis, or even New Orleans, without quadroons in it. He could understand why so many of them talked large, and why to their way of thinking Andrew Jackson, though he might not appreciate the nice points of international trade, could be counted on to put sense in the government. Trust a man who knew horses and cotton and plantation niggers to put the British and the British buyers in their places. He'd make Nicholas Biddle look like a stump-tail bull in fly time.

Every morning Captain Stankard made a point of hoping young Ames had been comfortable. Captain

Stankard was polite in the saloon, and it was gratifying to be singled out for his attention. Young Ames realised this when he saw the Captain raising Cain over one consignment of wood for the furnaces, or when he listened to him roaring at the nigger deckhands. At such moments he would spatter the sky itself with whole constellations of profanity. One wondered what the inmates of the ladies' cabin made of it. But when one saw the captain return to his office, wiping the last drops of profanity from his moustache, one understood that though he had two spheres of action, he did not mingle them.

"Playing cards?" he asked. "I hope you had good luck."

Young Ames felt pleased.

"I've been doing pretty well, Captain."

"I'm glad to hear it, Mr. Ames." He pushed at the rear door of the main cabin. "They tell me Andrew Jackson was a great hand to play when he was your age, sir. I guess you know your way around."

"I guess so," said young Ames.

He had to laugh when he recalled what Mr. Willoughby had said last night. They had finished up about eleven o'clock, and both Mr. Felton and Mr. Gratwick had said they'd had enough. "He can't do anything wrong," Mr. Felton said. "I never saw such luck played so close before."

Mr. Gratwick hadn't said anything at all. He had merely shaken his smooth dark face with a little smile that made young Ames feel almost sorry for him. They weren't used to playing with a New York clerk like Ames; they didn't realise that a man had to use his wits to get a living in New York. Poker was just another form of business.

He went outdoors to let the wind blow some of the tobacco and whisky fumes out of his head. He climbed up on the hurricane deck where he had only the stars overhead and the texas and the pilothouse and the two towering stacks behind him. The roar in them was like the breath of a racing horse magnified a thousand times ; but he had got used to the sound of the engines and the rush of the water and the occasional strokes of the engine-room bell that made a kind of punctuation, like commas, in the packet's course.

He took his place in the darkness, leaning on the forward rail and looked directly down upon the forecastle, and the bow slicing the dark river, and a solitary deck-hand sitting there. There was no moon ; but there were stars. It was a warm night for the season, and young Ames thought he could stay there till dawn without getting chilled. It made him wonder till he remembered they were getting south. Sometime to-morrow, maybe in the late afternoon, they'd be reaching Natchez.

It startled him when a voice said : " I trust I'm not disturbing you, sir. Oh, it's Mr. Ames, isn't it ? "

" Yes, sir," said young Ames. " You're not disturbing me."

He turned, recognising Mr. Willoughby's voice. The stacks were letting out sparks ; they gave a faint light, and he saw Mr. Willoughby's tall hat and his intelligent face faintly outlined. Then, as the darkness shut down, he had a glimpse of the tip of the pilot's cigar, like a firefly in the pilothouse.

Mr. Willoughby was silent a moment. Then he said : " I don't think you've travelled much, Mr. Ames ? "

" Not much," said young Ames.

" I was watching your play to-night," said Mr. Willoughby. " You seemed to be doing well."

" I had pretty fair luck to-night, sir," young Ames said, making his voice as modest as he could.

" You're playing again to-morrow, sir ? "

" They wanted to play to-morrow afternoon. I promised them they'd have a chance to get some back." Young Ames felt like a man of the world.

" It doesn't surprise me," said Mr. Willoughby. " Mr.

Ames, I'm enough older to give you a piece of advice. I'd go right careful in my play to-morrow."

"Thank you, sir, I will." Young Ames listened to his own laugh. " I guess they thought I was an easy mark. They don't know that you've got to be pretty sharp to get along in New York City."

Mr. Willoughby flicked the ash from his cigar and the point glowed up in the movement of air.

" Well, sir, you'd better stop when you lose a little. I think those men are professional gamblers."

" I don't intend to lose much." Young Ames laughed again.

" I know," said Mr. Willoughby. " But you will. I've seen it happen before. Men like Mr. Felton mark their cards."

" How do you know that ? "

It occurred to young Ames that Mr. Willoughby did not think much of him. He knew himself those men were sharp, but they hadn't been able to handle him yet. Three days. Why, he had won almost two hundred dollars. And here was this old gentleman trying to tell him he was a fool. He might have been Mr. McVitty himself.

Mr. Willoughby said dryly : " You can't make a living on luck, sir. Not the living Mr. Felton wants, and if I were you, I'd quit while you have money in your pocket."

" They'd think I was scared."

" They'd say so," agreed Mr. Willoughby. " They have caustic ways of speech to keep a sucker playing on their line. I've seen them shame a man so he didn't dare come out of his stateroom from Baton Rouge to Vicksburgh."

" If they're trying to play sharp with me, they can look out for themselves," young Ames said. " I won't stop them."

Mr. Willoughby said patiently : " You may have noticed that most of your good hands come after Mr. Felton fixes the cards and Mr. Gratwick deals. Also your two heavy losses that brought you back to the two hundred dollars they seem to have fixed as your limit came at the same time. They don't bet much when you've done the shuffling."

Young Ames hadn't noticed anything like that.

He said : " I'd see them if they tried to fix the cards."

" You think so ? You've not travelled much, as you yourself admitted."

Young Ames was mad. He didn't want to be rude, for Mr. Willoughby seemed to mean well. He supposed he would have to listen to him, but he didn't pay much attention as Mr. Willoughby told him stories of gambling he had seen. " Just once," he finished, " did I see a gambler licked down solid. Just like in your case. One of them had fixed the deal, and then he went out for a minute and a gentleman who was watching took the top card off the pack and slid it under without the second gambler seeing him. It changed the order of the cards, you see, and gave their fish the aces instead of the kings."

Young Ames appreciated that. Catching a man at his own game was the kind of thing he liked to think of. But Mr. Willoughby went on, " To-morrow, if you persist in playing, I shouldn't wonder if you won at first. Then your luck will start going. Just a little. You'll win a few. And then they'll fix you for a big hand."

Young Ames made a move from the rail. " If it's all the same to you, sir, I think I'd better get to bed."

Mr. Willoughby made no effort to detain him.

" Good-night," he said. " I wish you well."

7

Just how it happened wasn't clear to young Ames. It had poured rain since eight o'clock. The air was heavy, and an hour after dinner he and Mr. Felton and Mr. Gratwick had sat down at the corner table they had come to regard as their own. There weren't many passengers in the main cabin ; another set of poker players ; and two old Southern gentlemen who played backgammon and drank juleps, each swearing a blue continual vapour at his own luck and complimenting his opponent's play.

Young Ames stared at the table and watched Mr. Gratwick smile a little as he pulled seventy-three dollars to his mounting pile. Mr. Felton hadn't been doing so well. He had won a couple of hands from young Ames, but lost them three times over to Mr. Gratwick. Mr. Gratwick had the luck all right. With his thin dark face and quiet hands, he looked almost drowsy. The waiter, Henry, appeared at young Ames's elbow with a whisky and young Ames drank some, and then said : " I didn't order that."

But Henry had gone away and nobody else noticed and he finished it. He had no idea what time it was, but he picked up his cards and saw three queens waiting for him cheek by jowl. He riffled through his bills. He had twenty-five dollars left. " I'll stand," he said, and Mr. Felton had three cards. Mr. Gratwick dropped his cards, so Mr. Felton and young Ames worked the betting up to twenty-seven dollars, and young Ames said : " I've got only twenty-five here. I'll have to get some from my stateroom."

He felt a little unsteady as he returned with the three hundred and fifty dollars he was going to owe Captain Stankard when they reached New Orleans.

He sat down feeling shaky and nervous. His face had paled so that the freckles stood out. It made him feel mad to see Mr. Willoughby walking slowly towards them from the bar.

Mr. Gratwick had dealt the hand, but it didn't run to much ; nobody liked it. It went to young Ames for three dollars. The next hand Mr. Felton won fifty dollars from Mr. Gratwick and young Ames sat back and watched them close. They didn't do a thing he couldn't follow. Young Ames dealt and won again, fifteen dollars this time. The play was high, he knew, it had to be high now. And there was no doubt his luck was turning. But everybody tossed out the next two hands. A big hand was making up. You could feel that. Young Ames dealt, and Mr. Felton shuffled for Mr. Gratwick's deal. The hand young Ames had dealt went out for seven dollars, nobody calling Mr. Gratwick. Mr. Felton excused himself from the next hand and left the cabin.

It happened while Mr. Gratwick was picking up and sorting the seven dollars. He smiled and said he would pay his barber with it. Nobody but young Ames saw Mr. Willoughby slip the top card off the idle deck and put it underneath. Mr. Gratwick was quite unsuspicious as he picked the cards up and dealt them to young Ames and himself. " I bet this hand is going to be a thunderer," he remarked in his smooth voice. " We've been pretty quiet lately."

Mr. Willoughby caught young Ames's eyes. He nodded. Then he drifted round the table and came behind young Ames's chair. He watched young Ames spread his cards.

For an instant they blurred before his eyes, then young Ames saw the four kings side by side.

" Cards ? " asked Mr. Gratwick.

" Not for me, sir."

." I'll have to have three."

He dealt them out to himself and fanned his hand.

8

Against four aces, there was nothing he could do. Nothing at all.

He sat in his chair and watched Mr. Gratwick pick up the money.

" Bad luck, Mr. Ames." Mr. Gratwick's voice was smooth, without a shade of expression. " We'll try again after supper, sir ? We'll wait till we've cleared Natchez."

Young Ames nodded. He knew he couldn't play. He was figuring how to tell Captain Stankard that he wouldn't be able to pay him the promised money. . . .

Mr. Gratwick had left the cabin. The waiters had lighted lamps. It was dark outside the windows. The rain still fell. Down below, the strokes of the engine-room bell sounded faintly. The paddles eased and the boat went suddenly quiet except for the slow gasping in the stacks. Then the whole packet came to life. Everybody was on the promenade except young Ames. The waiter Henry touched his elbow. " Natchez, sir. You want to go on shore ? "

" No thanks, Henry."

" Mr. Willoughby sent his compliments, sir. He say for me to tell you he had to go ashore here. He say for me to wish you luck, Mr. Ames."

Young Ames looked up.

" You feelin' sick, sir ? "

" I'm all right."

He understood now. He thought he had been smart. It wasn't Mr. Felton and Mr. Gratwick who had hooked him, but Mr. Willoughby. They must have planned the whole business from the start. He had swallowed the bait belly deep. It was so obvious now that even his ears got red.

He didn't know what Captain Stankard was going to do. He didn't like to think of it ; but he had better tell him right away and get it over with. " Where's Captain Stankard, Henry ? "

" He's down on de fo'castle laying out the dock niggers," said Henry. " You'll excuse me, sir. I got to tend the passengers."

Young Ames followed him to the promenade.

Captain Stankard was using his boot on a dawdling dockhand. He stopped to tip his hat to a passenger. Then his voice exploded and young Ames decided not to go down.

He called another waiter and told him to ask Captain Stankard whether he would see Mr. Ames in the office as soon as he was free.

It was half an hour before Captain Stankard came through the cabin. " You wished to talk to me, Mr. Ames ? "

Young Ames gulped.

" Yes, sir."

The captain's body seemed to fill the passage. He unlocked the door of his office, went in, offered young Ames a chair, and sat down at his table.

· " What can I do for you, sir ? "

Young Ames drew his breath.

" I've been a fool. I've lost the three hundred and fifty dollars I promised you."

Captain Stankard's eyes froze.

" I saw you were playing pretty steady." His voice was quiet. " I thought you knew your way around."

" I thought so too."

" Who'd you lose to ? "

" Mr. Felton and Mr. Gratwick."

" I never saw them before. I thought you were all right as long as you didn't tie up with Willoughby. I had him promise not to play with you."

" He didn't, Captain. Not at cards."

" Tell me what happened."

Young Ames did so.

Captain Stankard couldn't hold himself in any more. He broke his rule entirely. He hogwashed Mr. Willoughby from stem to stern and through his middle, and out the other side. " He broke his word," he said finally. " He made a fool of me. I'm not saying what I think of you. Every man's a fool at least once, and the worst ones lost other people's money. But if Willoughby thinks he can keep that money, he's a bigger fool than you are."

" I'll do anything I can to help."

" I don't need your help. You'd better stay on this

packet and keep your mouth shut, sir. And don't bother
me." He got up, unlocked his desk drawer, and pulled a
heavy pistol out of it. For a minute he looked down at
young Ames's miserable face. He snorted.

"You mean all right. I ought to have looked out for
you, but I thought any Jackson man would have sense
enough to care for himself. You can come with me if you
like, but keep in back, Mr. Ames."

Young Ames followed him down on to the forecastle.
The captain roared for the engineer. "Mr. Wales," he
said, "Willoughby has got away with three hundred and
fifty dollars owing to me. Never mind how, we've got to
get it back."

Mr. Wales was a hulking river man in a sweaty shirt.

"Just a minute," he said.

When he returned he had the firemen and all the deckhands in his wake, armed with fire hose, axes, and any
other tool that presented opportunities for mayhem. "I've
told the boys we're going to crack some gamblers' skulls,"
he said.

"All right," said the captain. "Henry, where did Mr.
Willoughby go?"

"He told a boy to take his bag to the Rose Cardine."

"That'll save us breaking in more than one door," said
Captain Stankard grimly. "Come along, boys."

The crew went stamping through the muddy road
along the river. A couple of houses shut their doors when
they heard them coming, but young Ames could see girls
hanging out of the upper windows. Music stopped when
they went by, with their lanterns swinging their shadows
against the house fronts.

It was his first sight of Natchez under the hill, but
he didn't like the look of it. As he followed in Captain
Stankard's wake, he hunched his shoulders against the
rain.

The Rose Cardine was a house at the end of the road,
with the river sucking almost under its wall. It stood square

against the darkness, unpainted in their lantern light, its windows shuttered and door barred.

Captain Stankard stamped up on the porch, and hammered the door with his fists. He got no answer. "Hey," he roared, "open up." He hammered again. "Does anybody know who runs this place?"

When nobody seemed to, he bellowed with rage. He called on Willoughby, Felton and Gratwick by name. He announced if they would come out and hand over the money they had stolen off his boat he'd leave the house alone. But the house might as well have been a cotton bale for all the answer he got. Three minutes of silence was enough for him.

"Break down the door, boys."

The door was heavy, but two darkeys had a short spar which they used as a ram. They swung it together, half a dozen times, and the door splintered. Captain Stankard stuck his head through the hole and roared for the owner to come out. This time he got an answer.

"You get the hell out of here," shouted a man. "What do you mean breaking my door down and bothering me?"

"Are you the owner of this house?"

"Yes, I am. And I ain't letting you nor no other thief break in. Get out!"

"I'll get out when you hand over those three gamblers."

"They ain't here."

"I know they're here."

"You're a liar."

"What's that?"

"I said you was a liar. If you don't get out I'll put a bullet through your head."

"Go ahead," said the captain. "I dare you."

He pulled back quickly. He heard the man laugh. "Finish her up, boys," Captain Stankard ordered.

The two negroes swung the spar again. At the first crash, a pistol went off inside and a bullet slugged into the upper panel. The negroes dropped the spar and jumped out of range. The voice inside said : " I warned you. If you don't get out I'll let you have it from the winder."

The hangers-on, who had been gathering in the street, began to evaporate ; but Captain Stankard had turned unexpectedly calm. " Mr. Wales," he said to the engineer. " Go back to the packet. Tell Mr. Kitchel to bring her down here. Get out the long hawser and we'll wrap it round this house. By God, if they don't pay over, I'll have them in the river." As Mr. Wales and a couple of his firemen went back up the street, he said to the rest : " Keep tight to the walls and ring the house, boys, I'll watch the door."

Inside a woman's squawk joined raucous laughter. The woman opened a window. " Are you wet out there, dearie ? " she asked, and half a dozen more joined her. Pretty soon there were titters all up the road at the way the Rose Cardine was calling the captain's bluff.

But Captain Stankard wasn't bluffing. In half an hour they heard the sound of slow paddles in the river and the clear notes of the engine-room bell. The *Independence* came drifting through the rain like a great careful water-bird upon the river.

She came in nearly to the bank and hung there, bows on. A darkey on the forecastle tossed a line ashore. In fifteen minutes the hawser was run out and wrapped around the house and the steamboat had backed out until the slack had been taken up.

Captain Stankard went up beside the broken door and yelled inside. " I'll give you two minutes to hand over that money," he said. " I've got a steam packet on the other end of this rope and she's fired high. You can take your choice."

" You go to hell."

" Let her go, Mr. Kitchel." The paddles began backing slowly. The hawser straightened and grew taut. It made a faint humming sound. The paddles moved faster. The wash rushed in against the bank and the stacks on the boat belched fire. A deep cracking sounded through the house. She seemed to rise a moment, but she came down solid. Only then young Ames saw that the house had moved a good five feet towards the bank.

" Give her more steam, Mr. Kitchel," shouted the captain. " Throw on a bushel of resin." Heedless of pistol fire now, he stood out by the corner of the house swinging his lantern like a madman. " Pull the rats in whole," he roared. " If the house don't sink, ram her down, Mr. Kitchel."

The wheels piled a wave on shore ; the house groaned again. It began this time a steady riverward movement, and suddenly the porch dropped off the front. Wild yelling broke out inside. The owner appeared in the porchless door. His pistol hung in his slack hand, but the other pointed a roll of bills.

" Take your money, for God's sake, Captain. Just leave me be."

Captain Stankard yelled to Mr. Kitchel to ease in.

" It's a good thing you didn't bust my hawser," he said. " I might have got mad at you."

The man started to step out on his porch and saw just in time that there was nothing but a cellar hole under him.

" My God," he said. " Oh, my God."

" Put the damages to Willoughby's account," suggested the captain. " and toss the money to this gentleman."

Young Ames caught it.

" Count it," said Captain Stankard. " Never trust a bastard is what my mother always said to me."

Young Ames's hands were clumsy. He felt the rain run down his back. " There's five hundred and fifty dollars here," he said.

" Well, don't jaw about it," growled Captain Stankard.

Young Ames said sullenly : " I don't want any money but the three hundred and fifty dollars I owe you."

" Will you shut your mouth ? " said the captain. He gathered his men around him. " Keep those fire hoses handy, boys. We ain't on board yet. Mr. Ames, you keep alongside me." As they walked back through the rain he began chuckling. He was in a roaring humour when they reached the landing and found the *Independence* easing in. " That was a right handy piece of navigating, Mr. Kitchel," he said. " By God, sir, it was creation pretty."

Mr. Kitchel said, in a supercilious voice, " First time I ever worked a tugboat," and lit himself a cigar.

" Top nasty, ain't he ? " asked Captain Stankard. " All pilots are. They've got to be. All they got to know is how to steer a boat, and learn the river. Take Mr. Kitchel, now, he don't know yet what a pitman is. If you told him it oscillated he would knock you down."

He bawled to Henry. " Fetch I and Mr. Ames a bottle of that champagne wine, boy. Bring it to my office. And tell Mr. Kitchel, if he's thirsty, to step on down."

In his office, Captain Stankard turned on young Ames. " You're a foolish man, Mr. Ames. I should have thought after what's happened you'd know enough to take any money you can out of men like Willoughby. No matter how you do it."

" I don't like to take it, and I didn't get it myself. I'm glad to get what's owing to you, but that's all."

" You're a fool, sir. But I like you, sir. Henry, ain't you pulled that cork yet, you lazy black dumbheaded thief? I'll tell you what, Mr. Ames. I'll take half the profit. Give me four hundred and fifty dollars and keep the other hundred. We'll say it's for straining my packet's boilers if that makes you feel better. And we'll say this champagne wine is on Andrew Jackson. Here's his health."

9

The *Independence* had tied up to the levee before dawn. Two hours later, young Ames sat opposite Mr. Henriquez, of Maitland & Henriquez, cotton brokers.

"From Chevalier, Deming & Post? You left New York on February second? That's fast travelling, Mr. Ames. Thirteen days! That's lightning fast, sir. Mr. Chevalier's fortunate to have you in his house."

"I had the luck to catch a fast packet at Louisville, sir. The *Independence*, Captain Stankard."

"Captain Stankard is a first-rate man," said Mr. Henriquez.

"Yes, sir," said young Ames. He meant it. He didn't feel his old self-confidence at all, even if he had beaten the Great Southern Mail.

Outside the office the street was full of negro voices and strange French and Spanish words. New Orleans wasn't the kind of place he would like, he thought. You couldn't figure out these Southern men at all. Like Mr. Henriquez, for instance : he didn't look like a business man to young Ames. He looked too fat and sleepy. Even opening the packet, he took his time.

· The packet contained several documents. One, a letter from Mr. Chevalier, Mr. Henriquez read through slowly after asking young Ames's indulgence. He folded it when he was through and glanced at the letter of credit.

"This is a pretty fine piece of work you've done," he said to young Ames. "I'm going to be as owing to you as Chevalier himself. But excuse me, sir, you must be pretty well played out. You'll spend a day or two in New Orleans? I'll be proud to have you as my guest, sir."

"No, thank you," young Ames said. "I'd like to start back as soon as the buying's over. Chevalier's will be anxious to hear about it, Mr. Henriquez."

"You're quite right. You can catch the packet *Constitution* in the morning. If I haven't bought in 10,000 bales by then I'll go out of business." Mr. Henriquez seemed to have come to life. He rang a bell. "Fetch Mr. Maitland in here," he said to his clerk. "Tell him to hurry." He gathered up the papers. "Why," he said, "here's something addressed to you, Mr. Ames."

Young Ames took the folded single sheet.

"John Ames, Esq.," it said on the cover. He did not recognise the hand. When he opened it, he was glad he had decided to go straight back.

"I knew you'd beat the mail. I hope my hasty stitches held."

IV

PAY TO THE ORDER OF JOHN AMES

IF young Ames had had any notions of spectacular promotion in the counting-room of Chevalier, Deming & Post, after his trip to New Orleans, they did not materialise in a hurry. The morning after his return, Mr. McVitty had taken him into Mr. Chevalier's office and stood solemnly, snuffling in his stoppered nostril, while Mr. Chevalier asked about the trip and expressed satisfaction with the report of Maitland & Henriquez on purchases made in his name. "An excellent piece of work, Ames," he said. "I have talked with the junior partners, and Mr. McVitty. I may say we are unanimous in agreeing that your term of probation in this counting-room has been successfully passed. We shall raise your pay from seventy-five to a hundred and fifty a year, beginning as of January first, last. Also we shan't expect you to run the small errands for the staff. The boy—what's that boy's name, Mr. McVitty?"

"Finnegan."

"Finnegan will relieve you of those chores," said Mr. Chevalier.

He stood up behind his mahogany desk and held out his hand to young Ames. Mr. McVitty looked on with an air of pride, as if he felt entitled to most of the credit.

"Very few young men have had your opportunities, Ames," he observed.

"There aren't many would have made use of them so ably," Mr. Chevalier said quickly. The two old gentlemen smiled at each other and Mr. McVitty took snuff up his free nostril. Young Ames, remembering the mess he had got into on the Mississippi steamboat, flushed and mumbled his thanks.

But after two weeks of watching cotton kite skyward, seventy-five dollars a year increase in salary began to seem a picayune reward. The whole Exchange was in a ferment over Chevalier's corner. It was universally agreed to be the smartest deal since the famous Black Ball corner of '25. Little Pinky Finnegan, whose short jacket and tight trousers always had trouble connecting, brought in a goggle-eyed report of having seen Pruyn, of Pruyn & Co., cut Mr. Chevalier dead on the corner of Wall and Pearl.

"Howland bought at seventy dollars the bale this afternoon," young Ames burst out as he and Gibbs shared supper in his room at the top of Number 42. "It must be close to eighty now in Liverpool. Chevalier stands to make half a million." He jumped up and went over to the window and stared bitterly down at the dark line of the river. "And I did it. You can't deny that. You'd think that was worth more than raising my pay to a hundred and fifty a year. Even Cummings gets more than that!"

Gibbs, his dark face sympathetic, tilted the bottle of Marseilles over his empty glass. He remembered the evening a month after being hired, when young Ames allowed himself three years in which to become a junior partner, and it was easy to imagine how he must have planned on his future during the long trip back from New Orleans. Gibbs's thin lips twisted one-sidedly. Having to wait might be hard on a cocksure youngster. But it wasn't like starting one's majority with plenty, throwing it away, and facing a long downhill to the end of one's life.

" Listen, Johnny. Old firms like Chevalier don't do anything in a hurry except grab the profits. And that's only a habit."

" By God, Gibbs, you ought to hear Westerners talk about people like us." Young Ames's eye lit up.

" You haven't become a Jackson man, have you ? "

" I could pretty easy."

" America's Robin Hoods," said Gibbs. " Take from the rich and give to the poor. But those stout-hearted boys are never willing to admit that you've got to keep poor people poor to make it work."

Young Ames grinned. " They're right about one thing though. New York City isn't America."

Gibbs laughed.

" No," he agreed. " The eagle screams a damn' sight louder over Bean's Station than he does over Broadway. You'd better sit down and finish this cheese pie before I do."

He rose and crossed the hall for his pipe. When he returned, young Ames had pulled his stool before the grate and was brooding over the small fire.

" Dreaming, Johnny ? "

Young Ames glanced suspiciously at his friend, his face reddening under the freckles ; but as Gibbs sat down quietly in the jerky rocker, he let his glance wander round the room.

The ceiling sloped past the window, indicating the steep pitch of the roof towards the East River. On winter nights he could hear the wind whistling up the slates. It gave one a feeling of the weight of beams above the plaster. When he had first come into it he had thought it was a wonderful room. But he had not been to New Orleans then, travelling on a crack Mississippi steamboat with a thousand dollars expense money in his pocket. Now all he could see was the cord bedstead with its faded patchwork quilt, the chair and stool and rickety table, and the bureau whose missing leg had been replaced by an inverted piece of chamber crockery.

Gibbs broke in on his thoughts. " Want to make a bet, Johnny ? " he asked.

" What ? "

" I'll bet five dollars that fifteen years from now you'll be telling your son about this place. You'll even tell him about the chamber pot under the bureau, and you'll be proud it was cracked, too."

Young Ames gave a scornful laugh. " You think so ! What girl with any sense would marry a man with a hundred and fifty a year ? "

Gibbs blew a cloud of smoke towards the grate and watched the draught draw it up the chimney. Young Ames hadn't mentioned Christine Chevalier's name since his return. It was natural, he thought, for a young man to feel discouraged in the month of March.

"You can't haul a cart by kicking the dashboard, Johnny. You've done pretty well as it is."

" You sound like old McVitty," retorted young Ames. " All you need is a verse from the Bible." He turned restively on his stool. " If I had a thousand dollars, I'd know what to do with it." His face brightened at the thought. " Two thousand is what I need but a thousand would do. I figured it out coming back from New Orleans."

2

With little Finnegan, who had been hired in his absence, running the counting-room errands, young Ames found himself tied to his desk for most of the day. He had not been back four hours before Mr. McVitty handed him for copying letters to Constable & O'Hara in Liverpool concerning the sale of Chevalier cotton and discussing with great fullness the matter of brokerage fees. " If anything occurs to your expert mind, Ames," the chief clerk said with ponderous sarcasm, " you might take it up with the partners."

Young Ames had not outgrown his bitterness, and there were days, working overtime to catch up on the outgoing files, when he almost wished he were back at his old job running the docks. But the steady climb of cotton in the Exchange fascinated him. Mr. Chevalier apparently was holding on. However he felt about Mr. Chevalier's acknowledgment of his services, he could not help admiring the old gentleman's nerve.

The main problem arising from this policy was the matter of storage. Many of the warehouses ordinarily available to Chevalier were now closed to them ; for rival firms were not inclined to be helpful except at exorbitant rents and Mr. Chevalier wasn't the man to submit to highhanded tactics in others. As for Mr. McVitty, even a triple inhalation of snuff failed to express his wrath.

" ' And there shall the vultures also be gathered.' A man would be safer carrying a thousand dollars through the Five Points," he exploded.

As the cotton continued piling into New York, young Ames pinned a Burr map of the city over his desk and marked down all warehouses known to the firm. The appearance of it with its red and blue ink crosses roused great admiration in little Finnegan. It was, as a matter of fact, the first map of any kind he had ever seen and he got young Ames to show him the block of Elizabeth Street between Walker and Hester

" Gee, Mr. Ames," he said through a strong breath of liquorice. " It's exact, isn't it ? "

" What did you want to find that block for ? "

" That's where I live. I and my uncle, Mike Dolan. He married my sister. He's got the best ratter in Elizabeth Street. She beat the Cross Street champion in Morley's pit last month. She's pure-bred Manchester. He's give me one of her pups. Gee, Mr. Ames, I'd like you to see that pup."

" I'll have no dogs in this counting-room," said Mr.

McVitty. " Nor no lallygagging. Take these letters to the
Post Office right away. And say ' given,' not ' give.' "

" Yes, sir," said Finnegan, grabbing the letters. " But
he did given him to me anyway."

Mr. McVitty said " Faugh," with a retching sound.
" He's been chewing that damn' black dope again. I
don't know where he keeps it. Ames, there's a letter from
Maitland this morning ; they've shipped 750 bales on
the *Shakespeare*, and she's due in, the end of the week.
Have we got any space left ? "

Young Ames consulted his cards.

" We've a hundred in Bailey's on the corner of Beekman.
We're shipping five hundred out of his lofts on the fifteenth.
That still leaves us a hundred and fifty short."

" It's abominable," said Mr. McVitty.

Cummings, who was always ready to solve other people's
problems for them, called across the room : " Have you
tried A. & D. Brown ? "

" ' The dumb ass, speaking with man's voice . . .' "
Mr. McVitty muttered viciously. " Don't be a fool,
Cummings. They're connected with Pruyn and would
steal drawers off of infants. Ames, you'll have to get out
and just hunt us up something."

Young Ames dropped down from his stool without
optimism, and reached behind the counting-room door
for his hat.

" Ames ! " The chief clerk was mending a pen. Without
looking up from it, he said : " Mr. Chevalier wants a word
with you in his office when you get back. He's had a
letter from Mr. Henriquez that concerns you some way,
I believe."

3

Young Ames tramped gloomily down the stairs ; and all the way to the bottom he felt sure that, one way or another, Mr. Henriquez must have picked up the story of his gambling away his expense money on the boat. But as he opened the door on South Street, he suddenly remembered something Mr. Henriquez had said : " I'm going to be as owing to you as Chevalier himself."

The weather had turned suddenly warmer. The cobbles were dry and in the gutter a pigeon was puffing his chest at a biddy. There was a new free note in the shouts of the stevedores, matching the high-dropped cries of wheeling gulls. The wind, blowing in over Brooklyn, was soft to breathe.

Young Ames stared at the long webs of rigging spun against a blue sky and puffed his own chest. By God, he thought, they can't hold me down.

" Hallo, Mr. Ames. You hunting warehouses again ? "

Little Finnegan, with an important wiggle of his rump, walked up and took a stand at young Ames's side, facing the shipping.

Young Ames said : " Hallo, Pink. You don't know of any warehouses, do you ? "

" No, sir. Not myself. But my Uncle Mike might." He gave a hitch to his trousers, closing the gap for the moment, and went on : " I just saw him driving through William Street. Finishing up Williamson's morning deliveries, I guess."

" What were you doing here ? "

" Oh, just running around." The boy cocked an impudent eye. " McVitty says running is good for boys." He grinned. " You looking for warehouses on masts ? " he asked.

Young Ames grinned back.

" It looks as if spring was coming soon."

" It's here now," said little Finnegan seriously. " Uncle Mike says he saw Rowley's pig crossing Broadway this morning. He says when Rowley's pig heads for the North River it means spring's got here. Beats geese, Uncle Mike says. Say, why don't you go see him ? He'll be at Begg's now for his ten o'clock gin. It's four doors up on Gold Street. If you see Williamson's spotted horse in the alley you'll know where Uncle Mike is. I'll give you a card if you want." He fished inside a trouser pocket and brought out a grubby card on which he had written his name. With a stub of pencil he wrote on it, " Introducing our Mr. Ames."

" Thanks," said young Ames. He watched Finnegan bolt in through the door and heard his feet clatter upstairs. Going through Gold Street wouldn't take him out of his way, and he had no idea of where to find more space himself. Besides, Pinky Finnegan talked about his Uncle Mike so much that young Ames was curious to meet him.

He turned the corner of Maiden Lane about ten past the hour and had gone only a few steps beyond when he saw the spotted face of a bony horse peering out of an alley. Almost under his nose, cellar steps emitted a strong smell of stewed oysters and gin. Young Ames went down, pushed open the door, and found himself in a three-cent saloon.

The room was small enough to have been put into the strong room of Chevalier, Deming & Post complete with its bar and the blowsy woman behind it. There hardly seemed space for the patriotic engraving of the capture of Major André and the interesting picture of rats eating the belly of a Chinese prisoner, let alone the three men sharing an oyster pie and enjoying their own gin. All three were wearing leather jackets, narrow-brimmed hats, and short aprons. They all turned inquiringly at young Ames's entrance.

" Good-morning," he said. " Is one of you gentlemen Mr. Mike Dolan ? "

The middle one of the trio tossed off his glass and, admitting to the name, accepted the grubby card.

"Hallo," he said. "Pleased to meet you." When he moved he exuded an interesting compound odour of horse sweat, gin, oysters, grocery goods, and Meyers' Venetian Pomatum. It was obvious to young Ames that Mr. Dolan would make a good show among the Bowery boys on a Sunday Broadway promenade. "Boys," said Mr. Dolan, "this is our Mr. Ames Pink's been telling us about. Mr. Ames, this here is John Foggarty, who drives Artiguenave's cart, and Patrick Rowley of Clark & Cargill (they're hardware). You'll have a gin and lemon? Or name your own? Gin and lemon, Mrs. Beggs." He handed the glass himself from Mrs. Beggs's moist hand to young Ames. "What's that young tiger been up to?" he asked.

Young Ames grinned.

"Nothing at all. I'm looking for storage space for our cotton and Pink said you might know of something. The whole city is holding out on us," he explained. "Mr. Chevalier won't stand for that, you know."

"Pink told us about that," said Mike Dolan, while his two friends nodded. "You understand, Mr. Ames, Pink don't spread trade secrets. No, sir, he's a tight button. Just us. But I don't blame Chevalier. Where would Tammany be without a few hard-fisted old Federalists like Chevalier? Live and let live is what I say." He let out a little gin on his breath and wiped his mouth, while his eyes rolled. "That's what I keep telling Pink. You get into a good, dumbheaded Whig concern, like Chevalier, I said, or like Howland, I said. But don't get mixed up with no new-come business like Fish. You've got to learn the other side to lick them. No offence to you either, Mr. Ames. But Pink's going into politics, you see, and you've got to make friends all over town to go in politics. Finnegan, the people's friend. He ought to be mayor. Well, make it an alderman, if you like, Foggarty. How about Josephs' on the North River? Tried him?"

"He won't take any more," said young Ames.

Mr. Rowley took a drink.

"Mike!" he said. "You remember helping me hunt that damn' pig of mine three weeks ago?"

"Didn't I, though?" said Mr. Dolan.

"We found her in Merry Street. She'd gone and farrowed under the floor of that warehouse."

"For God's sake," said Mr. Dolan. He seemed struck by the recollection. "Seventeen spotted bodies and all of them squealing. And O'Conlon had to complain about the smell they were making in Davison's hearse. We couldn't use one of our grocery carts, you understand, Mr. Ames, and O'Conlon had only bargained on the sow, for he's a religious man and nearly got fired when Mr. Davison smelled it on Monday and O'Conlon tried to tell him it was mice."

"I seen O'Conlon driving them by and took off my hat with the other bystanders," said Foggarty.

"The old pig was that low she was groaning like a corpse herself," said Mr. Dolan.

Mr. Rowley swallowed another drink.

"Well, that's it," he said simply.

"So it is," exclaimed Mr. Dolan.

All three stared at young Ames, who stared back. Except for exhibiting the powerful resourcefulness of the Irish race in New York, he didn't see where it had got them.

"Have another drink," suggested Mr. Foggarty, after a minute.

Young Ames rallied himself. "This is my round," he said. Mrs. Beggs smiled at him and set them up and then, as if she had just been reminded of it, went to water the three pots of Youth-and-Old-Age in the area window. Reaching up to accomplish this task made her skirts lift over a surprising pair of ankles. The men watched them detachedly. Then Mike Dolan explained.

"That warehouse was pretty near empty, I'm thinking."

" Except for the pigs."

" Whose is it ? " asked young Ames.

" We didn't inquire," said Rowley. " We heard that damn' pig making her death groan under it and went in after. But it was between Water and Pearl. There's an alley runs in towards the back of the Walton House. Maybe John knows."

" It happens I do," said Foggarty. " With the widow Sheehan coming round to my old woman and complaining of the pigs that had stunk up the warehouse and the dirty rats that had robbed her of the pigs. She went to the magistrate wailing for a warrant. ' What for, woman ? ' says John Bloodgood. And she told him. ' Well,' he says. ' Do you want to sue the pigs ? ' ' Yis,' she says. ' What's their names ? ' says he. ' I don't know, your honour,' she says, ' but the dirty thieves that took them should be put in jail.' ' Who are they ? ' he says. ' I don't know,' she says. ' Then what are ye blathering about ? ' he says. ' What you don't know won't hurt you.' ' It's the stink, your honour,' she says. ' Have you tried soap ? ' says his honour. ' No,' says the widow Sheehan. ' I wouldn't dirty my hands with it.' So he thrown her out. ' Git out of here,' he says. ' If you wasn't a handsome woman, I'd have ye in contempt.' She stuck up her nose at him. ' I niver let no man lay hands on me but Daniel Sheehan,' she says. ' And not him till he married me. God rest his poor soul,' she says, and went out."

Young Ames began to see the drift.

" Do you know her address ? "

" Her ? What man doesn't ? Seven Batavia is the number."

4

The widow Sheehan had been widowed less than six months. She lit the gas in her dark back parlour and smiled at young Ames and said it was too early in the morning to do business ; but when he explained that his interest was purely commercial, she broke out in exclamations. " For the love of God ! Oh, the poor man ! He thought he'd make a fortune with it, and now the poor fool's ruined me."

It took several repetitive questions for young Ames to discover that only the bottom of the warehouse was empty, and not all of that. Shortly before his demise (because he had mistaken the points of the compass one snowy night in January when he was leaving Eno's Saloon on Roosevelt Street, and instead of going north had headed south and walked square off the end of Pier 28 into the East River— " The poor man was always left-handed," explained Mrs. Sheehan) Mr. Sheehan had bought three hundred tierces of rice and a hundred bales of upland cotton at very low prices and laid them into his warehouse. She would be only too delighted to oblige a young gentleman like Mr. Ames, but what could she do ? She had no head for commerce in rice. It wasn't the natural line of business for a woman. She didn't see why Mr. Sheehan couldn't have sold it before dying, but he hadn't and the warehouse was like to kill her with the worry as it was.

Young Ames let the stream pass over him. When Mrs. Sheehan had wiped her eyes on the hem of her petticoat, showing a knee that was round and nicely covered, he asked whether Mr. Sheehan had ever done business with any of the commercial houses of the city. " Only Pruyn's," she said. " And they sued him because the roof leaked, in the great north-east storm in December."

" It's Pruyn who's keeping us from finding storage," said young Ames.

She could, indignantly, believe it, for Dan Sheehan had
said they were all rats in Pruyn & Co.

Young Ames smiled at her.

" Would you trust me with the key of your warehouse,
Mrs. Sheehan ? I'd like to get an idea of its size and also of
the shape your rice and cotton's in. It's possible I might
find a buyer for you."

" You'd want a commission ? " she asked suspiciously.

" Only the promise to let us have your warehouse at a
just rent."

" It's easy to see you're a gentleman, Mr. Ames," she
said and, smiling herself, went for the key.

A small dog was running a pig from Oak Street down
Roosevelt, a crimson-faced woman with staring eyes was
pursuing the dog with a broom, and a little boy, his face
smutted with tears, brought up the rear as young Ames
emerged from Batavia. He watched the chase pour round
the corner into Cherry Street, then saw two negroes,
half-way up some cellar steps, watching him. He walked
deliberately past them and saw them look at his shabby
beaver. They didn't do anything, but he was relieved when
he turned the corner of Water. It wasn't like the Five
Points, but it was bad enough. He hurried, for it was
getting on towards noon.

The warehouse was easy to find. He let himself into the
loading door and found the cotton in fair shape, except
for some of the rear bales which the rats had burrowed into
for nests. One of them, a lean scarred veteran as long as
a cat, confronted him on the loft stairs, but when he
flourished his hat, it dropped off into the shadow, going
like dirty water down the wall. Young Ames checked the
rice in the loft. What in the devil made a man like Sheehan
buy rice ? he wondered. The man was dead, so nobody
would ever know. It was there, which was an incontro-
vertible fact, and as he looked at it, young Ames ran over
the last quotations from Marseilles in his mind. His
freckled face was thoughtful. Everybody was so worked up

over the cotton deal and Liverpool prices they weren't paying much attention to Marseilles. Except maybe a few ; but if they were they were keeping quiet about it.

As he went down the stairs again he saw a dozen rats working round over the bottom floor. He thought mechanically that something would have to be done about the rats—possibly bring Pinky Finnegan and his pup in for a few evenings—but his mind was rearranging the upland cotton. There'd be room for a hundred and fifty bales, maybe two hundred, with a little work. If they got rid of Sheehan's cotton and rice, Chevalier's entire surplus could be taken care of. The question was, who would buy it ? As he locked the door, he figured that fifteen thousand would be a good price for the buyer, even sixteen thousand would be all right.

He stopped for a slice of mutton and a mug of beer in an eating place near Fulton Market and then walked back along the docks. The sky was hazing and the sun was really hot. Rowley's pig obviously knew what she was about.

As he entered the counting-room door, Mr. McVitty turned on his stool with an unenthusiastic eye. " You're back, Ames. You haven't blistered the streets, have you ? Did you find anything ? "

" Yes, I found a warehouse."

Mr. McVitty sniffed, and climbed down stiffly. " I'll tell Mr. Chevalier you're here," he said. As he opened Mr. Chevalier's door and closed it behind him, young Ames hung up his hat. After a moment he got up on his own stool and pulled out the copying he had left. He let Mr. McVitty call him twice before he answered. " You needn't pretend you're so busy," said Mr. McVitty. " Mr. Chevalier's been waiting long enough as it is."

5

" Come in, Ames," said Mr. Chevalier. " Thank you, Mr. McVitty. That's all."

Mr. McVitty gave a long sniff, and went out. Young Ames stood in front of the Dominican mahogany desk and looked at Mr. Chevalier. The desk was bare except for a single letter with a second sheet pinned to it. Mr. Chevalier picked these up, laid them down, and then stared at young Ames with his blue imperious eyes.

" Sit down, Ames. I've two or three matters to discuss with you."

Young Ames obeyed. In spite of himself he sat on the edge of the chair. Mr. Chevalier had the trick of making a clerk nervous.

" First, did you find us a warehouse ? "

" Yes, sir."

" Empty ? "

" No, sir. It belongs to a widow, Mrs. Sheehan ; and there's some upland cotton and rice. But there's room enough for us."

" Who's she connected with ? "

" No one. She'll take a fair rent. If she gets rid of the cotton and rice, we can use the whole place."

" Rice ? " said Mr. Chevalier thoughtfully. " How much ? "

" Three hundred tierces," said young Ames. " I think she may have a buyer, though." He didn't know why he had said that, and he glanced quickly at Mr. Chevalier. But Mr. Chevalier was looking down at the letter in front of him. " No matter," he said. " If she can't sell it, we can make her an offer ourselves."

" Yes, sir."

" I've got to get room for my cotton. Maitland & Henriquez are shipping a good deal direct to England, but we must be careful not to pour it into Liverpool." He cleared his throat, and then glanced up at young Ames.

"You're a very young man, Ames," he said. "And I don't doubt you've felt that we haven't shown proper appreciation of your work on this cotton deal." His mouth twitched almost imperceptibly under his large nose. "Even considering our raising your salary a hundred per cent."

Young Ames was silent.

"I'm prepared to admit there would be something in your view," said Mr. Chevalier after a moment. "It's hard, naturally, for you to realise that there was a great deal of good fortune involved in your part."

"The boat didn't capsize," young Ames blurted out.

A frosty look came into Mr. Chevalier's blue eyes.

"I was right then," he said. "I appreciate that the boat didn't capsize. But perhaps you haven't stopped to think that our firm put up a million dollars and that you merely carried it to New Orleans." He tapped the desk with his fingers. Young Ames kept silent. After a proper interval Mr. Chevalier resumed. "However, this letter from Mr. Henriquez has rather forced my hand. I need not read it to you. He expresses his appreciation of what he terms your enterprise, and wishes, on behalf of his firm, to present you with the profit of the first fifteen bales. I regard that as generous, Ames, for they are under no obligation to you."

Young Ames drew in his breath. Mr. Chevalier continued without taking notice.

"Chevalier, Deming & Post, of course, cannot allow themselves to be in debt to any one. We've decided to give you the profit on fifty bales. The figures have come in. At $30 a bale that makes $1500 on our lot. Mr. Henriquez figures $25 a bale on his fifteen, or $375. The total is therefore $1875."

His blue eyes stared hard.

"For once," he commented dryly, "it seems that you have nothing to say."

Young Ames stammered and turned red.

"Thanks," he said. "I'm very grateful."

Mr. Chevalier's voice lightened. "So am I." He opened a drawer of his desk and drew forth a draft on the Manhattan Bank. "I've made out the whole sum in one draft," he said. "Mr. McVitty has instructions to take you round when you wish to cash it."

Young Ames felt his hand shake as he took the cheque. He mumbled more thanks and rose.

"Just a moment," said Mr. Chevalier. "There's one other matter to take up. Have you made any plans for investing this money?"

"I've hardly had time, sir."

"Perhaps not." Mr. Chevalier's eyes narrowed quizzically. "It's not any business of mine. But you haven't had much experience in business, and I should hate to see you throw this away. It's a very large sum for a man of your age to have made in his first year. I can't recall a single other instance to parallel it." He cleared his throat and looked out of the window. "I think you'd be wise to put it in a savings bank. The earnings are small, but you've no need of the income in your position. Eighteen hundred dollars after all is hardly a big enough sum to go on the market with."

Young Ames said: "Thank you, sir," in a non-committal voice.

Mr. Chevalier glanced at him quickly.

"I'm on the board," he said. "The bank's thoroughly sound, in spite of General Jackson's criminal manipulation of the national credit. If you care to you can go up with me at four o'clock, and I'll introduce you myself."

It was a handsome offer for Mr. Chevalier to make. But young Ames's freckled face set stubbornly.

"I think I'd prefer to handle the money myself, sir."

Mr. Chevalier stiffened noticeably.

"It's your money, of course. I hope you won't lose it, that's all." He pulled some papers from his desk.

" Excuse me, sir."

Mr. Chevalier glanced up.

" Well, Ames ? " he asked shortly.

" I wanted to say that there's only one place I'd like to invest this money."

" Yes ? "

" In Chevalier, Deming & Post, sir."

" That's impossible, Ames. The stock is entirely controlled by me and my partners. We've no room for small holders."

Young Ames flushed. " I know that, sir," he said. " I merely made the remark. I hope to stay in this firm and some day I'd like an interest in it. That's all, sir."

Mr. Chevalier looked up.

" You've shown some aptitude for business, Ames. You're sharp. You're inclined to be impudent at times. And I believe I've already said you were unscrupulous. You also have $1,875 which we weren't obliged to pay you. I think that covers your case." He smiled coolly. " You haven't shown that you can handle money yourself, which is a very different matter. When you've saved up five thousand dollars it will be time enough to continue this conversation."

There was no question of his dismissal this time, but as he returned to the counting-room he was grinning. Mr. McVitty, taking snuff, remarked : " You've got these letters to O'Hara to finish yet before closing."

" Yes, sir." Young Ames wondered whether Mr. McVitty, in all his life, had ever received an eighteen-hundred-dollar bonus.

6

His head was too full to notice Gibbs's preoccupation at supper that night.

"All I've got to do is persuade the widow Sheehan to accept a down payment of 10 per cent," he pointed out. "That leaves me $375. I ought to have six hundred, but maybe I can squeeze through."

Gibbs made an effort to interest himself.

"Hadn't you better think it over a little longer, Johnny?"

"I thought it all over on the way back from New Orleans. I worked the whole thing out." He didn't observe the expression almost of chagrin on his friend's face.

"You mean to say you spent all your time figuring how to work this particular deal?" Gibbs asked.

"I didn't know that Mrs. Sheehan had three hundred tierces of rice, naturally." Young Ames's voice sounded rather like Mr. Chevalier's. "That's sheer providence. But Goddard is sure to make the advance." He rumpled his sandy hair and jerked his stool up to the table. "This is how it works," he said. "I go to Mrs. Sheehan and offer her fifteen thousand dollars for the lot. It's a fair price for her. I give her 10 per cent down. Then I go to Goddard and tell him I know rice is high on the Marseilles market and that I have a chance to pick up three hundred tierces and a hundred bales of cotton cheap, but I can't put the deal through immediately without an advance. I know this firm, Leach & Tardy, are after rice, and cotton is bound to fetch a premium in Marseilles with everybody pulling the sticks out of packets to get everything they have to Liverpool. If Goddard will advance me seven-eighths of it, say fourteen thousand, we can put the deal through."

"You'll just walk in and ask for fourteen thousand?" Gibbs asked incredulously.

"Why not?" demanded young Ames. "He won't advance, of course, until I hand him the invoice and lading bills, but the *Fermoy*'s having a hard time to find a cargo, so Burgess will wait a day for his money. I insure the shipment for cost and profit. Goddard draws for the fourteen thousand and sells the bills on Leach & Tardy's Paris bank. I can't lose. It's just a question of timing the business. There's just one thing I haven't figured out. How I'm going to get a day off from Chevalier's. And then I'd like to have that two hundred dollars extra."

Gibbs looked into the fire for a few minutes.

"Johnny," he said, "it's a neat scheme. I happen to have two hundred laid up in the Manhattan Bank you can have."

"By God, that's good of you," said young Ames. "You'll get the same profit I do."

"Never mind about that. I'm glad to lend you the money. This deal means a lot, doesn't it?"

Young Ames was silent for a moment, his face blank.

"Yes," he said then. "I figure it will mean a lot. But I insist you take the same profit I do." He drew in a long breath. "That leaves the question of getting McVitty to let me off for a day."

Gibbs scraped out his pipe.

"Maybe I can fix that up too," he said thoughtfully. "Day after to-morrow's the twenty-ninth of March, isn't it?"

Gibbs gave a short laugh.

"Chevalier always lets me have the twenty-ninth off. I'll ask him to let you off too. I generally go out of town for the day."

"You think he will?" asked young Ames.

"I think so."

Young Ames stood up.

"Then I've started," he said. "They can't stop me now." He went over to the window and looked down at the river. He wasn't aware of Gibbs's watching him.

Reading his face, Gibbs relit his pipe and turned back to his contemplation of the fire. " I'm getting sentimental," he thought. The twenty-ninth of March was his birthday. On the twenty-ninth, too, he had come into his money. Three hundred dollars was all that was left of it.

" I ought to go up and talk with Mrs. Sheehan to-night," said young Ames.

Gibbs looked over his shoulder. He had to rally his thoughts. " See Mrs. Sheehan to-night? I wouldn't. Wait till to-morrow. You'll probably be sent up there anyway to arrange for the rent. From your description I should think the chances were she'd be engaged. And right now she thinks you're a gentleman of tact."

" I guess you're right, Howard." He grinned. " I don't ever think of things like that. We ought to be partners."

7

The unseasonable heat kept on over the twenty-ninth. When, at midday, he turned into Gold Street, young Ames was hot and tired.

It had been a busy morning, beginning with Mr. McVitty's introducing him at the Manhattan Bank and leaving him there with the testy admonition that " he that getteth rich and not by right, at his end shall be a fool."

" Yes, sir."

" I will say good-day to you, Ames." Mr. McVitty stalked out of the bank, striking each step with the point of his umbrella.

The day before, Mrs. Sheehan had accepted his offer of fifteen thousand cash, payable in twenty-four hours with 10 per cent down. His next call therefore was at the office of the agent for Leach & Tardy. Mr. Goddard, after a few questions, agreed to make the advance of fourteen thousand dollars, to be paid as soon as young Ames handed him the invoice and ladings, and had suggested the State Marine Insurance Company with whom his firm did business. The policy was now waiting for young Ames's payment of the premium. Mr. Burgess, one of the owners of the *Fermoy*, had eagerly accepted the shipment of cotton and rice, even at the low rates he had been advertising in the *American*. The *Fermoy* lay at Pier 24, next above Peck Slip, a short haul from the warehouse. It only remained to find enough cartmen willing to move his rice on two-hour notice on a Saturday afternoon. In this connection he had remembered the resourcefulness of Pinky Finnegan's Uncle Mike Dolan and Mr. Rowley in the matter of Rowley's pig. He hadn't dared go back to Chevalier's to find Pinky, since he was supposed to be having an outing in the country with Gibbs, so he had taken a chance of trying Beggs's three-cent saloon.

When he saw the spotted face of Williamson's cart horse sticking out of the alley with a nose-bag on, he knew that Mike Dolan would be four steps down.

"Hallo," said Mr. Dolan. "It's our Mr. Ames! Coming to dinner?"

"I'll have some oysters and beer," said young Ames. "Can I offer you gentlemen anything?"

"You can," said Mr. Dolan, checking off nods from Mr. Rowley and Mr. Foggarty and a fourth man in a black top hat whom he introduced as Mr. O'Conlon. "But you can't have beer."

Mrs. Beggs made a blowsy slap at a fly with a wet bar rag and said there was no money in beer.. "Beer gents drink too slow for a place this size," she pointed out. "Will you try gin and lemon?"

Gin and lemon seemed to be the stock drink at Beggs's, though young Ames hadn't yet seen the hide of a lemon anywhere in the place. He agreed and turned to Mr. Dolan.

"I'm very grateful for your suggestion of Mrs. Sheehan's warehouse."

Mr. Dolan waved his glass with a nice judgment to the effect of inertia on gin, and asked whether the woman had obliged.

Young Ames nodded over his fried oysters. "Our shipment docked this morning. We'll move it on Monday."

"I'm glad to hear it," said Mr. Dolan.

"It leaves me with the problem of moving my own goods out in time," said young Ames.

"Yours?"

"Yes, I bought Mrs. Sheehan's rice and cotton. I'm taking a flier myself and I can't pay for it or the carting till I've got it on board the boat."

Mr. Dolan exchanged glances with his three friends.

"I didn't know you were a man of business yourself," he said guardedly.

"I wasn't till yesterday."

Young Ames finished his oysters. He was aware that the atmosphere of Beggs's had changed, and he decided suddenly that the thing to do was to take Mr. Dolan entirely into his confidence. If he could get him interested, he might get help. In a few words he explained the whole transaction, and then asked whether Mr. Dolan or his friends could round up or put him on the track of a likely group of cartmen.

But Mr. Dolan ignored his request for the moment. "You hear that?" he exclaimed admiringly. "Fifteen thousand dollars' worth of goods bought, shipped, and insured with only two thousand dollars. That's what I would call business!"

Mr. Rowley nodded.

"What would you expect to make on the deal, Mr. Ames?"

"If I can get the cotton on the boat, I'll hope for a return of 25 per cent," young Ames explained.

"On two thousand dollars?" Mr. Rowley whistled, and even the sad-eyed O'Conlon held his gin in his mouth. "How much would that make?"

"Twenty-five per cent of $2000 would be $500," said young Ames. He couldn't help smiling. "But I expect

25 per cent of, say, $16,000." He wrote the figures down for Mr. Dolan. " You see, it makes $4000."

An aura of silence enveloped him so densely that the crunch of Williamson's horse's teeth on his last oat was audible through the open door. Mr. Dolan removed his hat and borrowed the bar rag to wipe his forehead. He turned accusingly on his friend Rowley. " I said that was what I called business. What do you mean, with your talk of two thousand ? "

Mr. Foggarty raised a cold question.

" What happens if the boat sinks ? "

" My shipment's insured, for the cost and the profit."

" My God," said Dolan. " He's even beat the insurance company ! Rowley's brother-in-law tried it with arson, but he went to Sing-Sing Prison with a seven-year sentence."

" They aren't being beat. I've paid the premium."

" Do you see, you poor blockhead ? It's honest, too."

" Well," said Mr. Foggarty. " If the thing is true, and I'm not saying it isn't a fine piece of work anyway, why isn't the whole world rich ? "

" Because men like you and me don't know the prices and the ports," Mr. Dolan said with scorn. " Why do you think I told young Pinky to get into a high-class firm ? To cut pens and buy snuff for that old crow of a chief clerk ? No, my boy. You've got to learn the tricks, I said, and all the fine dishonesties of trade as practised by the best people if you want to be a great man. Study how a gentleman like Mr. Ames diddles the insurance companies, I told him, and you'll never lose a cent by fire, or owe the laundress a penny. Pink's smart. He works under you, don't he, Mr. Ames ? " Mr. Dolan turned with a sweep of the arm.

" He sent me to you," said young Ames.

" Do you hear that now ? " demanded Mr. Dolan. " It would be a fine thing, wouldn't it, if we didn't help out Mr. Ames ? O'Conlon, your cousin's in the carting business."

" I don't want to speak to him ! " said O'Conlon.

" You can tell him Dolan's friend the alderman will see
he don't get his licence next year unless he turns out ten
carts, can't you ? "

The sad-eyed O'Conlon brightened slightly.

" Yes, I can."

" Do it now," said Dolan. " You said yourself there's
no burials this afternoon."

" I will," said O'Conlon.

" Make it four o'clock at Sheehan's warehouse," Dolan
shouted after him. " And no extra pay for late hours
barring drinks at Clancy's. Clancy will give you a dis-
count, Mr. Ames. You don't mind that ? I caught
O'Conlon's cousin coming out of a slavery meeting in
Chatham Street Chapel a while back and he's scared I'll
get him throwed out of the Party." Mr. Dolan shook his
head, soberly. Then he brisked up. " Rowley," he said,
" you and Foggarty had better round up some of the steve-
dore boys. Tell them it's a matter of obliging Dolan's
friend. Say it's our Mr. Ames and there's politics in it and
free drinks at Clancy's if the shipment's on before to-night."

The two nodded and, after accepting another drink from
young Ames, departed.

Young Ames turned to Dolan.

" I'm very much in your debt, Mr. Dolan. How can I
pay it ? "

" Don't mention it," said Dolan. " But keep your eye
on Pinky and give him a shove now and then. Maybe
some day you can cast your vote for Finnegan, the people's
friend, for alderman. Or maybe President, who knows.
Andrew Jackson was a bootblack after all," he added
seriously.

" I'd do that much anyway," young Ames said, grinning.
Dolan grinned back.

" Well," he said, " I don't forget favours, given or
taken. . . ."

The loading was finished an hour after dark under the

noisy supervision of Michael Dolan. Young Ames paid off
at seven-thirty, using one end of Clancy's plank bar for
his desk, with Pinky Finnegan, to Mr. Dolan's inordinate
pride, acting as his assistant. By nine o'clock Mr. Goddard
had the lading bills and invoice complete and the insurance
premium had been paid by a special arrangement through
his agency. At ten o'clock, while Pinky and Mike Dolan,
the latter full of amazement and interest at the vastness of
the inside of Number 42 and the private offices of the
partners of Chevalier, Deming & Post, were enjoying a
steak and kidney pie and a crock of Mike Dolan's favourite
gin, Gibbs returned. He stopped for a moment in the
door. Young Ames saw that he was drunk.

" Did you work it ? "

" Yes. Join us, Howard ? "

" I've done my own celebrating," said Gibbs. " But
I'll drink to the budding millionaire anyway."

Mike Dolan nodded approvingly and filled a glass.

" It's good gin," said Gibbs. " Your selection, I take
it, Mr. Dolan."

Mr. Dolan looked pleased.

Gibbs downed his glass and went to his own room.

" He's a sad man," observed Mike Dolan.

" He gets moods," said young Ames.

8

April and May went by. Cotton held up at Liverpool
and Mr. Chevalier suddenly began to sell, in warehouse
at New York. He judged the moment nicely. The firm
cleared at a uniform profit of better than twenty-seven
dollars. Young Ames had seen a million dollars made.

But the amount was not nearly so exciting to him as the
note handed on to his desk by Pinky Finnegan the third
of June. Mr. Goddard suggested that Mr. Ames call at
his convenience. He took the lunch hour for it. When he

returned he carried in his inside pocket a draft for $6800, representing $4800 profit and $2000, which he had advanced on the deal.

"You're late," said Mr. McVitty.

"I'm sorry," said young Ames. He hung his hat on the peg and went to his desk. He wrote a moment and then took the sheet to Mr. McVitty.

"It's a memorandum for Mr. Chevalier," he explained.

"I'll take it in in a minute."

Young Ames tried to work, but he could not do more than keep up a feeble appearance of it, until Mr. McVitty called him into Mr. Chevalier's office.

Mr. Chevalier looked up.

"You wish to continue our conversation?" he asked.

"I don't recall it."

"You said that when I had made five thousand dollars you would discuss the matter of investment, sir."

Mr. Chevalier sat back in his chair.

"You have five thousand dollars?"

"Yes, sir." He lost some of his cockiness under Mr. Chevalier's stare. "As a matter of fact I have sixty-eight hundred, but I should like to keep eighteen hundred for future operations."

"How did you make this money?"

"I invested it in rice and cotton, and sold in Marseilles."

"Ah," said Mr. Chevalier. "You were Mrs. Sheehan's possible buyer."

"Yes, sir."

"With whom did you do business?"

"Leach & Tardy."

"I see. You must have operated on margin. It's been done before, Ames, and it's not a sound way of doing business. Suppose the market had dropped in Marseilles."

"I had two thousand leeway, sir." Young Ames swallowed. "There was no chance of the market dropping, though. Not for six weeks."

"There have been known to happen things called, by

careful merchants, acts of God. Or did you consult the Deity ? "

Young Ames swallowed.

"I had to take a chance there," he admitted. "I was insured of course, sir."

"I should hope so." Mr. Chevalier tapped his desk. "Did you use my name in this transaction ? "

"No, sir." Young Ames swallowed again. He didn't feel as sure of himself. "I knew there was some risk, sir. But I had to take it, you see. That's why I'd like to put five thousand into something safe."

"Like Chevalier, Deming & Post ? It's sound because it doesn't operate beyond its means. But suppose a man like yourself, a reckless, cocksure, unscrupulous man, was in my place, would you feel the same ? "

"No, sir."

"Very well. You'd better get to your desk. Mr. McVitty reports you were late getting back." Mr. Chevalier looked down his nose at his desk. "I'll attend to your five thousand, Ames. Cash your draft to-morrow."

"Yes, sir."

He returned feeling considerably chastened.

He felt more so at closing time when Pinky Finnegan was called into Mr. Chevalier's office and came out directly with a slip of paper which he laid on young Ames's desk. "Memorandum for you, Mr. Ames, from Mr. Chevalier," he said.

Young Ames opened it.

It said :—

June 3, 1834.

John Ames, in account with George Chevalier.
One coat .... $125.00.

V

YOUNG AMES FIGHTS A FIRE

ARRIVING at Chevalier, Deming & Post's early in the morning, Pinky Finnegan made a hasty inspection of the premises to be sure that the chief clerk had not beaten him to it, and then hid his day's supply of liquorice in the spare umbrella Mr. Chevalier had hanging behind the counting-room door. Mr. McVitty had positively prohibited the chewing of liquorice ; the smell, he said, was nauseating.

This concealment accomplished, Pinky performed the usual cleaning-up, and ended the work by getting down the spirit lamp for Mr. McVitty's hot water. Not even the heat of mid-June was allowed to interfere with the morning cup of hot water. As the chief clerk entered, Pinky struck a locofoco and bent suggestively towards the wick.

" No ! " cried McVitty, taking the match away. " I'll light it myself. It's not," he continued, drawing back from the igniting like a successful elderly Guy Fawkes, " that you couldn't try to be careful. It's a question of nationality. The Irish are a notoriously unstable race where ardent spirits are concerned."

Little Finnegan hitched up his trousers.

" My Uncle Mike says he would rather have a barrel of whisky than the blood of forty patriots to start a riot any day."

" Your uncle's opinions may be important in the Bowery, Finnegan, but they don't concern Chevalier, Deming & Post. Come here and breathe," the chief clerk said sternly.

Pinky approached and exhaled dutifully. Mr. McVitty grunted.

" Last night," he said, giving Pinky a hard stare through his grey eyebrows. " I looked up an entry in the '27 cash-

books. The shelf smelled like a sidewalk candy pedlar.
Can you explain that ? "

Pinky's aplomb was not shaken.

" No, sir. I wasn't here in 1827." He looked out through
the narrow window into the back court, and immediately
was interested in two pigeons on the top of the opposite
roof. But his voice turned pathetic for Mr. McVitty's
benefit. " My father was killed in 1827. He was standing
on the cornice at the Bowen fire when it fell, sir," he said.
" I was an orphan when he hit the street. But the fire
department took up a collection for me, and my Uncle
Mike told me I could live with him."

Mr. McVitty drew a long breath.

" Yes, yes, Finnegan," he said, pulling out his tortoise-
shell watch. " No doubt." Finnegan had a way of flus-
tering him. " Get upstairs, will you, and tell Ames I want
to see him. It's opening time anyway," he added.

Finnegan ducked out and clattered delightedly up the
flights to the top floor of Number 42. In Pinky's opinion
young Ames was the only person in the counting-room
worth noticing, with the possible exception of Mr. Chevalier
himself ; and the two rooms under the roof seemed
spacious and romantic apartments compared to the single
small room on Elizabeth Street which his uncle and aunt
called home.

He saw Gibbs shaving through the open door and said :
" Good-morning, Mr. Gibbs. Is Mr. Ames up yet ? "

" Hallo there." Gibbs grinned crookedly through the
lather. " He's up, but he's not in. He went to a fire."

" Fire, sir ? "

" Yes, he got the bell at five o'clock and went out like
a monkey. It's his first since he joined Number 11."

" Gee ! ", exclaimed Pinky. " Number 11 ? That's
Oceanus Company, ain't it, Mr. Gibbs ? What'll I tell
Mr. McVitty, sir ? He wants Mr. Ames right away."

" It might be advisable to tell Mr. McVitty that Mr.
Ames has gone to a fire," said Gibbs.

" Yes, sir." Pinky was dubious, but he couldn't think of anything except a dead aunt, and that wouldn't go for Mr. McVitty. Mr. Ames had no relatives in New York.

" He's gone to a fire, sir," he told Mr. McVitty. " They got the bell at five. It must be a good one."

Mr. McVitty practically reared on his stool.

" It's preposterous ! " he exclaimed. " A clerk has no business being on the Fire Department. I'll speak to Mr. Chevalier about it. Fires ! Coming in at all hours and then making bird's nests of the cash totals." Mr. McVitty set down his cup with a clash on the saucer and helped himself indignantly to snuff.

2

When young Ames reached the engine-house off Old Slip the doors were open and enough firemen to make a starting complement were rolling Oceanus on to the street. Rock Doyle, the Fenian butcher from Franklin Market, claimed he had heard the bells begin in the south-end of the Third Ward, and the foreman set the route up William Street to Liberty accordingly. The fire was going to give their chief rival, Bolivar Engine Company Number 9, a block advantage.

" They'll be laying for us at the corner of Nassau," yelled the foreman through his speaking trumpet.

A couple of sailors on a brig in Pier 11 gave them a hooraw and young Ames, galloping along behind the painted shield of the engine, was proud to belong to Number 11. She had the finest painted shield of all the engines : the burning of Troy and Achilles being shot in the heel in the foreground. Eagle Company of course had the famous one of a mother getting her baby back out of an eagle's nest on a crag, but that wasn't classical. He only wished he was old enough to be regularly enrolled and therefore entitled to a place on the drag rope.

Carts jammed back against the kerb as they rumbled by Franklin Market.

Three more firemen, in their leather helmets and boots, but still working at their buckles, stumbled out of Water Street, and the foreman called for more rope on the drag as they took their places.

Oceanus picked up speed with each additional arrival. By the time she entered the long curve of William Street, she was going full blast with thirty-five men on the drag ; and when she levelled out, forty-four were wheeling her, and the foreman was yelping : " Pull together. Lay her down, boys. Lay her down and die."

The man carrying the lantern with Number 11 painted on the glass was half a block ahead. In the dawn, the light was unnecessary. He sprinted to reach Wall and caught the watchman in his box. The leatherhead complained that he didn't know where the fire was except it was somewhere near the North River. How could a man tell where a fire was with every church bell ringing over the whole damned metropolis ? He was supposed to keep his beat and take up vagrant children and arrest prostitutes for a dollar. Nobody had told him where the fire was. Why didn't the department find out for themselves, he wanted to know. He kept right on talking even though Oceanus was all the way past Cedar.

Oceanus took the turn into Liberty with a dismal screaking of her kingbolt. As soon as she got around, the company saw the Bolivars rounding into Liberty from Nassau, their engine's pink belly shining like cold boiled trout meat.

" Get over on your side, Number 9," roared the Oceanus's foreman.

The Bolivar foreman yelled back for Number 11 to come and make them. The two engines rocked along the crown of the street. Half a dozen volunteers behind Bolivar rushed like chickens to the left, but Rock Doyle, at the head of the drag, threw his shoulder into the last

one, sprawling him over the kerb, and roared to his own
volunteers to come up fast and pick off the crumbs.

Young Ames with six or seven more rushed up and
started imitating Rock's technique. But they hadn't his
bull-shouldered force and the volunteers' rivalry degener-
ated to a kind of wrestling match that straggled back and
forth across the kerb until the two engines were crossing
Broadway.

Young Ames let go of his particular enemy and saw
Tibbets, who, like himself, was making a first run, with a
shut eye. " Come on," yelled Tibbets, and he and Ames
launched themselves along the street.

The two engines were full force and going neck and neck.
They could catch glimpses of Rock Doyle bent down
against the rope, looking as if he dragged the crew and
engine both. The lantern carriers were shoving each
other and yelling at the crossings. A hackney coach went
over the sidewalk at Greenwich Street and the driver
cursed as he lost his hat and begged the volunteers to hand
it up to him. " The fire's back of the Northern Hotel," he
offered as a bribe, and then swore at them, demanding at
large what a driver could do with a horse just over from
Hoboken.

Oceanus's foreman had sprinted ahead to Pier 17, and
with his lantern carrier was standing off the rival foreman.
It was a good mix while they were at it. Rock Doyle called
for a last heave and Oceanus sprung Bolivar, and wheeled
thundering on to the pier beside Engine 21, which was
already pumping. Rock Doyle finished the dispute by
picking up the Bolivar foreman by belt and shirt collar
and dropping him into the river. Purdy had already
dropped Oceanus's suction into the water. The foreman
called an order to man the brakes just as young Ames and
Tibbets pounded out on the pier.

Their blood was up. Twenty-one was flashing her brakes
with twenty men. Bolivar was all milled up. A man with
a hook from the Number 3 Ladder Company was fishing

Bolivar's foreman out. As he came over the edge of the dock half-drowned, Oceanus's foreman asked, " Will you take our water ? "

The Bolivar foreman gathered up his company and took them into Cortlandt Street in the hope of finding the front end of a hose line, muttering what he would tell the chief engineer.

Tibbets, Ames, and the volunteers all booed lustily, and Rock Doyle roared at them to unreel. " This isn't a game, you fools," cried the second assistant.

Sweat was pouring down the back of young Ames's neck. It all seemed like a wild and intoxicating form of madness to him. He had often seen fire companies take hold, but he had never thought they seemed anything but orderly. Now things happened so fast he could not keep up with each step of rigging a line to the fire. He and Tibbets had hold of the third length of pipe. Purdy and Staats Mead had the end of the fourth. They looked to him like lunk-heads standing there, bellowing with the foreman, saying : " Will you take our water ? "

There was a great roaring down Cortlandt, and Purdy muttered : " It's Number 15. They won't look at us."

" Who's Fourteen ? " young Ames asked Tibbets.

" Peterson. Old Maid. From Elizabeth Street. Bowery boys."

" No talking on duty," Purdy said in a sharp voice.

Young Ames wiped his eyes with the back of his hand and watched them come. They didn't preserve the customary rule of silence on a run, but were all exhorting each other in wild Irish voices. Their engine looked a dandy ; it had more silver plates even than Oceanus, but the men were red-faced, big-built devils. They looked tough enough to split acorns with their fingernails. He remembered Pinky Finnegan using that phrase to describe them.

Volunteers were supposed to mind their own business, but young Ames thought he'd go up and speak to the foreman. It seemed a dirty cheat to have beaten Bolivar, dropped your suction, and then find nobody to take your water. " Sir," he began.

" Get back where you belong," said the foreman.

" I've got some friends on Fifteen," said young Ames. " I think they'll take our water."

" The devil you have." The foreman, who was growing anxious himself, glanced at young Ames. Young Ames looked like just another volunteer. He had lost his hat in the fracas on Liberty Street, and his sandy hair was stuck to his forehead. His eyes were full of sweat, and he blinked like a book clerk. But just then Rock Doyle came storming up from the pier foot. It was a terrible thing for an engine not to find someone to take its water. They couldn't make the distance alone either, even if they had a hose cart handy, and the carts were all round the corner waiting for the pressure pipes to come up to them.

" What's the trouble, boss ? " he asked.

" This volunteer says he can get Fifteen to take our water. They never do. They'll probably try to dump us in the river."

" Let them if they can," said Rock Doyle.

" I know Mike Dolan," said young Ames.

" Dolan is a rabbit," said Doyle. " Don't trust him."

Fifteen rolled up. There wasn't room on the pier for her. " Take our water, Fifteen ? " asked the Oceanus foreman, pocketing his quid. " Git out of our way."

Rock Doyle spat into his cupped fists. Young Ames, looking at the gathering crew of the Bowery engine, felt a cold prickle in the sweat between his shoulders. " Dolan," he yelled.

" Who wants Dolan ? " said Mike Dolan, coming round from unlimbering his suction. " Hey, it's our Mr. Ames. I didn't know you was in the department. You looking for someone to take your water, Eleven ? We'll take it, but if we suck on, we'll make you change."

" You suck on ? " said Rock Doyle. " All you ever

sucked on was a nipple, and a hell of a lot of water you
ever got out of it either."

He jumped back to the engine and laid hands that
spread like wet liver on the brake. Number 15 rolled
round at the corner of Cortlandt, presenting her butt.
Purdy and Mead of Eleven held their hose. Fifteen ran
out her hose and the chief engineer appeared to order
their pipe through the alley and side-door of the barn.
" It's a slow hay fire," he said. " But the cartman says
somebody brought in four kegs of powder last night and
now he can't locate them."

Young Ames, having helped couple Eleven's line, went
back among the rest of the volunteers to be ready to step
in on the brakes. A crowd was already gathering and the
windows of the hotel were filled with interested occupants,
and one harried individual with a wife, five children, and
a basket of rabbits was trying to emerge from the front
door. A cloud of smoke rose leisurely behind the building,
spreading in the still air like an umbrella. The river was
turning pearl colour and a drift of mist hung smokily a
little north of Canal Street. A bell was ringing in it, and
all of a sudden young Ames caught sight of the stacks of
the Albany night boat swimming through it. She would
have to wait to dock, for the engines had her pier. Then
he remembered that Mr. Chevalier was due back from
Albany, and he wondered whether he was aboard. He
could imagine Mr. Chevalier getting enraged at the delay.

" Ready on the brakes, Eleven." The foreman's voice
blasting through the speaking trumpet jolted him. " Start
her lively." His voice was reassuring, calm. " Shake her
up, boys."

Rock Doyle's great arms brought the brake down. The
opposite brake went up. Ten men on a side. Their backs
bent with the effort, and old Oceanus rumbled in her
bowels. There was a suck like a foot of an old cow in a
bog. At Fifteen's butt, Mead and Purdy braced their legs
around the leather pipe. Fifteen was watching them.

Their foreman yelled, " Ready ? Take her now," and the Bowery Irish raised a yell and bent their backs. Up and down, up and down. Westerfield, the Methodist class leader, called the stroke for Oceanus with his eye on Fifteen. He had a voice to fill a camp grove, high, nasal, and fine. Rock Doyle's grunts came with each down stroke. Forty, forty-five, fifty . . . eighty strokes to the minute, ninety-four. Water spurted through the couplings ; the hose lay solid and hard along the planks. Fifteen was pumping full blast but Rock Doyle was like a crazy man, the sweat dripping off his whiskers ; his face, his arms, even his great hands were scarlet. And Purdy on the butt unexpectedly began calling the levels of water in the rival engine. She went to within three inches of a full tank. The Bowery boys had left off cursing and worked de-mentedly to keep their engine from overflowing. If Rock could have held out for two minutes more, Eleven might have washed her.

But he couldn't hold out. Young Ames saw him reel off the brake and lie down gasping. A man jumped into his place. One by one the replacements took over without letting the flash of the brakes alter a beat. But the power wasn't the same without the Fenian butcher on the bars. Young Ames's heart thumped to see him lie there. His own turn was bound to come soon ; with both engines pumping over a hundred strokes a minute, the men on the brakes were changing at minute intervals.

He heard his name and sprang in. The descending bar tipped his fingers before he caught it, and he thought all eight were broken. The brake sprang up under them and he put his weight on it, bringing it down with the nine men alongside him. He stopped thinking at the fourth stroke. The motion whipped all the blood into his head. His ears sang so that he no longer heard the rush of water, the shouts from round the corner of Cortlandt Street, where the fire was being fought, the ringing of the bell on the Albany boat, which was backing on and off the pier, cutting circles against the tide. He felt his knees shaking under him. He thought he had gone beyond his own limits. He couldn't hold out. He felt ashamed, thinking he had done only half a minute. Then somebody yanked his shirt collar, his legs filled with blood as if they had been asleep, he reeled and sat down and found himself beside Rock Doyle.

Rock Doyle was getting up, stretching his arms.

" You did a minute and a half," he said. " Fair pumping for a squab."

" What you lying down for ? " The foreman was prodding him. " Get over to the pipe and line up with the others. There's some Five Pointers hanging round and I think they're going to cut us."

Young Ames staggered up and found himself reeling. Over by the pierhead were seven or eight ruffians with high battered hats, all of them carrying cudgels, except for one who was cleaning his nails with the point of a jack-knife. Looking round at his companions, young Ames thought dazedly that there wasn't much they could do if the Five Pointers decided to cut the pipe. He didn't feel like fighting at all. He felt like lying down with his head over the edge of the dock.

But they didn't have to fight. The attention of the foreman of Fifteen was drawn to the group by Mr. Dolan. He let out a roar. " Cut the pipe, would you ? " he bellowed, rounding up a dozen of his fresher volunteers. He caught sight of the Oceanus volunteers and yelled to come on. " Don't let them kick you, Mr. Ames." Young Ames found Mike Dolan fraternally rushing to the attack beside him. The rest of Fifteen's volunteers were ahead of them and a shout of " Plug-Uglies " went up like a battle cry.

Young Ames knew the Plug Uglies were one of the organised Five Points gangs ; they were reputed to carry firearms. But if they did, these specimens decided not to use them. They were facing nearly twenty men ; there were leatherheads round them ; and the fire companies had a way of forgetting private feuds when a gang tackled them. Without a sound they started moving off.

They ran down West Street, but they did not give the appearance of flight. Their size and their huge plug hats lent them a kind of dignity. Round the corner of Liberty Street, the firemen let them go, and turned back to the engines.

Mike Dolan said : " You've got a good company, Mr. Ames."

" We can't wash you, I guess."

" It's only happened once, and then only because we got some gravel in our valves."

" What were those toughs trying to cut the pipe for ? " young Ames asked.

Mr. Dolan spat contemptuously.

" Those dumb Irish fools don't know which end of a bullgine the water comes out of," he said. " They thought it was ours. The Five Points is always laying for the Bowery anyway."

Back at the pier the engines were still pumping full blast. Rock Doyle was at the brakes again and the members of Fifteen acted harried. But the shouts behind the hotel seemed to be dying down. The chief engineer appeared at the mouth of the alleyway and reported the fire out. " 'Vast playing," he said.

The men let go the brakes, which cocked up and down for a half-stroke and stayed up. The firemen sat down. Oceanus's foreman said to Fifteen's, " Thanks for saving our pipe."

" Keep your thanks," said Fifteen shortly, ordering his men to reel in. " We'll try you again some day."

" Anny time," bawled Rock Doyle, hauling the heavy suction out of the river and slinging it under the engine.

As young Ames's head cleared of blood, sounds and voices became audible. He was drenched and exhausted. It was hard labour merely to bend over and steady the suction. The other engine companies were heading off at a leisurely walk, and he wondered what had become of the Bolivars. He felt proud of Oceanus : there weren't many downtown companies that could have played successfully into Fifteen ; and he had worked his own trick on the brakes. It was pleasant to think of walking home slow through the early morning streets with the first pedestrians stopping to see you come by, admiring the engine and the tired but determined firemen. Even the prospect of spending a morning on a counting-room stool was pleasant. He felt fine as a small line of hotel waiters came out with beer mugs on a tray and passed them round with compliments of Mr. Harrison, the manager, and he turned to see why the bell was jangling so close.

3

The Albany boat had drifted into her dock, and hackney coaches were already crowding the pierhead. The passengers were coming off. Tibbets, his black eye completely closed by this time, plucked young Ames by the elbow.

" Here's someone who seems to know you, Ames," he said.

Young Ames wiped the sweat from his eyes and found himself blinking at Mr. Chevalier, who was standing just in front of him with his niece on his arm.

" Good-morning, Ames," he said, his blue eyes flicking over his junior clerk. " I hadn't been informed of your joining the Fire Department."

Young Ames gulped foolishly.

" No, sir. I only knew it myself yesterday."

Tibbets said : " We were elected together, sir. This is our first run."

Mr. Chevalier turned slowly to him. " I don't believe I have the honour of your acquaintance, sir."

Young Ames said stupidly, " Mr. Chevalier, Mr. Tibbets," and stopped short. He had never introduced a gentleman to a lady. He glanced helplessly at Christine Chevalier.

She wore a dress of flowered material, with a straw bonnet, and as she looked at him she twirled her parasol slowly on her shoulder. Her brown eyes were calm, faintly curious ; her mouth was composed. He thought he had never seen any one look prettier, but he saw too that this time she was not going to offer him any help, and he realised all at once what a fool he must seem in her eyes.

But Mr. Chevalier said : "Why, you must be Josh Tibbets's boy."

Tibbets said : "Yes, sir."

It made young Ames start. No one would have guessed that Tibbets was the son of Josh Tibbets, and heir to half a million dollars, they said on the Exchange. He looked at him uneasily.

Mr. Chevalier said in a dry voice : "I did not recognise you. I believe you have met my niece."

Tibbets bowed.

Christine Chevalier dropped a slight curtsey.

"I know Miss Ellen Pierce very well," she said. "She has told me about you, Mr. Tibbets."

Young Ames saw Tibbets flush. He felt unhappily that he was being shut out. He felt more so when he caught Miss Chevalier's eye. It was merely a flicker. "Perhaps you would introduce your friend, Mr. Tibbets."

"Good Lord," said Tibbets, "I'm sorry. I didn't realise. This is Mr. Ames. We're both volunteers."

Young Ames did not know what he should do. He could not read her face at all.

She said to Tibbets : "Won't you bring Miss Pierce round to our house next Sunday, Mr. Tibbets? And perhaps Mr. Ames could be persuaded to come also?"

She and Tibbets were smiling.

"To supper," she added.

Mr. Chevalier glanced at her and cleared his throat. "Yes, yes. Come by all means. There's Tom with the carriage, Kisty. We'd better get along to breakfast." He offered her his arm. " I like to see young men taking their part. I used to run with Number 6 in my day."

" Old Bean Soup," said Tibbets. " Father ran with Dry Bones. Those must have been good companies."

" They were. But no better than yours, my boy. I was watching you." He raised his white hat. " Remember if you see a man sitting on a barrel, you want to make sure there isn't a hydrant underneath him."

He led his niece away, leaving the two young men to finish their beer and follow the engine home. As they went, Tibbets said : " He's a fine old fellow, isn't he ? It's funny your not having met Miss Chevalier, though."

Young Ames started indignantly to say that he had met her, but he stopped himself. It would be impossible to explain to someone like Tibbets why she had been making fun of him. For she had been. He got hot when he thought of it. " Perhaps you would introduce your friend, Mr. Tibbets." She had looked so completely cool, bending her head towards him, such a picture of feminine courtesy. " Perhaps Mr. Ames could be persuaded to come also." As if he had never been in the house before, or she had not slipped a message into Mr. Chevalier's letter of credit when she sewed it into the lining of his waistcoat that evening three months ago. She couldn't· laugh that off. " To supper." Her voice, clear, cordial, and casual, exactly the note for a man she was meeting the first time. Some day, by holy, he could pay her back !

Naturally, when Tibbets had accepted for them, he had been too dumbfounded to say anything. He was committed now, and she knew it. He could tell by the way the corner of her mouth had twitched. It was the only sign she gave.

Tibbets seemed to notice nothing out of the way in young Ames's silence. He had too much to talk about. Ellen Pierce, it appeared, was the girl he was engaged to marry—Tibbets men always married Pierce women, he

said laughingly, and Ellen thought Christine Chevalier a
mighty fine girl. He thought young Ames ought to like
her. They could tell the two girls about their first run.
Hadn't it been a dandy, though? Springing the Bolivars,
standing off a gang of Five Pointers, Plug-Uglies at that;
and holding their own with Fifteen. And to top it all to
have got a black eye to show for it.

4

The window over the river was open. The rigging of the
ships along South Street hung in shadow, except those
docked in Old Slip, down which a shaft of the afternoon
sun still shone. But the thunderheads piling up in the East
caught the full sunlight against their bellies. They looked
threatening to Gibbs.

He was sitting with his feet on the window-sill, his chair
tilted at a comfortable angle and a glass of iced gin and
lemon balanced on his shirt front. There was a kind of
wistful amusement on his thin dark face as he listened to
young Ames's violent voice. " Whistling past the graveyard," he thought. Well, he had whistled past two or
three himself.

Young Ames, who was standing stark-naked in their tin
tub while he dried himself, stared hard at the back of
Gibbs's head, which told him nothing at all.

" Probably they think they're being nice to me," he
said.

" They probably don't think about it at all," said Gibbs.
" She wouldn't have asked you if she hadn't wanted you
to come."

" Maybe she thought I wouldn't," said young Ames.
" Well, I am. I'm as good as any one else who'll be there.
I'm a damn sight better, if it comes to that. I'd like to
know how much money Tibbets ever made in his life.

" What's wrong with Tibbets, Johnny? " Gibbs asked.

" There's nothing wrong with him. I'm just saying, that's all."

He glowered down at his naked legs. In the dim light, they looked as white as skinned eel. They made him feel a little sick ; in half a minute he was going to smell fish.

" If you don't quit rubbing yourself so hard," Gibbs said, " you'll have to take your bath all over again. Can't you see that those people aren't much different from any-body else ? They love you or hate you. Money hasn't got anything to do with that. Lord," he added, tilting his glass, " I sound like a preacher ! " He got up, refilled his glass, and leaned out the window, where they had a crock wired, for another piece of ice. Young Ames said at his back : " I thought the same thing the first time I went to the house. But I found it wasn't so. They can do what is worse than hating, they can think nothing of you at all."

" Maybe the fact that you were wearing a stolen coat had something to do with your feelings," Gibbs said, drawing his lank body back through the window. " I remember the first time I went to propose to a girl, I felt just the way you do, Johnny. I was afraid she'd think nothing of me."

Young Ames flushed.

" What do you mean by that ? Who said I was going to propose ? "

" It's just an academic statement of fact," Gibbs said. " I didn't say anything about what you were going to do. I just said I felt sick." He sipped at his glass and sat down and adjusted his feet again. " I was shaking so when I got out of the carriage I could hardly let go the knocker."

Young Ames looked up. " What did she say ? "

" She didn't. Because I never asked her. You see I was so anxious to make the right impression I didn't dare say no when her brothers offered me drinks. She had nine brothers," Gibbs added. " I managed to behave all right, but I knew if I tried to propose I could never get up again.

And I was ashamed to go back. By the time I was getting over it, one of her brothers told me she was engaged to be married. A man much older than I. One of her father's friends. She sent me a nice little note saying she counted on my understanding. A very nice little note," Gibbs said, crossing his feet. " I wonder what she thought I thought."

Young Ames glanced at him curiously and pulled on a shirt. It was the first white linen shirt he had ever owned. He had got it during the week, for he had made up his mind that, as long as he was going, he was going to be as well-dressed as anybody. He could afford it, too, he told himself.

" Didn't you see her again ? " he asked.

" If you mean optically, yes. You can see her yourself any Sunday when she promenades with her children in St. John's Park. She has ten of them, just like her mother, and a house on upper Broadway, a carriage, a box at the Opera House, a pew in St. John's, and a double chin. They say she's a very sweet character," said Gibbs. " And she always bows to me when we happen to pass on the street. Her name is Tallbut."

Young Ames was impressed ; Tallbut had been on the board of practically every first-class insurance company. He glanced at the back of Gibbs's seedy coat. Gibbs's shoulders looked a little hunched.

" Why did she marry him ? "

" God knows." Gibbs tilted his glass again. " If you're feeling sorry for me, you needn't. I don't want a box in the Opera House. Or a double chin for that matter. As long as I can get what I need." He got up and said : " That white satin tie is too dressy. Better put on a black one. You're going to a Sunday supper, not the Bachelor's Ball, you know," and walked out of the room.

As he tied his tie young Ames could hear Gibbs desultorily moving about his room at the back. But when he returned, he had the old sardonic gleam in his eyes.

" I only hope you don't get rained on," he said.

Young Ames cast an anxious glance at the window. The thunderheads had been moving up while he dressed. Lightning was playing in them. He could feel a hush in the air ; the river beyond the docks lay like dull glass, and gulls were squalling out in the bay.

"Good Lord," he said, "I never thought of buying an umbrella."

"Even a man of means has responsibilities," Gibbs said solemnly. "First he buys himself a new suit, but then he finds he has to have an umbrella to preserve his costly investment." He grinned and settled himself in his chair. "Well," he said, lifting his feet to the sill, "while you're enjoying yourself in the fashionable purlieus of St. John's Park, I'll sit here and watch the rain fall on Brooklyn."

"Go to the devil," said young Ames.

As he went down the dark stairwell, he could smell the mustiness exuding from the walls of the old house, as it always did in close weather. It gave a feeling of impending storm like nothing else he knew, and he found himself listening for the fall of rain. But all he heard was the echoing clatter of his own heels.

5

Outdoors the air seemed fresher and he set off briskly for Whitehall Street where the Tibbetses lived in their huge old house near Stone Street. Though it was no longer the fashionable neighbourhood it once had been, old Mr. Tibbets refused to be driven away. He had started his fortune in leather, shifted to drygoods, and ended up in coffee with side interests in the China Trade ; but he liked, as he often said, to sleep in a familiar place.

His son was waiting in the hall for young Ames.

"I'd ask you to come in and meet my mother and father. He thinks you must be the clerk who engineered the

Chevalier corner in cotton," Tibbets grinned. "He said he wished I had that much get up and git. But you'll be late if we don't push right along."

Young Ames was started out of the sense of pleasure that Mr. Tibbets's knowing who he was had given him.

"What do you mean, I'm going to be late? Aren't you coming?"

"No. Ellen's indisposed, so I'm going to spend the evening at her house. I just heard or I'd have let you know. She sent word to the Chevaliers and they sent word back that they'd expect you just the same. We can walk uptown together anyway," Tibbets said cheerfully. "It's a damn' nuisance the stages don't run Sundays, isn't it?"

Young Ames walked on alone from the corner of Greenwich and Jay Streets. His freckled face was serious and a little pale. He had made up his mind. Maybe she thought he was a fool. Anyway he was going to find out. He didn't know how he would, but there would be some way.

The wind struck his face as he turned east on Beach Street. There was going to be a storm all right; it would be one of those typical summer storms that seemed to hang in the bay, and then came over New York like an angry man suddenly turning on his heel. As he reached the corner of Hudson Street he saw the limbs of the trees in St. John's Park swinging in and out of the dim light of the street lamps. The flowing sound of wind in leaves hushed his footfalls. Through the high iron rails he could see the light from the open door of the Chevalier house across the Park, and he quickened his pace instinctively like any traveller who sees his destination in the moment of storm. Lightning edged the belly of a cloud. He reached the door as the first hard pelting drops whipped down to make dust puddles in the cobble cracks.

Amber, the coloured butler, was coming down the front hall on shuffling feet to close the door.

"Good-*evening*, Mr. Ames," he said, not quite controlling

an African roll of his eyes. "Seem like you just beat that thunder to Laight Street, sir."

He put young Ames's hat on the marble hall table among several others. "We all in the living-room, Mr. Ames," he said.

Young Ames drew in his breath. He could hear their voices.

6

The windows were open and the curtains stirred. Beyond them was the sound of rain falling in the back-yard garden, and a voluble middle-aged lady with a bosom that would have balanced a bird cage was begging someone to close the windows.

New York in a thunderstorm, she said, always terrified her, because they were so much more liable to get struck. It made her feel like poor General Braddock and the Indians. It wasn't at all like being in the country where the houses were so much farther apart.

Nobody seemed to be inclined to pay much attention to her except a thin studious young man who tried to tell her a little of the nature of lightning. Immediately she thought he was like Benjamin Franklin and said that Benjamin Franklin had always had women friends because he treated them like *human beings*. If a man treated women like human beings, she said, it was natural that they just couldn't help *loving* him. If it hadn't been for his good Boston upbringing, she felt sure that Benjamin Franklin might have been a notorious courtesan.

When the studious-looking man, who appeared to have a passion for fact, asked whether Mrs. DePeyster did not mean Casanova, her bosom swelled. "No, indeed," she said sharply. What a ridiculous thing to ask! She knew Cazenovia intimately herself. Had been there dozens of times to visit her cousins. Her voice merged in the other voices, and young Ames saw Mr. Chevalier coming forward to greet him.

"Good-evening, Ames," he said. "I'm glad you came."

He led him towards Mrs. Chevalier, who smiled comfortably at him and was glad he had come. But he mustn't stay with her. He must join the younger people. She turned to devote her attention again to Reverend Mr. Berrian's gout as described by Mrs. Berrian, who seemed barely able to discern young Ames's presence.

He felt Mr. Chevalier put a hand on his shoulder.

"Ames." His voice sounded strangely preoccupied and rather sad. As young Ames glanced at him, he went on, "I can't help thinking of Lafayette. He died in his house May twentieth. The *Silas Richards* brought the news yesterday."

"I knew she'd docked," young Ames said. "She must have made a fast passage for her."

Mr. Chevalier smiled. "Bad news makes even the *Silas Richards* sail, apparently."

Amber, the butler, appeared beside them with a huge silver tray bearing sherry glasses.

"It's Yriarte," said Mr. Chevalier. "It should be Château Margaux, but let's drink a silent toast." He turned to young Ames. "I suppose it doesn't mean much to a young man. We've been apt to think of the political Republican, in late years. I like to remember him as he came to this country, full of ardour and a belief in Liberty. I was thirteen when he landed."

He lifted his glass, and young Ames, a little puzzled, followed his example.

After a moment of standing in silence, Mr. Chevalier said to him, "You'll find my niece in the corner." He inclined his head towards the group at the other end of the room. "But you'll have to find your own way."

Young Ames moved aside, glass in hand. He did not see how a person could politely penetrate the group of backs, and he could not see her at all.

There were two or three young ladies, full of laughter and exclamations, and half a dozen men, one of whom he recognised as Mr. Atwood. At the moment he was doing all the talking, doing it easily, in a quiet, slightly drawling voice; and they were all listening to him and laughing when he wanted them to laugh. As young Ames looked on from the windows he remembered a conversation he had had with Gibbs in the latter's room. It was in his second month at Chevalier's, the night, as a matter of fact, after he had seen Miss Chevalier sing for the street beggar.

"And there's one thing you might as well face," Gibbs had told him. "Men like George Chevalier hire people like you and McVitty, and me for that matter, and they speak civil to us. But they don't like us mixing up in their families."

He hadn't believed it then; but now, for the second time in the Chevalier drawing-room, he felt the truth of it, and he wondered why he had been asked. There were certain things you knew and talked about, if you had the proper kind of breeding; and you knew how to say them; and you knew what to wear and when it was proper to sit down; and what to laugh at and what not. In their eyes you might be free, but you were never born equal.

He had felt it that first night, when he had got into the house by wearing Mr. Chevalier's coat. In his miserableness he had even blurted it out to Miss Chevalier. "I thought everybody was like everybody else and only the clothes were different," he had said. "I thought if I had on a coat like this I'd be just as good as him."

And suddenly he remembered her answer.

"Him? Oh, Mr. Atwood. And now you find you aren't? Doesn't it make you mad?" she had asked.

He felt an almost electrical shock. It was queer not to have remembered that. And suddenly he recognised the story Mr. Atwood was telling.

He was telling it very prettily, too, teasingly perhaps;

but he was making Miss Chevalier sound nearly as lovely
as she was. He conveyed the very feeling of that kerbstone
encounter. The frosty morning, the shawled street singer,
the lady getting out of her carriage and starting to sing,
and the gentlemen, recalled to their better natures,
returning.

One of the young women clapped her hands and said
it was just like the opera. " But there should be a buffo,
Mr. Atwood. You've forgotten the buffo."

" Upon my word," said Mr. Atwood easily, " so I have.
But he was there, you know. A man with a freckled face
and out-at-elbows coat. She charmed him, just as she had
charmed the rest of us. As a matter of fact, he stood right
beside me and gaped at Christine, with his hand in his
pocket as though he held his heart in it."

As Mr. Atwood sipped his glass, young Ames felt himself go hot. He stepped forward impulsively so that his
shoulder touched Mr. Atwood's and that gentleman was
forced to give way. He said : " Good-evening, sir," and
stood there confronting them, his freckled face flushed. He
thought they must be fools if they could not see for themselves, but to make certain of it he deliberately put his
hand into his coat pocket.

The young lady who had asked for the buffo put her
fan to her lips to smother her slight gasp, and glanced at
her companion on the sofa. Ames looked at her too.

" Good-evening, Miss Chevalier." He knew his bow
was awkward.

He could see that she also was angry. She sat quite still,
her hands holding the folded fan on her knees. But her
colour was high. Her lips were parted, as if she had
breathed sharply ; her dark eyes frozen on his face. In her
white dress, her figure was like a statue ; but the bodice
looked tight to young Ames, as though her breast were
swollen against it. It was the first time he had seen her in
white. He had not realised before the warmth of colour
in her skin.

Then, without moving her eyes, her lips smiled, and from them he drew a sick consciousness of having acted wrong. Had one of these people been impelled to do what he had done, he would have carried it off lightly, making it almost a pretty thing. But none of them would have been in his position. It was not a pretty thing at all ; it was ugly. He felt as if he were all alone, a long way from them all. He was baffled when he had expected them to feel confused ; and he had hurt her.

He could see that as her lips moved ; for an instant they quivered and her fingers trembled on the handle of her fan.

" Good-evening, Mr. Ames. I'm so glad you could come."

She had control of her voice. She rose from her sofa.

" Amber is announcing supper," she said. " Let's go in."

7

Young Ames was not conscious of what he was eating. There was a cold turkey at Mr. Chevalier's end of the table and Amber at the sideboard pontifically presided over a monumental ham. His gestures were modelled on Mr. Chevalier's, but when he laid the edge of his carving knife to the meat, the contact seemed to have a pleasurable effect that nearly closed his eyes, and his lips pursed gently while he stroked towards the bone.

Being supper, the gentlemen served the ladies, so young Ames, in imitation of the others, fetched a plate for an innocent-faced young woman whose name he had not learned. As soon as he was settled beside her, she asked him whether he went to Saratoga in the summers. He said that he did not, and she said she thought it was sad that gentlemen's business confined them so. The watering places would be so much less enervating if the men came also. It must be strange in New York during July and

August, she added, with no women one knew. Didn't he
find it so?

Young Ames was thankful that she did not seem to
require answers. He let her talk for them both, which she
did nobly. He thought she was a fool, until, glancing at
her, he found that she was studying his face and he realised
that she was being nice. Looking quickly across the table,
he found that Christine Chevalier also had been watching.

At the moment every one else was laughing at something Mrs. DePeyster had said and the young woman
whispered, almost savagely : " Can't you speak, Mr.
Ames ? You might at least help Kisty's feelings that much."
She gave him a pretty smile and said aloud : " Kisty says
you are with Chevalier, Deming & Post."

" Yes," he said.

" It must be exciting, Mr. Ames. I mean when things
come up like cornering the cotton market."

" That was," he admitted.

" My father has wondered ever since how Mr. Chevalier
beat the mail to New Orleans," she said.

" It was just a matter of bribing stagecoach drivers and
boat captains not to stop," he said. " I hadn't much
trouble."

She said : " Oh," almost incredulously. Then : " They
sent you ? Weren't you excited ? "

" Yes," he said, and closed up. He ought not to have
told her. But she was no fool, he found ; her voice returned
to its light note of chatter and she was speaking about
New Orleans. She had heard so much about it, but had
never been there herself. Did he see the quadroons, such
a scandalous thing to think of ; and did he attend the
French Theatre ? He said he had had no time.

She managed to breast a way through supper, but at the
end she was reduced to the subject of food. " Kisty," she
said, as they started to file out of the room, " Mr. Ames
is *so* interested in food. I think it's so unusual. He was
telling me about the seedcakes they used to have in his

home. You must get him to tell you the recipe for them."
Her glance at young Ames was malicious, but he bowed
and smiled.

Miss Chevalier stopped.

" Did your mother have a special recipe for seedcake ? "

" I don't know if it was special," he said. " They didn't
taste as good as these."

She raised her brows.

" Oh, you liked these ? "

" Very much," he said. " Miss . . . I don't know the
lady's name."

Miss Chevalier said : " That was Miss Terry, Lavinia
Terry. You seem to have had a lot in common."

He looked at her.

" Nothing but a dislike for John Ames," he said. " But
Miss Terry thought you might give me the recipe. So I
could send it home when I write."

She was looking at him curiously, then threw a quick
glance towards Miss Terry's back.

She said : " Oh," slowly. Then : " Aunt Chevalier
keeps the recipes in her desk. If you'll come with me,
I'll get it for you."

Young Ames glanced back as they left the room. No
one seemed to be noticing their departure except Miss
Terry, and she appeared to be listening sweetly to Mr.
Chevalier. But as he went round the door, he wasn't
sure ; he thought she made a mouth at them.

8

" The recipe for seedcake is in the black notebook in
the right-hand pigeonhole. Under *C*. If you copy it out,
Mr. Ames, it will save your doing it later when you write
home to your mother. You write to her frequently ? " she
asked.

He said : " No. My mother died years ago."

She was standing a little to one side of the desk, close to the open window. It was still raining outside. As he spoke she lifted her chin and turned back into the room.

" You don't want the recipe ? "

He said stubbornly : " Yes, I do. I have an aunt in Troy. She'll be interested."

He reached for the book, opened it to the letter *C*. CARAWAY CAKE, he read. " Take one pound of flour, three-quarters of a pound of sugar, half a pound of butter, a glass of rose water, four eggs, and half a cup of caraway seed—the materials well rubbed together and beaten up. Drop them from a spoon on tin sheets, and bake them brown in rather a slow oven. Twenty minutes, or half an hour, is enough to bake them."

He said : " It sounds simple."

" Yes," she said.

He pulled out a slip of paper, dipped a pen, and wrote. He wrote methodically, exactly as he would have copied a letter, checking each sentence. All the time he was conscious of her standing at the window. She stood perfectly still, but he knew she was watching him.

He put away the book, stuck the pen into the shotwell, and waved the sheet to dry it. He knew he would have no other time to say what he wanted to.

" I'm sorry I did that to-night," he said.

She said quite calmly : " We all lose our tempers sometimes. Mr. Atwood was being unpleasant, but, of course, he did not know you'd be there."

" I don't suppose he did."

She looked at him quickly.

" I didn't mean to say that," he said. " I wanted to tell you that I got your note." She said nothing at all. " In New Orleans," he said. " I was glad to get it."

" That was quite a long time ago, wasn't it, Mr. Ames ? " Some hidden movement of her body made her skirts sway. Her voice lifted slightly. " We'd hoped you would come to the house and tell us about the trip," she said. " Uncle said you hadn't told him much."

" I didn't know," he said. " I didn't want to come without being invited."

" Oh," she said. " You wanted to be invited ? "

" How was I to know you expected me to come ? " He felt that she had all the weapons, but as she answered, her cheeks brightened.

" I think Uncle was a little hurt. He has a high opinion of you, Mr. Ames, you know. He told me about your deal in rice. He said it was very clever."

" He didn't say so to me."

" Do you want people to tell you everything ? " she asked with a little laugh. " To humbly send you invitations and say how important you are ? "

" That isn't so ! " His face whitened under the freckles. " You know it isn't so. I'm a junior clerk in Chevalier's. How am I to know I'm wanted in his house ? "

" A matter of natural politeness, for one thing, I should think. And intelligence for another. My uncle sent you to New Orleans, didn't he ? He had you in his house overnight before you left. We thought we were treating you like a member of the family. I sewed a pocket for you. I even wrote you a stupid note, which you never bothered to answer. That's nothing to me, but I don't think you behaved well towards Uncle."

" He didn't show it."

" What do you expect ? To have him go round with a sullen face avoiding every one ? I'm afraid you're right, Mr. Ames. You are a junior clerk and likely to stay one."

They stared at each other for a long minute, he pale, she with her colour high. Then she made a movement towards the door. But he did not step back, and there was no room to pass him without the obvious gesture of moving the desk chair. She halted and pointed with her fan.

" You have your recipe, Mr. Ames. I think it's time we

returned to the drawing-room unless we wish to stage another little scene there."

"I have the recipe," he said. "The directions are simple, aren't they?"

"So you said," she replied impatiently.

"It seems to depend on the ingredients."

"Yes, of course, though the way they're put together is just as important." Her forehead wrinkled. "What on earth are you talking about?"

He looked white to her, a little drawn round the eyes, completely upset. Well, she had intended to upset him; she could still feel her heart racing.

"You haven't left much out," he said. "But you're wrong about one thing. I'm not going to stay a junior clerk all my life, not by a long shot. I made Mr. Chevalier a million dollars, whatever any one says, and I'll make myself a million before I'm done. Please don't get mad again. That was part of my job, if you like, and I'm not mad about it myself."

She turned to look out of the window.

"I think I was wrong about that."

She didn't say anything more. She was utterly still, but he felt a queer alertness in her, and he felt himself begin to shake.

"I haven't had much chance to learn manners. Mr. Chevalier doesn't give you much time off." He hesitated. "He told me last month that it wasn't safe or honest or good business, either, to operate on margin."

She seemed completely absorbed in her contemplation of the back-yard garden.

He said: "That time I saw you first, on Beach Street, it was just the way Mr. Atwood described it. I didn't know who you were, but I thought I would get rich in a few years. It seemed easy. I thought it was going to be easy when I started off for New Orleans. I thought so when I read your letter there. But I see it isn't, now. You just said a junior clerk doesn't amount to much. I saw that myself in New Orleans, and coming back on the steamboat. Mr. Chevalier made me see it, too, after I made that deal in rice."

She made no motion. The curls lay still against the back of her neck. Her shoulders were turned a little forward from the way she held her arms. For a minute he looked over her shoulders into the dark glass. It was still raining, but there was a little fog in the rain and he thought that before morning it would stop. He drew in his breath.

"I fell in love with you that morning."

"I know that," she said.

9

He heard the wet clop of horses' hoofs and saw the carriage lamps like dimmed eyes in the rain. It went by close enough to the kerb to throw the spray from the tyres against his trousers. The light of the street lamp on the opposite corner showed him a man and a woman in the carriage. He swung on his heel to look after it, before resuming his way down Hudson Street.

He turned off Broadway into Maiden Lane and followed it down to Front Street ; and suddenly it occurred to him that this was the route he had followed his first day in New York. But then he didn't have the street to himself. It was crowded that morning, and people kept bumping into him. He grinned suddenly, remembering how solitary he had felt. " WANTED—A BOY." He remembered seeing the sign tacked to the door of Number 42 and working up his nerve to go in.

Of course they would have to wait, probably a long time. Her stepfather was ill. She thought he was dying, and Mr. Chevalier would be her guardian. " Uncle thinks you are going to succeed," she had said. " I think so too. But I wouldn't make such a bad wife for a poor man, either. I can cook, you know. Things besides little cakes.

Mother and I didn't have any money before she married again." That was when she let him kiss her. "Perhaps that's how it happened," Christine said. "We're climbers too." It would be proper to call her Christine now, he thought, when they were alone together.

The watch flashed his lantern at the corner of South and Old Slip. "Oh, it's you, Mr. Ames."

He had on his short coat and the rain dripped from his leather hat.

"Hallo, McPhail."

"It's a wet night," said McPhail.

He held his lantern to shine on the keyhole and then went on his way, knocking his pine stick against the walls to give fair warning to any malefactor that he was coming. It was the kind of night the watch didn't feel like trouble.

VI

PROFIT, NETT

Winding between the Hudson and the cliffs, the gravel path had led them nearly three miles north of the Hoboken Ferry dock. This was the wilder part of the Elysian Fields. Young Ames had long since lost sight of Tibbets and his fiancée, Miss Pierce, whom they were to rejoin at five o'clock at the northmost bench on this same path; but the bench too was behind them. It was several minutes since they had encountered any one at all.

"I suppose it's too hot for most people to come so far," Christine observed. The path was now so narrow that they could no longer walk abreast; every little way she had to turn sideways to navigate her skirts between the bordering shrubs. She too had been silent, as if like himself she found it enough to walk under the shady trees while the birds made any talk there was to make. They were content just to be by themselves with no chance of interruption. He had to clear his throat to answer her, but all he could say was, "I suppose it is."

She walked easily; her sunshade, twirling slowly on her shoulder, now hid her head from him, now lifted to show the edge of her bonnet and the cluster of dark curls beside her ear. But he was satisfied merely to watch her move, to see how she managed her wide skirts, bending her slim waist to swing them past a tree.

"I love walking in the country," she said, lifting her skirts above a shoulder of the rock and giving him a glimpse of the laced hems of her petticoats and the heel of her black shoe. "See, John. There's a piece of grass down there, where we could sit. We've nearly an hour before we have to go back and join the others. Wouldn't you like to stop?"

He cleared his throat again before he could say "Yes," and followed her steeply down. She didn't need his hand, and neither of them spoke.

It was a shady corner, screened from above by a small tree. One could look out at the blue water and listen to the sound of it. There were white clouds. A sloop, moving north, had a breeze to curve its sails, and the voice of a wheeling hawk came faint, and thinly piercing. Young Ames placed the picnic basket in a bank of ferns, and turned to find her seated, her skirt spread round her, her waist, rising from the centre, curved slightly as she tilted her face to look at him. Her bonnet lay beside her on the grass; but she still held the ribbons in one hand.

She seemed to catch his silence from him, her dark eyes raised to his, as if the same spell snared them both; then, as their eyes encountered, the colour deepened in her cheeks, and her wide mouth bent a little. She smiled almost tremulously, and her voice was quiet. "You may kiss me now, sir. If you like," she told him.

2

She said : " You must have been a funny little boy,
John."

" Why ? "

" I don't know. All freckled, and sandy-looking, with
your hair on end."

He scrubbed his fingers through his hair. " I guess
I was."

" Coming home with your clothes in tatters and tracking
mud into the house. You used to do that, didn't you ? "

" My aunt used to scold me for it."

He felt shy with her. A week ago he wouldn't have
thought it possible for them to be like this. Tibbets had
suggested the excursion to Hoboken. " We'll pick the
girls up at their houses, and catch the three o'clock ferry.
Ellen says they'll provide the supper, and we can come
back on the evening boat." It had been as easy as that.
Leaving Tibbets and Miss Pierce snug in the hackney
coach, to mount the stoop of Louis Chevalier's house and
ring the bell, young Ames had wondered if he could be
identified from George Chevalier's house on the far side of
St. John's Park. What would they think if they knew that
the junior clerk of Chevalier, Deming & Post was taking
the senior partner's niece for an outing in the Elysian
Fields ? But they didn't have time to find out, for Christine
herself answered his ring, the picnic basket ready on her
arm, and in half a minute they had stepped into the coach
and started off up Hudson Street behind the rapid dusty
clop of hoofs. It didn't matter what they would have
thought, now he and she were here.

" I hope if I have a son, he'll look just the way you did."

" I don't. I never had a decent coat, or shoes. I never
had any money to spend. We were always poor."

She raised her hand quickly. " I don't mean that. I
mean coming home all hot and dirty and angry to tell me

what's happened to him. Thinking even if he's beat he
still can whip the world." She gave a low laugh. "You
looked a little like that the other night at Uncle's house."
Then her eyes dropped, and she bent her head, and he
saw the colour in her cheeks.

"I'd like to tell them you are going to marry me," he
said. "So they'll know."

She said coolly : "You mean Mr. Atwood ? "

"Yes, him. And Mr. Chevalier too. Then I could come
to see you when I want."

"But you can see me Sunday evenings at Uncle's. I'm
always there."

He said impatiently : "I can't talk to you there with
everybody else trying to too. I can't even talk to you at
all. I don't belong with those people."

"It's silly to feel so."

"It's true, though. They're all related to each other,
and they all know what every one does. And they know
I'm just a junior clerk. I can see what they think even
though they don't say so. They only speak to me because
I'm in his house."

She glanced away from him, out over the river. "You
must learn to feel differently, John. I just said I didn't care
much about money ; but I do care what people think of
you—all kinds of people. You'd probably like them if you
gave them a chance to like you."

He gave a short derisive laugh.

"Them ? Dandies like . . ."

"Like Mr. Atwood ? " She looked back at him. "But
you like Mr. Tibbets, don't you ? "

"He's different. He runs with our machine."

Amusement showed in her eyes. "You know, John,
when I first came here I hated oysters. But I had to eat
them to be polite."

"What's that got to do with it ? "

"Well, after a while I found they went down right easy,
and now I really like them very much."

She watched him laugh and laughed with him, her eyes shining. It was the first time they had ever really laughed together.

"All right," he said. "I'll try to like your oysters. But it's going to be hard sometimes. Just standing around while they take all your time."

"Won't it be some comfort to know that I don't like it, either, John?"

"No," he said. "But if I had money we wouldn't have to wait. I could ask your stepfather, and if he said no, I'd marry you anyway."

"He can't see any one. Mother probably wouldn't care what I did," she said thoughtfully. "But Uncle George would, and I wouldn't want to hurt him. He's been good to me." Her hands joined in her lap, and looking down at them she told him a little about herself. "We were poor too. Not honest-poor like you, but pinching to keep up appearances. I remember Mother's selling Tom, our butler, to buy new clothes when she met Mr. Chevalier. And then, after he'd proposed, she sold Mammy too." Her voice dropped lower. "Perhaps that's why I don't think so much of money." She could not remember her own father, and Louis had not taken any interest in her. She was kept out of the way, staying in the kitchen with Mammy. "He seemed to me like somebody's grandfather, till Mother told me she was going to marry him."

Young Ames recalled what Gibbs had told him about the young widow casting her snares for the old buck in Charleston; and he could imagine the bewildered little girl looking on with the old Negro Mammy. He had never seen her mother, but he imagined her, cool-eyed and calculating, filling Louis Chevalier with flattery and juleps.

Even now, Christine went on, she saw less of her mother and stepfather than of the George Chevaliers. The old husband and the young wife hadn't wanted an awkward, half-grown girl along to spoil their fun.

"When I first saw Uncle George, his eyes scared me."

(Young Ames knew how frosty those blue eyes could be.) "But he made me a bow as if I were a grown lady." Now his house seemed more like home to her than her own mother's. "That's why I couldn't bear to disappoint him, John. And he's so worried about my stepfather. He doesn't see him because Mother and he dislike each other."

"Why do they?"

"I don't know."

Young Ames let out his breath. "George Chevalier'd never let you marry me if he could help it. Not unless I had a lot of money."

"I think you're wrong," she said quietly. "He likes you. If we give him time, he'll think it natural when we want to marry. He barks a lot worse than he bites."

"To you, maybe." Young Ames could see the dreary wait ahead of them. "It'll be a long time before I have enough for us to live on, the way things are now in the city. A hundred and fifty a year salary isn't anything. I won't get many chances like that Sheehan rice deal and I don't want to touch the five thousand I made on it, now it's invested."

She said: "Uncle George wouldn't have put it in the firm for you if he hadn't liked you, John."

"Maybe," he said. "If I tried to touch it, though, he'd find out why."

She said: "But it will be making money, won't it? How much will it earn a year?"

"Five thousand at 6 per cent? Three hundred dollars. But that isn't much, either."

"Three hundred dollars?" she said thoughtfully. "Some of those new Bleecker Street houses rent for that."

It made the possibility of marriage seem enticingly closer, and suddenly they were quiet, almost solemn, with the thought. Watching her, young Ames let his imagination rush ahead to the door of a Bleecker Street house, entering it with her, closing the door behind them, she and he alone. He wondered whether she thought of it the same way. She

was so still, her body rising out of the wide spread of skirt
and petticoats, her face a little bent, so that he saw the
rounded white part in her dark hair. Then she glanced
up at him, lifting her chin.

" I don't care about being rich. As soon as it's right for
us to marry, you'll find I'm easy to bargain with." Her
lips twitched at the corners. " In fact, I think you could
name your own price, sir."

He said : " I don't see why a girl like you wants to
marry me."

" I suppose because I've fallen in love, John. . . ."

A little later, she told him that she was going to go to
Rockaway with her uncle and aunt for three weeks. Mr.
Chevalier planned to come back to town after a few days,
but he would rejoin them on July third and stay till they
returned together on the eleventh. It would be wiser,
perhaps, not to write.

Young Ames would have agreed to anything.

3

But she had written, a short note that Gibbs brought
up to him on July seventh. Gibbs had a grin on his satur-
nine dark face. " Here's something for you, Johnny. A
billet-doux, I should judge. She writes a nice hand, too."
But he let young Ames read it in peace in the sun-filled
room, while the pigeons pattered the hot slates on the roof
outside and the morning dock sounds drifted slowly up.

ROCKAWAY, *July fifth.*

" DEAR JOHN,—We are here at the Marine Pavilion.
The Hones have gone back to the city, but poor Mr.
Lamar is here still. It is sad to see him, now he is old and
has no prospect of making more money. He seems quite
broken. Uncle is trying to find him a position in the
customs.

" We promenade along the beach every day if the sun is not too hot, but sometimes I go out with my sunshade anyway, to be alone, and then I can think of you without risk of seeming ' vagueish ' as Aunt tells me I have lately become. See what you have done to a girl ! I watch the gulls fly in along the shore and wonder if one of them does not look in your window sometimes. I have never seen where you live. Will I ever ? I know I said we must not write, but I am too naughty, and had to, to send you my love.

" Ever,

" CHRISTINE."

Young Ames shifted restlessly on the top of his high stool. It was packet night, past nine o'clock ; the heat of the day still clung to South Street ; and the counting-room was airless as the inside of Mr. McVitty's snuff-box.

Next to him, Gibbs was working on the translation of an order from Rio that Chevalier, Deming & Post was handling on commission ; behind him Cummings was using his squeaky pen that made almost as much noise as a whistling gaslight or the chief clerk's stoppered nostril. It was hard to concentrate when your mind was occupied with a love letter and you had been racking your brains for ways to turn a thousand dollars into something more than 6 per cent. Rather than leave it idle young Ames had picked up here and there a few odd lots of merchandise auctioned off by broken firms and sent them out on speculation with acquaintances who were supercargoes in the Pacific trade. But hundred-dollar lots could not be expected to make a man's fortune.

All trade was slow. Though Chevalier's had done well by grace of the corner in cotton, other people had suffered, and old firms that had been hanging on all winter started to give out at the very end. Some went under with scarcely a ripple. Others might have friends who would try to rescue them, as Mr. Chevalier had tried to help Lamar's.

He had taken a second ship off their hands—the *Unity*,
411 tons—but that had only served to delay the end.
Lamar & Phisterer had folded on the twenty-ninth of
June and all Chevalier's had to show for what Mr. McVitty
disparagingly called their romantical notions of friendship
were two as sluggish vessels as ever rubbed their snouts
in Pier 14.

June, 1834, the chief clerk claimed, would stand for
ever on the pages of American history as the Black Month.
The Senate had passed the Clay resolution for restoration
of the Federal deposits, but the House had tabled it. The
last hope for the United States Bank was gone. It was
dead, dead as the guts of a gutless herring, and whatever
one thought of the House's action, the prime eviscerator
was still that murderous madman, Andrew Jackson.
" 'The murderer rising with the light killeth the poor
and needy.' Job 24, the fourteenth verse," and Mr.
McVitty inhaled a cavernous quantity of snuff. " Have
you finished those invoices, Ames ? "

He peered round young Ames's elbow.

" You've scarcely started," he said severely. " Get to
work. Leaning and lallygagging like a lovesick swan." Mr.
McVitty's metaphors were apt to be as erratic as his
accounts were accurate. He rustled the papers in his
hands and stalked off to the office of the junior partners,
where young Ames could hear him heavily asserting that
there were three things that ruined annually more junior
clerks in New York City than alcohol or arson : going to
fires, falling in love, and attending abolition meetings.
Young Ames grinned as he met Gibbs's sardonic eye. The
last fatality at least had not yet overwhelmed him.

It infuriated Mr. McVitty to have a clerk run out to
an alarm ; but he couldn't stop it, for Mr. Chevalier had
run with Old Bean Soup, Number 6, in his own day, and
approved of young men's joining up.

The invoice was as dull a piece as he had ever hoped
to copy. McChesney, Finch & Sons : Liverpool. He

wondered if the sons were Finches or McChesneys. Cotton, upland, 300 bales ; naval stores—rosin, tar, and turpentine ; red-oak barrel staves ; pearl ashes ; treenails ; flaxseed ; beeswax. . . . In the slack and stuffy summer heat, the routine of the counting-room had staled for him. The three weeks Christine had been away seemed deadly long and the city itself had become a dust-covered maze of sleeping houses. The only excitement had been the printing-house fire in Pearl Street and the occasional rumours of gang fights in the Five Points and Cherry Street that Pinky Finnegan brought in to them. The Dead Rabbits, he said, were after the Native Americans and the Bowery Boys had beaten up three negroes in Oak Street. Sometimes the morning papers confirmed these stories with a brief paragraph about a " disturbance in Cross Street," but more often they reported nothing at all. The Five Points worked under its own dirty crust. It was only when a gang fight became violent enough to spill over into the outer streets that you knew trouble had begun. Pinky's uncle, Mike Dolan, said it was the heat started the boys brawling. Later, the dogs would feel it, and there might be another dog-killing in August.

Mr. McVitty returned for the invoices and young Ames finished the third or shipper's copy with a spurt. It didn't please the chief clerk. " The writing's like a sidewalk auction for a Jewish haberdasher," he said. " All sizes. You'll have to show an improvement, Ames."

Young Ames mechanically said : " Yes, sir."

Cummings had fetched his hat from the pegs behind the door and started for his little house in Henry Street ; Gibbs unfolded his long legs off his stool ; the junior partners emerged together from their office and said good-night— Mr. Post stiffly, Mr. Deming with his usual easy good nature. Outside they could hear Pinky Finnegan's heels clattering over the cobbles towards the packet berth in Pier 18. Mr. McVitty, the lassitude of heat and age suddenly overcoming him, slowly locked the strong-room door and fobbed the key. The day that had begun at half-past seven that morning was done at last.

Gibbs said : " It's been hot. I think I'll buy a lump of ice. Want to come, Johnny ? "

Young Ames shook his head. He had no taste for gin and lemon, even iced. Gibbs said : " I'll be right back," then, glancing over his shoulder, he grinned. " There's to-morrow coming, Johnny. Cheer up."

Young Ames let him go without a word. Climbing the steep flights slowly, he gloomily lit a candle and got out Christine Chevalier's note to read again.

She would like to see his room. He glanced distastefully round him at the stained plaster, the stool and chair and rickety table, the narrow bed, and the bureau with the cracked chamber pot under one corner replacing its missing leg. She'd never see it if he could help it.

He cocked his feet up on the table and brooded darkly over last Saturday's *Journal*. There was nothing in the market news. Hides—market remains 'dull. Ashes—remain at $4 a $4.30. Cotton—fair. Naval stores were up a cent in North Country turpentine. " Freights to Europe remain very dull." Even in Ducks—" there is little doing."

BUSINESS GENERALLY.—The sales of the week were not large, yet the feeling in the market is getting better, and the best-informed merchants expect a fair business for the fall.

That was nice to know, for the best-informed merchants. For a clerk with a thousand dollars to play with, the news-paper might as well have reported a prospect of an increase in the city's mice. He heard Gibbs returning with his lump of ice. " There's to-morrow coming," Gibbs had said. To-morrow, at this time, young Ames felt, he might as well be dead.

But to-morrow at that time he was running hell-for-

leather behind the shield plate of Oceanus, Engine Number
11, towards a fire somewhere in the region of Bridge Street.

4

The leatherhead, rapping his stick along his beat on
Front Street, obligingly roared the location as they ran
the gooseneck out of the engine-house. It had been a quick
turnout and the foreman paid out the drag for thirty men.
With Rock Doyle heaving powerfully on the tongue and
Staats Meade lunging wide on the tail rope to swing her,
they took the corner into William Street and went up it
with a dizzy roar of wheels upon the cobbles.

The signal lantern was bobbing half a block ahead and
the foreman was shouting back to " jump her, boys, jump
her." Young Ames had a place on the drag for the first
time. He had been second to Rock Doyle at the engine-
house, and no one had offered to displace him, though
he ranked merely as a runner. He saw out of the tail
of his eye Tibbets's admiring stare as the latter pounded
up to them at a dead run when they took the bend into
Pearl Street. Rock Doyle grunted, " Beat your wings,
squab," and the thud of his nailed boots sounded like
destruction just behind. A fire in Bridge Street would
give Oceanus's chief rival, Bolivar Number 9, a start of
several blocks.

But as they straightened out down Broad, they heard
the commotion straight ahead and realised that as usual
the watchman had been wrong. There was a fire all right,
though. Purdy, whose nose was celebrated in the company, said he smelled hay smoke. If they had taken Water
Street they would have made the conflagration in a two-
blocks sprint.

Broad Street, however, offered them a fine chance for a
real burst. They had old Oceanus rocking on her small
wheel, the iron tyres knocking sparks from the cobbles as

they slewed to pass a hose cart careening in from Pearl Street ; but as they cramped into Water Street, they saw the Bolivars already working the brakes at the corner of Coenties Slip.

Oceanus dropped her suction under a schooner's cut-water and, while the Bolivar's runners hooted derisively, ran their line up a narrow alley. They caught up with their foreman and Staats Meade, who carried the pipe, in the doorway of a small barn.

The inside of the barn was a turmoil of yells, smoke, and the piercing whinnies of horses. Wiping the sweat from his eyes, young Ames tried to see in, but he could not make out anything except the smoke, nor hear anything intelligible except Vredenbergh's speaking trumpet bellowing for Oceanus to start playing. Then he made out two of Bolivar's vamps playing a fair stream from their pipe on to the burning litter on the floor.

A swish sounded under him ; between his feet the leather hose of his own company swelled and hardened. Staats Meade, who had the reputation of being a sala-mander, stepped directly into the burning mess. Heavy smoke and steam rose chokingly before him and the hiss of quenched flames drowned out the sound of burning. It looked as if Meade were cutting the fire in two.

The tall figure of Gulick, the chief engineer, broke out of the smoke beside young Ames. He spoke through his silver trumpet. " Well played, Meade," and young Ames saw the back of Meade's neck turn red.

The chief engineer coolly surveyed the scene.

" This fire's about whipped now," he said to Vreden-bergh. " It's lucky, with those horses back in the stalls and no way to get them out. I wonder how the hell it started."

He had his explanation almost at once. The thinning smoke showed a hackney coach cramped against the wall. The horse, still in harness, must have thrown himself when the fire started, for he lay cast in the corner, his head turned back on his shoulder. His eyes rolled wildly. It was sheer luck that the first run of flames had been away from him.

As the fireman went up to him, however, a loud uncertain voice bellowed inside the cab : " Go on, go on. Damn it, driver, can't you go faster than this ? " A clenched fist was thrust out of the window, followed by a gangly, intoxicated face. The man craned towards the driver's seat, saw it was empty. " My God," he said, looking round to meet the cold stare of the chief engineer with vague and startled eyes. " Fire ! "

" That's right," said Gulick.

" Where is it ? " His voice was eager. " I haven't been to a fire for three years."

" The fire's here, but it's out," said Gulick.

The passenger stared at him a moment, hiccoughed deeply, and suddenly fell back inside the coach.

Gulick put his silver trumpet to his mouth. " 'Vast playing, Number 9. Eleven can wash down."

Meade glanced at him, and as if by accident the nozzle swung in his hands and the stream went unerringly through the window of the coach after the vanished face. The chief engineer had turned his back. He held the pose for a full minute before saying : " I said wash down, Meade. The straw."

Meade said, " Yes, sir," and dutifully began to flush his hose over the floor.

" Get the horse up and bring that man out of there," Gulick ordered.

The horse was a job to handle ; he was badly scared. But the passenger needed no bringing. A wild yell issued suddenly from the coach, the door burst open, and his lank figure emerged like a rising duck. He hit the floor with both feet, lost his balance and clung wildly to a wheel.

" Where'd that water come from ? " he demanded.

Meade said, " Here," and turned the hose for an instant into the man's waistcoat. The force of the water against his belly folded him completely. He sat down in a wet, charred mess of straw. " I'll sue you," he said. " By God, I'll sue you."

Gulick said : " Will you ? What's your name ? "

" Funk." He coughed. " What business is it of yours ? "

" I have to report how the fire occurred. You seem to be the only human in here. Horses don't strike matches."

After a moment's consideration the man agreed. " That's right. Horses don't wear pants. . . . Say, mister, you trying to say *I* started this fire ? "

Gulick said boldly : " See if he has matches on him."

Funk scrambled to his feet as Vredenbergh and Rock Doyle, who had just entered the barn, approached him. " Sure I got matches. But I don't use 'em to set fire to barns. I use 'em to light a cigar, see ? Smoke. God damn it, they're all wet." He stared at them disconsolately. " Just lit one riding down Broadway. Threw the match out. Then I threw the cigar out, mister. I didn't set no fire."

There was a commotion in the doorway and one of the police entered with the driver. The latter was inflamed with injury and indignation. Shaking his whip at his late fare, he asked every one to look at his clean cab, and his horse, the poor dirty beast that never did any one any harm at all.

" What do you mean by leaving a fare in a barn ? " demanded the chief engineer.

" Sure he was that drunk he thought he was driving down Broadway." They had been doing it, he explained, half the evening, up and down between Bowling Green and the Parade, and that one inside drunk as a smelt in a whisky barrel. " Is that a bar ? " he says. " Shtop and fetch me out a double whisky. Again and again, your honour. And did he offer me the wet of a lip from the bottom ? He did not ! " That had started around six-thirty. Before that the gentleman had been sober enough to navigate his feet and his package in and out of half a dozen auctioneer's offices. He bought a drink after each of these visits and looked angry, which was what had gotten him drunk in the second place. " It's my belief he wasn't sober when he hired the cab at the head of Peck Slip in the first place. A bad hour." And then after a while the gentleman just wanted to drive up and down Broadway, and when the driver asked didn't the gentleman want to go home, he said this was as good a home as any. So when the horse and himself got tired at it, the driver brought him into the barn and left him there while he went off for a glass at Murdoch's. The gentleman thought he was riding down Broadway so what did it matter if he was in a barn. Him and his package, by God !

At mention of the package, Mr. Funk, who had been showing a little more intelligence, lurched back into the coach. He emerged with a parcel done up in damp wrapping-paper, which he examined with unsteady hands. " I guess it isn't wet through," he muttered.

Young Ames had watched the process curiously. " What's in it ? " he asked.

" Picture books," said Mr. Funk. " Beautiful picture books. Chinese picture books. But I can't get a man in New York to look at them."

" Chinese ? "

" Yes, sir." Mr. Funk smothered a hiccough. " Bought 'em myself in Canton. Got a thousand. Thousand picture books. But nobody'll look at 'em."

He sounded sad. Young Ames said : " I might. What are they of ? "

Mr. Funk made an elaborate gesture. " Flowers, *beautiful* flowers. *Beautiful* birds too. Beetles. . . ." His pale eyes examined young Ames's freckled face almost shyly. " I like you," he said. " I'll show them to *you*."

" Not here," said young Ames.

5

When Gibbs came home near midnight, he found young Ames beside the window poring over the books of rice paintings. Each book contained twelve plates of Chinese scenes, birds, flowers, insects, as Funk had claimed, and besides those there were books of whipping scenes and Chinese tortures, bloody, gruesome, and fascinating. Gibbs went into his own room to fix himself a glass of iced gin and came back tinkling it.

" Where've you been all night ? " he asked.

" Buying these," said young Ames. " You'd better look at them."

But Gibbs said : " Pictures, eh ? Well, here's one I found."

Young Ames took it casually. It was a handbill showing a slave driver on horseback flogging on a negro, while a coloured woman and a little child tried to hold him back. LOOK OUT FOR KIDNAPPERS, it read.

" Will men who love Liberty, and believe that all innocent men have a right to it, tamely see such villainy perpetuated by law in this city ?—a man would be hung for it if committed on the coast of Africa ! Opposition to Tyrants is Obedience to God."

" Looks like some of Tappin's work," young Ames said.

" That's what they're saying along the Bowery. These handbills are up all over, and the crowd was tearing them down. They had a real row over at the Chatham Chapel. Threw the negroes out and busted up the place."

" I know about it," Ames said absently. " That's why the watch was willing to let Funk out of the watch-house."

" Funk ? Who's Funk ? "

" The man I bought these books from. There are a thousand altogether." Young Ames pointed to a large box in the corner of the room. "You'd better look at some. I'll make you a present of one. I'm going to give this one of the whipping scenes to Mr. McVitty. But you can have your pick."

"You've got a thousand of these?" Gibbs asked curiously.

"Yes. I guess I've a few over."

Gibbs picked up a second. "They're pretty," he said. "But what are you going to do with them, Johnny?"

"Sell them."

"How? I never saw anything like them."

"That's how," young Ames said. "Funk couldn't sell them, but he took them to the wrong places. He tried to sell them as novelties and he was glad to let me buy them to-night."

"What did you pay for them?"

"I paid him a flat hundred and eighty dollars. That gave him a 50 per cent profit. They only cost twelve cents apiece in Canton. I expect they ought to bring six or seven hundred, handled the right way."

"Do you?" Gibbs asked. "That seems to let your friend Funk down pretty low."

"Oh, Funk. He's a fool and I guess a rogue. He'd been a clerk with Olyphant in Canton till they sent him home. Probably he's been playing with opium—they're against it, you know; and I don't think he wanted to come up before a judge. I got Pinky's uncle, Mike Dolan, to speak for Funk. I couldn't have done it if Constable Hayes had been around, but some of the watch are in Dolan's district and he's boss. They let him go. That's how I knew about the riot, Hayes not being there. I got the books from Funk's boarding-house on Fulton Street, and he's clearing out of town to-morrow. He says he doesn't like New York."

"You just about know everything, don't you, Johnny? Pictures and Olyphants and opium and Canton."

"You have to keep your ears open if you're going to

make money in New York," young Ames said complacently. "I've got to make a lot. The trouble with Funk was he handled these books as notions. He had one bright moment though, and took them to Cooley, the book auctioneer. But you don't want to treat them as books. You want to sell them as art."

"What do you know about art?"

"I know Aaron Levy wouldn't be handling it if there wasn't money in it," said young Ames.

"Do you ever think about anything else, Johnny?"

"I don't like being poor. I want to get on top. It's going to take longer than I thought, maybe, but I'll get there." He stared past Gibbs at the open window. "And I'll carry you along with me too, Howard."

"You told me that once before." Howard Gibbs smiled wryly at the earnestness in the freckled face. He wondered what future young Ames thought he saw. His own thoughts always reached back towards the images of the past. In a way, that was what brought them close to each other. "Thanks, though, Johnny," he said softly. He knew young Ames meant what he said, but he had seen too many people drift away from another man's misfortunes.

Silence flowed between them into the candlelight, and Gibbs turned to look into the thick dark beyond the roof. "The Five Points was making a lot of noise to-night. The police were keeping clear of it." He tinkled the ice against the side of his glass. "It's hot," he said. "God, it's hot."

6

The morning papers all carried a story on the riot in the Chatham Chapel. It sounded like trouble; and the *Journal of Commerce*, even, called it A REAL ROW. Reading the papers, Mr. McVitty declaimed vehemently against the behaviour of the ruffians masquerading as the New York Sacred Music Society, who had thrown benches

and chairs from the gallery on to the heads of a negro
congregation, and he inveighed against what he termed
the African presumptions of the blacks. But he acted
downright rabid about the abolitionist handbill with its
incitement to violence which he ascribed to the Tappan
brothers. "They're merchants," he cried, "but you'd
think they were Jackson Republicans. If we don't watch
out they'll cut the cotton trade out from under New York's
feet. What do you want extra time for lunch for, Ames?
Half an hour is plenty for any man to eat or drink. Why,
Arthur Tappan himself could go to the devil in less time
than that."

"I have some business, sir."

"Business to transact on Chevalier's time! What
business?"

Gibbs said solemnly: "Johnny's going into the art
business."

"Art!" snorted the chief clerk. "Show me a picture
to beat a clean column of figures with a credit carried
forward, and I'll show you the portrait of a solvent merchant, and the painter would be a matter of no consequence
either." He took snuff with obvious self-satisfaction, and
granted young Ames permission to buy the National
Academy if he chose.

Young Ames had never had occasion to visit the sales-
room of Mr. Aaron Levy and, as he climbed the stairs of
the house on Broadway, he hardly knew what to expect.
The quietness amazed him. The stairs had a carpet and
the showroom on the second floor had another, and as he
looked round on the gilded frames of paintings hanging on
the walls, he hugged the package of sample books defensively.

The hushed atmosphere was intensified by a pale youth
who asked him his business in a hushed, bored voice.

"I'd like to speak with Mr. Levy," said young Ames.
His own voice seemed loud, but he let it be loud. "On
business."

"Mr. Levy is engaged," the youth said, with a super-cilious glance at the brown paper parcel. "You've probably been misinformed. We deal only in old masters here."

"Do you? Well, I came on business. I'm supposed to be back in the office of Chevalier, Deming & Post in half an hour, but if Mr. Levy's busy, I'll wait."

The pale youth said contemptuously : "If you want to show your sketches, it's no use. We see thousands of them every year. We only handle old-master paintings."

Young Ames had caught his backward glance, however, and he fixed his eyes on the nearly closed door. It opened at once. A small, smooth-faced man slid silently into the room. He was dressed with fashionable conservatism, in a well-cut dark coat and a black tie and dove-grey trousers, but the coat and trousers needed pressing and the collar of his shirt showed where he had perspired either that day or the day before. He tapped his pursed lips with a ranged finger and regarded young Ames with shrewd, shining black eyes.

"Yes, yes," he said, in a silky sort of voice. "Quite right, Bernard. That is quite right. Old-master paintings, yes, exclusively of course. Except we handle sometimes the best masters as well. This gentleman wants to see me from my good friend, Mr. Chevalier? Mr. George Chevalier? Yes, I haven't the advantage of his name. Bernard, you should always inquire the gentleman's name. So, Mr. Ames? What can I do for you, Mr. Ames?"

"I've got something to show you, Mr. Levy. They just happened to come my way. They may not be in your line, but I know your reputation and I'd like your opinion."

Mr. Levy's voice was indulgent. "Yes, I am happy to," but his eyes, young Ames noticed, were brightly fixed on the package. "Come into my other room," he said. "Bernard can handle the gallery." It was obvious that he wasn't going to commit himself, and though he had already made up his mind that young Ames wasn't anybody important, he wasn't going to miss anything either.

The back room was as confused as the gallery was orderly. There were pictures stacked in ranks along the floor, framed and unframed ; boxes stood in tiers against the walls ; a feather duster hanging from a hook spun slowly in the suction of the closing door, but the duster did not appear to have been used on the books that were piled helter-skelter on the shelves. A bare, unfinished, cracked table held a mess of varnish and oil bottles and a nest of rags from old linen garments. There was an accountant's desk with a drab ledger, and in a corner by a sunny window a small, dusty grey parrot. The parrot was gripping its perch with one foot and thoughtfully stroking the lid of one eye with the other. It coughed at their entrance and watched Mr. Levy unostentatiously remove a canvas from one side of the room to the other. " Excuse me, Mr. Ames, while I move this Canaletto fine oil-painting of Venice. It's not quite maybe a superlative, but it is a nice fair Canaletto which Mr. Chevalier might examine for a thousand dollars, if you should happen to remember, Mr. Ames."

The parrot shook its feathers at this point and squawked : " *Old-master paintings.*" Then, as Mr. Levy turned round : " *I always come halfway.*"

Mr. Levy said, " Incessant bird ! " with smooth indulgence and rapped its beak wickedly with the large stone in his ring. The parrot sidled, shaking its head. It stretched its toes and regripped the perch, and as soon as Mr. Levy was out of reach said hoarsely, " *Slit his belly, God damn it,*" fluffed its neck feathers, and closed its eyes.

Mr. Levy ignored it. He pulled a chair for young Ames to the table, swept back the rags, and sat down himself. His eyes, watching young Ames unwrap the parcel, were bright as the parrot's. His face, however, settled at once into blankness when he spied the picture books. He took up a couple and began flipping the pages with agile, round-tipped fingers. "Rice paintings," he observed. "I've seen one example of them before in Mr. Rogers's beautiful home: They are curious, but I was informed personally by Mr. Rogers that in China you can buy them cheap. I handle exclusively old-master paintings, Mr. Ames. I am not a stationer."

"I suppose I could take them to Cooley's." Young Ames saw no point in telling him that Cooley's had already refused to handle them. "But I thought a man who understood the picture business could do a lot better."

Mr. Levy said bitterly: "Cooley's. Ink-smirching booksellers with their cheap engravings at half-price! What do they know about art! You take my advice, Mr. Ames, and don't go to Cooley's."

"That's what I thought. But you do know about art, Mr. Levy, and if you wanted to put your name to these, they'd sell like fury."

Mr. Levy put the ring to his pursed lips and delicately wet the stone with the top of his tongue. There was something almost approving in the cock of his head as he regarded young Ames. "I could, Mr. Ames. But what has Aaron Levy to do with offering cheap Chinese picture books? Now, when I sell one of my old-master paintings to the right purchaser, it makes me five hundred, a thousand, two thousand dollars. What would I look like offering a dollar book? Even twelve books? What would Mr. George Chevalier say, or Mr. Auerbach, or Mr. Hone? Will you kindly inform me, Mr. Ames? Speechless, like you! Well, they would think Levy's old-master paintings maybe they aren't so good if he has to sell cheap Chinese picture books," he concluded, looking down at young Ames.

But young Ames wasn't impressed. The mention of a dollar price had been a give-away. He said, with a smile: "I guess even the picture business gets a little slow these days. Of course, old-master paintings aren't listed in the price current . . ."

"Price current! Listen to me, my young friend from my friend Mr. George Chevalier. Let me tell you something educational. Consider a piece of earth to begin with and what does a man do with it? Construct a railroad perhaps? Or maybe he thinks he will grow some grass for hay or maybe feed a cow with it so he can remove the skin, a nasty mess, so then he has to tan it, and what becomes? Shoe leather on an Irishman's foot! But now look at the old-master painter and what does he do with this earth, perhaps? He makes a paint colour, a pigment out of it, like sienna, and he puts it on his canvas, and there becomes an old master painting, maybe a Rembrandt, for sale by Aaron Levy's gallery on Broadway between Liberty and Cedar Streets, and maybe it is John Jacob Astor coming to examine it."

"I see," said young Ames, deliberately gathering up the books. "I thought you might be willing to auction off a thousand of them. I thought you might say they were unusual specimens of an interesting art-picture style, or something like that, and it ought to draw people into your gallery in a slack time. . . ."

Mr. Levy placed a moist, reproving finger on the last book and held it. His eyes were reproachful. "You didn't inform me it was a thousand books. You didn't talk that way. You talk beautiful, Mr. Ames. You ought maybe to get a job with me in the gallery. That Bernard Baumgart is a fool." He leaned forward. "'Mr. Aaron Levy offers a thousand bound volumes of genuine Chinese rice paintings at his gallery on Broadway. Examples of a famous style of a strictly popular Oriental art, interesting specimen-depictions of flowers, birds, landscapes, tortures. . . . Etcetera,' Mr. Ames. How much will you sell them for?"

"I won't. I'll let you handle them on commission."

"No."

"Five per cent."

"Five per cent!" Mr. Levy quivered. "You try to

commission-merchant me ! Me ! I will pay you ten cents apiece."

" I paid more than that for them."

" Then you were foolish. I will pay you fifteen cents."

" You'll do nothing of the kind." Young Ames stood up and took hold of the last book.

Mr. Levy wouldn't let go of it. " We were talking about per cents," he said smoothly. " Twenty-five per cent, I think was what you no doubt intended mentioning to start with as a price ? "

" Five."

Mr. Levy sighed. " You are a young man, and young men like the moon in their watch-pockets with a fob on it. If you was in my career, Mr. Ames, my young friend, and I was your friend from Mr. George Chevalier, what per cent would you sell them for, being such a judge with such a reputation of old-master paintings ? "

Young Ames grinned.

" That's different, isn't it ? I'll make it 10 per cent."

" Yes," sighed Mr. Levy. " Well, I will come half the way. Twenty per cent."

They settled on 15 per cent and drew up an agreement which Mr. Bernard Baumgart superciliously witnessed. Mr. Levy seemed a trifle wistful as he said that he wished Mr. Ames was in the old-master paintings business. " Just so long as it is positively Aaron Levy's gallery you work for, Mr. Ames."

7

The books were to be delivered that evening, and young Ames, packing them after hours, outlined the entire trans- action for the benefit of Mr. McVitty, who was fascinated by some of the pictures. The old chief clerk stopped long enough to jot down a column of figures.

Levy sells 900 books at $1.00 - $900.00
do.   do.   100   do. at   1.50 - 150.00

Proceeds of sale - - - 1050.00
Levy's commission at 15 per centum   157.50

Credit to Ames - - 892.50
Cost of books - - 180.00

Profit, nett - - - $712.50

" It's a nice profit," he said, feathering one nostril with
the tip of the pen. " I would almost go so far as to say it
was an ingenious profit. I think I'll attend the sale myself.
One or two of the items are interesting."

Young Ames grinned. " I was going to make you a
present of one, Mr. McVitty. I thought of it especially for
you." He handed over a book containing the goriest of
the whipping scenes.

The chief clerk hesitated and took snuff defensively.
His voice was plainly shaken with pleasure and surprise.
" It's the very one I had my eye on, Ames. I hadn't
expected it." He hesitated, then, after clearing his throat
once or twice, said : " I think there's one point you have
not considered, here." At the foot of his column of figures,
he wrote below :

Profit, nett - - $712.50
Paid to Funk - 180.00

Funk's loss - - $532.50

" Mr. Funk," he pointed out, " sounds like the plausible
kind of man who might consider he'd been diddled."

" What of it ? " Young Ames's face showed his annoy-
ance. " He made 50 per cent profit. He said he was
satisfied."

"I just thought I'd mention it. No man can get as ugly as a fool who finds he is one. 'Let a bear robbed of her whelps meet a man, rather than a fool in his folly.' That's Scripture, Ames." He tucked the book under one arm, picked up his umbrella, and departed with an unaccustomedly pleasant good-night.

Young Ames chuckled. But Gibbs said : "You know there's some truth in what old Aloysius just said, Johnny."

Young Ames said : "Oh, Funk ? He said he was leaving town. The only thing I'm worried about is old Levy's not getting his price."

Gibbs said nothing as they lugged the box downstairs and hunted up a late porter with a barrow who wheeled the books over to Broadway and up to Liberty. It was a hot still night, and when he first stepped out of Number 42, young Ames had an odd sense of quiet in the city. It wasn't anything he could lay his finger on ; there were hoofbeats coming down William Street and he could hear the rap of a nightstick a block away on Water Street. Sounds seemed to carry clear. It occurred to him that the city, after nightfall, underwent a change. By day you knew the people in your neighbourhood, but now you had no idea of who might be out upon your street. Working in the commercial district and living as he and Gibbs did at Number 42 South Street, it was easy to forget the numbers of people who went to work every morning in shipyards and ropewalks and foundries and manufactories of all descriptions ; they looked normal enough by daylight, but what became of them at night ?' Who knew, any more than who besides Gibbs knew what became of John Ames between dark and daylight ? He wasn't thinking of the Five Points so much as of the great generality of the poor quarters of the city where the people tried to segregate themselves as well as they were able, Germans, Irish, Jews—nearly twenty thousand of them, many without knowledge even of the English language. Andrew Jackson's private constituency, Mr. Chevalier called them when Lawrence had been elected mayor during the riotous April balloting. What, for instance, did he know about the porter, beyond the number of his leather badge? He was probably a hard-working man with a big family staying out long after most on the bare possibility of making an extra twenty-five cents. But you didn't know, and as young Ames looked at the man's muscled shoulders he felt glad of Gibbs's company.

There was a bill posted on Mr. Levy's door board.

As advertised in the Newspapers
Beautiful Chinese Paintings
A SPECIAL SALE
Never before offered in this city
at such prices
1000 Bound Books of old master
·*Chinese rice paintings*
$1.00 & $1.50
Open to view of the public on and
after July 10

"Levy's losing no time," Gibbs said.

Mr. Levy himself was enthusiastic in his silky way.

"I have sold seven already out of those twelve I had. They will become a rage. If you get me any more, I'll handle them. I could have asked twice as much, but now I have the advertisements in the papers coming out to-morrow."

As they went down the stairs, Gibbs said: "If Mr. Funk sees one of these advertisements, he'll be able to figure out for himself what he's missed out on."

"To hell with him," young Ames exclaimed. "He's not your worry, anyway. Let's do something, Howard. It's too hot to go home."

Gibbs glanced down at him as they walked along up

Broadway. Young Ames was taking quick steps, but for Gibbs's long legs the pace was easy enough, and he thought : " It's true. Johnny hasn't a thought in his head about Funk. He's just part of a deal and it's closed, so Funk is closed out too." Some day, he was afraid, young Ames was going to get a shock.

He said : " All right. How about going to Niblo's ? "

" I'd like to see something. Not just sit around."

" The Bowery Theatre's putting on Forrest in *Metamora*," Gibbs said. " It will be hot up in the gallery."

" We'll buy pit tickets," young Ames said. " My treat."

" You're pretty extravagant, aren't you ? "

" I'm going to make some money out of these pictures," young Ames said. " I feel rich."

They had plenty of time. Walking up Chatham Street, they passed the alley in which the Chatham Chapel stood. There was nothing to see down its dark narrow gullet. Chatham Street, behind its shuttered haberdashery store fronts, looked blank and innocuous. But as they crossed Pearl Street into Chatham Square, a wave of sound came towards them down Orange Street.

It had a vague humming quality, drowsy, indecisive, suppressed, that reminded young Ames of swarming bees ; but it also contained human indications. Now and then the flow of sound was punctuated by a shriller note, like a woman's voice, or the sudden bleat of a child's crying ; as he crossed the street opening, he smelled the rank mustiness of neglected drainage, filthy streets, and the sense of teeming heat it conveyed made Chatham Square seem cool and fresh. A troop of pigs came out of the dark gap, quick feet tapping hornily as they reached the cobbles, and a lean terrier-like dog backed away from the corner and fled silently.

He looked round for signs of the police ; it would have been reassuring to see a squad of the watch in their leather helmets ; but there were none. For a moment he felt his

skin prickle. Then Gibbs said : " Here we are. In plenty
of time, too." Ahead of them the Bowery Theatre raised
its lofty white façade, and carriages were still drawing up
to its door.

He paid his seventy-five cents for two pit tickets, and
they went in with the other people to take their places. It
was nearly time for the curtain. The footlights made a
ribbon of brilliance. Suddenly, without knowing why, he
drew a sense of comfort from the fact of other people
sitting close around him, and he looked about him
curiously. A few of the box parties looked elegant, but
the people in the pit seemed less fashionable than those
in the pit of the Park Theatre. They looked like trades-
men, mechanics, clerks like himself. Then he remembered
that Gibbs had said that Edwin Forrest could draw all
sorts of men to see him.

Gibbs touched his elbow. " What did you say Funk
looked like, Johnny ? "

Young Ames jerked away.

" I told you," he said impatiently. " He's a kind of
gangly with a hangdog face. Why ? "

" There's a man looking at you from the gallery."

Young Ames turned to look up to the right. At the
very end of the balcony rail, his elbows on it and his chin
resting on his hands was Mr. Funk. His hat was tilted at
an angle that seemed to indicate the continuance of his
drunken spree. But his wavering eyes seemed steady
enough now, and he was staring down directly at young
Ames.

At that moment the lights dimmed and the curtain
slowly lifted.

8

At first, as the play was getting under way, young Ames could feel Funk's eyes still staring down from the gallery to where he sat. The stage lights did not illuminate the upper part of the theatre sufficiently for him to pick the man out, but he knew that he must be visible to Funk. It annoyed him to be made uneasy. He owed the man nothing, and there was nothing that Funk could do to him. He made an effort to fix his attention on the stage and lose himself in the fate of the last of the Wampanoags.

He did not need to be told who Forrest was. As soon as the actor appeared, a wave of applause broke out with cries of " Forrest ! American Forrest ! " all through the theatre. The actor received them without a sign, standing with folded arms. As a physical specimen, he was magnificent. And when he began to speak, his utterance had an almost brutal force. It filled the auditorium ; even in its quieter moments it took hold of both men and women. They could hear the prowling hunger of the natural man barely in leash, the thwarted passions, the sorrow, the disdain for anything less strong, the instinct to reach out beyond the confined areas that man created for mankind and mankind for the individual man. Even a man like Gibbs, sardonic, living within himself, reacted to the hammering thunder of that rolling voice, and young Ames was utterly lost in the unfolding of the Indian's story.

It seemed incongruous, then, when the confusion started at the back of the pit. He was suddenly conscious of having heard pounding at the doors. For a moment there had been silence while the great voice rolled on undisturbed ; then as Forrest made an exit, leaving the stage to the other actors, bedlam broke loose and the aisles were suddenly jammed with men who ran down clear to the edge of the stage. Others packed in on their heels. There was a shout of " Farren ! "

"Throw out the Englishman!" somebody bawled.

Young Ames rose from his seat with the rising wave of the audience. He could see the faces of the mob packed in the aisles, their sweaty cheeks reflecting the shine from the footlights. They looked wild. Their hooligan clothes showed that they had been on the loose for some time. A man near him kept wiping blood from the tip of his nose.

The audience was still quiet, standing, like the mob, as if poised for an explosion. Nobody made a move. He glanced quickly at the stage. The actors were huddling back towards the wings. The paint on their faces stood out, giving their features the appearance of old paper. But one of them stayed near the centre of the stage, staring out at the audience as if fascinated. Then, in the dead silence, his eyes shifted to the wings and you could see he was going to bolt. At the same instant a man lifted his arm, a woman in one of the boxes screamed, and the air was full of missiles—eggs, potatoes, bricks, stones, cabbages, pelted the stage. The yelling was universal, the audience adding its voice to the mob's. The lone actor went like a scared rabbit, leaving a bare stage.

The sight of the empty stage seemed further to infuriate the mob. They began stamping in the aisles, milling up and down, while a sudden battalion rose in the gallery and a fresh volley of missiles came showering down over pit and stage alike. The woman in the box had stopped screaming; an elderly gentleman suddenly popped an empurpled face up over the rail to shake his fist. Another woman, however, had gone hysterical and her crazy laughter began to rise through the men's voices. It was impossible for any of the original audience to move out of their places. The packed ranks of the invading rioters jammed every exit, and in the brief lulls young Ames could hear in the street outside the rising mutter of voices.

He felt his heart beating slow and hard and suffocating, and he grabbed Gibbs's arm and yelled to know who Farren was. "An English actor," Gibbs yelled back.

" He was the fellow on the stage. He's been talking like a
Trollope. The *Evening Post* printed something, anyway."
Gibbs's dark eyes moved over the crowd. " Just keep
still, Johnny."

It seemed for a minute that the crowd was baffled. Then
on the right side of the theatre a howl broke out. It immediately became universal as a man walked on to the stage
carrying an American flag. An egg squashed against a
scenic boulder, and the yolk spread and slowly coagulated
in the artificial moss. The man raised the American flag
over his head with one hand and pointed at it with the
other. The gesture brought a brief volley, and suddenly
the old man in the box raised himself on to a bench and
shouted " Shame ! " in a surprisingly loud and apoplectic
voice.

There was a moment of silence in which the man on the
stage wiped some egg from his cravat. Then from the
gallery a hoarse voice bellowed : " He's another dirty
Englishman, boys. Come on ! "

The man was leaning far out over the railing near
where Funk had sat. Funk was still there, but he wasn't
watching the stage ; he was still staring at young Ames.
He did not turn his eyes when the man raised himself to
his full height, swinging a dead cat by the tail. The spotted
shape spun from his hand, missed the figure on the stage
by a couple of feet, struck the artificial boulder with a
limp thud, and skidded off towards the wings. The man
with the flag gave it up. The stage was again empty.

There was a sudden splintering of wood from the back
of the theatre as the mob started tearing down pictures
and ornaments in their search for ammunition.

Then, still in his Indian costume, Edwin Forrest walked
on to the stage. He was in no hurry. He stared into the
pit with his arms folded for a moment before deliberately
walking forward to the footlights. All the mob seemed to
recognise him. They yelled his name, applauding, cheer-
ing, calling him " American Forrest," while he impas-

sively confronted them. Suddenly his chest swelled and his great voice broke over the hullabaloo, drowning it, and as the noise stopped his voice lowered with it, and when they could hear him, he said quietly, "Farren's gone. He won't appear again to-night."

"I bet," shouted someone.

"You'd better go home, those of you who haven't paid. We're giving a play, and we have to finish it." He paused. "We're all good Americans here."

There were calls for three cheers. For Forrest, for Jackson. The quality of the voices had changed. They were pleased, warm, elated. Somebody cried, "Police!" A stampede began for the doors. In two minutes the theatre was cleared of rioters. Nothing was left except the sound of their retreat down the Bowery. The doors were closed.

The voice on the stage suddenly recalled the audience's attention.

"Ladies and gentlemen, if you will be patient for a few minutes more, the play will proceed. I only ask your indulgence for the gentleman who will substitute for Mr. Farren." He bowed, and it was as though a greater man had spoken to them. The audience waited in silence. As far as young Ames could see, almost no one left the theatre, not even the empurpled old gentleman, whose female companion had fainted. He had propped her up in her chair and was fanning her gently with one hand while he glared with gallant eyes at the gallery. When young Ames glanced up, he could see no sign of Mr. Funk.

9

"If we're sensible," Gibbs said, "we'll go right home."

The audience was showing a disposition to linger together in the theatre portico. They watched the nervous horses in the waiting line of carriages. The coachman on the box of the foremost carriage was saying excitedly, "It's terrible, Mr. Ogden. They say there was a regular battle in Rose Street. They broke into Mr. Tappan's house and burned the furnishings right in the street, sir. I heard one of the watch say they quit only a few minutes ago. They had to call the fire engines out."

"Stop babbling, Bob," said the empurpled old gentleman. He handed his lady in and got himself, his hat, and cane in after her; but he leaned out of the door before slamming it. "If any of those ruffians so much as lift a finger, lay your whip across him, do you hear?"

The coachman touched his hat with the thumb of his whip hand and started his horses nervously.

"I didn't hear the alarm bell," young Ames said.

"I didn't either, Johnny. But they had the theatre shut up tight." Gibbs stepped on to the sidewalk. "We'd better get moving ourselves."

A group of watchmen stood on the sidewalk below the theatre. They had their sticks in their hands, and the assistant captain carried a lantern. Their varnished leather helmets shone faintly under the street lamps. Their faces looked worn. All of them were drenched with sweat.

One of them told Gibbs that the mob had broken up itself. "We could chase them out of Rose Street, but in Pearl, where it was wide, they had the best of us. There were more'n a hundred of them."

"Where'd they go?"

"Over into Madison, some of them. I guess they'll run a nigger or two."

He cocked his head.

There was a faint sound of yelling over on the left.

"They've started," he said gloomily. "I guess we'll have to go after them."

One of the officers said: "We've got orders to protect the theatre. We're staying here. Let the niggers look out for themselves." He flashed his lantern on to Gibbs's face. "Where are you gentlemen going?"

"Home," Gibbs said. "Forty-two South Street."

"If I were you, I'd go right along. No telling when they'll head back."

"Are they out of the Five Points?"

"Some are," said the watchman. "But it was a queer mob. They sounded young at first; they handled easy enough; there's no harm in them. But they draw the gang out, you see? And that's something else. We had to send two men back to the watch house, both hurt."

Young Ames was anxious to leave. They walked rapidly, in spite of the heat. Crossing the mouth of Orange Street, they heard again the sound of troubled life in the close alleys, only now it seemed fitful, with a sharper tendency to raise its pitch, and young Ames suddenly thought of the faces in the theatre aisles.

Then Gibbs remarked that he had to have a drink, not at home as young Ames suggested, but right away, and he led off through Spruce and Ferry Streets and turned down Pearl past the shuttered fronts of the drygoods stores. Here and there an upper lighted window showed where a back-country buyer was still up, but most of the boarding establishments were dark too.

A lighted strip on the sidewalk gave evidence of a gin shop still open for business. They went down the steps and found that, with the barkeep, they had it to themselves. Gibbs ordered an iced gin and lemon, but young Ames wanted nothing either to eat or to drink. He waited restlessly, cocking his head to listen when footfalls sounded outside. A watchman looked in. Gibbs offered him a quick one.

"Can't. High Constable's out and prowling and he can smell gin a mile." He looked round. "I saw a feller sneaking along. Did he come in here?"

"No."

The leatherhead went on, rapping his stick to warn malefactors. He was willing to give any one a chance to get out of the way; trouble, when the Five Points was moving, was the last thing a leatherhead wanted to find.

Finishing his second glass, Gibbs stared over the rim at young Ames. He said abruptly : " I'm not going home to-night, Johnny." His voice had an edge in it.

" Where are you going ? "

Gibbs said briefly, " Thomas Street. Come along if you want to."

" No, thanks." Young Ames stared at his friend's face. He'd had a feeling that Gibbs was getting himself set on something, but studying the long dark sardonic profile, he couldn't make out any of Gibbs's thoughts. And then Gibbs gave a short laugh. " It's better than nothing." He got up briskly, paid the barman, who looked interested, and led the way out. He stood at the kerb, his back to young Ames. " You've got something," he said. " Well, good-night, Johnny." He stepped off across the street.

For a minute or two young Ames watched the tall figure striding away from him. He had known well enough where Gibbs was headed. He felt like a fool to have asked. Then he swung on his heel and started in the opposite direction. The rioting was uptown and east of Pearl Street, and there was nothing for him to worry about. But just the same it seemed a long way back to Number 42 South.

10

His heels rapped on the flagstones, and the blind store fronts echoed them behind him. It was dark between the street lights. They made small yellow pools into which a man could step or which he could walk round, and they seemed far apart. About two blocks ahead he saw the watchman's figure wade slowly through the light and disappear to the right up John Street. He kept a steady pace, neither fast nor slow. When he came to John Street he looked for the leatherhead, but the man had vanished. Nothing was left in the street but the echo of his own feet.

It was when he was crossing Wall Street that a queer thing occurred to him. At an intersection, the echo ought to stop. But it hadn't. He had passed six intersections without the openings making any difference in the echo ; and he realised that someone must have been following him ever since he had left Beekman Street behind.

Hot as the night was he felt the sweat prickle coldly on his neck, and he stopped and whirled round between two lights. But the street stretched empty behind him. There wasn't a sound. He decided that he was a fool and that crossing streets could make no difference in the echo. He started on again, slowly, and the echo followed suit. Still walking, he looked over his shoulder, but he could see nothing. He lengthened his stride suddenly, but the echo suited itself to the change of pace. " I'm acting like a fool," he thought, and then, as he came to Beaver Street, he thought of a good test. For six paces he walked on his toes, and the echo sounded just as plain as though his heels were rapping the stones.

Without knowing why, he thought suddenly of the man who had slung the dead cat at the stage. But he could remember nothing out of the ordinary about the man's appearance. The man had nothing to do with him. He had never seen him before. The man had been standing beside Funk, and had thrown the dead cat, and had disappeared. Funk had disappeared too. There was no reason for his being worried about Funk, he told himself. And if the man, whoever he was, wanted to catch up with him, he could have done so before now.

Young Ames halted on the lower side of Beaver Street and looked back again. This time he saw the man enter the light on the corner of Wall, turn down Coffee House Slip, and disappear at the same even pace. Young Ames realised that he had been scaring himself like a boy passing a graveyard. He felt like laughing as he went ahead. He was glad that Gibbs hadn't been along to see him.

Hanover Square was quiet and he turned down Old

Slip, whistling under his breath. Seeing a light in the engine house, he stopped for a minute to find Rock Doyle, who lived in, smoking a final pipe before closing up.

" Where've you been ? " the butcher asked. " We had an alarm."

" At Mr. Tappan's ? "

" No. It was a fire on a canal boat in Number 7. A bit of a blaze. A mouse couldn't have warmed his tail in it. But we heard about the trouble at Tappan's."

" I was in the theatre. They broke into it and chased an Englishman off the stage."

" Did they, by God ? " said Rock Doyle. " It's those wild Irish fools from the Five Points, the poor ignorant scuts. They don't know how to behave in a free country. With the liquor so cheap."

" They don't all look Irish," young Ames said.

Rock Doyle pointed his pipe stem.

" Listen to me, young pigeon. If there's a good riot, there's an Irishman at the bottom of it every time. And another one on top of it too, don't forget," he added complacently. " But I'm guessing we aren't through with them yet and the Mayor'll have us all out along with the police before it's done." He folded his arms. " One fireman with a spanner is worth six leatherheads any time," he said. " I've seen it proved."

Young Ames left him in the door and went down Old Slip. The rigging of the ships made a webbed shadow against the sky. But in the breathless dark, no sound came from them. There were no lights anywhere in the counting-houses—only the few street lamps that touched the bowsprits reaching over the paving. He looked up at the three-story front of Number 42, but he could not see his own window, still higher, on the roof. It would be stifling hot up there, he thought, and he wondered whether it was cool at Rockaway.

The Chevaliers would be in bed by now : it was past midnight. Christine, probably, was sound asleep. He thought of her with a quick loneliness, feeling himself solitary. A cat suddenly started miyawling way up among the chimneys. But it did no good to get sorrowful, and he would have something to tell Christine the next time he saw her. Seven hundred dollars on a single deal was a profit even Mr. Chevalier wouldn't sneeze at. He reached into his pocket for the heavy key, and stopped short.

He could just make out the figure sitting on the brown-stone step. The man lifted his gangling body and asked : " Is that you, Mr. Ames ? "

II

" What do you want ? "

Young Ames stood his ground as Funk approached. It was obvious that the man had been drinking, but he wasn't drunk.

" I saw you in the theatre," Funk explained. " I was going to speak to you outside, but your friend was with you, so I thought we could talk here."

" What do you want ? " young Ames repeated.

" Couldn't we go inside ? "

" It's against the rules."

Funk hesitated. He seemed to be making a real physical effort to speak.

" I need some money, Mr. Ames."

" I haven't got any," young Ames said shortly. He started to move past the other towards the door. But Funk put out his hand. He didn't touch young Ames. At the last moment, he pulled it back. His voice was shaking.

" I've got to have some money."

" What do you come to me for ? I paid you a hundred and eighty dollars yesterday."

" That wasn't enough. I needed over three hundred."

" What you need's not my business."

" Listen, Mr. Ames. I have to have it. I've had a hard

time. It's hard being away two years. You come back
and you don't find things the way you expect. My wife's
got to have money. She's sick. She owes a lot. She
borrowed to pay the rent. I need three hundred dollars."

The fact that Funk had a wife was in a strange way
shocking to young Ames. It angered him also. It had
nothing to do with him. It put the whole business on a
false plane.

"I was drunk last night," Funk went on. "I had to
sell those paintings. I didn't have any pay saved up.
They didn't pay me when they let me come away from
Canton." His voice went higher. "I hadn't cheated them.
It was none of their business what I do. But they said I
was lucky to be given passage home. They let a man work
two years for them and then they don't pay him."

"They probably had reason."

"They told me that. But a man has to live. I thought
I could make something on those paintings."

"You made a profit. I paid you cash."

"I know you did, but I was drunk."

"What's that got to do with it?"

"I didn't know you would take them to Levy's. I saw
his sign. I was looking for work all day. Look, Mr. Ames.
I don't ask you to give me a share of the profits. I just
want the money loaned to me. That's all. If I don't get
it they'll put my wife out of the place."

"Why not pay them what you made off me? That
ought to make them give you time."

"I tell you, I lost it. I tried to make something more
with it. I lost some and then I was robbed."

"You're a fool. What sense would I have lending money
to a fool?"

He could see Funk stiffen. But the man controlled himself and said with a kind of desperate quiet, "I know.
But I'd go steady. I was trying to get a job. It's hard
without a reference. They all want to know where you
were last."

Young Ames heard him swallowing.

" I can't tell them that. What I did wasn't so bad. Olyphant's didn't lose . . ."

" It doesn't matter what you did. I won't lend you money. Right now I haven't got any to lend."

" You'll make seven or eight hundred on those pictures." He hesitated, then said more quietly, " I'm not complaining about that, Mr. Ames. But I hadn't been home when I let you have them. If I'd known how bad things were I might have held on. I might not have thought of taking them to Levy's . . ."

" I don't think you would. But I did."

" I know that. Listen to me, Mr. Ames. My wife's got no family to go to. I haven't. If she's turned out, she'll probably end up in the Five Points. She makes a little, sewing. But she can't work out with the baby to mind. She's been sick . . ."

" You had money to spend on a theatre ticket."

" All right." Funk spoke sullenly. " But what if I did ? I've been two years out in China. I just got back. What difference does twenty-five cents make ? " He stopped himself. " Won't you lend me the money ? "

" No, I won't. I made you an offer and you took it. I paid you cash. That's all there is to it. You had your chance to sell them to Levy—if you'd thought of it."

He stood still, watching the other man. And Funk suddenly said : " I tried to ask nice. I don't say you cheated me."

" You'd better not."

" But I'm not going to be responsible for what happens. I did the best I could." Young Ames could see his head still turned towards the river. " I did the best I could," he said again.

Without looking round, he started to walk away. He went slowly, as if he were not sure of where he was headed, moving into the darker shadow under the bows of the docked ships. Once he seemed about to stop, but he kept on going, and young Ames waited until his footsteps had petered out.

His hands were shaking and the key rattled against the keyhole as he unlocked the door. It was pitch-dark going up the four flights, through the smells of coffee and dry-goods, and brandy, into the hotter dark under the roof. He had a hard time finding his candlestick, and when he struck a match the flame seemed reluctant to lay hold of the wick.

The room slowly took shape in the strengthening light, the cracked plaster of the sloped ceilings, the window framing the black night beyond the roof, the bed in the corner, the door opening on the head of the stairwell. The candle burned without wavering and the light fell brightest on the small table top with Christine Chevalier's letter where young Ames had laid it. Looking down at the clear handwriting, young Ames said :

" How do I know he has a wife ? " And then, after a minute, " It's not my fault."

12

Little business was transacted Thursday in the counting-room. Even Mr. McVitty seemed inclined to talk about the riots, for besides the one centring around the Bowery, there had been half a dozen petty outbreaks through the city. Houses of abolitionists had been stoned. The watch had been kept on the run all night.

" They should call out the military," Mr. McVitty said, and several merchants dropped in in the course of the day to enlist Chevalier's support with Mayor Lawrence to do just that. The Mayor, it seemed, was reluctant to do so. " It's purely political," said Mr. McVitty. " He's afraid of losing votes." He fumed and took snuff, but when, late in the afternoon, a rumour went through the city that the Mayor had said it was pointless to call out the militia for they could not legally fire on any one without the presence or written order of the Governor, the old chief clerk went off like a bomb. " He's given them licence to murder, rape, and arson," he declaimed. " He's worse than Andrew Jackson himself. You've got to admit the President isn't afraid to bring out the army, whatever else he is." Even Mr. Deming looked grave at the news.

Young Ames listened with only half his attention. Most of the rumours were purveyed by little Pinky Finnegan. Pinky was in his element, because, for once, Mr. McVitty displayed an interest in Mike Dolan's opinions. Mike Dolan, it appeared, had been present at the rifling of the Tappan house.

" It was a fine terrible sight," Pinky reported. " They were bringing out the furnishings and flinging them on the fire, when my uncle seen one of them throwing a pitcher on to the burning flames." His little body became taut and erect, and Mr. McVitty said, " Pitcher? Was he trying to put it out ? "

" Pitcher," Pinks said importantly. " In a gold frame. And my uncle says wait. What's that, he says. It's George Washington. Would you burn the Fayther of your country, you ignorant murdering blackguard, he says. And he took it away, knocking down the man in the disorder, he told me, and called up four or five of the boys out of the engine company and put them and the pitcher across the street and stood guard on it till the watch came up and gave him great credit, he said." Pinky accepted Mr. McVitty's approval complacently. " I'm going into the political life myself," he announced. " The trouble with being in the political life, my uncle says, is to get credit on both sides when there's a riot."

Nine of the rioters had been arrested and were in jail under a thousand-dollar bond apiece. The newspapers listed their names and spoke of them as the ringleaders ; but the Five Points was still seething, according to Pinky. His Uncle Mike said it was a poor ringleader who would let himself get arrested in a genuine riot, which Mr. McVitty admitted was an observation of intelligence.

" I don't like it," he said. " I wish Mr. Chevalier was here." But the junior partners had decided there was no reason to call Mr. Chevalier home. He would be back to-morrow in any case.

And the day passed quietly enough in the city. The old chief clerk, indeed, felt slightly reassured at closing time, though he cautioned Gibbs and young Ames to make certain they left the door locked if they went out that night. " You look more sober than ordinary, Ames," he remarked. " What's the matter with you ? "

Young Ames said there was nothing the matter. The rice paintings were selling in spite of the disturbed condition of the city. He had come to Levy's in the noon hour, and Levy had reported fifty-odd sold that morning. But after McVitty left, he told Gibbs about Funk's visit.

" How do I know he isn't lying ? "

" You don't."

" He didn't sound as if he was, though." Young Ames rubbed his head irritably. " It's not my fault if they're bad off."

Gibbs said dryly : " A conscience is an inconvenient thing, isn't it, Johnny ? "

" I don't see what conscience has to do with it."

" Well, it's sometimes upsetting to find that the other man in a deal is human, too." He smiled at the back of young Ames's head. " Here you've made him an offer and he's taken it and it's square all round, and even if he was drunk, he probably would never have taken the books to Levy. Why, you even paid him more than another man might."

Young Ames nodded. " Yes. I bet Cooley wouldn't have paid him more than fifteen cents apiece. Maybe twelve."

" And yet," Gibbs went on in the same dry voice, " you can't help thinking what it would feel like, hindside to. If

Mrs. Ames-to-be, whoever she is," he said with malicious tact, "had to take in sewing."

"*She* won't have to," young Ames said angrily.

"But you can't help thinking about it." Gibbs walked out of the room to get his pipe. When he came in he was blowing smoke ahead of him. He spoke through it. "Johnny. Sometimes it pays to do something that isn't strictly businesslike, even in business." He walked to the window, and when Ames made no reply, he said : " I wonder if there'll be more trouble to-night."

"I don't know," young Ames said moodily. "Are you going out ? "

"No. I feel domestic." Gibbs turned back from the window, and said quietly, "Johnny, you know sometimes a man who's dropped to the bottom gets pretty crazy ideas."

Young Ames laughed scornfully.

"You mean Funk ? There's nothing to him. Why, he was practically crying last night."

"That's what I was thinking of," Gibbs said.

13

The idea that Funk could do anything to him seemed fantastic to young Ames. The man lacked inwards. If any one was crazy, it was Gibbs.

He tried to shake off the notion on his way to the engine house, and getting there he lost himself in the flurry of running the engine out. The alarm had sounded at twenty minutes to ten, the bell starting in the fourth district. Rock Doyle said it must be the rioters again, and the watchtower beam pointed the lantern towards Chatham Street.

Going down Frankfort from William Street, they heard the yelling of a mob, the raucous, high-pitched bedlam of men running, and as Number 11 wheeled into

Chatham, young Ames had a glimpse of the last of the rioters streaming across the Park and leading off up Broadway.

There was no fire. The mob had broken into Chatham Chapel and held an impromptu anti-abolitionist meeting. A man named Wilder had taken the chair and made a speech while the hoodlums applauded him by pitching whatever benches remained in the gallery on to the heads of their fellows.

Half a dozen machines lined the street with the companies milling around, waiting for orders to drag home and getting some fun out of the spectacle of the redoubtable Petersons, who had seized the only hydrant and had nothing to play their water on. There was some talk from Black Joke of starting a fire for the sake of putting it out, but nobody took it seriously. It was too hot.

Young Ames, standing at the mouth of the alley with Tibbets, heard Rock Doyle say, " Why don't they let us go home ? " But nobody made a move.

Tibbets was full of talk. He wanted to make another excursion like the one they had had to Hoboken. When was Christine Chevalier coming home ? Young Ames told him, to-morrow.

" Father bought a couple of books of Chinese pictures at Levy's this afternoon," Tibbets said. " You ought to see them. I bought one myself for Ellen, just flowers, but they're mighty pretty things. They had some books about torturing scenes though. I couldn't buy her one of those, but you ought to see them."

" I know," young Ames said absently. " They belong to me."

Tibbets wouldn't rest then till he had found out where young Ames had bought them.

" A clerk from Canton had them," young Ames said. " He couldn't sell them and I bought them on spec."

Suddenly he found himself looking round over the bystanders. He didn't expect to see Funk ; but he did see the huge muscular figure of High Constable Hayes coming through the Park.

Every one knew Constable Hayes. His size, for one thing, identified him, though probably no more than the solid calmness of his face. He borrowed a speaking trumpet from one of the machines and called for the foreman to join him. The vamps stood by watching the group. It broke up after a few minutes, and the foreman came back to report.

Hayes informed them that half a dozen gangs were out. The Mayor hadn't called the militia so the watch was doing the best it could. But six hundred men was a small number to cover the city. He wanted the Fire Department to stand by till the streets were quieted. The foremen had agreed, he told them, but it was really up to the vamps themselves. They had never failed the city yet, he didn't think they would now, and he asked them how about it. They gave him three cheers. That was the beginning of Thursday night.

The companies coming from the Sixth, Fourth, Seventh, Tenth, and Fourteenth Wards, where serious trouble was most likely to start, returned to their engine houses, but Oceanus, which stood in the First Ward, was one of the companies assigned to a sort of patrol duty, and it was four o'clock the next morning before they finally hauled the engine home to Old Slip.

Before they returned they had been as far afield as Charlton Street, where a demonstration was made against the home of the Reverend Dr. Cox, the minister of the Laight Street Church. Garrison was reported to have praised one of his sermons.

The watch caught the mob before the door, but there was no serious difficulty, and the mob dispersed after breaking in the ground-floor windows. Most of the rioting that night was more noisy than destructive. The bands roving the streets were mostly small. It was only when two or three of them merged that there was real danger of violence. And finally, with the first hint of daylight, they just seemed to melt away, leaving the streets to the worn-out watch and the engine companies. They couldn't stand another night like it, Rock Doyle said. And young Ames, stumbling up the stairs of 42 South Street, knew it was true.

He stayed by his open window, too exhausted to undress, and watched the beginning of daylight over Brooklyn. He had seen niggers working on his trip South ; and they seemed better off than most of the negroes in New York, yet people wanted to free them so they could be as well off as the New York negroes. He wondered if the abolitionists had ever seen some of the cellar holes their negroes lived in. He had never been down in one, but he had smelled the fetid breath of them rising up the steep steps out of the ground. He didn't want to be troubled with such things. All he wanted was to make money. Perhaps they ought to be free. When people were as poor as he had been they had to work harder than slaves did. They had to get ahead. If they didn't they just went down like Funk. Where would Funk be at this time of day? Probably drunk. Maybe trying to find his way home. Young Ames wondered where he lived and what kind of woman married a man like that. Damn Gibbs for saying that about his wife having to take in sewing.

He saw the rigging of the docked ships beginning to take form.

A gull swung in from the harbour, all alone, pursuing his silent flight upriver towards Corlear's Hook. Christine had written that she watched for gulls along the beach at Rockaway. . . .

" You'd better get to bed, Johnny."

Gibbs was standing in the door, his feet showing bare under the nightshirt.

" Yes, I'm tired," young Ames said.

14

When he awoke, Gibbs was sitting at the foot of the bed and reading a sheet of print.

"The Mayor's issued a proclamation. Pinky brought it up a minute ago. The militia's to be called out."

"It's time enough."

Young Ames felt stale and shaky as he got out of bed. Below the window, Pinky Finnegan was already sweeping the sidewalk and the street, his broom making a swift faint whisking in the stillness. It was hot again.

"Fire Department's under orders too," Gibbs said. "And all patriotic citizens are asked to report at the arsenal to-night at nine o'clock. I suppose that means me. You'd better get a move on. It's nearly seven. McVitty will turn up any minute."

Mr. McVitty did. He stamped into the counting-room a good ten minutes before young Ames reported and he was breathing fire. "The city's disgraced, but thank God the Mayor's stopped playing Pontius Pilate. Good-morning, Ames. Gibbs says you've been out all night. The department's been a credit to the city, by all accounts, and I'm proud the office has one member in it." He glared round at the inoffensive Cummings as if he had never in his life inveighed against clerks wasting their time at fires. "If you feel the fatigue this afternoon, you can quit half an hour early."

When Gibbs asked him whether he intended to report to the arsenal, the old chief clerk shook his head.

"I'll not leave the counting-room to-night."

Solemnly he shook open his umbrella, fished into it, and drew forth with a mysterious air a navy pistol.

"I stopped by Pine and Van Antwerp on my way down," he said. He laid it gingerly on the back of his desk above the office ledger.

"Do you know how to load it?" Gibbs asked.

"No. I had them do it for me there. It's my idea one discharge should prove sufficient. Cummings, you can enter it on the day-book. Twelve dollars and forty cents."

"Under what heading, sir?"

"Under running expenses," said Mr. McVitty grimly.

Young Ames climbed up on his stool and took up his first task, copying the lists of a consignment of Birmingham ware to Lalage & Co., New Orleans. It was hard going. At half-past ten Mr. Post's daily mail was turned over to him for copying, dry, neat, factual letters, totally unlike Mr. Chevalier's. Reading the senior partner's mail was as good as sitting across a desk from him with his china-blue eyes staring at you. Mr. Deming's letter usually contained at least one story to offset the difficulty of deciphering his sprawling hand. But with Mr. Post's, young Ames had to struggle to keep himself awake.

At half-past one the junior partners went on change and the counting-room atmosphere let down. Even Mr. McVitty made small effort to pull the staff together. " I'm thankful Mr. Chevalier's coming back this afternoon," was all he had to say. Pinky Finnegan, sitting on his chair behind the door, said, " My uncle, Mike Dolan . . ." when the sound of heavy footsteps on the stairs interrupted him.

They were neither hurried nor slow ; they ascended deliberately, as if the maker were memorising the individual characteristics of each tread. Mr. McVitty twisted round on his stool and peered over his glasses, and for some reason every one else left off work.

Entering the counting-room with the same sure deliberation, the visitor passed young Ames, whose desk was nearest the door, and took his stance in the middle of the floor.

"Who's in charge here?" he asked. He was a solid man, filling his blue coat tightly.

"I am," replied Mr. McVitty. "My name's Aloysius McVitty. What can I do for you, sir?"

The man felt in his coat pocket, drew forth a battered

leather folder, and extracted a piece of paper from it. He peered at the paper for a minute before asking : " Does John Ames work here ? "

Mr. McVitty looked across at young Ames.

" We employ a junior clerk of that name."

The man turned slowly. His red smooth face looked oddly youthful. He handed the paper to young Ames. " Would that be you, do you think ? "

Young Ames took it from him. Someone had scrawled in pencil on it, " John Ames, 42 South Street."

" It might be," he admitted. " I'm the only John Ames here."

" Ever see that handwriting ? "

" I'm not sure. Why ? "

" I'm Constable Sparks." He paused. " I must ask you to come with me."

" He's at work," Mr. McVitty broke in.

" I won't keep him over an hour, sir," Constable Sparks said with perfect politeness. " The High Constable wants to see Mr. Ames. On business."

" Have you a warrant ? " Mr. McVitty asked.

" No, sir. None needed, as long as Mr. Ames is agreeable."

" What do you want me for ? "

" I'm not at liberty to say. I can say it is purely a matter of police business. Routine, you might say." Sparks seemed gifted with patience.

Young Ames stared at Mr. McVitty. Beyond him he could see the other members of the staff watching in a complete hush. Even Pinky's jaw was open.

" All right," he said, as Mr. McVitty nodded. " I've finished the letters, sir."

" I'm obliged to you, Mr. McVitty," Sparks said equably.

Mr. McVitty took snuff with a snort.

Feeling utterly nonplussed, young Ames accompanied the constable down the stairs. As they turned north in South Street, he asked : " What's happened ? " But the constable only repeated his former statement. He walked phlegmatically beside young Ames. He looked slow and smelled of tobacco, but young Ames had the idea that he would be a quick man in an emergency. " I've got a coach in Beaver Street," he observed. " Ordinarily we'd have no right to put the city to the expense, but Mr. Hayes wants to finish up this business as soon as possible."

The hackney coach was headed away from the river. Mr. Sparks said to the driver, " Take us to the corner of Elm and Anthony," opened the door for young Ames, and got in after him. He took off his hat and balanced it, bottom up, on his knee. It was an old hat that had seen some rough usage, but it was neatly brushed. The knee under its crown was broad. " It's been hot," said Constable Sparks, wiping his forehead with a handkerchief which he took out of the hat. " It was hot last night. Were you out at all ? "

" I was out with Number 11," young Ames told him. " I didn't get home till four."

" You must have been tired out," Sparks said in a friendly voice, and put the handkerchief back into his hat. " It's hard to get rested after a night like last night."

" I couldn't seem to get to bed till Gibbs—he lives in Number 42 with me—came in and got me started."

" I know how it is when you're dog-beat. Gibbs, you said ? "

" Yes, Howard Gibbs. He's the translating clerk."

While Sparks unobtrusively took out a small notebook and wrote in it, young Ames looked out the window. The coach jiggled them rapidly over the cobbles. They passed the Park on their left, crossed Chambers Street, and entered Elm. The buildings rapidly changed character, becoming shabby, with limp-looking women and children sitting on the baked doorsteps. Their lustreless eyes followed the progress of the coach.

" Here we are," Sparks said as the coach drew up. He got out ahead of young Ames and paid off the driver. A

couple of men in ordinary clothes moved out of the shade
of a drink-shop doorway and returned Sparks's nod.
Glancing casually at young Ames, they led the way off
down Anthony Street.

"Mind the pigs, sir," said Sparks.

15

Three long-legged, spotted hogs were watching a butcher
dress out the carcass of a country pig in front of his store.
Their little eyes gleamed knowingly. Sparks kicked one
aside but he merely grunted and made slow room on the
narrow sidewalk. He had lost an ear at one time in a
battle with dogs and he wiggled the stump as a fly buzzed
towards him.

There were flies everywhere, buzzing heavily in the heat
and crawling on the windows, on the hand rails, on the
house walls. Young Ames could see them moving as high
as the third story. Suddenly his gorge rose. Black children
peered at him out of the cellar doorways and the negro
men lounging along the sidewalk made room as sullenly
as the pigs.

At the corner of Centre Street they had to leave the
kerb and go round a cart that was unloading barrels into
a saloon. Two more men joined them there, falling in
behind with the same casual exchange of nods to Sparks,
and young Ames suddenly had a feeling of being trapped.
There was a shout of "Suds!" and a tubful of dingy
water cascaded down over the sidewalk just in front of
the officers.

They stopped for the drip to cease, and then went on,
taking the next right-hand corner into Leonard Street.
The bystanders looked on without interest. The dirty
water spread only a little way over the roadway before
the dust absorbed it. A pig moved out to investigate.

Down Leonard Street the two men in front turned into

an alley less than three feet wide between the walls of two
wooden buildings. Sparks said quietly : " Here we are."

The alley had a rotting footboard laid on chunks of
wood down the middle. It smelled mouldy. There was
almost no sunlight and it looked to young Ames as if there
had never been any. The eaves of the two buildings nearly
touched overhead. The windows opening on the alley
were closed. The place seemed hushed ; but ahead was a
continual mutter of sound. He could not see where the
alley led, for a third building, its wall blank, projected
across the opening. Sparks said : " This takes you into
Little Water Street, if you know your way. You have to
go underground."

He opened a door in the left-hand building and led the
way up a stair so narrow that only one person could mount
it at a time. Going up, young Ames felt that the building
was full of people. It was quiet, but there were smells of
boiling cabbage and old stews, stale washing, tobacco, and
liquor. The doors on the landing were all closed. Sparks
passed them and led the way up another flight.

One of the officers followed behind. The other three
must have stayed in the alley. They came out on the second
landing, and one of the closed doors had a sign : " Room
to rent."

They climbed a third flight in almost complete darkness.
The heat was stifling. Sparks said, for the third time,
" Here we are," and knocked on a door. It was opened
by a white man. Young Ames recognised him as another
officer.

He found himself in a small room with a window looking
south out over the roofs. He had a glimpse of crumbling
chimneys, of wash hanging from strings between them. On
the roof of the next house a boy was throwing out crumbs
for pigeons, but the birds looked wary. After the climb
through the dark stairwell the light was dazzling.

But the room itself was hot, and smelled of stale bedding.
A negro was lying on it. He neither moved nor spoke. A

negro woman huddled at his feet, three children close beside her, and a baby in her arms. Her eyes rolled at Sparks, showing the whites ; and then swung towards the ramshackle door in the other wall.

Sparks led the way across towards this and rapped on it. " It's Sparks, Boss. I came as quick as I could." He stood to one side as the door opened. " This is Mr. Ames," he announced.

The bulk of High Constable Hayes filled the door. He looked down at young Ames for a moment, his eyes imperturbable. He said : " Sorry to bother you, Mr. Ames. I want to see if you can identify a man."

" Identify ? " young Ames asked.

" Yes, we found a paper in his pocket with your name on it. That was all we did find. He'd been robbed."

Back of young Ames the negro woman cried shrilly from her corner : " 'Fo' God we didn't rob him. We foun' him on de stairs. We done brought him in hyar. Didn't do nothin' to him but give him dat room and he was all right. 'Fo' God, Jesus, mistah. . . ."

" Shut your mouth, mammy," Sparks said calmly and the woman said, " Yessah," in a moaning voice.

Hayes said : " I'm sorry to bring you here. But I don't want to bring out a dead white man at this time of day. It only needs a bit to start the gangs going again." His eyes were on young Ames's face. Sparks shoved into the small room behind young Ames and closed the door.

It was a closet of a room, with bare space for a bed, and a window only large enough for a single sash. On the bed was a figure of a man under a dirty quilt.

" You just have to look at him," the High Constable said, with a note of kindness in his voice. Young Ames started swallowing. He felt as if his throat clattered, it was so dry. He walked unsteadily beside the big hulk of Hayes, watched his heavy hand lift a corner of the quilt, and looked down at the dead man's face.

It was Funk.

16

" I see you know him."

Hayes had instantly let the quilt fall back over Funk's face. He did not wait for young Ames's faint nod. " Come over to the window," he said. " Take a couple of breaths. It depends on what one's used to."

Sparks said : " Here."

He held out a small flask and Hayes, taking it from him, urged young Ames to take one swallow. It set him coughing. He thought for a moment that his stomach would refuse the liquor ; but it took hold. " I'm all right," he said shakily. " His name is Funk. William Funk."

" When did you see him last ? "

Gathering his wits, young Ames told him : " Night before last. He came to ask me for money."

Hayes let the silence hang.

" Known him long ? " he asked after a minute.

" No." Young Ames told of how he had seen Funk at the fire, got him free of the watch-house, and bought the Chinese paintings. " I didn't know anything about him, except that he said he'd worked for Olyphant's in Canton, and they'd sent him home."

" We can find out about that at their counting-room," Hayes said. " Did he have any claim on you for money ? "

" He thought I was going to make more than a fair share on the paintings," young Ames said. " But he sold them to me outright. I've got his receipt."

Hayes nodded.

" He had no claim against you that I can see. But when he asked you for more money, did you give him any ? "

" No," young Ames said.

" Well, he was beaten pretty badly. But the woman out there," he tilted his head towards the other room, " swears he was able to walk when they found him on the stairs. She put him in here. She was afraid he'd be found there and she and her husband would be accused, because some white roughs had beaten her husband on his way home. They'd say it was revenge. When they found Funk was dead this morning they knew they couldn't hide him so they sent for us."

Sparks said : " They've got a right to be scared. It would take less than this to turn the whole Five Points into the negro districts."

Young Ames asked : " But if he could walk last night, what did he die of ? "

Hayes said calmly : " It's funny how a man or woman who's been hit can get up and walk home sometimes. They'll go a dozen blocks, they'll even think they're all right, and then, all of a sudden, they'll keel over. I've seen it happen before in riots. Probably that's what happened to this Funk. Either he thought he was going home, or somebody brought him this far and left him in the first handy door." He led the way into the other room. " We'll have to get a coach, Sparks. And we'll take him down as if he was sick. Maybe we can get him out without any one even seeing him." He stood over the huddled woman and the prone negro. " It's all right, Mrs. Jones. You've acted all right. Just keep quiet and we'll get him out."

She called down a blessing on him, and on Sparks, and then on young Ames, as if she attributed this kind treatment to his arrival. Seeing the sheer animal terror in her face made him feel sick and ashamed. He turned quickly towards the stairs.

Sparks touched his arm.

" Just a minute, Mr. Ames. Where are you going ? "

" I'm going home."

" Well, you'd better wait for me. I'll send two of the boys out to Centre Street with you. It's not good for a man's health to walk around this neighbourhood by himself. By the way, do you know if Funk has any relatives ? "

" He said he had a wife and child. I don't know where they live."

Sparks nodded. " We'll find that out." He led the way out on the landing and down the steep stairs. Again young Ames had a sense of a household of people, all listening, all lying quiet, behind the closed doors. But Sparks, treading heavily down through the darkness, acted as if it were the most natural thing in the world. Beyond the doorway even the musty air of the alley seemed fresh. Young Ames's heart pounded as he breathed deeply of it.

" Will it take long to find out ? " he asked.

" Find out what ? Oh, the address of Mrs. Funk. I don't expect so. Come around to the City Hall watch-house to-morrow if you want to know."

Standing solidly in the middle of the alley, he gave the impression of listening, almost as if he were able to absorb surrounding conditions through his skin. Then he turned to young Ames, looking down on the pale face.

" It's too bad to drag you here," he said. " It was the quickest way. You'll understand we'll have to check up with your engine company and Mr. Gibbs. It's no signifi-cance. Just to get the whole story, that's all."

" Why did he die ? " young Ames asked. His voice sounded high-pitched even to himself.

Sparks filled a short pipe. " Some people just die, that's all. You can't tell. He'd been beaten, you know, hit on the back of the head, two or three places. But sometimes a man just lets himself die. It's hard to say. Don't worry about it, though, Mr. Ames. You've got nothing on your conscience."

He gave a soft, low whistle. Two of the men came in from the alley mouth. " Take Mr. Ames out to Centre Street," Sparks ordered, " and fetch back a hackney coach. Make it quick, boys." He held out his hand. " I'm pleased to have met you, Mr. Ames," he said stolidly. " If you come round to the watch-house, ask for me. T. Sparks."

Walking along the baking street, young Ames stared straight in front of him. The two officers offered no con-versation until they reached Centre Street. Then one of them said : " You'd better keep on as far as Elm. There's an ugly feeling here to-day."

Young Ames thanked them and went on all the way to Broadway. It was comforting to hear the clatter of passing omnibuses, to be jostled by people in decent clothes with normal faces. A pig, scurrying to the kerb, was just a pig, harassed and a little comical. This was the city he was used to. It seemed incredible that the other place was only three blocks over. He couldn't get it out of his mind, and he knew he wouldn't feel right again until he was back in Chevalier's counting-room. He began to hurry, cutting through the shopping crowd in Maiden Lane to get back on the waterfront. But even when he saw the webs of rigging against the blue sky, the picture of that top-floor room stayed with him, the view over the dingy housetops, the silent beaten negro man and the terrified woman, and the thin shape under the quilt.

17

As young Ames entered the counting-room, he saw Mr. McVitty emerge from the office of the senior partner with a sheaf of letters in his hand. The chief clerk spotted him at once. " You're back," he said, coming over to young Ames's desk. " What did they want ? "

" They wanted to see if I could identify someone. He was dead."

" You mean Funk ? "

Young Ames nodded.

" I thought it would be something like that." Mr. McVitty peered over his glasses and cleared his throat. " Mr. Chevalier's here and he wants to see you as soon as you come in. You'd better do it now."

He led the way to the office door, knocked, and said : " Ames has just got back, sir. If you want to see him."

" Send him in."

Y.A.   H

Young Ames entered with a sick feeling that he would have to go on telling people about himself and Funk for the rest of his days. He looked up as Mr. McVitty carefully closed the door behind him. Mr. Chevalier was seated at his desk. In spite of the heat, his coat had held its press. He looked neat and self-possessed, his face a trifle more red than usual—that would be the sun and sea air at Rockaway—his blue eyes steady and cold.

" Come in, Ames," he said. " Maybe you'd better sit down." He waited till young Ames was seated opposite him. " Mr. McVitty's told me about this latest exploit of yours, quite properly, since the firm's reputation is involved."

" I don't see how you can say that, sir," young Ames said in surprise. But Mr. Chevalier ignored him.

" What did the police want with you ? "

Young Ames stared at the desk top as he told him. But when he finished and glanced up again, Mr. Chevalier was looking out of the window. " It's a nasty business, Ames. but Hayes obviously thinks you're all right, or he wouldn't have let you come back here."

" I don't think Mr. Hayes wants it in the papers. He thinks it's likely to start the Five Points rioting after the negroes."

" It will probably do that whether it gets into the papers or not," Mr. Chevalier said. " Somebody must have left him there. The point is, though, that I don't want Chevalier, Deming & Post mixed up in a story of this sort."

" There's no reason why it should be," young Ames said. " It was a private deal."

Mr. Chevalier's cold blue eyes swung round to him. His voice was biting. " The newspapers aren't going to be satisfied with John Ames, in the story—the Jackson newspapers aren't, however much importance you may think they attach to the name. Not when they can say ' clerk in the employ of Chevalier, Deming & Post,' and slip in the fact that I support the Whig Party. It doesn't matter if there's no valid connection. They'll just mention the name as frequently as possible, and in two days it will be 'that Five Points murder Chevalier's was mixed up in.'"

"I'm sorry. I didn't realise."

"Young men don't," Mr. Chevalier said shortly. "I don't believe you've done anything unseemly, from what Mr. McVitty tells me. He considers it a clever piece of business. He stood up to me just like a good, mothering hen." Mr. Chevalier smiled grimly. "Only, you'd be a much more comfortable clerk to have on the premises if you had a little less of what he calls 'enterprise.' To me it smacks more of close dealing, or possibly taking advantage of a drunken man. No doubt he's a rascal," Mr. Chevalier added.

"I paid him a fair price," young Ames said. "I didn't know how bad off he was, sir, or about his wife. I still don't know if he has a wife."

"A wife? McVitty didn't mention her."

Young Ames told him. "Not knowing it, though, I wasn't to blame for making what I could out of my own knowledge, was I, sir?"

Mr. Chevalier said more kindly: "I suppose not. Though it was a gamble."

"So was your corner in cotton, sir. And that was based on your own private knowledge, wasn't it?"

"You're an unscrupulous fellow," Mr. Chevalier said in a short voice. "I've said it before, Ames. The point is, as far as I know, no one suffered from my deal. They merely made less money than I."

"That's how I thought of it with Funk, sir. But I didn't know the rest, about his wife and all."

Mr. Chevalier glanced at him.

"What about her, if it's true?"

"I don't know, sir."

Mr. Chevalier's fingers drummed on his desk.

"Ames," he said after a moment, "I don't believe in

trying to dictate my clerks' lives for them the way the Tappans do. I'm not considering the firm now, either ; but I think you'd be better off if you let things go along as they are."

Young Ames couldn't get away from the figure under the dingy quilt.

" Mr. Chevalier, have you ever seen how people live in the Five Points ? "

" No, I can't say I have. But there used to be other places. Peck Slip, Dover Street, part of Gold Street, and the edges of the Swamp. Some of them have changed, and it's the Five Points now. As long as there are indigent people, there will be such places. I don't say I approve of them, but people in a large measure create their own surroundings. Some may be unfortunate, but some live that way because they are that kind of people. There's not much the rest of us can do except run societies for aiding the first class."

Young Ames stared at him. " He said, if he was put out, she'd have nowhere else to go."

Mr. Chevalier studied his set face.

" Very well," he said. " It's your affair." He changed the conversation. " Mr. McVitty says you were out with Number 11 most of last night."

" Yes, sir. We have to report again to-night, at nine-thirty."

Mr. Chevalier said : " That's fine. I'll be watching for you."

" Are you going out, sir ? "

" Of course. The Mayor's called for every man who believes in law and order to report. It's high time these blackguards were taught they don't own the city in spite of their instigators in Washington and City Hall." His eyes kindled. " Once they're faced, they'll run fast enough."

Remembering the faces he had seen that afternoon, young Ames felt not so sure.

18

The counting-room was closed at six. The partners left early. Mr. McVitty had announced his intention to stay on guard, and would not budge an inch from his resolve in spite of Mr. Chevalier's protests. He seemed to be imbued with a kind of Spartan heroism. Let the Persian hosts of the Five Points come, he would defend the counting-room stairs as if they were Thermopylæ. Even Pinky, fetching him a chicken pasty and putting his hot water to boil on the spirit lamp, was impressed.

"I'd like to stay with you, sir," he lied with an artless expression on his face. "But my Uncle Mike wants me to stay with my aunt while he's out."

"It's your duty," Mr. McVitty grunted. "Pay her my respects."

Pinky's jaw gaped as though Mr. McVitty had suddenly turned into a species of musical waxwork with bells on the back of his neck. "Yes, sir," he said, and turned and bolted.

Mr. McVitty stirred sugar into the hot water and laid his supper on young Ames's desk, with the pistol laid ready to hand on the pen rack.

"I hope he won't shoot us when we come in," Gibbs said. They had stopped beside Old Slip. The streets were getting dark, but the river still gleamed faintly with the twilight.

"Are you going to the arsenal, Howard?"

"I'm going to buy myself supper and then go sit on the Battery," Gibbs said carelessly. "Take care of yourself, Johnny."

He went off alone. It was characteristic of him; if society owed him nothing, he owed nothing to society. In a way, young Ames felt envious as he turned off to the engine-house.

The company had arranged a chowder supper to eat

on the premises. It was a full turnout, packing the engine-house, and many of the company took their bowls outside to eat on the sidewalk. McPhail, the watchman, did not put in an appearance as he usually did. The watch were all uptown.

Neither young Ames nor Tibbets had much to say. Every one seemed grave, even after the beer keg was tapped. Rock Doyle passed among the younger runners urging them to confine their thirst to a single drink. Running on a hot night with a skinful of beer, he said, was something no man should try for the first time in an emergency.

He and the foreman made a final inspection of the engine. She stood in the middle of the floor between the hose racks, every last quarter-inch of her brass gleaming in the lantern light.

" God, I hate to take her out, Rock, and maybe get her all marred up," the foreman said. " But the chief engineer passed out orders and we've got to do it." Young Ames saw Rock lean against the blue and black engine and talk back earnestly. The foreman listened a minute ; then he lifted his speaking-trumpet and called the men into the engine-house. " Boys," he said, " if the crowds get ugly, you leave any fire there may be, and come round the engine. Meade's going to fill the toolbox with old pipes and spanners, but if you can't get one, find yourself a brick. Now, that's about all. Haul her out. We're supposed to show up at the Park at nine-thirty. We'll go up slow."

It was like taking her out on parade, except that they wore their regular clothes. There was no sense wearing a red shirt to a riot. The vamps manned the rope and the runners walked in the rear. It was practically a full turnout, and their numerical strength impressed them ; but it felt uncanny to be trundling the old gooseneck through the streets at a walk. She didn't sound right. There was nobody looking at them.

Yesterday's hard night and the emotional pressure he had undergone that afternoon made young Ames light-headed. His legs moved under him with a sensation of floating, and his thoughts hovered from point to point without any logical coherence. At times, the whole business of the pictures, the riots, Funk's death, the squalor in Leonard Street, and the interview he intended to have with the man's widow seemed to stem out of himself, as if he had started the whole queer web, and as if everything he had done had added to it.

But it wasn't so. It wasn't so simple. If there was any web, he was more like a fly, or maybe Funk, or the Tappans with their abolitionist notions, or even Chevalier's, were the flies. Mr. McVitty could rationalise it all by saying Andrew Jackson was the spider and letting it go at that. But that was nonsense—the Five Points existed before Jackson, and before the Five Points there had been other places like them, according to Mr. Chevalier.

While he was talking to Mr. Chevalier things had started to clear themselves in his mind. Now he wasn't sure that Mr. Chevalier wasn't right. Let things go along. As long as you hadn't been dishonest you could keep what you made. And then a crazy idea popped into his head : that if Olyphant's had not had scruples against the smuggling of opium, which all other Canton firms considered a perfectly proper form of investment, Funk would never have been sent home without pay ; he wouldn't have bought rice paintings in an effort to have something to show for his two years in China ; there would have been no fire in the barn of Coenties Slip, and young Ames would never have been involved or even known of Mrs. Funk's existence. Then the idea recurred to him that Funk might have been lying about her, that there was no Mrs. Funk at all. But it wouldn't do, that way. Until he knew that she didn't exist, she did, she and her baby, and he kept wondering what kind of a woman she was.

Tibbets said : " Hold on, John," and he saw that they

had reached the Park and that Oceanus was drawn up at the kerb opposite City Hall. He looked round dazedly.

There were half a dozen other engines there, a small crowd of citizens, a few leatherheads near the watch-house door. It looked queer to him. Then he realised that there were no women in sight, and he began to pick up the rumours going round.

Two squadrons of cavalry had been called out. The 27th Regiment, four hundred strong, was drawn up at the arsenal, but Colonel Stevens had refused to let them move unless the Mayor issued ammunition. The Mayor had refused, and some of the leading citizens had gone to put the double pressure on him. The leatherheads had no idea where trouble would start first, if it did. There had been no general exodus from the Five Points.

The engine company's lamps gleamed here and there through the Park as young Ames moved over towards the City Hall. The officer in command of the leatherheads was Sparks. Sparks recognised him. " Hallo, Mr. Ames," he said. " I've got something for you." He handed young Ames a piece of paper. " Found out this afternoon. It was easy. Olyphant's had the address. She's been notified."

So she did exist, he thought. He took his way back to Oceanus engine and read the writing on the slip by the light of Purdy's lantern :

" *Note for Mr. Ames*
    " Mrs. William Funk
      43 Elizabeth Street
        (2nd floor front)
    Her maiden name was Amelia Briggs.
    She says she comes from Pittsburgh.
           " T. SPARKS, *Asst. Capt.*"

He knew roughly where the house must be—between Walker and Hester Streets. It was the same block the

Dolans lived in, and Pinky Finnegan would probably know the house.

Vredenbergh was yelling through his speaking-trumpet. "Number 11. Number 11. Oceanus this way."

19

The gangs were running and they had caught the leather-heads flat-footed. Arthur Tappan's house was one of the suspected rallying points, and so it turned out ; but the mob had filtered through to it from all directions, suddenly ; and then at the first show from the watch had started off pell-mell down Pearl Street yelling : "Hanover Square," and obviously headed for the Tappan store.

Most of the watch were uptown, expecting demonstrations against the abolitionist churches ; the 27th Regiment was still near the arsenal. Beyond the handful of men that had been posted as a sort of scouting force before the Tappan house, Spark's squad was the only available force.

Rock Doyle grunted as he heaved the tongue of Oceanus engine round. Here they had come all the way uptown, and the trouble was going to begin only two blocks from the engine-house, and the mob had a good lead. A single squad of watch wasn't going to drive them either. The word came back that there were over a hundred men out.

Vredenbergh's hoarse shout to lay her down and die came back to them, and in a hundred feet they had her rolling. They picked up the pace, roaring down Broadway, and wheeled her into Maiden Lane and took her round the corner into William Street like a scared cat. Behind them the watch came pounding. Young Ames could see Sparks running heavily, his leather hat pushed back and his elbows tucked against his thick sides. But they drew away from the leatherheads, and young Ames suddenly wondered what they were going to do when they reached Hanover Square. The Bolivars were putting up a fair stern chase, but the Bolivars were never anything to shake a sheep's tail in a real row.

The uproar in Hanover Square became audible over their own thunder as they wheeled round the bend of William Street, crossing Exchange Place, and headed for the river. Then as they plunged into the square, young Ames saw the mob rushing under a wave of torches against the Tappan store. A small knot of leatherheads valiantly stood up to them for an instant ; but the mob went right over them. The leatherheads had simply been submerged. Stones volleyed against the shuttered windows and bounced harmlessly off. A thwarted roar broke out of the throats. It was like a snarl. Then young Ames saw a man on the stoop waving his arms. Someone shouted : " He says there's spring guns inside." A group with a ship spar stopped short of the door, and Vredenbergh was shouting through his trumpet to pack in and keep her rolling.

Young Ames closed up behind her. He even heard Rock Doyle's heavy grunt. They had the slight grade with them. A shout broke out. The vamps in front butted their helmets low and dug against the rope. He had a confused glimpse of wild faces, heard the yelled oaths, and felt a man cannon off his shoulder. The mob parted like water. Oceanus bucked and a man screamed and Tibbets tripped over him. Young Ames caught Tibbets by the arm and brought him up, and the next moment they were through ; Oceanus was standing by the kerb ; Vredenbergh was yelling to close up ; and Meade was passing spanners and pipe out of the toolbox as cool as a halibut on ice.

They formed up round Oceanus with their weapons in their fists and looked back at the mob. They had shaken the toughs. One man was rolling in the gutter and yelling and the rest had backed off from the store. " Look out for bricks," Rock Doyle said and caught the first rock as it came and sent it back with interest. It fetched a yelp. The mob massed up and started coming just as the Bolivars wheeled into the square.

The arrival of a new engine gave them pause. They didn't want to be taken in the back again ; and they turned, facing Bolivar, so that she pulled up.

The mob were still two to one and the two fire engines were on opposite sides. But in the pause Sparks arrived at the head of his squad of leatherheads, and stamped up the steps to the man by the front door. He had a speaking-trumpet. " We've got orders to shoot," he said. " Alderman Lalagh says there's armed men inside ready to shoot. You'd better break up."

The mob wavered. The torches made a heavy smoke in the still air. Young Ames could smell the burning pitch smell, acrid, choking, as it drifted towards him. It seemed to reflect the light on the faces turned towards the shuttered windows.

He saw hate in them like a kind of sickness. They had a chilled suspense like men balancing on wires. Some of them looked as if they must have jobs. They wore decent clothes. He saw half a dozen who might have been apprentices from the yards, delivery boys, or mechanics. But the mass at the front of the crowd were the same sort he had seen in the theatre.

They did not look different, and yet they did, and he could not put his finger on the difference. But seeing them he felt his neck prickling. They did not look just riotous ; they looked reckless and deadly, and he knew they were Five Pointers from one of the gangs that preyed on the poorer storekeepers, the negroes, and the immigrants who didn't know how to protect themselves.

There was also a curious sense of defensiveness. They kept moving their heads like animals surrounded. " Like rats," Rock Doyle grunted suddenly, and it seemed so.

It was touch and go. They had begun yelling again. A voice here, another there. " They dassn't shoot if they come. They can't without the Governor." A hoot of laughter rose high. The stones began to fly against the store windows again. But they didn't move themselves.

They weren't sure, yet ; but they howled when a leather-lead ducked and shifted their aim to the group at the front door.

" We'll have to go after them," the foreman said at young Ames's elbow. His face was set, the skin tight over the jawbone. He didn't like the idea any better than the runners. " Stick close," he said, " and hit for the heads. It will be us or them."

In that minute, however, there came a pause. The stones stopped and a leatherhead picked himself off the stoop. Then young Ames heard the sound, the beat of running horses coming down William Street. " It's the cavalry," somebody shouted.

The next moment, without a word spoken, the mob was scattered across the square and filtering into Pearl and Water and Front Streets. When the cavalry clattered into the square the last of the rioters were tailing out of sight. There were left only the watchmen that had been over-whelmed in the first rush and the man the engine had run over. He was crawling along the sidewalk, dragging his broken leg. Some of Sparks's men set after them. He got up and tried hopping and then turned on them, yelling at them, and one of them knocked him off his good foot and he went down under them.

The officer in charge of the cavalry squad rode up to the stoop. " You've got them out," he said. " I have to report back to the arsenal. Which way did they go ? "

" Most of them went into Water Street."

The officer saluted with his sabre and said : " Maybe we can drive through some of them. They don't like horses." He wheeled his men and took off up Water Street, and presently, as the firemen helped pick up the fallen leatherheads and laid them on the stoop, they heard shouts uptown. Sparks turned his head. " That'll take some of the ginger out of that bunch," he said. He glanced over Oceanus Company. " You boys must have done a pretty fair job."

Alderman Lalagh wiped his forehead with a shaking hand.

" They certainly did."

Rock Doyle grinned at him. " Maybe the city will give us a medal, boys. What do we do now ? Walk her back uptown ? "

20

That was what they did do, taking their time about it, and hoping that if there was more of such work to be done, some of the other companies would have put their fist in first. The Park was nearly empty when they hauled up at the kerb. Oceanus and Bolivar were the only machines in sight. But off back of City Hall they could hear the distant uproar in the Five Points. Sparks sent up to the arsenal for orders, while his men rested outside the watch-house.

In twenty minutes they got news. An alderman came down to the Park in a carriage, the driver whipping all the way. The alderman was scared ; you could tell that from the way his voice got away from him.

There seemed to have been a definite plan to the riot, and the attack on Tappan's store was only a diversion. Half an hour after that started, the mob began to show up in groups in the area formed by Canal, Chapel, and Franklin Streets and Broadway. It was hard to say how big it was. It had been filtering into those streets for ten minutes before the watch got on to it. They couldn't surround the Five Points. There were underground passages, sewer openings, and bolt holes that even thief-chasers like Hayes, Lowndes, and Sparks did not know. Anyway the Five Points made up only part of the mob, which was two or three thousand strong by the time it began to move into Varick Street. They had surrounded St. John's Park and attacked and broken into and demolished the Laight Street Church. Before the troops could move over there, however, the mob had split and the troops had taken after the main gang. But they should be coming back to the arsenal. That was the plan—for the troops to base on the arsenal ; and in the meantime the mob had moved up to Dr. Cox's house in Charlton Street—or some of it had. Hayes, though, had expected that and had the house filled with armed men. That was the alderman's last news—it was like the French Revolution. God knew where the cavalry were. The last he'd heard they were being sent to the Coloured Zion Church on Leonard Street. God knew where Colonel Stevens had taken his militia. God knew . . .

You could hear the bell start pealing even in the Park. It had a wild tumbling beat as if it were rocking to the top of its beam, and ringing that way, alone, it sounded clamorous. The older firemen tilted their heads : they knew the city bells ; but they waited for Purdy. He said after the third note, "That's the Spring Street Church," and Sparks nodded. "Reverend Ludlow's," he agreed.

A cab came dashing up to the Park and a watchman leaned from the window to yell for the location of the troops. The mob was building barricades in Spring Street. They had broken open the church, there were nearly four thousand of them. He'd been to the arsenal but the regiment hadn't come back. If the troops were going to do any good, they'd better show up quick.

"The troops will do all right," Sparks grunted. "You take that cab back up the Bowery and if you find the troops, just tell the Colonel that we're having difficulty in Spring Street."

He directed the two engines to go up Varick and report to the watch nearest the scene of the disturbance. Himself, he headed for Leonard Street.

Going up Varick Street the two engine companies saw the wreckage of Dr. Cox's church littering Laight Street the length of St. John's Park. Young Ames wondered whether the Chevaliers had had any trouble. It must have been terrifying to hear the mob right outside one's door. But as far as he could see, the houses had not suffered damage. He couldn't take time now anyway to find out how they were. The foreman was calling to the runners to close up.

They took the engines across Canal Street at a fair pace but slowed when they got across it. They could hear the roar of the mob and see the line of their torches now, four blocks away, across the opening of the street. As they came closer they made out the barricade, constructed out of carts and pews and furniture and area fences. Behind the barricade the torches swayed with the sheer pressure of jammed humanity.

But the rise and fall of voices was like nothing human ; it had no more articulation than a wind-torn sea. Before that noise, under the eyes of the swaying faces that lined the barricade, the silent watchmen looked baffled and helpless. " There's nothing we can do," they told the firemen. " You'd better pull up on the sidewalk." Every now and then a storm of cobbles and bricks would fly over the barricade.

Young Ames felt his heart beat slow and hard, high in his chest. The barricade looked to him impenetrable. The idea of breaking it down was simply inconceivable. Even troops could not get through unless they did it shooting. This was no casual riot, but an organised defence with a power for violence that he had never dreamed existed. At times the roar of human voices shut off the sound of the bell, yet when he looked up between a gap in the houses, he could see its swinging lip come into the glare of torchlight and rock out again unceasingly. And then after a moment the unutterably solitary clangour of it would swing over their heads again.

As he heard its voice come back, he had a queer sense of his own detachment. There was nothing he could be called upon to do now unless a fire started. And even if a fire started no engine company could break through that barricade. The mob, as it was now situated, could set fire to the surrounding blocks if they cared to with not a soul to stop them. He looked on at a little knot of watch officers and aldermen in a house doorway just beyond him. And then he heard the military coming.

It was like a scene in a play. The troops marched up Varick Street in close order with dressed ranks, their steps precise, and halted fifty yards from the barricade and grounded arms. Colonel Stevens stepped ahead to speak to the watch and young Ames was near enough to hear the alderman arguing that the regiment had better retreat to the arsenal. They were only four hundred strong and the mob four thousand.

The nearer portion of the mob must have learned of the arrival of the troops for the din seemed to subside for an instant, and in the lull young Ames heard the colonel say, " There is no retreat in this case. I am here with my regiment to disperse this mob and quell this riot. Until it's done, I shan't return."

He walked coolly forward and studied the barricade. Then he returned and sent an officer back. Orders were barked and the soldiers moved to the sidewalks, leaving the street bare except for the colonel. If he was baffled he didn't show it.

Presently a captain of cavalry trotted towards him up the street and they conferred, saluted, and the cavalryman cantered his horse back. In the meantime the squadron of horses had formed across Broome Street. A trumpet sounded, piercing the clamour of the mob, and the horses moved. They had two short blocks in which to gain momentum and they came fast. Passing Oceanus they were going at a gallop, moving solidly, the men leaning forward over their horses' necks as they neared the barricade.

Young Ames thought they must stop ; but they hit it ; he saw it lift before them, totter and crash ; and they rode through with only one horse down ; and there was a sudden awful high-pitched screaming from the mob. He heard it travel back along the block in one ascending wave and then it broke and the cavalry wheeled after it. In the street before him the 27th Regiment formed precisely and marched ahead, wheeling squad by squad into Spring Street. All that was left was the broken barricade, which now looked ineffectual, shoddy, almost forlorn. It seemed to have no point, no sense ; it was impossible to say that it had stood for anything ; it was pathetic ; and staring at it, young Ames was suddenly aware of his own unimportance.

To his right he heard the receding yells down Sullivan Street and imagined the broken rioters fleeing before the steady tramp of the militia.

21

It was past midnight when he dropped out of the company and cut through Laight Street to the Chevalier house. The butler opened the door on its chain, and young Ames saw the white of the terrified eye peering through the crack. He gave his name.

"Thank de Lawd !" said Amber, opening the door. "Come right in, Mr. Ames, sir. You come right in. Mr. Chevalier say when he went I'se to keep this do' on de chain," he explained, and then, forgetting his dignity, he bawled, "Oh Mis' Chevalier, Mis' Kisty ! Hyer come Mr. Ames ! "

Young Ames heard the rustle of her skirts as she got up ; the quick feet running through the dining-room and parlour, and her voice saying, "John ! " And then she stopped, her skirts swaying, her cheeks pink at the sight of Amber's startled eyes.

"You're all right ? "

"Yes," he said. "Are you all right? Amber says Mr. Chevalier's out."

"Yes." Her eyes travelled over him, amused, moved, smiling. "It was awful for Aunt, with those men yelling outside. But they didn't do anything to the houses. John, you're sure you didn't get hurt?"

He became ruefully aware of the sight he must make, sweat-stained, dirty-faced, and one sleeve out of his coat torn from the burst through the gang in Hanover Square. "I'm not fit to be seen here," he said.

He saw her voice tremble in her throat. "Oh, Mr. Ames," she said shamelessly, "you look fine to me."

"Does to me, too, Mis' Kisty." Amber grinned. Then he covered his teeth soberly and whispered, "It's all right, Mis' Kisty. I ain' seein' nothin', nor is I hearin' it."

"You shiftless darkey! Leaving the door wide open for the whole Five Points to walk in."

Mr. Chevalier was standing in the doorway. He was white-faced, his blue eyes like ice, and his hat was broken on one side and he carried his gold-headed stick by the middle. When he handed it to Amber they saw that it too was broken.

"The badges of Jacksonian democracy, Ames." A glint of satisfaction came into his eyes. He touched the stick. "For services rendered, though."

Mrs. Chevalier had come breathlessly into the hall. "Mr. Chevalier," she said. "They've hurt you."

"A few bumps. I'll survive, my dear. A bunch of them thought they'd try for the arsenal after the troops left. But there were plenty of us. When I left the regiment was coming back down Centre Street and Hayes said the riot was broken. Maybe they've learned this time that there's law in New York if not in Washington."

"You come upstairs with me."

"I want a drink," he said.

"Amber will fetch it up. I insist you come up and let me tend to you, Mr. Chevalier."

He gave an amused glance at young Ames.

"Christine can look after Mr. Ames," his wife said.

"I don't doubt it," Mr. Chevalier said dryly. "Very well, my dear. But Amber can wait on them."

"Yes, Mr. Chevalier," Amber said.

Young Ames hesitated. He knew it would be better to go home now. But Christine's fingers were touching his arm, and he followed her into the drawing-room.

"I'm filthy," he said.

She stood looking at him.

"I'm not made of sugar, John," she said. "Are you always going to be scared of me in this house? You'll have to get over it, you know, for we'll live in one like it some day." Her face was tantalising and she lifted an impudent mouth.

"There," she said, "now we can be as decorous as you like. Uncle will be down again presently. Did you get my letter?"

"Yes."

"I was naughty to write. But it seemed dull and lonely there, so far away."

But he was tongue-tied. How could he tell her that he had read and re-read her note? He was suddenly dog-tired, and to help him she said: "Tell me what's happened these three weeks."

It was a relief to tell her about the fire off Coenties Slip and the affair with Funk. It was a relief to find someone he could talk to. He had thought it would be hard to tell her, it had all been so muddled in his own mind. But she was quick to understand, even when he slid over the business of Funk's death.

"It must have been awful for you," she said, watching him compassionately. "Of course, you must go to see Mrs. Funk and help her if she needs it, John."

"I kept feeling I was to blame for it."

"That isn't so, and helping her isn't saying you are, either, John."

" I suppose not."

" And if there is anything I can do to help, you'll tell me, won't you, John ? "

" Yes."

" I wonder," she said thoughtfully. " John, when we get married, I don't want to be just someone you keep in a pretty house. I'd rather live poor than be like dear Aunt Chevalier." Her cheeks flushed as she went on, " Of course, she's perfectly happy. She's had everything all her life, she goes to the resorts, and she reads all the *Ladies' Journals* and *Repositories*, and she's perfectly sweet to Uncle George. But *I'm* going to know what you do—what you're planning, and what you're afraid of. I won't let you just walk out of our house in the morning into another world and come back at night into ours again. I want to know about it and feel it even if I can't be in it. Maybe I could help, even if it was only by listening."

She looked so earnestly into his eyes that he smiled.

" Don't do that ! "

" Don't do what ? "

" Don't smile at me that way, please, ever, John ! I couldn't bear it. There's nothing on earth that shuts a woman out of life like that kind of smile."

" I didn't mean it that way," he said, puzzled.

" I know. But you might get me used to it. I might learn to feel satisfied with it. It might even make me happy."

" Would that be bad ? "

" Yes," she said. " I think we ought to get married soon, John."

" But how about Mr. Chevalier ? "

" If Uncle George objects, we'll elope," she said fiercely. Then, as she watched him, her lips twitched. " Don't look so dismayed ! What's the matter ? Wouldn't I be a good risk ? Hush, John. I think he's coming down."

They heard Mr. Chevalier briskly descending the stairs.

Christine smoothed out the lace on her dress and let her hands arrange themselves in her lap. But she asked in a lowered voice, " You'll see Mrs. Funk to-morrow ? " And when he nodded, she gave him her whole-souled smile. " Don't be afraid of being generous, John, will you ? Because you really want to be."

Then she turned her eyes, solicitously affectionate, towards Mr. Chevalier as he came into the drawing-room. He had put on a printed cashmere dressing-gown.

" Your aunt's had a shock, Kisty. I oughtn't to have left the house."

Christine said : " Poor dear. But she'll be all right to-morrow, Uncle George."

" You think so ? Maybe you're right," he said, smiling at her. " Weren't you scared ? "

" I ? Yes, but I got mad as hops," she said. " I wished I'd had a gun."

Mr. Chevalier's eyes kindled. The colour had returned to his face, and his white hair seemed fairly to bristle. " I had to get in some work of my own against those hoodlums," he exclaimed. " It's time they saw people like us aren't afraid of them. Ames, they say Oceanus broke up the mob in front of Tappan's. Lalagh was talking about the city's making a presentation to Number 11. I'm proud Chevalier's was represented in the company. Was that where your coat was torn ? "

" I suppose it was," young Ames said. " I didn't notice at the time."

" Amber's bringing up some whisky," Mr. Chevalier said. " Bourbon. My contacts with Mr. Jackson's demo-cracy have given me a democratic kind of thirst."

Amber entered with juleps on a tray.

" What's more," said Mr. Chevalier as he sipped his glass with satisfaction, " it's damned good democratic drink. Jackson or no Jackson, the South's given us four things that can't be beat—juleps, cotton, horses, and women." He made Christine a little bow. Then he said, eyeing them one after the other, " I'd give a pretty to know what you two young people were talking about."

Christine's eyes were demure.

" Mr. Ames was telling me about some Chinese rice paintings he had bought and sold while we were at Rockaway. The ones you spoke about, I expect, Uncle. He wished to make me a present of one of them and I thought it was proper to accept. Wasn't it ? "

" Of course, of course," said Mr. Chevalier. Suddenly he caught himself up and stared haughtily down his nose at her. " Minx ! " he said. " It depends entirely on the book."

" This one is of flowers, sir," young Ames said seriously. Christine caught his eye and turned suddenly pink and Mr. Chevalier stared hard at young Ames.

" Are you two making fun of me ? " he demanded.

Christine laughed. " Oh, no, Uncle. Mr. Ames was telling me about the deal and we were discussing what to do about the poor man's wife."

" Indeed. May I ask what you decided ? "

" He should help her, of course," Christine said.

Watching them, young Ames had an uneasy feeling that she was skating on thin ice. He wondered how much Mr. Chevalier had really taken in when he surprised them in the front hall. It was impossible to tell. Those china-blue eyes of his gave away no secrets. Young Ames still had no inkling when, after Christine had said good-night a quarter of an hour later, Mr. Chevalier showed him to the door.

" Good-night, Ames," he said, surveying the littered street. " It was good of you to come round. I appreciate it. But let me give you a word of advice. Don't discuss your business with a woman. It only worries her, and then you have to worry for both." He met his clerk's eyes without expression. " By the way, if you want time off to see this Mrs. Funk to-morrow, arrange it with McVitty."

" Thank you, sir." Young Ames said good-night. He didn't dare look up at the windows as he walked away, for

Mr. Chevalier stayed on the stoop. He wished he knew what Mr. Chevalier meant by his advice. But he felt more like himself. He couldn't tell precisely why, for he had made no new decision, and he felt that Mr. Chevalier had taken in a good deal more than Christine would admit.

He looked back after he had turned the corner of the Park. Over the top of the iron fence he saw her window light come on. She came to the open sash carrying her candle in her hand and waved her handkerchief. He couldn't wave back, for Mr. Chevalier was still staring after him. But his elation grew. Her thoughts were with him all the time, and her belief in him, and her heart. That was the clear, indisputable fact that had come out of all these troubled days.

He felt them with him next afternoon when he went to find Mrs. Funk. He had been to see Mr. Levy first, and collected three hundred dollars from the enthusiastic dealer, who expected to get rid of the rest of the books within a week.

Number 49 Elizabeth Street was a two-story frame house with a liquor store on the ground floor. To the right a covered alleyway led darkly back. On the left an outside staircase ascended to a small door in the side of the second floor. Young Ames mounted and knocked. While he waited for an answer, he looked down the street at a squad of watchmen slowly patrolling towards him. It seemed as if the riots were broken, though the papers said that the 27th Regiment would remain under arms.

Then a woman opened the door.

" Mrs. Funk ? " he asked.

She nodded.

" My name is John Ames. Could I talk to you for a few minutes ? "

" Come in," she said quietly.

She was a small, bright-looking woman, almost pretty. She led him into a tiny room with a grate, a bed in the corner. The room was poor, but he could see that she was self-respecting. There were a few pots of flowers in the window and the baby on the bed was neatly dressed.

" Please sit down," she said.

He had thought it would be simple, but it wasn't.

" I feel badly about your husband, Mrs. Funk."

" Poor William," she said. She sounded sorrowful, but she wasn't particularly grieved. " He never could make anything come right. I thought when he went to China he might have a chance to do better."

" I feel badly, though. I bought the paintings in good faith."

" Paintings ? " she asked. " William didn't say anything about them."

" Didn't he ? " Young Ames stared at her. Then he said : " I bought them from him and agreed that we should share the profits. I paid him a hundred and eighty dollars down. But there's a hundred and ninety due you."

" Oh ? " She looked away, first at the baby, then out of the window. Then she said quite calmly, " Is that true, Mr. Ames ? "

" Yes," he said.

" Poor William," she said. " I didn't know what we were going to do. I've supported myself for two years, but I became ill and had to go into debt. They said I'd have to leave here."

" Mr. Funk said you owed three hundred dollars."

" Not that," she said. " I need a little over a hundred, and this will take care of it. Oh, it's kind of you, Mr. Ames."

" What will you do now, ma'am ? "

" I'll go home," she said. " I come from Pittsburgh. I could do very well, there, I think, by dressmaking. It's hard for women there to keep abreast of the fashions, you know."

" You mean, to start a clothing store ? "

He could see that she was capable and intelligent.

She gave a rueful little laugh. "Hardly that, for a while. I'd have to make a little capital first, wouldn't I? But I've thought of it."

"How much would you need to start a store with?"

"I hardly know. But I could rent cheaply. A hundred dollars would go a long way if I had a buyer here who could pick up small lots," she said. "You know our buyers are men, and they come East here and try to get things cheap. Not clever things, but what they're used to handling. I'm not very clear, I'm afraid, Mr. Ames."

"I think you are." Young Ames felt his excitement growing. "Mrs. Funk," he said. "I'd like to make you a proposition. I'll advance the hundred dollars, and you'll write back what you need. I have opportunities of buying sometimes, small choice lots that wouldn't bring me a profit here. But out there they might sell well. You'd have to keep me informed of what you need." He thought rapidly. "And I have a friend, a woman friend, who could send you the latest fashions and might help advise us both."

She was looking at him earnestly.

"You don't know anything about me, really, Mr. Ames."

He grinned and ran his hand through his sandy hair.

"I'm willing to take a chance, Mrs. Funk. Will you do it?"

"Yes," she said. "Oh, it's wonderful for me. I hardly knew where to turn, but I'm sure I can do it, Mr. Ames. And half an hour ago, I was wondering where on earth my son and I could move to. It was so frightful all last night."

"When could you start?"

"To-morrow, if you like. There's nothing to pack."

"I'll buy your place on the train and coach," he said. "Here's my name." He wrote it down, with the address.

"Ames and Funk," she said.

"I'll draw up an agreement in duplicate." He pulled a chair up to the bare little table while she brought him paper and pen. After a moment he glanced up from what he had written. "Ames and Funk doesn't sound just right.

Do you think it's a suitable name for such an establishment ? "

" Why not ? " She wrinkled her forehead as she repeated the names. " Oh, I see. You think it ought to sound more feminine ? Of course, you're right, Mr. Ames. Let's see." She smiled. " You're not married, I suppose ? "

" No," he said.

" Have you any preference for a girl's name ? "

He grinned.

" How about Christine ? " he said, guardedly.

" It's perfect," cried Mrs. Funk, clasping her hands. " It sounds French. Madame Christine and Mrs. Amelia Funk, dressmaking and millinery. Paris, New York, and Pittsburgh ! "

She signed her name, and then, as he pocketed his copy, she offered her hand.

" You've been wonderfully generous and kind to me, Mr. Ames. Perhaps reckless. But I won't let you regret it."

22

He slipped his copy of the partnership agreement between the leaves of the book of rice paintings, next to the picture of the cherry blossoms on the last page. It wasn't the kind of present he had intended to buy Christine; but he knew she would like it better, and it would make something to talk about on their next picnic to Hoboken.

Pinky Finnegan, who had an errand uptown, was waiting to take it. " It's for Miss Chevalier," young Ames emphasized.

Pinky wiped the knowing expression from his face as he said, " Trust me, Mr. Ames."

" It's important, Pinky," he said again. Then he grinned as he remembered Mr. Chevalier's doorstep advice.

VII

THE GIRL FROM DUBLIN

SUNLIGHT slanting through the high back windows presented the counting-room of Chevalier, Deming & Post in a busy aspect for an August afternoon. The *Grosvenor* had docked that morning from Dublin and the clerks were at their desks making lists to be sent round to the drygoods merchants for a private viewing. Pinky Finnegan, who had returned from delivering one batch already, sweated gratefully on his low stool by the door and listened to the tramp of porters in the hallway below.

Outside on the sidewalk young Ames was enjoying his respite from the close heat of the counting-room. As each item was taken in, he checked it against his list and jotted down the number on the porter's leather shield. Chevalier's consignment was not large, and he had time enough to watch the river front between arrivals of barrows and handcarts that now lined the kerb as the porters waited for their pay in the shade against the wall. It was a clear day with white clouds massed above the rigging of the docked ships. He could smell salt ; and he thought a south-east breeze might be on the way to cool the evening for them.

A pedestrian stepped round them with a muttered apology. He possessed what Mr. McVitty would have called a plausible face. The nearest porter eyed him contemptuously, spitting juice from his pipe and nodding when young Ames said, " Runner ? "

Boarding-house and railroad runners clustered the docks whenever an emigrant ship arrived. Young Ames had grown used to their aggressive voices, their loud friendly manner. He thought of them chiefly as nuisances, getting in the way of the proper unloading of a ship.

He watched the man move rapidly up South Street,

dodge in front of a rumbling cart, and jump out of the way of a pair of greys. The greys came at a brisk trot, and as they drew close he saw that they were the Chevalier horses. They swung in to the kerb beyond the line of barrows ; the door opened before the coachman could get down, and Christine Chevalier stepped out. " I won't be long, Dick," she called to the coachman.

Her clear voice and the cool soft grey of her dress caused a stir of interest among the porters. She came back along the sidewalk towards Number 42, her furled sunshade in her hand and a leghorn bonnet on her dark hair. Her brown eyes lit at the sight of young Ames. She made him a little curtsey as if to ask him whether he liked the way she looked, and she found her answer in his face.

" I wanted to see Uncle," she said. " Do you suppose he's too busy ? "

" Lord, no," he said. Telling the nearest porter to hold the remaining bales at the door till he got back, he led her into the counting-house. She breathed deep of the mingled smells of coffee, drygoods, and brandy. " It's wonderful, John. I love it down here, but it's seldom I can think of an excuse to come."

" It's hot and dirty. You'd better mind the walls," he said, eyeing the crisp wide skirt.

" I'm not afraid of dust ! It's fun to be where something's going on. When you have your own counting-house, John, I'm going to come down every afternoon to fetch you."

It was something to think about. Young Ames didn't have a doubt in his mind it would be so ; he only wondered how long it would be before the name—Ames—was put into the firm. In the dusky stair hall he felt the pressure of Christine's fingers taking hold of his ; and he had an electrical sensation of its being his house in fact, that what she said was so ; and he returned the pressure, suddenly hard, so that she looked at him with a quick motion of her head.

They did not say anything for they were then on the landing. Mr. McVitty appropriated her with a rusty bow. From the door young Ames watched the effect of her progress through the counting-room. She seemed to carry light into the room with her. Pinky was open-mouthed ; and young Ames saw with pride the open approval on Gibbs's dark face. Gibbs was a judge.

He went downstairs reluctantly, but he had scarcely started to check in the waiting items of the consignment before Cummings came out. " You're wanted in Mr. Chevalier's office," he said enviously. " Mr. McVitty told me to finish up here."

2

" Come in, Ames," Chevalier said. " Sit down. My niece says she met you downstairs."

" Yes, sir. I was checking Knox's consignment."

There was an impenetrable gleam in Mr. Chevalier's blue eyes. " She seems to have an idea that you know more about the workings of the city than any one else in this house." His voice was dry. " I don't know where she got that impression, but I suppose she's right. I seem to remember that you've made some Irish connections."

Christine was seated in the window, and the light, coming over her shoulders, outlined the curve of her chin. She caught his eye, and the corner of her mouth twitched.

Mr. Chevalier picked up a letter. He looked troubled and impatient. " You'd better read this to begin with, Ames," he said, handing it over.

It was a note to Mrs. Chevalier from a lady signing herself Angela Knox. The heading was Dublin, the date two months ago.

" All Ireland seems to be emigrating to America, men, and women and children, even young unescorted girls. It is about one of them I am writing you. I have taken the liberty of giving her a letter to bring to you, for she doesn't know a soul there.

" Her name is Delia Mahoney and her mother has been in my service for seven years. I offered the child a place in my house, but she would not have it, for the news is that a woman, even a servant, can make twice the money in America that she can here. She is besides ambitious and though she cannot read or write seems to have dreams of improving her station. So she has bought herself a passage on the *Grosvenor*, bound for New York. Mr. Knox thinks she will be all right on the boat, as Captain Blanchard is a gentlemanly man and a thorough officer. But it is quite possible that she may forget my letter, or lose it or be afraid to take it to you—our lower-class girls are such unresponsible creatures. But I have told her to wear a red-and-white striped shawl I made her a present of. She seems very pleased with it, so she may remember to wear it. However, in case she does not, I had better describe her. She is of middle height, eighteen years old, and well-favoured in a healthy, country way. She has dark brown hair, very heavy, and blue eyes, and a bright complexion, and though she is headstrong about going to America, her manners are modest, almost timid.

" If you can arrange to have her met, I shall be most grateful, especially for her mother's sake. . . ."

The rest of the letter was of a private nature, and young Ames handed it back.

" Naturally, Mrs. Chevalier was happy to look after the girl," Mr. Chevalier explained. " She sent the carriage to the pier and Kisty went down with it. But the girl never showed up. At least, Kisty didn't see her."

Christine said : " I didn't see anybody wearing a red-and-white shawl. But there were so many coming off, and so many people on the pier, and everything was so confused, I might have missed her. Dick was looking too."

" She probably forgot to wear it," Mr. Chevalier said testily. " They're all alike. As soon as they land here they lose all sense of how to act, if they ever had any. I wouldn't bother except that Knox is a friend of long standing. He and his wife were very cordial to us, some years ago, when we were abroad." He glanced at Christine. " And then my niece doesn't like the idea."

" It must seem terrible coming here all alone," Christine said. " What do you think we ought to do ? "

Young Ames took a minute to think. It was a new kind of problem.

" Did you stay till they were all ashore ? "

" I asked one of the officers and he said they were. He said he hadn't noticed any Delia Mahoney during the voyage. But he seemed interested," Christine said demurely, " and he went back on board to check over the lists. He told me she'd sailed on the ship beyond a doubt, and she must have landed.

" She might still turn up at your house."

" But that was before ten this morning, and she's had all day ! "

" I suppose you could advertise in the newspapers," young Ames suggested. " Even if she can't read, someone else might know about her and tell her or answer on their own hook."

" I doubt it, but we can try," said Mr. Chevalier. " I can notify the watch, too, but I don't suppose they'll bother much unless she's done something criminal, which hardly seems likely." He seemed irritated. " I'd thought of those points myself, Ames. Have you any other ideas ? "

Christine was looking at him.

" Suppose she was your sister. What would you do ? " she asked.

" I'd go aboard the *Grosvenor* first," said young Ames. " I'd begin asking there, and see what I could find out. But it might take quite a while."

" Well, go ahead, Ames. Report to me if you find anything, or come round to my house to-night. My wife will be anxious to hear as well as my niece. When you go out, tell Mr. McVitty I want to see him."

Christine rose too. "You're good to give me so much time, Uncle George. But Aunt was so upset."

"Tell her not to worry," Mr. Chevalier said dryly. "There's nothing to worry about. Ames will find the girl."

"I'm sure he will, Uncle," Christine said serenely. But young Ames, meeting Mr. Chevalier's eyes, felt his face get hot.

"It's not going to be easy," he told her as they went down the stairs. "Have you any idea how many foreigners there are in the city?"

"No."

"Well, nearly forty thousand emigrants landed last year. A lot of them go on, but a lot stay."

"Whatever becomes of them all?" Christine asked.

"A lot of the men get jobs on the docks. The women work in houses and hotels, I guess."

"But the poor girl can't just disappear. You'll have to find her, John. I told Uncle you could."

"Oh, I'll find her," he said, but he didn't feel sure. They were out on the street now, the bustle of trade surrounding them, and he thought, "I can't just walk up to every woman and say, 'Are you Miss Delia Mahoney?'"

Christine was saying, "Aunt doesn't want the carriage this afternoon. Shall I drive you to the pier?"

"It's only a little way. I can walk."

"Don't be stupid, John. Here I've managed to get us by ourselves, and you want to walk! Tell Dick to drive to the pier."

Young Ames gave the order and sheepishly got in after her. The wine-coloured leather upholstery made a glowing frame for her face. She leaned slightly towards him.

"If you kiss me quickly, John, I don't think any one would notice you."

3

Threading its way through the dock traffic, the carriage disappeared up Dover Street, and young Ames turned to the ship. The *Grosvenor's* crew had mostly gone ashore, but stevedores were still at her and the first mate was standing by the forward hatch.

" Is Captain Blanchard on board ? " young Ames asked him.

" No." The first mate bent over to bellow orders into the bowels of the ship. He was anxious to finish up, to turn the ship over to the ship's watch and go home.

" Where is he ? "

The first mate straightened. " How should I know ? " he asked in a level voice. He was a heavy man and he stared with contempt at young Ames. " He took the lists to the Recorder's office an hour ago."

Young Ames decided he would not care to work before the mast on the *Grosvenor*. But the mate couldn't do anything to him here. " I'm trying to trace one of your passengers. Delia Mahoney. Did you notice her ? "

" No." The mate wiped his face with a blue handkerchief. " Do you expect me to keep track of every biddy on the boat ? "

" Is the second mate on board ? "

" I don't know." A note of resignation had come into the mate's voice. " All I know is I've got to get this hold empty before I can go home. Why don't you look for yourself."

There was nothing else to do. Pushing through the line of dockhands, young Ames found his way between decks to the gentleman's cabin. It was hot and desolate with the litter of departed passengers. The *Grosvenor* was not a new ship. The mahogany columns looked heavier than those you would find in a Liverpool packet ; the olive-green upholstery and hangings were shabby ; and the long table showed the scars of ocean service.

" Mr. Smith ! Is Mr. Smith here ? "

His voice had a hollow sound, and for a minute there was no answer. He moved slowly aft down the fifty-foot length of the cabin, trying to make out which of the doors that lined each side might belong to the second mate. Between each door was a latticed window opening. It was impossible to see through.

Then, as he was nearly at the end, one of the doors opened and a voice asked : " Looking for me, mister ? "

Young Ames saw a chesty young man, no older than himself, without shirt or coat, in the process of shaving.

" Are you Mr. Smith ? "

" Yes."

" My name's Ames. I'm trying to find out what's become of one of your passengers."

" Sit down out there, while I finish shaving."

Mr. Smith jerked back into his stateroom and started whistling. " What was the passenger's name ? "

" Delia Mahoney."

" You don't say ? Why, a young lady was asking about her this morning. Damned fine-looking young woman she was, too."

" Miss Chevalier."

" You know her ? "

" I'm a clerk in her uncle's firm. Chevalier, Deming & Post."

Mr. Smith whistled. " Wish you luck," he said. " What's all the business about Delia Mahoney ? "

Young Ames briefly explained the circumstances. " Maybe you noticed her," he said. " She's young and good-looking ; brown hair and blue eyes. She was supposed to wear a red-and-white striped shawl."

Mr. Smith soused his face and appeared with a towel. " That's funny," he said. " I do remember seeing a girl like her. Remember noticing her the first few days out.

She wouldn't tell me her name. Seemed shy when I spoke to her and went off on a course of her own. Then we ran into a three-day blow and the weather was dirty for over a week. I sort of lost track of her." He grinned. "Some of those Irish girls scare easy."

"Well, I'm supposed to find her. Who'd be most likely to know about her on board?"

"Boatswain. He measures out their water and food to them every morning. Maybe the cook."

"Where's the boatswain?"

"Gone ashore. I can give you his name—it's Robert Whelden. I can't tell you where he lives, though."

"How about the cook and steward?"

"I don't know where the cook is, but the steward's skipped. You can tell by the looks of the cabin."

Young Ames stared at the skylight. He said: "It's queer how a girl like her can take passage, come aboard, and then just disappear."

"Nothing queer about it," Smith said, working into his shirt. "Thousands of them do it every year. God knows what becomes of them. They pay twenty dollars for their passage—but we don't get that. Our owners sell the steerage space, lump sum, cash down, to an emigrant office. It's generally Rawson & McMurray, though other firms have bought us out once or twice. After that we supply the water and try to keep them from getting drowned. We ain't supposed to take more than two passengers for every ton, and in this ship that figures out at eighty, including cabin passengers. But that don't stop the emigrant-office boys. We had 150 this trip. And for three days we had to keep the hatches on them. There were twenty down in the orlop, and one of them died, an old woman. She was probably sick to start with." He buttoned on his coat. "Look here. I've got a few minutes. Suppose you come and see where they bunk."

He led young Ames, who was curious, forward. They had to go on deck and then down through a forward companionway. As soon as young Ames started down, he smelled the reek left by packed bodies and dirty bedding. It was dark there, too, even with the sunlight coming through the hatches. There were no portholes, nor, as far as he could see, any means of ventilation except the companionway and the hatch. Three days, Smith said, they had had to keep them shut. " A hundred and twenty people in here," Smith pointed out. Young Ames could see the bunks built so close together that a person could barely have found room between, and though there was less than six feet of headroom, all the bunks were doubledeckers. The only floor space was the seven- or eight-foot alley left down the middle. Three hanging lamps served for light. " Men, women, and children," Smith said. " Once in a while we have trouble about a girl—then it's my job to clean up the trouble-maker. So I know what it looks like."

Young Ames could imagine for himself. He stood peering round, trying to forget the odour.

" Have any trouble this time ? " he asked.

" No. The old man won't stand for that. Of course you don't know what happens, but there weren't any complaints about it," Smith told him.

" You said a woman died. Did you lose any others ? "

" One child. But we had another born. It was a healthy voyage. Three sick. We had to leave them at the quarantine hospital. But your girl wasn't one of those. She was checked off as going ashore. Mr. Cantwell did that, I looked up the list for Miss Chevalier."

" Could there have been a mistake ? I mean could Delia Mahoney have been put off at Staten Island and then somehow someone else been checked here under her name ? "

" I suppose so," Mr. Smith said carelessly. " There's always a lot of confusion. It's not very likely, though. She's probably gone to some boarding-house."

" With a runner ? "

" Sure. Her kind make easy pickings."

They had come out on deck. The afternoon sun burned in their faces, but it was good to breathe clean air. Staring at the houses, the movement along the piers, the busy streets, young Ames saw the city as a stranger might have, remembering how it had looked to him when he came to New York two years ago. But emigrant runners did not meet a Hudson River boat.

She had walked off the pier, with someone, into those streets, and somehow he had to find her.

Mr. Smith was pulling out his watch.

" What time is it ? "

" Three o'clock. . I've got to meet my girl in half an hour. Sorry I can't help you."

Young Ames shook hands and watched him pass a few words with the first mate and swing ashore. He didn't have any illusions about Mr. Smith, but he liked· him.

He stood still for a few moments and his freckled face seemed to sharpen. Then, guided by the galley stovepipe, he made his way between decks once more and after a brief search unearthed the cook.

4

The cook was a strapping negro, nearly six feet tall, rigged out in a tight blue coat with full skirts. In the confined space off the galley where he bunked, he was making his own preparations for going ashore.

" What's your name ? " young Ames asked sharply, sizing the man up.

" It's Bert."

He didn't talk like an ordinary negro ; young Ames decided he must be West Indian. He said : " Well, Bert, I'm looking for an emigrant girl who went ashore and disappeared. You see a good deal of the emigrant passengers, don't you ? "

Bert narrowed his eyes.

" Those emigrants," he said. " They're trashy. They won't spend no money. They always want to use my galley, when it's dirty up top." His nostrils spread suddenly.

Young Ames said : " Remember seeing a girl named Delia Mahoney ? "

" No, sir. I don't want to learn their names."

" This girl was kind of short," young Ames said. " Brown hair and blue eyes. She might have worn a red-and-white shawl." He thought he saw a careful light slide into the cook's eyes. They swung towards Ames, passing over the bed. There was a paper parcel lying on the rumpled bedding.

" Might have seen her," he admitted.

Young Ames eyed [him silently, watching him get uneasy.

" No, sir," he said after a minute.

" Let's see it," young Ames said.

" See what ? "

Young Ames said : " You know the people have been rioting against niggers here, Bert. They killed one man last month. Killed him right on the street. And they beat a lot more. I'd hate to tell the watch you robbed a white girl."

" I didn't rob her. She didn't want to eat the beef raw, she wouldn't give me a dollar, so I took the shawl. I took it and told her she could use my galley." He showed his teeth ingratiatingly.

" I guess that was all right," young Ames said. " I want the shawl. I'll give you a dollar for it."

" I'm going to give it to a lady."

" No, you're not. You're going to give it to me for a dollar. Or you'll have to give it to the police for nothing."

" She offered me a dollar for it," the cook said.

" When was that ? " Young Ames could imagine the girl frightened by the big black cook.

" The last day out of port," the cook said.

" She wasn't sick ? She wasn't one of the ones put ashore at Staten Island ? "

" No, sir. She went off right here."

" How do you know ? "

" I seen her myself. She was looking in the galley and she saw me and took off across the deck." He licked his lips, his tongue looked pinkish. Young Ames could see the way he had relished having the girl scared of him— not because he wanted anything of her ; just because it gave him something pleasant to think about, having one of the passengers scared of him. He was getting back his nerve. He said arrogantly, " I didn't think nothing of it. I just thought she was trash."

Young Ames deliberately reached out for the package, opened it, and took out a fine red-and-white striped shawl.

He said as he re-wrapped it : " Did you see her go on the dock ? "

" Yes, sir, she went right off in the crowd. She kept looking round. She was scary, that girl was. Then I see her talking to a white man, and that's the last I seen of her."

Young Ames got up.

" How about this man ? What did he look like ? "

" I don't know," Bert said sullenly. Young Ames decided that Bert thought he didn't amount to much. It made him grin.

" What was he wearing ? "

" I don't know."

" Did he look like a ticket agent or a boarding-house runner ? "

" Maybe he did."

" You're a fool, Bert," young Ames said. " But if Miss Mahoney turns up, I guess you won't get into too much trouble." ·

" What you mean, trouble ? " The negro's cockiness deflated. " I ain' done nothin'."

" Only robbed a white female passenger," young Ames told him. " Here's your dollar." He tossed the bill on the floor and walked out. He went to the gangplank, and down it, and off the ship. The freckles stood out on his face and he felt his hands turn cold with anger. " Suppose she was your sister. What would you do ? " Christine had asked. He didn't need to suppose. He stared at the entrance to Dover Street, trying to feel to himself whether the girl had gone up that way. There was a gin shop on the corner.

5

It was a small place, with a layer of sand on the floor, a plank bar, and gin kegs lined on two shelves behind it. The bartender was in his shirt sleeves. A couple of men stood at the bar and three or four more lounged at two small tables near the window. A strong smell of clam broth and raw onions floated out of a hole in the wall at the back. Young Ames didn't want food or drink, but he laid three cents on the bar and asked for gin.

" Get any sailors in here ? "

" What do you think ? " said the bartender, drawing the gin from the keg.

" I don't suppose there's anybody off the *Grosvenor*."

The bartender glanced through the window. " That the one in 26 ? " He looked at his customers. " There were plenty a while back. You take a man likes gin and keep him on rum five weeks and he comes to the nearest shop. This is it."

" I'm looking for a steerage passenger," young Ames explained.

" Female ? "

" Yes. A young one. Good-looking. She's disappeared."

The bartender shrugged.

" You're a fool to bother. If she's good-looking." He slapped a fly with a neat snap of the bar rag. It was delicate. " Jerry," he said.

One of the customers at the tables came over to the bar. "Anybody off the *Grosvenor* here now?"

Jerry, a watery-eyed, grey-faced individual, shook his head. The bartender explained: "This gent's looking for an emigrant girl."

"Wants to break a leg?"

Young Ames stared at him.

The bartender saw he was green. He explained, and young Ames felt his face get red. "No, I'm trying to trace her."

Jerry looked interested but incredulous.

"What's her name?"

"Delia Mahoney. Middle height, blue eyes, brown hair."

"Bleak?"

The bartender interpreted.

"He means is she pretty?"

"Yes," said young Ames.

"I didn't see her. I might. How much ochre's in it?"

"She worth any money to you?" the bartender interpreted.

"Five dollars if we find her," young Ames said. He hadn't been authorised to offer money, but it would do no harm.

"I'll look," Jerry said, moving off.

The bartender said in a low voice: "Jerry's a nose. He might hear. Come around to-night or to-morrow morning."

So far he had accomplished nothing except to find Delia Mahoney's shawl. He had the cook's word for it that she had gone ashore at Pier 26. The lists also indicated as much, if the second mate was to be believed.

To be thorough, he ought to look at the steerage list himself, and he went over to the Recorder's office in the City Hall. But he was unable to make any headway with the clerks, who didn't regard it as their business to show lists to anybody who asked for them, and hoping to get

help he went down to the watch-house and asked for
Constable Sparks.

Sparks was not on duty, but a young officer, who gave
his name as Homans, took an interest. " Mr. Sparks would
get them for you all right," he said. " But I guess if we
go to see Mr. Riker, I can do just as well."

Mr. Recorder Riker, an elderly, oily-looking little fat
man, swelled with indignation as soon as he learned from
Ames that the girl was good-looking. It was general knowledge that the Recorder, who would savagely sentence a
delinquent female to the workhouse, would no more than
gently admonish a pretty girl who knew enough to smile
at him. He summoned the clerk, who summoned a
junior, who looked startled when he saw young Ames,
and fetched the lists on the run.

Delia Mahoney's name stood on the second sheet with
a cross marked clearly beside it, exactly like the names
above and below. There was no evidence of hesitation on
the part of Mr. Cantwell. " I don't think there's much
doubt of her coming ashore," said Mr. Riker.

Young Ames thanked him and walked out of the
building with Homans. The constable wrote down the
girl's name and the slight description young Ames had
to offer and promised to pass them round. " There's not
much we can do," he said. " But she may turn up, somewhere. If you want to talk to Mr. Sparks, he'll be round
about seven."

6

It was nearly closing time when young Ames returned
to 42 South Street. In his office, Mr. Chevalier was ready
to start home. He had his white hat in one hand, the
other rested on the gold head of his cane.

" Well, Ames," he said, " you haven't found the girl ? "

" No, sir. But here's the shawl Mrs. Knox gave her."

He put the parcel on Mr. Chevalier's table. " I thought Mrs. Chevalier might like to see it. It would show her I was on the girl's track."

Mr. Chevalier slipped one finger under the string. " That's not a bad notion. Mrs. Chevalier's upset, and my niece seems to have taken the affair to heart also. Well, I don't suppose you've found out much in this time."

" Only that she must have landed in New York." Young Ames briefly reported his activities. " I'm afraid I'm going to need money, sir."

" I expected so," Mr. Chevalier said dryly. " How much ? "

" It depends on how much you are willing to spend, sir."

" Whatever's necessary, but no more." Mr. Chevalier's blue eyes hardened. " This girl will probably cost me ten times what she's worth to the world," he said. " But in a way, I've been made responsible for her." He laid his hat and cane on the table and sat down. " Do you think you can really find her, Ames ? "

" I don't know."

" I think it's pretty hopeless myself. She's obviously in the clutches of some of these emigrant sharks." He paused for a moment, staring at his junior clerk. " I'm told they always prey on their own races. The Germans go after the German emigrants, the Irish after the Irish."

Young Ames said : " Yes, sir. Would fifty dollars be too much to spend ? "

Mr. Chevalier's head perked. " It's a lot of money. But if you need it, go ahead. I'll speak to Mr. McVitty as I go out. Do you want it to-night ? "

" Yes, sir."

" How are you going to use it ? "

Young Ames had worked out a plan on his way back from City Hall ; but he hesitated to tell Mr. Chevalier. " It may sound queer to you, sir."

" What do you mean ? "

"Well, the watch can't do much to find a girl. The chances are she's in some house on Mott or Mulberry or Orange Streets, if she hasn't been taken to Paradise Square." He paused. "But I don't believe that would happen, though a girl like Delia might end up there. The point is, even if the watch were willing to hunt through the Mott Street houses, they wouldn't learn anything."

"You'd think a girl with any spunk and decency would walk out and ask a watchman the way to my house."

"I don't think it's a question of that, sir. In the first place, she may have forgotten your name."

"She has a letter addressed to me," Mr. Chevalier said indignantly.

Do you think they'd let her keep it—once they'd taken what money she had? That's probably the first thing they'd take away from her, sir." He wondered how he could make Mr. Chevalier see what it felt like to land in a strange city. "It's quite likely the runner told her he was taking her to your house."

Mr. Chevalier made a brusque gesture.

"Even a fool could see she wasn't going there."

"He could have said you were out of town, and that she could stay in a nice cheap boarding-house for a day till you got back. Then when she's inside, the landlord tells her it costs three or four times what the runner says. If she tries to leave, he takes her bundle or whatever she has to pay for the room which has been held for her. It's easy enough, if she's alone, and scared. If she's old she just gets turned out. If the emigrant's a man and makes trouble, he's beaten up, or if he has a good deal, he's just got rid of. It's easy enough."

· Mr. Chevalier said : "You needn't elaborate it, Ames. Every community has an ulcer of some sort. I don't see, though, how you can go looking for her where the watch can't."

"I'm not going to look for her myself, sir. I'm going to hire Pinky Finnegan to do that."

"You mean our office boy?" Mr. Chevalier asked incredulously.

"Yes, sir. Pinky's smart. Boys like him can go any-where." He glanced at his employer. "Besides, they won't cost as much as men."

Mr. Chevalier thought it over. Then he picked up his hat. "You might as well try it. I wouldn't have thought of it myself," he said. "I'll speak to Mr. McVitty."

7

Two hours later, young Ames and Gibbs were finishing their supper in the former's room. Over Brooklyn a lone cloud reflected the last of the sunset. The dock sounds had thinned away, and on the slates outside the open window pigeons made murmuring sounds of settling down for the night. The twilight was already in the room.

Young Ames cleared away their few dishes and started to lay out twenty-five-cent pieces in a row where the candlelight would shine on them. Gibbs cocked his head. "What's this?"

The sound of pelting feet flowed down South Street. Young Ames leaned from the window. "That you, Pinky?" Pinky answered, "Yes, sir," and ran out over the cobbles while a knot of small boys swarmed after him and craned their necks to look up. "All right, Pinky, I'll toss the key down."

The boys, a fluid, excitable mass in the dusk, went after the key like chickens. Pinky yelled: "Hand it over to me, O'Brien," and then disappeared under the eaves; there was a brief silence; and in the next moment the stairwell echoed with their stamping feet. They poured round the corner and over the landing and materialised in the candlelight.

There were two dozen of them, ragged and barefoot for the most part. They lined up awkwardly inside the door while Pinky, stiff with importance, bristled. " Here we are, Mr. Ames."

Young Ames kept his face sober. " You see those quarter dollars ? " It was an unnecessary remark. From the moment they had lined up behind Pinky the eyes of every one of them had seen nothing but those twenty-five-cent pieces. The money must have looked like John Jacob Astor's fortune to them.

" Every one of you can take a quarter when he leaves," young Ames told them. " And to-morrow every one of you'll get another." He let the fact sink in. A lone voice said : " Gee ! Fifty cents."

" What I want you to do," said young Ames, " is to see if you can find a young emigrant woman. Now listen. She's Irish, about eighteen years old, and has brown hair, and blue eyes, and she's pretty, and about as tall as me. Her name's Delia Mahoney. She's probably in some boarding-house. I'll leave it to you where to hunt, but you ought to look in every boarding-house where an emigrant might go. I'll give a five-dollar bill to the one who finds out where she is. If you find her to-night, every one of you'll get fifty cents extra. Will those terms satisfy, Finnegan ? "

Pinky said : " Yes, sir. Where will we find you if we find the woman ? "

" I'm going to go out for a while," young Ames said. " I'll be uptown. Is there a good place you can think of ? "

Pinky frowned. " If you don't mind drinking beer, maybe the Columbia Gardens would be a good place. They'll let in a boy there. Take a table near the door, sir. It's where my Uncle Mike Dolan goes," he explained, " when my aunt wants a taste of beer, so it's respectable."

" That's the one above the Bowery Theatre, is it ? "

" Yes, sir."

" Then I'll be there by nine o'clock, and I'll stay there till midnight. You'd better get along."

A boy, taller than the others, with a single string holding

up a ragged pair of trousers and lacking the sole of one
shoe, asked how they would make their inquiries. " If
they've took her to a cab house, mister, they'll hide her
if they think someone's looking after her."

It was a good question, young Ames said, in spite of
Pinky's scowling at any one but himself daring to speak.
" What's your name ? "

" Torbie O'Brien."

" Have you any ideas, O'Brien ? "

But Pinky wasn't to be put down. " You can say she's
dropped something in the street and can have it for calling
at—at Mr. Mike Dolan's, 49 Elizabeth Street, to-morrow
morning."

" And they'll say what is it's been found," O'Brien said.
" What will I say to that ? "

Young Ames came to Pinky's aid.

" As a matter of fact, she lost a shawl, which I now have.
A red-and-white striped one. You can say it had her name
in it, if any one asks you. Do you remember the name ? "

" Delia Mahoney ! " The chorus was unanimous.

" All right," said young Ames. " Take your quarters."
In two minutes they were gone.

8

" Pinky's got them organised like Sixth-Ward voters,"
chuckled Gibbs. He had decided to accompany young
Ames for the sake of the walk, and also because the idea
of a Bowery beer palace appealed to him on a hot night.
" Do you think they can find her, though ? "

" They can if any one can," said young Ames. " That's
the gin shop on the corner."

The place was occupied by two customers and the bartender. The latter, recognising Ames at once, beckoned
him over to the end of the bar.

" Jerry was in about seven," he said in a confidential

voice. " He says he's sure he knows who the runner was took her. But he ain't found out where yet. He's got to work for the pigs to-night——" His voice dropped to a husky whisper. " The watch. It's a water-front job."

There was no point in waiting for Jerry. Going out again, Gibbs and young Ames followed Roosevelt Street to Chatham Square and the Bowery. Here the quiet of the lower streets gave way to the slow packed movement of the summer crowds. They moved in a steady stream, filling sidewalks and overflowing on to the thoroughfare, their voices blending with uproar from the saloons, the slow shuffle of their feet on the pavement an undertone to the stamp and music from the dance halls. They looked like a careless crowd, but there were occasional evidences of tension left over from the July riots as men came together at the entrances to side streets, keeping a watch on the Five Points. Down these streets from time to time was audible a seething clamour, shriller when it rose, where the Five Pointers were parading Paradise Square.

" Come on," said Gibbs. Turning into the Columbia Gardens, he led the way to the right of the door and appropriated a table from under the noses of two other men with a coolness that young Ames would never have been capable of.

The interior of the Columbia Gardens was a cavernous place. Hundreds of people sat at the tables ; but the hall could have held thousands. The air waved with drifting tobacco smoke. From a balcony an orchestra of three fiddles and a French horn make squeaky, cheerful music. Waitresses in short white skirts and red boots that came nearly to their knees and had bells in the tassels passed among the tables. One of them, who looked no more than fourteen years old, took their orders for two beers.

Young Ames said : " I'm afraid you'll get bored waiting."

" Not here." Gibbs stared round at the drinking couples. " Besides, do you think I'd miss seeing Miss Mahoney fling her arms round your neck when you rescue her from sin ? "

From where they sat, they could also watch the promenade of the crowd beyond the windows. It seemed to gain in numbers as the night grew older. Carriages appeared for the theatre audience and there was a quick infiltration of small boys offering to hold doors, find your carriage, mister, want a cab ? A portion of the gallery audience entered the Columbia Gardens. Among them young Ames suddenly saw Pinky's Uncle Mike Dolan.

He appeared in the doorway, magnificent in a tan hat, grey coat, and broad-striped waistcoat, with a young woman on his arm. Catching sight of young Ames, he immediately came forward with an air, and said, " Goodmorning, Mr. Ames," recognised Gibbs, and remembered his name. He turned to the girl. " Bessie, this is our Mr. Ames," he said, " Pinky's boss. Gentlemen, I'd like to introduce Mrs. Dolan."

Gibbs made a bow and pulled up a chair for Mrs. Dolan. She was dressed to the nines in a rose-coloured dress, a fan to match, a Neapolitan scarf, and an immense quantity of green gauze round her bonnet.

" We've been to the play," said Mr. Dolan. He shouted for beer. The small waitress came on the run, took the order for four with four more to be brought in five minutes. Mrs. Dolan laid a ripe red lip to her mug and pulled like a man. She was a bright, cheerful-looking girl, with a shy but effective manner of using her eyes. " And what brings you here, Mr. Ames ? " asked Mr. Dolan.

Young Ames's recital roused Mrs. Dolan's indignation. " The poor ignorant creature," she said. " To think of her coming ashore—oh dear ! And her bothering a gentleman like Mr. Chevalier and the two ladies, and keeping Mr. Ames up to all hours ! It's a shame. Can't you help, Mr. Dolan ? "

Mike Dolan shook his head. " Not until we find her," he said. " I can't find her if the boys can't. And it's hard to get them out of the hands of such people and no wonder, with thousands of them pounding into the city every year trying to take the honest work away from honest Americans. It's no more than they deserve, indeed, making so much trouble." He finished his first mug by a single tilt of his head that turned his throat into a conduit for the beer. "If you don't mind, though," he said to Ames, "Bessie and me'll stay a while and see what the boy turns up."

"That's him now," said Mrs. Dolan. Her quick eyes had spotted Pinky at the window, nose to glass, with the nose of O'Brien similarly pressed at his right. She waved her hand, shrieking to them to come in and be quick now, and in a moment they had pelted through the door.

"Torbie's found where she was taken," Pinky said. "It's on Orange Street above Howard, and the house belongs to Downey McConnor."

Mike Dolan grandly placed his hand on the top of Torbie's head. "You're O'Brien's boy," he said, and explained to young Ames, "O'Brien's a butcher in Mulberry Street and a useful man to me."

"Yes, sir," said Torbie. "But the woman's gone."

"Gone?" asked young Ames.

"They turned her out when she said she wouldn't stay and kept her money in payment and her bundle. They don't know where she's gone. They said she went down the street."

Mike Dolan stared at young Ames.

"That's bad," he said. "If she kept to it, she'd fetch up at Paradise Square." He turned to Torbie. "When did that happen?"

"Only an hour ago," he said. "That's what they told me, anyway, Mr. Dolan. It was just before I got there and I might have passed her in the street if I'd been coming the other way."

"So you might," said Dolan. "You're a smart boy. But you wasn't, and if you had been you wouldn't have recognised her. What made her leave?"

" They said she acted like a fool."

" I don't doubt it. We'll have it hard to find her now."

Pinky said : " I've collected the rest of the boys and sent them in round Paradise Square to look out for her. Torbie found out the clothes she was wearing. She has a brown dress on with a white ribbon round the top and no hat."

" Would she come with them if they found her, do you think ? " young Ames asked.

Pinky hesitated. " She might. I told them to tell her Mr. Chevalier was here with you waiting for her and drinking his usual pint of beer. I thought that would sound easy and natural to her. "

Gibbs chuckled. But Mrs. Dolan was shocked. " Mr. Chevalier wouldn't do any such thing and you oughtn't to mention it if he did."

" She wouldn't know that, Aunt Bessie."

" Well, you should guard a nasty tongue just the same," she said, rearranging the scarf and glancing primly at Gibbs.

Young Ames said : " I think I ought to find Mr. Sparks and see if we can't get a squad of the watch to go through there."

" They wouldn't be able," said Mike Dolan. " There's been too much trouble and though they're orderly now for the time being, the Dead Rabbits would kill a constable drawing breath in the Five Points. I think we'll round up some of our boys who understand the constitutionality of the procedure. Pink, go round to Dugan's and send them here to me. About fifteen or twenty will do if they bring a few bats and wear their hats."

Mrs. Dolan said : " You're not going to start a riot, Mike ? "

" Why not ? To-morrow's Sunday."

" Well, I hate to go home," she said with a pout.

Gibbs rose to the occasion.

" If Mrs. Dolan would be content with the company

of an old man like me, I'll be delighted to entertain her here till you return."

She gave him an arch glance. "I don't know what to say, I'm sure, though it's very kind of you, Mr. Gibbs. But I would hate to go home thinking of that poor ignorant girl with her property taken away from her."

"That reminds me," said Dolan. "O'Brien, my boy, run up to Downey's and tell him to send her stuff and money around to me in the morning. Tell him it's political. He can keep a dollar for the rent. He's a valuable man," he explained to young Ames.

Young Ames felt that the affair had been taken out of his hands entirely, but he was sure that Mike Dolan's were far more capable than his. He began to have hopes of finding Delia Mahoney after all. Now that the boys knew what she was wearing and had narrowed the possibilities of her whereabouts, it seemed likely that they would pick up her trail before long.

9

Pinky returned with the report that only nine were at Dugan's, but that they would appear shortly with the necessary reinforcements. The True Blues were attending a wake in Chrystie Street.

"Whose is it?" asked Dolan.

"Danny Gallagher's."

"Bad luck to it, I should have been there! He was always getting obstructed in the riots," Mike Dolan explained. "I forgot he was dead. He was a valuable man."

Pinky went away to get in touch with his gang, accompanied by Torbie O'Brien, who had done his errand to Downey's. Downey, he said, was unfriendly, but he had agreed to restore the belongings except for the silver, which had been lost or stolen.

Shortly after the boys had gone, a procession of Bowery toughs began to assemble. They came in by ones and twos, received a nod from Mike Dolan, and took places at the nearest long table. " Pass out beer for the table." Dolan instructed the little waitress, who by now was beginning to look drawn and weary.

The men were all wearing their tall hats, which they kept on their heads. Some carried sticks, which they laid in front of their beer. Two who came late walked up to the table to shake hands with young Ames. They were Mike Dolan's particular cronies, Foggarty and Rowley, who had assisted young Ames in the Sheehan rice deal, and they looked solemnly pleased when he remembered their names.

" Where's O'Conlon ? " demanded Dolan.

" Putting away the hearse," said Rowley. " Mrs. Gallagher didn't like the looks of the coffin Davison sent round for Danny, and at eleven o'clock she ordered another one. He had to take it round. Foggarty tried the old one on the way back and said it was comfortable as a bed, but she wanted a different lining."

The time passed more slowly than the beer. A little before midnight, Mrs. Dolan began to show signs of weariness, patting her lips with the tips of her fingers and yawning heartily.

Then they got the first word.

Pinky had sent back O'Brien. Delia Mahoney had reached Fat Sue's in Anthony Street, asking a man at the door where she could find a constable. It was all over the streets. The man had been so amazed that he had failed to grab her, and she got away and run up Anthony towards Paradise Square. There had been a hue and cry with three or four bloods taking after her, but she had been lost. Pinky's cohorts were combing the small alleys.

Fifteen minutes later a boy appeared to report that the girl had been hailed by one of their number, but had been so scared she had run away. They were after her, going

back up Orange Street, when she had ducked into a narrow
passage that might lead into Cow Lane, from the back.
None of them knew it and they were scared to go in till
Pinky came along.

Mike Dolan looked grim.

" That's where the Plug-Uglies hang out. The Eagle's
at the end of it." He got up and went over to the long
table where his henchmen sat. There was a confabulation
of some minutes' duration during which a couple of lead
slugs were brought out and slipped into socks and restored
to the pockets of the frock-coats.

Then Pinky arrived with a black eye and an air of
excitement. He had followed the girl up the passage as
far as the Eagle, hiding himself in a nest of barrels of
garbage, and he had been too late. A man had accosted
the girl. She was like a rabbit, he said, too scared to
run, and the man had taken her by the arm. When Pinky
had gone up and said she was his cousin, the man had
knocked him down with the back of his hand. The man
had led her into the Eagle.

" Downstairs or up ? "

" Down," said Finnegan.

" Then they have her in the bar and we might get her
out if there ain't too many of them there. But it will have
to be quick work."

Pinky, who had recovered his breath, said that the Plug-
Uglies were holding a shindig in Paradise Square. The
Eagle seemed nearly empty. He had seen only four or
five men through the windows.

" That's good," said Mike Dolan. He seemed lost in
thought. " If we had something to put the girl in when
we get her," he said.

"A carriage ? " suggested young Ames.

" They'd pull the wheels off anny carriage. It won't
do."

The blank faces of Foggarty and Rowley reminded young
Ames of the absent O'Conlon, and that gave him the idea.

II

When she found what she had been put into, Delia Mahoney lost courage entirely. She started to wail like a wild woman, and nothing young Ames or Mike Dolan could say had any effect. It was a wonder the hearse wasn't stopped by the watch, but if they had tried, the pace O'Conlon kept up would have defeated their efforts.

"He's a timid man whenever he's driving a hearse," remarked Mr. Dolan, "and it's my belief he won't show any courage till he rides inside it himself. Shall I slap her one on the face, Mr. Ames?"

"No, I wouldn't. We're nearly there, and we've been lucky."

"We have so. It's a wonderful idea for a riot," said Dolan, "and I think I'll use it one of these days."

The Chevalier house was dark when they drew up in front of it; the butler had gone to bed; and it was Mr. Chevalier himself who came to the door.

"Ah, Ames. You come late. Have you got any news?" He stopped short. For the first time, young Ames saw him confounded. But the sight of Mike Dolan hauling a wailing girl from the back of a hearse would have puzzled any one.

"Stop your noise," shouted Dolan. "It's Mr. Chevalier's house. It's him himself. Have you anny sense?"

He turned her head so that she had to look at the house, and as soon as she saw Mr. Chevalier, she burst out of Dolan's hand and rocketed up the steps like a pheasant to hurl herself against the old gentleman's chest. "Oh, for the love of God," she roared. "Oh, thank God!"

Mr. Chevalier retained his balance by a supreme effort and made efforts to soothe her. "You're all right, Miss Mahoney. Quite all right." But she wouldn't let go her clutch of him. And that was how Mrs. Chevalier and Christine found them—not to mention the curious neighbours, who, as Mike Dolan remarked, had probably never seen a hearse deliver a live passenger in St. John's Park.

" You'd better come in," said Mr. Chevalier. " We're disturbing the neighbours."

O'Conlon, however, was not a party to the invitation, for the scene had been too much for him. He was making the circuit of the Park at a furious trot with the hearse doors clapping like hands behind him.

Mr. Chevalier turned the girl over to Mrs. Chevalier, and Christine brought sherry to the three men in the living-room. Mike Dolan sat on the edge of a chair eyeing her with embarrassed admiration, and saying, " Yes, sir," whenever Mr. Chevalier opened his mouth.

It took them half an hour to tell their story. By the end of it, however, Mike Dolan, having lost his embarrassment entirely, was doing most of the telling.

" It's a great honour for me to tell Bessie," he said, as they left the house. " They're fine gentry, and it's people like them our Party cannot get along without. And the girl is a very fine young lady, Mr. Ames, and you're lucky to be marrying her."

" Marrying her? " asked young Ames. " What makes you think that? "

" It was plain all over the both of you the way things were going. There's no doubt you're lucky, with Mr. Chevalier approving of the match."

" Approving of it? " young Ames grabbed him by the arm. " He doesn't know a thing about it."

" That wasn't my impression," said Mr. Dolan. " When you went out of the room to help her fetch in more of them pastries, I tipped him a wink round the stem of me glass. And didn't he wink back? " asked Mr. Dolan. " He did so ! "

VIII

ANDREW JACKSON AND THE AMERICAN EAGLE

In New York it had been raining since dawn ; the shipping along South Street was dark from the drenching ; cart horses were slow to move—they huddled their rumps against the wind whenever they had the chance and stood with dropped heads. Inside the counting-room of Chevalier, Deming & Post a fire was drawing in the stove and the fragrance of roasted samples of coffee had filled the whole building with an unaccustomed atmosphere of comfort. It was the noon hour. Only Gibbs, who was reading a novel, and young Ames were on duty.

Young Ames watched the rain streaking the windows and thought with anticipation of the week to come. Mr. Chevalier had gone to Washington to confer with leading Whigs on the possibility of restraining the expected violence of the President's forthcoming message to Congress on the collection of the French debt, or at least, since there was no actual hope of restraining Old Hickory, of neutralising the effect of the message. The last thing commercial New York wanted was war with France.

But young Ames wasn't troubling his head over Andrew Jackson. As long as Mr. Chevalier stayed away, he and Christine would have many more chances to see each other. Already she and Ellen Pierce had planned a supper party at the latter's house for to-morrow evening, with no other guests. For Ellen Pierce, being engaged herself, had become an ardent matchmaker. She thought falling in love with one's uncle's junior clerk unutterably romantic.

Downstairs the front door slammed. Mr. McVitty was flapping the rain from his umbrella in the lower hall. He was intoning a jingle with unharmonious satisfaction as he entered the counting-room.

> " Murky, burky, dank, and drear,
>   See this gloomy month appear.
>   Every trouble now seems double,
>   And the worst of all the year."

He went straight to the stove for a precautionary cup of hot water, sipped gingerly, and turned to face the two clerks. Gibbs closed his books and asked : " What's your good news, Mr. McVitty ? "

Setting down his cup, Mr. McVitty extracted a copy of the *Journal of Commerce* from his coat pocket and laid it on Gibbs's desk with trembling hands. " You'll note the communication on the second page, the first column, near the bottom, signed *Cincinnatus*. You might read it out, Gibbs, seeing we're alone. I've no desire for notoriety," he added with ill-concealed triumph.

Gibbs read soberly :

" GENTLEMEN,—Permit me through your patriotic journal to suggest the propriety of erecting public privies on the wharves of this city. The adoption of such a measure would not only be affording proper conveniences for a portion of our labouring classes, and strangers, but would also serve the cause of the social decencies which are now unavoidably violated, and would also add much to the cleanliness of these localities.

" Resp'y,

" CINCINNATUS."

" Did you write it ? " Gibbs asked.

Mr. McVitty nodded. " I've been trying to interest the public prints in the matter for seven years. Do you think it's all right ? "

" I'd never have thought of it myself. I don't wonder they published it. It's a masterpiece."

Mr. McVitty fairly beamed.

" I wanted to make it succinct. And I think you'll agree

with me it is. That's what gave me the idea for the nom de plume. Succinct—Cincinnatus."

"Congratulations," Gibbs said. "From the way you came in singing, I thought Andrew Jackson must have got shot."

"It's too bad he didn't," said Mr. McVitty, "before he puts us at war with the French. I suppose he thinks France is the size of Naples and he can scare the wits out of them just by ordering our navy for sea duty. One sloop of war probably looks big as God's thunder to a man whose previous maritime experience is confined to the creeks of Tennessee." He drew snuff up his better nostril with a withering snort. "Many a man wears a sailor hat who never owned a rowboat," he said sententiously.

Climbing up on his stool he shook out the skirts of his rusty black coat with a flourish and picked up his pen. The rest of the clerical staff were returning from lunch in damp groups, and the counting-room swung into its afternoon routine. By the time the junior partners came in, the sounding of hurrying pens made an undertone to the gust of rain spattering the back windows.

Mr. Deming was laughing. He had been on change in Mr. Chevalier's place and he said : " The whole Exchange is wondering whether Old Horse is going to kick or eat French hay."

Mr. Post said woodenly : " He won't eat hay unless it's got gunpowder in it."

"That's damned good, Henry," exclaimed Mr. Deming. It was so unusual for Mr. Post to say anything even remotely humorous that the entire counting-room woke up. But the second junior partner preserved his wooden expression.

"Has our pouch from the Havre packet come in yet, Mr. McVitty ? "

"Yes, sir. It's laid out on your desk."

They disappeared together into their office and young Ames went to work on the daybook. He made a notation for his own benefit to ask Christine what she thought of some Henegun merino shawls to add to the shipment of Canton flannels he planned to send Mrs. Funk in Pittsburgh.

He wondered if it would not be a good opportunity to ask Mr. McVitty for an extra hour at lunch on Monday. It would be easy for Christine to meet him at Austen, Wilmerding's and look them over. He could ask Mr. McVitty just before closing, uniting the request with a reference to Cincinnatus. Thinking it over, he watched Pinky Finnegan lighting the gas jets. Pinky had turned up the last to the exact point at which its whistle most nearly resembled Mr. McVitty's stoppered nostril when Mr. McVitty himself said at young Ames's shoulder. " Mr. Post would like to see you in his office, Ames."

The request flustered him. But if Mr. McVitty had noticed Ames's preoccupation, he offered no remark on wasting one's employer's time. The quill wabbled behind his ear as he led the way to the office of the junior partners and closed the door behind them.

Mr. Deming grinned but said nothing. Mr. Post stared solemnly from young Ames to a letter in his hand.

" You will have to go to Washington, Ames," he said abruptly. " We've just received a letter from Paris that Mr. Chevalier ought to get at once. You will have to start to-morrow morning."

Young Ames saw all the plans he and Christine had made for this week go glimmering. Mr. Post paid no attention to his dismay, but Mr. Deming grinned as he explained, " Neither of us can be spared in Mr. Chevalier's absence, and it's important for the letter to reach him as soon as possible. Mr. McVitty suggested you be sent, as you've had more experience travelling than our other clerks."

Mr. McVitty nodded sententiously. " It's an opportunity for you to see the capital, Ames. You ought to be glad of it. If Mr. Chevalier has no use for you there, you should be home again by Friday."

"Damn the capital," young Ames thought, but there was nothing he could say. Mr. Deming shook his hand. "Good luck, my boy," he said. "I hope you'll have some fun."

2

Sitting on the box of the Washington coach, young Ames bitterly surveyed the dripping countryside. He was bound to lose the week. He hadn't even had a chance to see Christine, but had had to leave a letter for her at the house. She would understand, of course ; she knew enough about business to realise that a junior clerk had less liberty than a plantation hand. But all the understanding in the world could not make up for his ruptured plans for the week.

The trip from New York had already consumed more than forty-eight hours. Sunday night had been spent in Philadelphia, Tuesday night in Baltimore. Now on the road from Baltimore to Washington the coach wallowed through a never-ending trough of mud, and it was nearly three o'clock in the afternoon. They had spent seven hours covering the first stage of the thirty-seven miles.

He had taken the outside seat when they changed horses, for no one else coveted the honour on this drizzling day. But even the penetrating dampness was a relief after the curtained pitching interior of the coach in which the long stogie of a Representative from western Pennsylvania enveloped the passengers in a rank fog.

The driver was as taciturn as he, and chewed tobacco with a gaunt jaw. But he had a touch on the reins. His team was well put together and buckled grittily to the work. In spite of the mud the coach was making progress at last. As he watched them haul through a heavier stretch than common, young Ames could not help exclaiming, " That's a first-rate team ! "

" You're right there, mister," the driver said at once. " They're Vermont bred. They know how to pull. You take the average horse here, and he'll flannel along like a Congressman." He emptied his mouth of juice to add clearly, " But you take Vermont horses and a Vermont man to drive them, and you've got a Yankee hitch."

" I take it you're a Vermont man."

" I am." The driver spat again with evident pleasure. " Where do you come from, mister ? "

" New York City, but I was born near Troy."

" Well, that's the right side of the Hudson, anyhow. This your first trip to Washington City ? "

" Yes, it is."

" Washington's a funny city," said the driver. Now that he had sounded off, he kept right on talking. He said there wasn't a city or town anywhere in the country like Washington. Only a shoemaker could feel happy in a place where houses stood so far apart. But the public buildings weren't too bad. The White House, for instance. At least they had a horseman in it, whatever you thought of Old Hickory's political notions. He had an unfortunate partiality for bigness in a horse, but then he was a tall man. And if it came to the Capitol—the driver pointed his whip. " Just skin your eye round the corner of that hill and you'll see it before too long."

The clouds showed some signs of breaking as the coach heaved over the top of the grade. On the other side the road wound down in the same red muddy trough, and then went straight across the flatland. At the end, the tollgate cast its bar across the ruts.

But beyond and above it young Ames saw the Capitol, its high dome reared dramatically against the damp sky.

The white mass of the building, so much bigger than anything he had expected, seemed to stand aloof above the sodden countryside. As the coach crept slowly nearer, its dimensions seemed to grow, and young Ames was reminded, strangely, of his journey to New Orleans, of the peaks of the Allegheny Mountains, of the high bluffs of the Ohio, of the ever-widening ceaseless current of the Mississippi River.

"Noticeable, isn't it?" asked the driver. "But some people here get used to it, so they hardly look at it at all."

3

At Gadsby's Hotel he was informed that Mr. Chevalier had gone out. Neither the house clerk nor the porter knew where he was. They expected, however, that he would return for dinner. Though young Ames would have liked to go out himself, for it would be his only chance to look the city over if he were going to take the coach back to Baltimore in the morning, his orders were to deliver the letter as quickly as possible. He decided to wait in Mr. Chevalier's rooms.

He sat in the window of the sitting-room watching the traffic along the avenue. He missed the hurry and noise of New York streets. Store clerks, closing up, took things easy; pedestrians were ready to stop at the drop of a hat for long leisurely conversations; even coloured servants seemed free to loiter. Their aimlessness irritated him. His whole trip, with its delays, the rain, the muddy road, seemed pointless. As the darkness stole in over the city and the thinly scattered lights appeared here and there along the avenue, he felt homesick even for his bedroom under the roof at Number 42 and Gibbs's sardonic company.

He did not hear the door opening until Mr. Chevalier said: "Ames! They told me downstairs you were waiting for me."

He scrambled to his feet.

"Yes, sir."

"I'm afraid you've had an unpleasant trip, Ames. It's been miserable weather." Mr. Chevalier was carrying a lighted lamp. He set it on the table and came forward to shake hands. There was nothing in his manner to suggest an employer greeting a junior clerk. "Mr. Webster promised it was going to clear, but I can never tell what the weather's going to do when I'm away from home." He smiled. "I feel like a fish out of water here. Is everything all right at 42?"

"Yes, sir. Mr. Post sent me down with this letter."

Mr. Chevalier took it with raised brows, opened it, and asked young Ames's pardon for reading it.

"Did Mr. Post tell you what it was about?" he asked.

"He said it was from Paris, sir."

"It is. As long as you've been to so much trouble," Mr. Chevalier said kindly, "you might like to know what it's about. Of course it's confidential. It's from a connection of ours who happens to be in the Paris legation. He says that the rumour goes round that Louis Philippe has assured Mr. Livingston of his personal belief in the justice of our claims against his government and has suggested that a strong message from the President might have a beneficial effect on the French Chamber." Mr. Chevalier folded the letter thoughtfully and put it in his pocket. "If that's true, the chances are that General Jackson has received the same report from Mr. Livingston."

Mr. Chevalier's blue eyes got icy as they always did when he mentioned the President by name.

"Do you think it would make much difference in General Jackson's message, sir?"

Mr. Chevalier grinned.

"I don't know. This might be just the match he needs to set off some of his fireworks. He's probably hunting some new excitement to entertain the nation, now that he has killed the Bank. Bread and circuses!"

Young Ames said: "But according to this letter, sir, a strong message wouldn't do any harm."

" I imagine there's a good deal of difference between the King's notion of a strong message and Andrew Jackson's," Mr. Chevalier said dryly. " Instead of bringing them to reason, he's just as likely to bring us to war. Mr. Post saw the point. Post is a sharp man. We've been holding that Chesapeake tobacco for a rise in price, but it may be better to start it over before Congress convenes. Once the President's message is public, every one is likely to get the same idea."

" The *Erie* sails December first, sir," young Ames said. Mr. Chevalier nodded. " We have till the twenty-eighth to make up our minds."

Young Ames said hopefully, " Then you'll want me to go right back to-morrow, sir ? "

" To-morrow ? " Mr. Chevalier's blue eyes were fixed on young Ames's anxious face. Suddenly his lips twitched. " That seems hardly necessary, Ames. I fancy that the counting-room can spare you for an extra day or so, and you may be useful here. But if nothing turns up for you to do, you can enjoy your holiday getting acquainted with the capital. Now, let's go down. It's past dinner-time. We'll see Gadsby about finding you a room."

4

That night, before going to bed in the small room the manager had provided for him on the top floor, young Ames finished a disconsolate letter to Christine.

". . . so I shall probably be kept here until Mr. Chevalier is ready to return, which won't be before the end of the week. He asked me to have dinner with him to-night and bought a bottle of wine to go with the venison. I suppose he thinks he is being kind to give me a holiday, but I would like to tell him how much rather I would be in New York. I can think of no excuse but the right one, and it is not

possible to use that. He says I should see Washington and
to-morrow I am going to look at the Capitol, the State
Department where they have historical documents on view,
and the patent office, all of which Mr. Chevalier says one
should see. There is also the White House, but I think
there is little to see or be done here. I think the United
States could get along perfectly well without Washington
and I don't see why the capital wasn't left in New York
which is the logical place for it. Maybe it is more lively
here when Congress is in session, but from what I have
seen of Congressmen they are not much and wouldn't
know the difference between a packet and a parcel unless
it was explained. I do not mean some of the Senators,
like Mr. Webster or Mr. Calhoun, or Mr. Adams who
dropped in to see Mr. Chevalier in the evening. They are
all talking about what the President intends to do about
French debt. (Mr. Adams is a Representative, of course,
but he comes from Boston, which is nearly the same as
New York.) I suppose the only way I could expect to get
home sooner, would be for Mr. Chevalier to learn what the
President is going to say. . . ."

He mailed the letter next morning, after parting with
Mr. Chevalier on Pennsylvania Avenue. Mr. Chevalier
went off as if he were the only man in Washington who
knew where he was going and intended to get there. As he
watched the blue coat and white hat moving briskly away,
young Ames felt a stir of affection. Mr. Chevalier had laid
himself out to be pleasant, both last night and this morning
at breakfast. He had asked young Ames unobtrusive
questions about his upbringing. Across the table his blue
eyes had grown kinder, the bold arch of his brows had
relaxed as young Ames somewhat haltingly described his
family's poverty and his father's impracticality. "It's
too bad he is dead," said Mr. Chevalier. "He would have
been proud of what you've accomplished." Then he spoke
of his own early days, before New York had been handed

over to the hoodlum vote, as he called it, and there were
snipe on the Jersey flats across the Hudson. He had had
his own struggle to keep the firm floating during the
second war with England. " Then we had a weak-kneed
President," he said. " I always thought it a pity that Mr.
and Mrs. Madison could not have sorted out their qualities
and sexes to better advantage. And now we have an
Indian-fighting, democratic, as he styles himself, back-
woods duellist. Our country's big enough to survive either
extreme, but in international crises it's better to have a
man of judgment. There's nothing like a merchant's
training to create a balance of mind, Ames."

Young Ames smiled as he remembered Mr. Chevalier's
face. It had been as fiery as any display one could imagine
the President's bringing forth.

He turned himself to the business of sight-seeing, for
there was nothing else to do ; and he did it thoroughly,
though historical documents meant little to him. He could
not see the difference it made now how Napoleon wrote
his signature. The only useful purpose in knowing a man's
handwriting was to guard against the possibility of forgery.

In the patent office, most of the patents that a patient
attendant turned over for his inspection seemed to him the
products of a wasted ingenuity. There was no money to
be made from most of them. Inventors notoriously died
in poverty, except for the few whose affairs had been taken
over by practical men, as, for instance, Robert Fulton's
had.

After lunch, he went to the Capitol, and as he mounted
the bold incline of steps, its impressiveness once more took
hold of his imagination. It was nearly devoid of visitors,
and his heels rang with startling clarity in the lofty rotunda.
As he stared at the paintings over his head—Washington
resigning the Presidency, Jefferson signing the Declaration
of Independence ; they seemed placed too high for him
to see them clearly—he had a sense of his own smallness.
Suddenly he was assailed by doubts of the ability of men

of the merchant classes, like Mr. Chevalier, to continue indefinitely their power in the national destiny. When, after two hours, he walked away from the Capitol, he felt himself dwarfed by what it represented.

He wished Christine could have been with him, for he had an intuition that her warmth of heart would have transmuted his own doubts. She had a gift for understanding what people looked for, as she had so quickly understood his own hunger and fright and lack of confidence the first time he had made his way to Mr. Chevalier's parlour. A small brooch in a jeweller's window caught his eye, and not letting himself be daunted by the cost, he went in and bought it for her.

The sun was setting when he came out on the sidewalk with his purchase and he walked on down the avenue, watching the colours spread and slowly fade. He felt happier ; he kept his hand on the little box in his pocket ; and wanting suddenly to examine it again, he cast about for a place where he could do so without attracting attention.

The White House was in front of him. He saw it in the waning light, white and pillared, surrounded by lawns and trees.

5

The brooch was merely a bar of gold holding an amethyst, but it was the first piece of jewellery he had ever bought. He knew that Christine had far more valuable jewels, but he felt no doubts of her liking it, and in a way it would take the place of the evenings they had expected to have together.

" Good-evening, sir."

" Good-evening." Young Ames looked up with a start. He had heard no one coming ; he had expected no one to come along this walk so far below the White House. It was nearly dark, and the bench was in an almost hidden corner. Then as he looked at the tall figure leaning on the cane, he scrambled to his feet.

The man raised his hand. " Sit down, sir. I didn't intend to disturb you. I saw you were looking at a pin."

" Yes, sir." Young Ames stammered a little. " It's just a pin I bought for a friend."

He stared at the thin pale face, with its straight features and clear eyes and white hair showing below the hat brim.

" Would you let me see it ? "

He took the box from young Ames's hand and held it close to his eyes.

" It's pretty," he said. " Whoever she is, she'll surely like it."

" Do you think so, sir ? It's not much of a pin."

" She will, if she's worth the gift, sir." His eyes went shrewdly over young Ames.

" She's worth a good deal more," young Ames said quickly.

" Then she's sure to like it. Sit down, sir. Do you mind if I sit down also ? I've done my walk and there's still a few minutes till dinner. My name's Andrew Jackson."

" Mine is John Ames."

Andrew Jackson sat down beside him and rested his hands on the head of his stick. For a moment he was silent ; his eyes were fixed on the line of trees, in the direction of the White House ; but he seemed to young Ames to be looking at something far beyond. " It's good to have a woman you can buy things for. The first pin I bought was simpler even than yours," he said, with a quick shy smile. " It had no stone at all. That was a long time ago, Mr. Ames," he went on. " Long before it had ever occurred to me that I might some day sit here. Well, I have only two years more, before I can go home."

He did not talk like the kind of man young Ames had pictured to himself. He seemed sad, and a good deal older in heart, and young Ames felt moved and a little shaken.

" Didn't you want to be President, sir ? "

" Not especially. That is, not till Henry Clay traded his constituents for the secretary's office. Then I had to be elected whether I liked it or not." His voice had a quick hard ring as he said that. " I didn't want it for myself ; I was past the age at which a man likes personal triumph ; I had to be elected to vindicate the people of the United States. Henry Clay had to be whipped." The knuckles showed whiter on his hands, and young Ames saw why the people called him Old Hickory.

" Dealing sharp is all right, if the deal is honest. Henry Clay is an able man, but when he licked me he licked himself. He still wants to be President, but he never will be now. The American people will never elect a man who has shown that he wants office for the sake of personal power. Once they've learned that about a man, they'll put him down, sir," he said more quietly. " Just as they've put down Nicholas Biddle."

" I should think you'd had a hand in that, sir," young Ames said.

The President stiffened. " I don't deny the imputation, Mr. Ames. But mark you, I couldn't have reached the first quarter-turn if the people hadn't backed me. Nicholas Biddle knows it now, but he learned hard. He tried to break the American people for his own ends, but they wouldn't be broken."

" Didn't you have any doubts of it ? "

" I was shaking in my shoes," said Andrew Jackson, " but I knew Nicholas Biddle was shaking in an Ionic Temple. I didn't have any doubts about the people. I've fought with them and drank with them and been black-guarded by them. No, sir, I shook with my own doubts. But that's a Presidential privilege." The warm smile returned, and he asked : " Is this your first visit to Washington, Mr. Ames ? "

" Yes, sir."

" I wish more young people like yourself came here. But you ought to come while Congress is in session. Reading speeches is not like hearing them and seeing the man."

" I can see that."

Andrew Jackson glanced at him sharply. Then he laughed. " You mean me ? "

" Yes, sir," young Ames said seriously.

" What did you suppose I was like ? "

Young Ames began to feel that he had ventured pretty far. But it was impossible to dodge the General's clear stare.

" I'd thought you were more . . ." He hesitated.

" Violent, perhaps ? "

" Yes, perhaps."

" Do you belong to the Whig Party ? "

" I don't vote."

" You're a politic young man." But he sounded pleased.

" You see, sir," young Ames explained, " I got most of my impressions on the Mississippi River. I once passed myself off as a confidential agent of yours, at least I allowed the impression to gain weight. I had been told by my boss to beat the mails to New Orleans and that seemed the likeliest way to get action out of the steamboat captain."

" Did you beat the mail ? "

" Very easily. Captain Stankard said he'd do anything to help you beat the Bank. He said you'd made Biddle look like a stumptail bull in fly time."

" Not Amory Stankard ? " Andrew Jackson asked with high delight. " There's your fire-eater. He's your real American. He can yell louder, fight harder, and laugh louder than fifty sinners, but he's as good a gentleman as John Forsyth. But you couldn't persuade some of a small class we have here in this country that he wasn't half an alligator. Those people haven't outgrown Europe yet, Mr. Ames. They got what they wanted out of the Revolution, but now they want to sit down on it. This country can't ever sit down. I've been in parlours in Boston and New York it was an honour to go into, but I tell you the knick-knacks on the mantelpiece had a better idea of the American Eagle than the human occupants. He's a bird you can't keep perched. He only looks like something when he's on the wing." He chuckled. " I'd like to confront Louis Philippe with Amory Stankard. Tell me about your trip with him, Mr. Ames. That is, if you have a few minutes to spare."

It was the first time young Ames had ever told any one the full story of gambling away Mr. Chevalier's money, but he had a feeling that Andrew Jackson would understand.

The General listened to it all in silence, only snorting to himself when Captain Stankard hitched his steamboat to the river house. " Amory must have taken a fancy to you," he said. " I guess he thought you'd take the lesson to heart."

" Yes, sir."

" This Mr. Chevalier of yours," pursued the General. " I've heard about him. He's led petitions for the Bank. In fact he brought one to the White House. When I told him to go to Nicholas Biddle, I thought he had a bit of the American Eagle in his eye. He'd do well wherever he was ; I could have used him at New Orleans. What does he think of the French debt ? "

" I couldn't say, sir."

" No. Quite right. But what do you think yourself ? "

" I don't know much about it. The city's worried over the possibility of war."

" Are you, Mr. Ames ? "

" I was," young Ames said honestly.

" Thank you," the General said seriously. " The money's not worth fighting for. Money never is. But we're a young country, and Europe, like some of our seaboard classes, still thinks of us as a small line of disunited states. They'll have to be shown we have a sense of our own dues.

No, Mr. Ames, you don't kill a man because he owes you
the price of a horse. You bring public opinion to bear
against him. Some people who speak of law forget that
law is only the expression, morally, of what the people
think is right. Public opinion is the one thing, no matter
what they say, that even emperors are afraid of. If it's
united. We've got to show ours is united. It will be on
this question, it will be evident even to the Deputies and
Louis Philippe. So there'll be no war, but . . ." the
General said dryly, " there won't be any doubt about
our views. The American people must learn that if they
stand together, they can lick the world."

He paused to glance at Ames, and young Ames, meeting
his eye in the gathering dusk, knew he had the answer to
what Mr. Chevalier would like to know.

6

" But I've been talking politics, Mr. Ames. You've
bought a pin and you were thinking of a lady. If not,
you should have been."

Young Ames realised with a start that he was still holding
the little box in his hand. He restored it to his pocket.

" Are you planning to be married soon, Mr. Ames ? "

His genuine interest made young Ames answer frankly.

" We've made no plans, sir." He hesitated. " You see,
I've only a little money saved up. My salary isn't a great
deal. And in New York, a junior clerk hasn't much standing unless he comes of an old family."

" That situation is not confined to New York," the
General said dryly. " You're not ashamed of your family,
are you ? "

" Of course not. They just didn't have money."

" Well," said Andrew Jackson, " I don't see what's
hindering you. I always believed it didn't matter whether
a man married early or late in his life. But once he's

found the right woman, he's a fool to miss a minute, sir. This girl of yours isn't the hesitant kind, is she?"

"No, sir."

"Hesitation in a woman is a pleasant enough form of coquetry. But a woman who says she's in love with a man and then holds back had better not marry at all."

"It's not for ourselves." Young Ames paused. But Jackson's obviously sympathetic interest overcame his doubts. "Our trouble's Mr. Chevalier," he blurted out.

"She's his daughter?" asked the General quickly.

"No, sir. His niece by marriage," young Ames explained. "But he thinks of her like a daughter. He's never had children of his own, and he's been kind to her."

"I understand." The General blew his nose. "Has he forbidden the marriage?"

"We haven't spoken to him yet."

"For heaven's sake, why not? He has a right to know." The General lowered his voice. "It's natural for a man to feel possessive about his daughter, or a girl he holds in place of a daughter in his affections. Perhaps even more so then, especially if he's old."

"Yes, sir. I think that's so with Mr. Chevalier. And Kisty wouldn't want to hurt him. Neither would I," he said, as he remembered Mr. Chevalier's kindness the night before.

The General was silent for a moment. His head drooped thoughtfully towards his folded hands.

"Has it occurred to you two young people that he might be far more hurt by your not having confidence in him? I've no right to offer you advice," he went on almost shyly, "but if I were he, that's how I should feel." As he looked up, young Ames could just make out the smile on the white face. It had a kind of tenderness he hadn't expected. "I should go straight to him, man to man, and tell him, if I were you. Tell him you love her and that she loves you. That's something he can't get around, Mr.

Ames, but if he says no, why, you can elope, can't you ?
She's old enough ? "

" Yes, sir."

The General stabbed the gravel with his cane.

" Come to Washington on your wedding trip," he said.
" *I'll* give you my blessing."

Young Ames grinned. It occurred to him that there was
a great deal in common between Mr. Chevalier and
Andrew Jackson. Impulsively, he said so.

" Is there ? " said the General. He got slowly to his
feet and young Ames rose with him. He towered a good
head taller than young Ames. In the darkness it was hard
to make out whether he was offended ; but with an abrupt
motion he held out his hand. " In that case, Mr. Ames,
I don't think you have much to worry about. Good luck.
And when it's settled, kiss your Miss Christine for me,
will you ? "

7

Standing in the entrance to Gadsby's dining-room,
young Ames hunted between the figures of the coloured
waiters for Mr. Chevalier's table. He sat there, by himself.

He sat erect, the shoulders squared under the blue coat,
his vigorous white hair rising back from his forehead, his
eyes staring into the glass of wine he held under his slightly
arrogant nose. It occurred to young Ames that it was
much easier for General Jackson to lay down the law than
for himself to execute it. He moved slowly towards the
table.

Mr. Chevalier's china-blue eyes picked him out at once.

" Well, Ames," he said, " you've made a long day of it."

" Yes, sir."

" Sit down," said Mr. Chevalier. " Jerry, bring Mr.
Ames a helping of the bluefish. It's very good. What
will you have for soup ? "

" I don't care for soup, sir. I never liked it."

" You should. A good soup is the soul of any dinner,
Ames. We merely fill our bellies with the meat. Nature
produces fowl and fish, but it takes man to make a
soup."

His voice brightened. Young Ames realised that Mr.
Chevalier had been lonely. He diffidently accepted the
soup Mr. Chevalier ordered, and at his request recited
the sights he had taken in.

" What have you done since five ? You couldn't have
been in the Capitol."

" I went to a store, sir," young Ames told him.

Mr. Chevalier smiled.

" You bought a present ? "

" Yes, sir."

" That's the only good part of being away from home.
Buying presents to bring back. As a matter of fact, I did
the same thing this afternoon. I found a first-rate shawl
for Mrs. Chevalier and bought a pin for my niece. It's a
coincidence in a way, isn't it ? "

Young Ames gulped and said : " Yes." He looked up
to find Mr. Chevalier's eyes studying him. Seeing his
embarrassment, Mr. Chevalier looked away. He was
smiling, however, as he said : " What did you do then,
Ames ? "

" I spent an hour with Andrew Jackson."

" You did ? Upon my word ! " Mr. Chevalier set down
his glass and stared. " What did you talk about ? "

" Henry Clay and our claims against the French, for
two things," said young Ames. A little of his confidence
returned.

" I'm confounded," said Mr. Chevalier. " What did he
have to say ? "

" He said the American Eagle was a bird you couldn't
keep on a perch. He only looks like something when he's
on the wing."

Mr. Chevalier snorted. " Demagogic phrases ! He's

right enough. It depends, though, which way he flies.
What did he say about the French ? "

" He said the American people have to learn that if
they stand together, they can face the world. I think he
means to use the business with France to do that. He says
no money is worth fighting for, not for its own sake. He
said there'd be no war if we showed France we stood
united."

Mr. Chevalier said thoughtfully : " Of course he's right
in that. The pity is that he's done more to divide the
country than any man since George the Third. But he
knows people." He glanced up. " Sometimes I have a
feeling he may prove right about the Bank. Mr. Biddle
showed a streak of ruthlessness that wasn't becoming."

It was the nearest to an admission that young Ames was
ever to hear Mr. Chevalier make.

" He told me once to go to Nicholas Biddle. The para-
phrase was obvious, and I suppose he believed it. He
might have been a great President if he had been willing
to take the advice of sound men in money matters. What
did you think of him ? "

" I liked him," young Ames said simply. " He was very
kind to me." He felt the blood rush to his face and his
heart begin to pound. For a minute he had the feeling
that the whole dining-room had withdrawn from their
table, and that he and Mr. Chevalier were sitting alone
on a high, precarious pillar. It seemed like a long jump
down. " He gave me some advice."

Mr. Chevalier was looking at him oddly. " Advice ? "
he said.

" It was personal advice," said young Ames hesitantly.

" How did he come to do that ? "

" He saw me looking at a pin I bought. You said, sir,
it was a coincidence that we both bought pins. As a
matter of fact, we bought them for the same person."

After a moment he looked up. Mr. Chevalier's eyes
stared expressionlessly at him.

"Christine," he said.

Young Ames nodded.

There was a long pause.

"Let's finish our dinner and go upstairs," Mr. Chevalier said, breaking it.

Eating the rest of his dinner was one of the hardest jobs young Ames was ever to tackle. But he was conscious of Mr. Chevalier's eyes, and he stuck doggedly to it, though the bluefish might have been Nashua Brown Sheeting, for all the taste it had.

Mr. Chevalier lit the lamp carefully in his sitting-room, pulled up two chairs beside it, and said : "Sit down, Ames." He waited till Ames was seated before seating himself. Then he said : "I suppose you think this has shocked me."

"I suppose so, sir."

"Has Christine any knowledge of your feelings ? "

"Yes, sir. She feels the same way."

"I've had an inkling of it. I didn't know it had progressed so far. I suppose it was Andrew Jackson who advised you to speak to me ? "

"Yes."

Mr. Chevalier smiled thinly. "It's the way he keeps the Eagle on the wing, I suppose," he said dryly. "You've done very well for a young man, Ames. Remarkably well. I have a high regard for your talents though I have always told you I considered you unscrupulous. It appears that Christine has succumbed to the same trend of the times. You realise, of course, that she is going to inherit a good deal of money ? Not as much as before the panic Mr. Jackson and Mr. Biddle engineered between them, but still a good deal of money."

"Yes, sir. But I shall make money for us both. We won't have to depend on what comes to her."

"It's not so easy as you may think from your first fortunate venture," said Mr. Chevalier. "What made you decide to speak to me to-night ? "

"General Jackson pointed out that it was hardly fair to you not to. Christine didn't want to hurt your feelings in any way, and I had thought in a year or two I would have more money."

"Money!" exploded Mr. Chevalier, rather illogically. "The money doesn't matter. Haven't I said she would inherit plenty?"

"Yes, sir. But it matters to me."

"I suppose that's so. But do you realise what it costs to support a woman like Christine as she has lived in my family?"

"Yes, sir. But she's going to live with me."

"And like it, I suppose."

"I hope so, sir." He looked up anxiously. "She says she would make a useful wife to a poor man. But we won't stay poor."

"But you would like my consent?"

"Of course. She says she won't marry without it."

For the first time, Mr. Chevalier's eyes showed signs of softening. "Blackmail?" he asked.

Young Ames grinned.

"No, sir. Not on her part."

"But it wouldn't be safe to push her too far?"

"I don't suppose it would."

Mr. Chevalier got up, and suddenly he changed the subject. "I think we can assume safely what the drift of the President's message is going to be. We'll start home to-morrow, and I'll ship our tobacco. Run out and get seats for us on the Baltimore coach, will you? And then come back here."

8

When young Ames returned to the private parlour, Mr. Chevalier was seated again with a small jeweller's box under the lamp on the table.

" Did you get seats ? "

" Yes, sir."

Mr. Chevalier was silent a minute or two.

Then he said : " I've decided I should talk to Christine herself before we discuss this affair any further. She's of age to speak for herself."

" I know, sir."

" May I see your pin ? " he asked. " I got mine out to show you."

He opened his box, and young Ames stared at a heart-shaped brooch of diamonds framing a single pearl. He knew what it must have cost, and his hands shook as he opened his own small box and laid it on the table beside Mr. Chevalier's. The contrast spoke for itself. He felt his face flushing, and he felt resentment rising, and he looked up angrily, and swallowed what he was going to say. Christine, he knew, wouldn't care a fip's worth.

Mr. Chevalier was still looking at the pins.

" They're both in excellent taste," he said. Then he looked into his junior clerk's eyes. " My wife is very fond of pearls," he said. " As soon as I saw it I knew I had to buy it for her. But I'm troubled about the shawl. I've never bought a scarlet shawl for Kisty. Do you think she'll like the colour ? "

Young Ames picked up the brooch.

" Scarlet ? " he said in a puzzled voice. Then, as he studied Mr. Chevalier's face, he caught on. " Yes, sir," he said. " I'm sure she will."

XI

A CHRISTMAS ROSE FOR AMES

IT had begun snowing at six o'clock in the afternoon. In the darkness below young Ames's window the East River flowed an utter black past the whitened piers ; the rigging of the docked ships made a silvery web ; and a lone cart, bound homeward up South Street, printed a noiseless track.

Sitting close to the fire, his glass of gin and lemon in his hand, Gibbs watched as young Ames gave up his attempt to brush his sandy hair into neatness and reached for his dress coat.

" Remember when you tried it on, Johnny ? "

Young Ames looked down with a grin. He knew the other's moods. Now that Gibbs had broken the silence, he could tell that his friend was not going to lapse into one of his morbid fits of solitary drinking.

" I tried it on in your room and you said it fitted too damned well, and so did a winding sheet."

" Did I ? I wasn't thinking of that." Gibbs drained his glass, set it down. His smiles were rare things, but his dark face was lighted now. " I was thinking of a youngster, too poor to buy a coat, who kept himself from acting scared by being cocksure he could lick the world." As the kettle started steaming, he hooked the crane forward from the flames to add water to his replenishment of gin. A vapour of lemon blossomed through the shabby room.

" I wasn't cocksure about going into Mr. Chevalier's house, especially when I found him there himself." Ames settled the coat on his shoulders and tried to see himself in the cracked mirror. " Every time I put it on I can see the way he looked at me. I don't see why he didn't fire me."

"I don't either," said Gibbs. "But I guess it was the same reason that made me lend you a shirt that day, and made your Christine look twice at you?"

"What's that?"

"That's a secret she and I are going to have in common," Gibbs said. "Maybe you can get it out of her, but I doubt it. I shan't tell you. When are you going to be married?"

"I don't know. Mr. Chevalier's going to talk to us to-night. He said in Washington he'd do it when we got back, but then when we came home, Christine's stepfather was dying, and we had to put it off. It broke Mr. Chevalier up. He hadn't seen his brother for a long time."

"I know," Gibbs said thoughtfully, "Louis's wife came between them, but she's let Christine practically live with the George Chevaliers. I've never been able to figure that out. It got so bitter that apparently George turned over the details of Louis's estate to Mr. Deming rather than have to see her himself. You haven't ever seen her, have you, Johnny?"

"No."

"She's got lots of style, and she looks young enough to be her daughter's sister. Before Louis had his stroke, she used to be seen all over town with him—horse races, sailing boxes at Niblo's. She started rowing parties round Manhattan Island. I remember her coming into the counting room with him; the old buck was proud as a peacock of her, and she was vivacious, very vivacious. You could hear her and Mr. Deming laughing through the closed door." Gibbs stirred his gin with the stem of his pipe. "It makes it all the queerer, the way she has shut herself up with the old fellow since he became sick. Long over a year, and nobody I know of goes to the house, except Deming when there are papers to be signed.

"Papers? Was he fit to sign papers?" Young Ames looked up curiously. "Christine told me he couldn't talk."

"I don't know about that. I overhead Deming tell Post
one day that the poor fellow could make himself understood all right."

"It sounds queer," said young Ames. "I don't see what
kind of papers he would have to sign."

"Leases, I suppose," Gibbs answered carelessly. "Most
of Louis's money is in tenement real estate."

"I didn't know that."

"Oh yes," Gibbs said dryly. "At first his real estate
must naturally gravitated into the tenement class, like the
negro section on Madison Street. He learned the advan-
tages from them, I guess, and he developed an eye for the
business. He even went into building here and there—
those six-story tenements on Mott Street, for instance. You
get the tax rate lowered on property like that, but if you
fill them full enough, they'll earn as much as a Broadway
mansion. More nett, for the upkeep doesn't figure to any
extent. Louis handled the business through agents, so his
name didn't come into it at all ; and he belongs to a
dozen beneficent societies, so his conscience doesn't either.
I doubt if it would anyway." Gibbs's voice grew wry. "I
doubt if the old fellow ever went through a street like
Madison in his life."

"How do you know about it, Howard ? "

Gibbs waved his hand.

"Deming tipped me once to copy some contracts after
hours. It was before you came here. The agents are
Vultee and Agate."

"Deming ? " young Ames asked. "How did he happen
to come into the firm, Howard ? "

"He had political connections in Albany. They were
necessary for licences, especially for a firm like this that
had worked actively against Andrew Jackson."

"I see." Young Ames hesitated. "He's always been
nice to me."

"I don't doubt it. He's a very pleasant man. He's
stood me a drink more than once, especially since he found

I was a distant connection of the family. But he don't give me any more copying." Gibbs put his nose in his glass.

" Have you any idea how much money Louis Chevalier had, Howard ? "

" Oh, about a quarter million, more or less."

" I wish he hadn't."

" Why not ? "

" It's not my idea how to get rich."

Gibbs understood. " It's got nothing to do with you, Johnny. Nor with your Christine. Hadn't you better cut along ? George Chevalier don't like dawdling clerks, and he won't like it any better in a son-in-law."

Young Ames grinned. " I'm on my way." But as he glanced back from the door, he saw something lonely in the slump of the lean back under the shabby, well-cut coat. " When I come home, Howard, I'll let you know when you'll have to be my best man."

Gibbs's head jerked.

" Johnny . . ."

But young Ames had closed the door. He was clattering down the dark flight ; and Gibbs was left to his gin and lemon, the fire, and the last heavy echo under the roof as the front door slammed.

· 2

The snow had silenced the city. Buses and hackney coaches rolled up and down Broadway with scarcely any sound. Drifting through the street lights, flakes whitened the shoulders of pedestrians and hushed their voices. Even the cries of newsboys and hot-cake girls had lost their stridence.

" Buy one." A girl opened her basket in front of Ames and fell into step beside him. " It's my last. Maybe it's lucky, mister."

He gave her five cents. " No change," he said. " That's

for luck too." He saw her smile under her shawl as he licked the sugar from his fingers.

"See, mister. Luck's sticking to you."

"I hope you're right."

He had been mulling over Gibbs's remarks about Louis Chevalier's investments ; but he could not figure out what part Mr. Deming had played in the business. It was hard to know anything about Mr. Deming. Mr. Deming was always behind a laugh, or a joke, or a clap on the back.

But the hot-cake girl's smile put the problem out of his head. It was late. As he hurried round the corner into the foot of Hudson Street, the bell of St. John's began to strike eight o'clock. The notes came with the snow through the dark sky, and other church bells over the city took up the hour. He was supposed to call at eight, and he still had seven blocks to go.

During Louis Chevalier's final illness, he had had only glimpses of Christine. But one evening when she was called back to her stepfather's house, they had stolen a few moments as he escorted her across the Park.

"Father Louis has been so ill, I didn't feel it was right to tell Mother about us," she said. "But I will as soon as he gets a little better."

"Do you think he's going to ?"

"I don't know. He's very ill, and he can't say any-thing," she had said. "Mother doesn't allow me to go into his room." She stopped walking, standing beside him for a moment in silence. Then she said : "It's a dreadful thing to say, John, but I don't want to. He makes such helpless sounds, and nobody but Mother seems to under-stand him." He thought she shivered. "I wish I didn't have to stay there so much. I want to see you all the time, John. But Uncle George has been sweet."

"Did he say anything about us ?"

"He only said you'd told him. He said he'd come to know you much better in Washington and on the way home. But he thinks we're young and he wants us to think seriously about ourselves."

" I have."

" So have I." She paused again. " John. Mother said something about some day going back to Charleston. She wants to buy back our old house and put it in order. She was full of plans of what we would do."

" You don't want to go ? " he asked in sudden panic.

" Don't be silly. I wouldn't go. She couldn't make me."

As they stood close to one another in the shadow of the high iron fence, young Ames had thought that it was easy to talk bravely. But suppose her mother insisted and suppose Mr. Chevalier, who had strict ideas of propriety, backed her up. He would be Christine's legal guardian, and her affection for him would be an added argument.

She read his thoughts.

" Oh, John, wild horses couldn't drag me away now ! " Looking up at his doubtful face she had twisted her fingers in his scarf and pulled his head down to kiss him. Her lips were cool in the frosty air. " Don't you believe that ? "

3

Scraping the snow from his shoes on the foot brush while he waited for Amber to answer his knock, he could see lights in the dead man's house across the Park. It was the first time he remembered seeing any lights in the downstairs windows, and he had an uneasy sense of something hostile in them. Until the last few days he had never given much thought to Christine's mother, but now she seemed to be coming into his life, step by step, in a way of her own, as if the entire sequence were of her choosing. Christine rarely mentioned her ; he didn't even know what she looked like.

" I wish you good-evening, Mr. Ames."

Amber had noiselessly opened the door and was bowing
with becoming gravity.

" Mr. Chevalier's expecting you, sir."

" I'm afraid I'm late."

" Oh hardly, Mr. Ames."

The coloured butler conducted him to the sitting-room.
" It's Mr. Ames, Miss Christine," he announced.

He had never seen her wear black before ; it made her
seem taller, and a small wave of excitement went over
him. She saw it in his eyes, and her lips curved. She came
to him without a word and kissed him.

" John, dear."

She looked up into his face from his arms and then
disengaged herself as Amber lifted his voice in the hall.

" Mr. Ames just came this minute, Mr. Chevalier."

" Yes, yes, I know. You needn't shout, Mr. Amber,"
said Mr. Chevalier.

" Amber's a dear," Christine said. " He knows all the
proper sentimental gambits."

" Gambits ? "

" Didn't you ever play chess, John ? I've something to
teach you then. You'll love it. Uncle, imagine ! John
doesn't know how to play chess," she said, as Mr. Chevalier
came through the door.

Young Ames turned, searching Mr. Chevalier's face.
Mr. Chevalier held out his hand.

" Good-evening, John."

Young Ames swallowed hard. It was the first time Mr.
Chevalier had called him by his first name. Christine's
eyes were shining.

" Sit down, Kisty. And you too, John. I want to look
at you both.. Stir up the fire first." Mr Chevalier spread
his coat-tails and took the chair on the other side of the
hearth. " I can see that you are still bent on getting
married, though I urged Kisty to think it over carefully.
You're both younger than I suppose you feel yourselves

to be. Kisty's not eighteen and you're how old, John? Nineteen?"

"Yes, sir."

Christine said : "Aunt Chevalier said she was sixteen when she married you, Uncle George."

Mr. Chevalier smiled.

"So that makes you a proper age, I expect, Kisty? But I was twenty, you see. I was a mature man."

"Aunt Chevalier told me she took that into account," Christine said demurely.

"She did, did she? You seem to have got her on your side," he said, smiling. He looked into the fire for a moment. "John," he said. "Some people might think it very soon after my brother's funeral to be discussing marriage plans, but what people think don't need to enter into our lives. I didn't want to keep you up on a wire through the holidays, for as Kisty and my wife pointed out, I actually was twenty myself once. But this morning my brother's will was read to the family by Mr. Duane." He paused. "It's caused me some surprise. I told you once that Kisty was going to be a very wealthy woman, John. Of course I knew the terms of Louis's will and they're the same. Kisty and her mother were to share the estate." He looked up. "I'm telling you this, John, because you are going to be a member of the family."

"Yes, sir." Young Ames was dazed by the matter-of-fact way in which Mr. Chevalier made this announcement.

"Something strange seems to have happened in the past few years. The will contains a series of codicils turning over practically all of Christine's share to her mother, outright."

Young Ames met Christine's eyes. She nodded.

"I'm really quite poor, John."

One of the logs hissed in the fireplace, and they all turned their eyes to it. When it had quieted, young Ames said slowly : "We don't need a great deal to live on. I've saved up six thousand dollars. And Mrs. Funk is making money in Pittsburg. She wants to send me fifty dollars, but of course I'll put that back in the business."

"Of course you should," Christine said seriously.

"What's this about Mrs. Funk?" asked Mr. Chevalier. "Oh, the widow of that fellow you bought the paintings from. I didn't know you'd set her up in business." He smiled. "It's always sound to feed your profits back into your firm. I don't doubt you two will get along if you have to, though it's always easier to do it in plans."

He brushed that aspect aside.

"I want to talk about Louis's will," he went on. "Kisty knows what I think, and I believe she feels the same way. I don't believe my brother was competent when those codicils were drawn. Christine's mother never allowed me to see him. She said he was too ill. And I didn't want to put my nose in where it wasn't wanted. Deming handled the details of the estate for the same reason and McVitty balanced his books and gave me a summary. Deming made a good record. I knew my sister-in-law disliked me, so I let things alone." He stared at young Ames, his china-blue eyes growing frosty. "The codicils seem perfectly proper, on the surface. The witnesses are honourable men. Field and Drinker, for instance. Lord knows how she hoodwinked them into believing a man who could neither talk nor write was competent, but they must have thought so or they wouldn't have signed. And the codicils were not entirely in her benefit. There were some bequests to Louis's favourite benevolent institutions. And another thing they include is naming new executors—a lawyer named Vultee and herself. The only thing, apparently, that she overlooked was the will's naming me as Kisty's guardian."

It was obvious to Ames that the old gentleman had been deeply hurt.

"I'm glad you still are, sir."

"Glad!" Christine exclaimed. "I'd be desperate if it were any one else."

"You're both good," Mr. Chevalier said abruptly. "But that's how it stands. I hate dishonest dealing. I'm not going to see Kisty done out of what is rightfully hers. I think the will can be broken and I'm going to do it if I can. It won't be a pleasant process. There's bound to be a scandal."

Christine said : "Why must we, Uncle ? John and I don't need the money."

"It's my duty to protect your interests."

"Even if I don't want them protected ? "

"You're too young legally to say what you want, Kisty. Besides, if you and John have children, they ought to be considered."

"John can provide for all of us," Christine said quickly.

Young Ames glanced at her. Her eyes were bright and her cheeks were flushed. She had never looked lovelier to him, even the first time he had seen her, singing to the street beggar's organ.

Mr. Chevalier smiled at her. "I don't think you realise all it means, Kisty. But she says she's going back to Charleston right away and she's taking Kisty with her."

Christine looked at young Ames. "I told her I wouldn't go."

"Did you tell her why ? "

"Yes." She hesitated and then went on with flushed cheeks. "She only laughed at me. She said she'd never give her consent to my marrying a clerk. When I said we'd elope, she said she'd have the marriage broken. I got quite angry, I'm afraid, but she was calm as could be. I told her I wouldn't marry any one else, and that I'd come back to New York as soon as I was over age."

"You see," said Mr. Chevalier, "from her point of view, it's less a matter of your marrying than of taking Christine away from my wife and me. But maybe if you did elope, she'd give up the notion of breaking the marriage. A *fait accompli* is something no one can get around."

He rubbed his nose. It was the first time young Ames had ever seen him baffled.

" I don't want to elope," he said. " I want to marry Christine with you there, sir, and Gibbs for my best man, and Christine's friends."

" I'm glad you said that, John," Mr. Chevalier said. " Kisty's like a daughter to us, and my wife and I always hoped she'd be married from our house. But if she has to go South with her mother it will be only for a little over a year."

Christine started to speak ; but she changed her mind, leaning back in her chair and letting her hands rest in her lap, a very picture of a young lady content to leave the settlement of her affairs in the hands of her menfolk. But young Ames detected a glint of amusement in her eyes, and grinned at her.

" I don't think we'll have to wait that long. I want to speak to Christine's mother."

Mr. Chevalier stirred himself.

" Do you think it will do any good ? "

" I think so, sir. We've your permission, which was what we wanted most."

" You'd better not tell her that," Mr. Chevalier said, with a note of bitterness. " But you have my blessing, both of you." He rose abruptly and offered John his hand while he kissed Christine. " Good-night. Will you see her home, John ? "

When he had left them, Christine said : " Poor Uncle," then, looking at young Ames with troubled eyes : " Do you mind, John ? "

" Mind ? About the money ? I'm glad it isn't ours."

" No, no. I mean all this. About the way she changed the will. It's not exactly her fault. She's always wanted to be rich more than anything in the world, and to go back to our old house and live the way she used to." She made a quick gesture with her hand. " You must believe she was kind to Father Louis. She was, and she nursed him devotedly. But all this planning to get the money in her own name. It's like stealing."

" It hasn't anything to do with us."

" It does with me. I'm her daughter."

" You're you," he said.

She leaned a little towards him, then came all the way. " It makes me feel ashamed. Even my skin feels ashamed. Do you mind kissing me, John ? "

After a moment she said : " You're so good. I felt sure you were that first time on the street ; I knew it when you came here to see me, wearing Uncle George's coat and looking so terribly scared. It's funny to think I felt sorry for you, and now I have to depend on you. You'll take care of me, won't you ? "

" Yes," he said, touching her hair. The pins came loose and the knot slipped with them.

" It's all at sixes, isn't it ? I'll have to take it down to fix it. Do you mind ? "

She plucked the pins from it and shook it down as she crossed the room to the mirror over the desk. Young Ames stayed by the hearth, watching her back as she re-coiled the knot, her quick fingers white in the dark plaits.

" You'll have to get used to this, you know," she told him round the last two pins. But he caught the forced gaiety in her voice and looked quickly at the mirror. Her eyes, regarding him from the glass, were almost desperately shy.

" You want to see Mother to-night, do you, John ? "

" No." He was going to have to plan for both of them. " You'd better ask her if I can come to-morrow, though. To-morrow evening."

" Yes, John." She left the mirror and came back to him. " Will you take me home now ? "

4

The scrape of a snow shovel woke young Ames. When he looked from the window, South Street stretched white and smooth in the light of a clear dawn. The line of the eaves hid the sidewalk, but the snow shovel scraped diligently on, and small loads of snow kept flying into view.

"That you, Pinky?"

"Good-morning, Mr. Ames." The office boy's voice floated up to him with shrill exuberance. Later he would regard all snow with dismal resignation, but the first fall was an event.

Ames dressed quickly, stirred his fire, and put on the kettle. He woke Gibbs. "I'm going down to shovel. Watch the kettle, will you?"

Pinky Finnegan, scarlet-faced, with a scarlet muffler wound around his throat, breathed on his knuckles and said: "Lord, ain't it fine, Mr. Ames? My Uncle Mike Dolan says we'll be on runners before New Year's."

They finished the walk together and cleared a space for carts and barrows along the kerb. Young Ames worked in silence. Since last night, when he had reported the state of affairs to Gibbs, he had been mulling over his method of approaching Louis Chevalier's widow.

"Pinky," he said. "Have you ever seen Mrs. Louis Chevalier?"

"Sure I have, dozens of times," said Pinky.

"What's she like?"

"Well," said Pinky, "she's what my Uncle Mike Dolan would call a fine female creature. She's pretty as Miss Christine—almost, that is. She wears handsome dresses. And she's scented lovely. It's Mounseer Leclerc's Bouquet d'Amour."

"How do you know?"

"Mr. Deming sent me to Hart's for it and the clerk let me put the stopper to my nose," said Pinky. "It's expensive. My Uncle Mike Dolan says you could buy twenty gallons of beer for the price of one small bottle of it. She's very nice," Pinky went on, "and she always sends me down to the kitchen for cookies."

"You must have been to her house a lot."

"Oh yes, Mr. Deming's always sending up papers for her to get signed, and she said it was a pity I wasn't older so I could witness Mr. Louis's signature. Not that he signs ; he only makes a cross and then she writes his name beside it for him."

"You're not supposed to look at the papers you carry," young Ames said sternly.

"I didn't. It fell out of my pocket and the seal was unstuck and the paper opened itself and I seen it picking it up," Pinky said at a straight gallop. "But besides that you don't have to see papers to know what's going on in a house. It's a wonderful fine house too, Mr. Ames. Will you live in it after you get married?"

"Hardly. In the first place she is against my marrying her daughter."

"She must be a fool," said Pinky. "Why don't you go up and drag it out of her, Mr. Ames?"

"It's hardly that easy."

Pinky wiped his nose thoughtfully along the handle of his shovel. "Uncle Mike says the way to handle a woman you have to know what she's afraid of, or make her afraid of something else. I suppose a lady like her would handle the same, being of the same female sex, Mr. Ames."

They had finished the shovelling and were walking in the front door. Pinky stopped on the stairs.

"Couldn't you elope and run off with Miss Christine? O'Conlon could stop for you in one of Davison's coaches and my uncle could bring along Williamson's cart for the baggage if it was after hours."

"That's a fine idea, Pinky. But neither of us wants to get married that way."

"It's to be in church then? It's better for business, and

if you put it in the papers beforehand there's nothing better than a wedding for drawing the interest of the voters, Uncle Mike says. Only he says it's safer to weed out the Dead Rabbits from the nearest bystanders so there won't be any brickbats among the shoes coming at you. There comes Mr. McVitty and I've not filled the sandboxes ! "

Young Ames went back upstairs to gulp his tea, which Gibbs had ready for him along with toast and a piece of smoked herring.

" Find out anything from Pinky, Johnny ? "

" Nothing except that Deming seems to have played hand in glove with her as well as sending her presents now and then. Perfume, for one thing. Pinky knew the name."

" He's a sharp little devil," Gibbs said.

Young Ames nodded. He still had no idea of what he would say to Christine's mother, and he hadn't made any progress when at eleven o'clock Pinky laid a note on his desk with a conspiratorial whisper that it was from her, herself, in the carriage.

He read it under cover of the daybook.

" DEAR JOHN,—Aunt Chevalier and I are on our way to see Mrs. Giraud, who has been so ill, for the day. Mother has consented to see you, though she refused for a long time, till I said you were coming anyway. So please come after supper to-night.

" My love always,

" CHRISTINE."

" P.S.—Aunt Chevalier says you must be very clever and will surely find a way to manage Mother ! She says you are the kind of man who naturally manages things— does that mean me, too ? "

He didn't feel clever ; he was afraid that Mrs. Louis Chevalier would leave him tongue-tied. She was the clever person. He had no more doubt than Mr. Chevalier himself that Louis was not capable when the codicils had

been drawn ; but she had foreseen obvious objections by
bringing in witnesses of impeccable standing, according to
Mr. Chevalier. Field and Drinker, whom he had mentioned, were both ministers.

Field. Young Ames pulled himself up on his stool.
Field was a crusader for abolitionist proceedings of any
sort. He was one of the leaders of the African mission of
which Louis Chevalier had been one of the officers, even
while he was landlord of one of the districts which the
mission served. No doubt that was why Mr. Field had
been called in. He would naturally feel sympathy for a
benefactor in such a sad state of health. Men like him
were too absorbed in the causes they worked for to see
the reality before their noses.

But it wasn't how Mr. Field had been led by the nose
that interested young Ames. It was what the preacher
stood for. What Pinky's Uncle Mike Dolan said about the
handling of the female sex made sense when you remembered that, he thought ; at least he would know when he
had seen Mrs. Louis Chevalier. But he wanted to see her
alone.

5

He was conscious of his own inexperience as he waited
in the front parlour on Beach Street. It was more richly
furnished than the George Chevaliers' ; and he was hot
from having hurried to get there after the counting-room
closed. Thank the Lord, he thought, that he had had
sense enough to put on his best coat.

The coloured maid who had admitted him announced
with a faint note of surprise that Mrs. Chevalier would see
him. Mr. Ames was please to wait. He dismissed her with
a nod and she tossed her head as she went down the hall.

But he was kept waiting, and after a minute or two he
got up from the gilded chair and went to the window. Just

up the street a cart was vending Christmas greens from house to house. It was fresh in from the country and had a powder of snow on holly, boughs, and driver. Snow had begun to fall again to-night ; perhaps Mike Dolan would be right about the city's being on runners by New Year's.

Behind him he heard a quick footfall in the hall ; but he stayed where he was, wishing to see her before she saw him. He had a shock when she entered.

She might for an instant have been Christine. She had the same dark hair, short nose, and full red mouth. But when she came under the chandelier he saw that her face was thinner and that her lips were set. Christine might look like that if she were angry or unhappy, he thought ; the mother's face showed none of her warmth of heart.

She stood looking round her ; she must have seen his hat on the hall table ; she knew he was there.

" Mr. Ames ? "

Her voice was clearer than Christine's.

" I'm sorry, Mrs. Chevalier," he said. " I was watching a Christmas cart, and I didn't hear you come in." .

" You're Mr. Ames ? "

" Yes."

" I thought you were coming at seven-thirty." He could see that she was annoyed, but it didn't sound in her voice.

" I know. Christine sent me a note. But I thought we could speak more freely alone."

" You must be aware that I am in mourning, and that your calling here is an intrusion, Mr. Ames."

" In that case, Mrs. Chevalier, you needn't have seen me," he said, trying to sound cool.

" I might have said offensive," she said.

" I think curious might have been a better word, madam."

She was still standing under the chandelier, her eyes now studying him openly. " You wish to marry my daughter," she said.

" I am going to do so," he said. " I thought that should be understood between us whether you decide to delay our marrying or not."

She smiled faintly.

" A year is apt to make a great difference in a young girl's views, Mr. Ames. I believe I understand Christine." She seated herself and tilted her face to look at him. The angle was becoming ; she seemed slighter, almost fragile, and completely feminine. No wonder, he thought, that Louis Chevalier had gone head over heels at the age of sixty. " Of course," she continued, " Christine admires your talent for making your way, and I must admit I do too. In this bustling vulgar city, it's inspiring to see a young man of no family or financial backing making money as you have. But there is a great deal more to marriage than a talent for making money. You see I know all about you, Mr. Ames."

" Yes, from Mr. Deming," he said bluntly.

" Why do you say that ? "

" It's fairly obvious, Mrs. Chevalier, I don't want to make an enemy of you ; I want to marry Christine. My people were as good stock as yours even though we class as Yankees. We just lacked money. The way you lacked money before you married Mr. Chevalier. I intend to make up the lack."

Her eyes became surprisingly frank.

" By the same means, Mr. Ames ? I mean by marrying my daughter ? That isn't very clever of you after all. My husband, you see, had money. Christine will never have a penny of that if she marries you."

" I don't expect it from her. I prefer not to make my money out of tenements."

" Indeed, Mr. Ames," she said coolly. " But I am merely taking what my husband willed to me. How he made it wasn't my responsibility. I shan't live here in any case."

" I know the terms of the will and how the codicils were made. I have my own informant too."

" Indeed," she said quietly.

" Yes. Pinky Finnegan, the office boy, admires me for some reason. He's insatiably curious about people like the Chevaliers. For instance, he even knows what perfume you wear. It's not queer, as he bought and delivered it."

Her eyes did not shift, but her hands smoothed her skirts slowly.

" You are even younger than you seem if you think you can frighten and upset me with innuendoes."

" I don't want to. Your arrangements with Mr. Deming don't concern Christine and me. I think myself that it would be a mistake to marry Mr. Deming."

" May I ask why, Mr. Ames? "

" Yes. What you have wanted more than anything, all these years, is to be able to live in Charleston in your old style. Isn't it? Do you think Mr. Deming fits the picture? " He did not wait for an answer. " You thought you could do that by marrying Louis Chevalier. But his brother induced him to come back here to live and you had to give in. They were fond of each other. And you were trapped, until Mr. Louis had his stroke. Then you made sure that once he had died you wouldn't have to stay here."

He waited. " Am I right? "

" Why ask? " She shrugged her shoulders. " It doesn't matter to me, you see, Mr. Ames, what a young man thinks or does not think about me."

" You've lived for it," he said quietly, " All these years. I must say I admire the way you've done it. You made a bargain with yourself and you've stuck to it to the last letter."

" You're a strange young man, Mr. Ames." She studied him with a new expression in her eyes. Then she said quietly, " I think my daughter is cleverer than I gave her credit for."

" I'm not strange at all. It's what I said, Mrs. Chevalier. We're pretty much alike." He remembered that Christine had once said the same thing to him. It wasn't exactly true but it did not matter, as long as he meant it now.

Her voice softened.

" It wasn't as hard as you think to be nice to Louis. You see, he had never been happy before, and it took very little effort to make him so. He had always been second fiddle to his brother, though he was the older. He wasn't as bright or as hard as George ; he knew it. I tried to get him away, but I couldn't. It, it was like . . . it doesn't matter what it was like. He liked to show off. I was a kind of achievement, probably the first he had ever engineered without his brother's help."

" Yes." Young Ames paused. " Now you're determined to go back to Charleston and set up in your old style. You still have the house ? "

" Yes. They wouldn't let me spend money on it. But I've kept the roof up, the outside of the house, out of my own allowance."

" You won't have to accept anything from any one now. Will you ? " He smiled suddenly. " But I have to accept Christine from you." He leaned forward, resting his hands on his knees and looking down at them. The colour in his face deepened. " Mrs. Chevalier, when I came here, I was going to point out two mistakes I'd thought you had made. I won't now."

She said quickly, " I wish you would."

" I don't think they're necessary. I want Christine, not her money."

She laid her hand on his for an instant, a cool light touch.

" Mr. Ames, you've been the second really friendly person I've met in New York. I don't know why you are, for I don't think you felt that way when you came into this house. I'd like to know my mistakes."

" They don't matter now, do they ? "

" I'd like to know."

He said, " Why ? If you give your consent to our

marriage, Christine and I shan't do anything to question the codicils of her stepfather's will."

" Yes," she said. " About them. I want you to believe me when I tell you that Louis would have wanted to make them of his own free will."

" I understand, and I do believe you."

" I suppose, since you're both young, you want to marry soon ? "

" We'll have to wait a year, out of respect for Mr. Chevalier."

" Yes, that's so," she said. " Though conventions seem less and less important to me."

He didn't need to answer her question. He wasn't at all sure if his plan would have worked. She had gone beyond easy fright. It seemed too obvious to have thought of threatening to spread tales of her playing hand in glove with abolitionist ministers where her Charleston people could hear them. He knew he couldn't have done it. It made him feel almost foolish.

When he got up from the chair and looked down again at her, she tilted her face ; and he found that she seemed like a friend for whom he felt desperately sorry. How much would her house and servants mean to her now, once she had them ?

Her lips curved slowly, like and unlike Christine's.

" You look troubled, Mr. Ames. Not about me, surely ? "

He knew he was a fool to say it, but he had to.

" Do you think a man who'll work behind his partner's back is to be trusted ? "

" Mr. Deming ? " she said at once. " Don't worry about him. I said you were the second friendly person I had met—I should have said you were, besides my husband. Mr. Deming isn't very intelligent, perhaps, or very resourceful, but he's honest in his feelings. I've learned to know. They mean more to me than morals."

" I hope you're right."

She rose beside him.

" I suppose you want your answer," she said. " I'll give it gladly, John. After all, you're going to be my son-in-law, so I may call you John? Will you kiss me before Christine comes in? I hear the carriage."

6

Mr. Chevalier said : " Perhaps this is the best way, as long as it makes you happy. I hope Deming doesn't turn out badly for her—after all he didn't play ducks with the firm."

There were no lights in the Beach Street house across St. John's Park; the new snow on the doorstep was un-printed. They had gone away the evening before, after dark, with a note from Mr. Deming announcing his resig-nation from the firm and the fact that Vultee and Agate would act as his financial agents.

" I wish she had said good-bye," Christine said.

" Think kindly of her, Kisty," Mr. Chevalier said. " I almost find I can. But I wish you had had her consent in writing, John. We don't know where they've gone, and Kisty being under age, I'd like it, even though I'm her guardian."

" I think she'll send it," young Ames said, and he found that he believed it.

It came, as a matter of fact, before they had left the room. Amber tapped on the door. " A gentleman left this letter to Miss Christine," he said. " He said he was to deliver it to-night ; but he wouldn't come in. He says there's no answer."

The letter was held to a small box by the ribbons round them both. Christine broke the seal. " It's from Mamma. The box is for you, John. Open it."

The box contained a single red rose and a card.

" DEAR JOHN,—I have sent Christine my consent to

your marriage, but she will come to you from herself, so
I am sending you this rose for Christmas with my love. If
you find thorns on it, try to remember that they are not
the rose's fault.

"Sincerely,
"FLORA C. C. DEMING."

X

THE DOWNEY ACCOUNT

MR. McVITTY had found it difficult to accustom himself
to the idea of a junior clerk of indistinguished antecedents
marrying into the family of the senior partner of the firm.
And except for the fact of being himself in receipt of an
invitation to attend the wedding of Christine Chevalier to
John Ames in St. John's Chapel on the nineteenth of
December, 1835, he would have refused to believe that
any such thing could happen to the counting-room of an
establishment like Chevalier & Post.

"I suppose it's her not being his actual own niece that
accounts for Mr. Chevalier's consent to the union," he
confided to Gibbs for what might have been the twentieth
time. "But you'd think Ames could see for himself that
wedlock's no help to a man of his age and position."

"Well," said Gibbs, "it's supposed to be a convenience
when you have children."

"I'll ask you for no more such loose talk in this counting-
room, Mr. Gibbs!" the chief clerk said indignantly.

"All right then, don't."

Mr. McVitty turned deliberately on his high stool. It
was hard for his old eyes to see across the counting-room
with only the two gas jets lighted. Gibbs's dark face was
bent over his work; his pen scratched busily; to all
appearances he was absorbed in translating into Spanish

a copy of the final invoice to Mrs. Widow Roberts & Company, Cádiz. Mr. McVitty stifled his impulse to retort. From long experience he knew Gibbs's knack for putting him on the wrong side of his own arguments ; and in any case there was no one to hear.

It was nearly nine o'clock. Besides themselves, Mr. Post was the only other person left in Number 42 South Street. The rest of the staff had gone home at half-past eight ! Mr. Chevalier was making an address on " Some Aspects of the Indigo Trade " before the American Institute ; and young Ames hadn't yet come in.

Gibbs eased his long legs off the stool and handed the copies to Mr. McVitty, who pretended to inspect them, though Gibbs knew as well as he did that he had never learned a word of Spanish in his life. " All right," he said, and clipped them to the wire that held the outgoing files.

Gibbs stretched. " That finishes me for to-night. I'm not used to these late hours, McVitty, and we seem to be getting a lot."

Mr. McVitty nodded complacently. The daybook on his desk bore witness to the volume of business Chevalier & Post were doing. An extraordinary wave of prosperity and optimism had swept the country in 1835. Even heavy goods in hardware, that rock-bottom indicator, shared in the boom. There were disquieting notes, like the gambling in stocks in Wall Street ; but cotton held steady, and cotton was the thing to tie on. Imports were passing all autumn records, and warehouse room was going by the foot instead of by the loft.

Chevalier's had been riding the wave for all it was worth. In September, Mr. Post had sailed for Liverpool to negotiate exclusive consignments to Chevalier's from some of the larger British manufacturers, and it was only three days since he had returned. As Mr. McVitty said, Mr. Chevalier wasn't a man to let the grass grow under his feet while he was making hay.

The door of the junior partner's office opened abruptly

and Mr. Post came through, carrying his hat in one hand and a letter in the other. He stood stiffly, staring round the counting-room, and asked, " Where's Ames ? "

" He's not come in yet," said Mr. McVitty.

" I gathered as much," Mr. Post said woodenly. " He seems to have pretty independent ideas for a clerk."

Mr. McVitty bridled.

" Is there something I can do, sir ? "

" Yes. Tell Ames to copy this letter to Bantry, Boyce, Limited—*to-night*. Or if he hasn't come in by the time you go home, leave a note for him. By the way, where is Ames supposed to be ? "

" I sent him to look for space for the Henderson consignment we're expecting by the *Orpheus*."

" He seems to be taking his time about it." Mr. Post pulled on his gloves, finger by finger, and there was no shadow of expression in his face as he added, " I suppose when you're going to marry the niece of the senior partner, you feel free to help yourself to extra time off. That's one way to get ahead. Good-night, gentlemen."

They heard him walk slowly down the stairs and close the front door solidly. Gibbs whistled.

" By God, he's a cold-blooded son of a . . ."

" Mr. Gibbs ! "

" I know," Gibbs said, grinning at the old man. " But I'd like to have kicked his . . ."

" Mr. Gibbs ! If you please." Mr. McVitty cleared his throat sonorously. " Mr. Post wasn't very happy when I recommended promoting Ames to the outside work last spring," he explained. " He didn't like it any better when Mr. Chevalier backed me up on it, either. Of course, you'll understand I knew nothing about Miss Chevalier at the time."

He peered at Gibbs over his glasses.

" Of course not," said Gibbs.

A momentary suspicion flickered in Mr. McVitty's eyes, but he let it pass.

"Mr. Post argued that seniority put Cummings, Smith, and Crockwell ahead of Ames. But none of them have talent for the outside. So we agreed to give Ames a trial." Mr. McVitty paused. "Of course I knew Ames would do well at it. I saw the promise of talent in him when he came through that door the first time." He helped himself to a reflective pinch of snuff. After fifty years at the head of a counting-room like Chevalier's, you developed an instinct for the pattern of ability and honesty that made up a man's mind. "Ames is making a good record, and this last month he's started bringing in accounts. Of course Mr. Post gets 25 per cent outright of any accounts *he* brings in and I suspect he doesn't like the way Ames is taking hold."

"I should say it was obvious," Gibbs said dryly. "I suppose the firm gets all of the accounts Johnny brings in."

"Naturally," said Mr. McVitty. "You don't pay a commission to any clerk till he's been five years with the firm."

"I suppose not," said Gibbs. "By the way, have you any idea what's keeping Johnny?"

Mr. McVitty's voice, issuing from the strong-room where he was putting the daybook to bed, had a cavernous quality.

"Considering the circumstances," he said, "it's possible it might be Miss Chevalier."

2

But Mr. McVitty was only part right. Young Ames had only then arrived at St. John's Park. He had to wait a moment on the stoop before the door was opened by Amber with well-concealed surprise. Miss Christine, he said, was in the drawing-room, and young Ames found her seated on the floor, surrounded by samples. She held up both hands for him to raise her, and kissed him then and there, to the coloured butler's obvious delight.

" John ! How wonderful ! "

" It's awfully late," he said, " but I had to come round. What are those things ? "

" Samples," she said, " for our house. I've decided on the green damask for the parlour curtains. Do you like it ? "

The house they had rented was tiny and stood on what Mrs. Chevalier considered the outermost fringe of responsibility on Bleecker Street, but Christine was taking its furnishing as seriously as if they intended to live there the rest of their lives.

Her eyes grew appraising as she looked at him. " Have you had anything to eat, John ? " And when he said he had eaten early, she rang for Amber and ordered sandwiches and whisky. " Uncle always has whisky when he comes home late and tired."

" I'm not tired," he said, and she could see by the shine in his eyes that he was on edge with excitement.

" John," she said. " What's happened ? "

" I got the Downey account. I got it this evening."

" The Downey account ? " She felt ashamed not to know what it was, since he thought it was so important. But she was too honest to pretend about it.

" Higgins & Downey. Pearl Street and Maiden Lane. They're the biggest drygoods wholesalers in the city, and that means in the whole country." He scrubbed his fingers through his hair in the old gesture that was a remainder of his boyhood. He was like a boy ready to whoop, now that his restraint was off. She could imagine how he had been, his freckled face intent, talking quietly to Mr. Higgins or to Mr. Downey, whichever it was. It was good for him to let off steam.

" I talked to Downey," he said. " Higgins is too old to be active in the firm. It was· part luck. I was looking for warehouse room for our Henderson consignment and

I found a corner in LeRoy's and was measuring it up when I noticed a lot of Henderson boxes made out to Higgins & Downey. We've got the exclusive consignment now of all Henderson lines for the American market, and that gave me an opening wedge. I got round to Pearl Street just as they were closing and I was lucky to get hold of Mr. Downey himself. He asked me what I wanted," young Ames grinned, " and I told him I wanted to do him a favour that might run into money. I guess he thought I was pretty fresh. But he listened."

He sat back in his chair as Amber came in with a plate of sandwiches, a glass, and a decanter. Christine leaned towards him to pour the whisky, but Amber took the decanter from her and arranged the tray on a small table before the fire.

" This 'yer's the way l usually fixes Mr. Chevalier when he comes home late," he said, arranging the chairs to suit himself. He poured the whisky then and departed with dignity.

" There's no tyrant like an old darkey," Christine said. Her eyes met Ames's across the table with the same friendliness that had first made him fall in love with her. He felt himself relaxing as he ate and to his own surprise heard himself say, " You must always wear a pink dress when I've made a big deal."

" Why, John ! I didn't know you noticed my clothes." The colour rose in her cheeks and her lips curved. " Is that a clause for the marriage contract ? "

" Yes. Though I don't know how you'll know before-hand when I've put a deal through."

" I'll know, John."

He grinned at her. He could have told her every dress she had ever worn when she was with him.

" You know, the firm's been after the Downey account for years. Mr. Deming was always having a try at it, and Mr. Post tried again in February this year."

" But you got it," she said.

"I said it was part luck."

"I don't believe that, John." She shook her head. "It must have been exciting though."

"It was," he said. "But it was all over quicker than I ever thought could happen. Mr. Downey knows when he's going to say yes. He kept me a while talking about his business and asking about the work I did at Chevalier's."

She put her hand in his. "Uncle's going to be terribly pleased. He was talking about how well you'd done this year and how pleased he was."

"I wish he'd feel pleased enough to give me a commission. The Downey account ought to be worth a hundred thousand dollars to the firm. Just think what even a 5 per cent commission would mean—five thousand dollars, Kisty." He set down his glass and leaned towards her.

"But we don't need it, John."

"Don't we? Do you know what I'd do with it? I'd put it all into Mrs. Funk's store. I thought about it when I was walking up here."

The store end of the little millinery venture in Pittsburgh had begun to overshadow the dressmaking side, and five thousand dollars' worth of first-class merchandise would turn it into a real store. Mrs. Funk would no longer have to depend on the odd-lot buying he had to do for her now. They could buy direct from importers, leaving out the wholesalers entirely; and Funk's could then act as wholesaler in dress goods for Western merchants, saving them the yearly trip to New York. Of course, in time, such a business would find itself fighting the New York wholesalers like Higgins & Downey; but, young Ames thought with a grin, that could be faced when the time came.

It wasn't likely ever to come, for it would take more than even the clerk's full salary he was now receiving to support Christine and himself. There was no chance of a commission. The lost opportunity was almost more than he could bear, and he looked up angrily to find Christine watching him.

"There'll be other chances, John," she said.

"They don't happen often enough for a man to get rich by waiting for them to happen."

"You'll make them happen," she said confidently.

She knew it was true. He would never be satisfied to sit back and let things come to him. His ambition would always drive him. It was the same instinct that brought a horse home first to the winning post, she thought, or that raised a man like Andrew Jackson out of obscure beginnings. It was money John wanted now ; but when he had money, she knew that there would be something else.

"It's easy to say," he said.

She raised her eyes to his. "You mustn't be impatient, John. Uncle believes in you." She hesitated. "I don't know how counting-rooms are run, but I should think one would have to go up step by step, not all in one bounce."

"You sound just like McVitty," he said caustically, and then, meeting the affection in her eyes, he felt ashamed of himself. "I don't want the damned commission just for the money," he cried. "I want it for what it will mean to you. And I want it because I know I'm worth it." He got up from his chair. "It's like waiting for molasses from a barrel. Look at the way we had to wait a year to marry."

"Am I like molasses ? " Her lips curved, and he thought she was going to laugh at him, but she was half crying, and when he touched her it was like touching someone he had never known. Her voice seemed to have a veil on it. "You mustn't take everything so hard, John." She lifted her flushed face. "It makes it hard for me, and I'm human too." She flung her arms round his neck, and as he held her he felt shudders come through her ; and all her reserves were swept off in a storm of crying, and she kept asking, "There, don't you see, John ? You do see, don't you ? "

There seemed to be nothing he could do except hold on to her until her crying checked and she found her voice shakily to ask him for his handkerchief.

" We mustn't let that happen again, John. It's better not. And we've only five days more to wait."

She managed to smile as they walked into the hall together, and she gave him his hat with a mock-wifely air. It had been like a storm that had begun and ended in a moment's violence, and it had left both of them shaken, he as much as she. As he went back down-town through the nearly empty streets he kept wondering what it was that had touched off in her such an emotional disturbance. He was amazed that any one could feel so strongly, and a little frightened. He didn't think of the Downey account at all until he was climbing the stairs of Number 42 and the light left burning in the counting-room informed him that work had been left out for him to finish.

He found the Bantry letter on his desk, a pencilled note attached : " Mr. Post expects this letter copied to-night. —McV." He saw at once that the letter was utterly unimportant and had been spun out as long as possible, and he realised what he had begun to suspect even before Mr. Post had sailed for Liverpool, that the junior partner wanted to ride him out of the counting-room. There had never been love lost between himself and Mr. Post ; from the first each had instinctively recognised the other's complete determination to be top dog. Mr. Post had a long head start ; but it was getting shorter, and he knew it.

Young Ames bent over the desk, determined to make his copy of the letter as near to Mr. McVitty's ideal of copperplate as his hand was able to fashion it. When he had finished it, he made out a memorandum of his own afternoon's work—the space he had leased in LeRoy's warehouse and the rent he had agreed to pay. Underneath he drew a line, and poised his pen. He headed his item : " Memo. Downey account," and wrote out his information in one brief sentence. Turnabout for Mr. Post.

He put the slip on Mr. McVitty's desk, turned out the gas, and climbed the stairs to bed. Gibbs was out ; but he must have built up the fires before leaving, and Ames kept gratefully close to the warmth as he undressed by the light of a single candle. He could hear the deep flooding rush of wind up the steep roof overhead ; and somewhere in the house below, one of the great beams creaked with the entering cold. It was going to seem strange, living in a small two-story house, and he went to his window suddenly to look down on the river, a dark belt beyond the docks with the shipping a darker shadow on it.

He had been lonely and half afraid his first nights in this room, before he made friends with Gibbs across the landing ; but he knew he would miss it. And he thought some day he must show it to Christine.

3

Mr. McVitty arrived next morning in a driving flurry of snow, and he shook out the folds of his greatcoat and gave it to Pinky Finnegan to hang behind the stove. He went through his usual ritual of inspecting the offices, sending Pinky out to sweep the sidewalk, pouring his cup of hot water, and getting the books from the strong-room. His eye fell on young Ames's memorandum, but he didn't read it until everything was in line for the day's work and he had drunk his hot water and helped himself to snuff. By the time he was ready to mount his stool, the counting-room force had arrived and already the day's work was beginning.

Mr. McVitty picked up the memorandum and adjusted his glasses and suddenly stiffened under his rusty black coat. He exclaimed simply and articulately, " Good God Almighty ! "

The entire counting-room revolved on its stools and stared at him, but he seemed totally unaware of what he had said.

" Ames, will you step over here a moment ? "

He pointed to the J.A. in the lower right-hand corner of the slip of paper.

" This is yours, isn't it ? "

" Yes."

" You're serious ? It's not a joke ? " Mr. McVitty asked suspiciously.

" No, sir."

Mr. McVitty was peering at him over his glasses.

" It's extraordinary," he said. He glanced over Ames's head as the counting-room door opened and Mr. Post entered, with a brief nod, and stalked to his office. His bell rang at once. Pinky answered it and came back to say that Mr. Post would like to see Ames's copy of the letter to Bantry. He wished to make a change or two.

Mr. McVitty produced a noise in his nose that resembled a snicker more than anything else. " You may go back to your desk, Ames," he said, and picked up the letter and left the memorandum. But five minutes later, when Mr. Chevalier entered, his shoulders powdered, and, according to his invariable custom, ordered a quart of brandy drawn from the oldest pipe in the cellar for celebration of the first snowfall, Mr. McVitty said he would bring it himself. And he went in with the bottle, glasses, and Ames's memorandum on the tray together.

It was only a moment before Mr. Chevalier's bell rang briskly and Pinky Finnegan was instructed to fetch Mr. Post. But it seemed a long time to young Ames till the bell rang again and Pinky said, " Mr. Chevalier would like to speak to Mr. Ames."

4

" Please stay a minute, Ames," Mr. Chevalier said, and waited for Mr. McVitty to follow Mr. Post out of the office. " Sit down," he said, pointing to the chair on the opposite side of his mahogany table. His china-blue eyes softened a moment as he looked at young Ames.

"This is quite a feather for a youngster to put in his cap," he said. "Kisty ought to feel proud of you when she hears about it."

"I told her last night," young Ames said.

"The minx! She never said a word about it to me." Mr. Chevalier stared out of the window at his side. The thinning snowflakes were driving on a north-west wind; and the sky was a dark solid slaty grey against which the spars of the shipping had acquired a whitish gleam. "John," he said slowly, "I don't know exactly what I ought to do about this. I don't see why Downey and I shouldn't reach an agreement unless you've filled him with some over-fancy ideas of price reductions." His eyes turned appraisingly back to Ames's.

"I told him just what I've told you I said, sir."

"It must have been good sales talk and you must have said it well." He hesitated for a moment and then made a slight gesture with his hand. "I'm going to be frank with you, John. I think you deserve a commission on this, though it's not usual. But Mr. Post thinks you don't and Mr. McVitty thinks it wouldn't be a good precedent. Mr. McVitty, for all his good points, lives and breathes and eats, and I've no doubt got born," Mr. Chevalier said with an unexpected smile, "purely by precedent. I only consider his stand as it seems to support Mr. Post. Post is a partner and has as much say as I do in the running of the business. He has a very considerable cash investment in the firm, and we've expanded to the point this year where cash assets are doubly valuable. I feel I can talk to you this way because you're about to become a member of my family, John, and some day I hope you'll take a place in the firm."

"I see," young Ames said.

What he saw was that he was not going to get a commission of any sort and that Mr. Chevalier had no intention yet of putting him on a commission basis for all his saying he would like to do so. He remembered that Mr. Chevalier had made no move to pay him a bonus for his work in the cotton corner until the firm's New Orleans correspondents had acted independently. There was no point therefore in talking about it.

Some of his resentment must have shown in his face, for Mr. Chevalier rose when he did and said, " You can't always measure success by your reward in dollars, John. Good will generally pays more in the long run than a quick cash turnover."

" Yes, sir," said young Ames.

He had the feeling of being thwarted, and he didn't know exactly what to do about it. The fact that the news had made a sensation in the counting-room and that every one, down to Pinky Finnegan, took time out to congratulate him, only seemed to make it worse. There was a tentative agreement to be drawn, which Mr. Chevalier took with him to discuss with Mr. Downey after a luncheon at Delmonico's. His cheeks were redder when he returned and he put the agreement on Mr. McVitty's desk. " I want three copies," he said. Mr. McVitty brought it to Ames. It was just, he announced loudly, that Ames should have the honour of making out the fair copies. To finish the day off, Ames was sent up to Higgins & Downey to obtain their signature.

5

Mr. Downey was in his small office off the display room on the second floor. The auction rooms were on the first floor and the rest of the big building was given up to lofts and shelf space. A clerk showed young Ames in, announcing him as " Mr. Ames, from Chevalier & Post."

" Come in," said Mr. Downey. " Sit down. This the copy ? "

He ran through it with a rapid eye, and signed it.

"That's that," he said. "It's a new departure for this firm, but I think you were right last night. People our size can do better buying from big manufacturers. We're too big to do our own window shopping." He was a thin-lipped man in his late thirties ; there was nothing distinctive about his appearance ; you could have seen a dozen of him any day along Pearl Street. But his voice had a whip-like quality and he had a trick of looking at his hands when he was speaking. His hands were always in repose. "Chevalier & Post are a fine old firm," he remarked. "They've a good reputation and they're daring operators and sound at the same time. Bit of a blood, the old man, I guess, in his time."

"I don't know," young Ames said.

"Good people to work for, I imagine," he said. "But these old firms are hard to work up in. I know. I did it myself here. Higgins & Pliny, before me ; Pliny was dead. Don't know what he was like but his name was still there. You could keep dead names in your letterhead then. We did a small respectable business, maybe twenty thousand a year. Well, it's different now. Things move here now, Ames. And this boom we're in has only just got started."

He still looked at his hands, and young Ames found himself looking at them also. They were sparsely haired, with long fingers and square knuckles. He wondered what Mr. Downey was getting at. It was time he himself returned to Number 42. This was packet night. They'd stay open past ten o'clock. Then he glanced up to find Mr. Downey watching him and not his hands at all.

"You know," Mr. Downey said, "I've been thinking about what you said yesterday about selling—building up big lines of merchandise by getting control of them and keeping them in your own hands, I suppose it's what I've been working towards all the time, though I hadn't thought of it just like that. But Higgins is no good to me. He's old-fashioned. Hates advertising."

" I know. A merchant shouldn't buy more than two
inches of space in a paper for the year, and stick to it," young
Ames said with a grin. "Announcing, Mr. Chevalier
calls it. The firm name is what brings people in."

" Well," said Mr. Downey, "that's all right for Chevalier,
who sells to me. But I've got to sell to Mr. Tripp of
Trapp's Corners and what does *he* want to know about
Higgins & Downey ? He identifies names with merchandise. Like Henderson's British Printings. You could sell
them right across the country. There's a big job there,
waiting for someone to work it out. It's a job for a man
who ain't afraid to move, Ames. And I'm willing to pay
him what he's worth." He paused, and then went on
coolly, " I could promise you 50 per cent more salary
than you're getting from Chevalier, with a percentage of
any increase our books show over our past three-year
average."

" You don't know what my salary is," young Ames
pointed out. He needed time ; and he didn't want
Downey to see his surprise.

But Mr. Downey didn't bat an eye.

" It don't matter what your salary is. What I said was,
you'd get 50 per cent more. To start with."

For an instant, young Ames felt himself on the edge of
closing. But he couldn't quite do it. He spoke slowly :
" I'll have to think it over, though it's a good offer, Mr.
Downey. You see, I'm getting married Saturday."

" I know," said Mr. Downey. " To Miss Chevalier.
Congratulations." He met the inquiry in young Ames's
eyes with a small, tight smile. " I'm a thorough man,
Ames. I don't make an offer like this without looking up
the whole record. I like people who move, but you're in
a delicate position. Let's put it this way. The office of
manager of Higgins & Downey will stay open to January
1, 1836. That ought to give you time to look at every
angle of it."

6

There was a heavy mail to make up that night ; it was a quarter to eleven when Mr. McVitty pouched the last letters with the remark that they wouldn't expect another mail like it until 1836. The notion brought a seasonal feeling into the counting-room that was heightened by the kettle singing on the stove, the frost tracks that showed on the windowpanes, and the uninterrupted blowing of the wind. One could see thoughts of Christmas and New Year's coming over the clerks' faces, and somehow Pinky Finnegan's eye suggested snowballs and beaver hats. But Mr. McVitty punctured the holiday spirit in its incipience. There was the inventory left to do, of course. He would lay out the work himself to-morrow, and the staff would begin on the seventeenth. He saluted with his umbrella and disappeared down the stairs.

"Life with McVitty is just a whirl ; never an idle moment," Gibbs said. "Come along upstairs, Johnny. I want a drink." He lit candles in his own room and threw some extra chunks of coal on the fire, fished out a couple of glasses and lifted a jug from under the table. "It's old Kentucky whisky, and good for what ails you. It'll solace me after you've got married and it will cheer you up now. Getting married isn't so terrible after all, Johnny. Others survive it." He poised the jug in his hands and glanced at young Ames. "Something on your mind ? " he asked.

Young Ames shook his head. Downey's offer was something he ought to think out for himself. From the point of view of income, there was no question of what he ought to do ; and he didn't feel that Chevalier & Post had any real claim on him either. But as Mr. Downey had said, there were angles for him to look at. There was Christine and the way she'd feel about it, to begin with.

He glanced up, hearing Gibbs chuckle.

"Getting married during the inventory is the smartest

idea that's been worked in generations. Poor old McVitty told me this noon that in all his years here no other clerk ever tried it on him. I'd like to propose a toast to Christine without whose encouragement it could never have been put over," he said. As he watched young Ames down his glass, his dark face was lighted by one of its rare smiles. " She's a fine girl, Johnny ; she's lovely ; and what's better yet, she's intelligent. If something's on your mind, why don't you take it to her ? "

7

When she looked into his face, she imagined that he must have looked much the same way coming home to confess a boyish escapade to his mother ; and her eyes grew tender. If she was upset, she didn't show it. " Why, John ! " she said. " It's wonderful."

He stared at her, thinking she had not understood him. " I'm thinking of taking it," he blurted out. " Even at the start I'd be making more money than I am right now."

" You'll have to decide that, John."

" You wouldn't mind if I took it ? "

" Not if you honestly think you'll make more of a success there than at Chevalier's. You ought to make sure of that," she said earnestly. " Uncle George says you're doing wonderfully well."

He said truculently, " Mr. Downey's willing to pay me for my work."

She didn't let herself be nettled. " I don't know what kind of work you'd do at Downey's."

" It would be selling," he said. " To small buyers, but selling on a big scale. It's not the same kind of work."

" Would you like it as well ? " she asked. " Wouldn't you miss South Street ? "

" I don't know." He had been asking himself the same question, and he hadn't got anywhere, all day.

" I don't know what kind of man Mr. Downey is," she said.

" He's smart as a trap. And he's willing to pay."

" I'm sure he's smart," she said, her colour rising. " But would he stand by you if you were down ? That's one thing Uncle George would do, and has done before."

" That needn't come into my case," young Ames said. " I can look out for myself."

Her eyes searched his, and she said, " Dear, it's something I can't solve for you, really. It's a man's problem."

" I know that. But I didn't want to go into it if it was going to make you feel badly."

" You needn't think of my feelings, if it's what you really want to do. I only want you to be sure of that, and then go into it for all you're worth. I want you to get on top, no matter what it is, even if it's chimney sweeping."

" I don't want that," he said, grinning at her. She hadn't helped him make up his mind, but she had let him know that whatever he decided to do, she would stand behind him. He realised suddenly that he ought to have known that all along.

" I've got to get back. I promised McVitty I would. He wants to see me, about the inventories, I suppose." He looked down into her face and said : " I don't really have to decide till New Year's. So don't worry."

She put both her hands on his arms. " I know you'll decide it the right way, John."

She had taken him to her aunt's upstairs sitting-room, for there were dinner guests. Now they stole downstairs together and kissed good-night in the hall, with the blur of voices just beyond the drawn portières. She waved to him from the door and closed it softly, and he turned into the cold.

He still had his problem with him on the long lonely walk back from Laight Street. Almost the whole city seemed to have gone indoors, and no wonder, considering the bite of the wind. It must be near zero-cold, he thought.

In all the way he encountered but one hackney coach, the horse hunched, blanketed, and breathing steam in front of a three-cent liquor store. When he turned down South Street the waterfront was utterly deserted. Not even a ship's watch was in sight. But the ships themselves were full of frosty creakings ; the slap of the waves against the dock pilings had an icy note that was accentuated by the low level of the water in the slips, due, it was said, to the long-continued north-west wind. It had been increasing steadily and had now reached a near-gale force.

But the heavy walls of the counting-house shut it out ; the counting-room itself was warm from a red-hot fire drawing in the stove. No checking of Mr. McVitty's frugal devising could hope to hold a fire on such a night ; and at times, above the steady popping of the whistling gas jet, they could hear the wind sucking at the mouth of the chimney three flights above them.

" It sounds wild," Mr. McVitty said, with a glance at the taut red spots of cold on young Ames's cheeks. " You'd better stand by the stove and warm up. I'm well up with the work anyway. We can afford to lally-gag awhile." He climbed down from his stool, helping himself to snuff on the way. " You'll be married Saturday, won't you ? "

Young Ames nodded, and Mr. McVitty nodded back at him. It's a wonderful thing," he said. " The way you've come up in the firm. It's happened to others, but not often in a firm of Chevalier's standing. I wouldn't wonder some day to get the signboard changed," he went on, looking into his snuffbox, " to Chevalier, Post & Company."

Young Ames looked into Mr. McVitty's grey eyes. They were watery, and a little faded, from a lifetime's reading of other people's profits. It occurred to him all at once that Mr. McVitty might have had some of the same dreams and ambitions he had himself and an uncontrollable impulse made him say, " Why not Chevalier, Post & McVitty, while we're about it ? "

" Don't be a fool," Mr. McVitty said. " What would I

do with a partnership now ? And what would Chevalier's
do if I wasn't chief clerk ? That's more to the point." But
his voice had shaken for a minute, and young Ames said :
" Fifty years is a long time. I was thinking of that on my
way back here to-night."

" Were you ? " Mr. McVitty closed the snuffbox with
a deliberate click. " Well, you needn't think so. I've been
well treated, I may tell you. Many a merchant right in
this city has less cash and credit with the bank than I have.
At your time of life fifty years seems a long time, I suppose.
But I haven't a year to regret of them." He raised his eyes
suddenly. " No, when I said ' & Co,' I was thinking of
John Ames."

" Me ? "

Mr. McVitty smiled.

" I won't be surprised if it happens inside of the next
four or five years."

" Five years ! " Young Ames could see the kind of hope
that had fed a younger McVitty. Well, it wasn't the kind
that would keep John Ames going down a single rut. The
scorn was in his voice for McVitty to read, but the old
man remained unruffled.

" I was meaning to talk to you sometime. You've done
so well in this counting-room that you're beginning to get
known in the city, especially now you're on the outside
world. No doubt you'll begin to get offers from others,
offering better pay, or promising immediate advancement.
There's some men always after other people's clerks, and
this counting-room," with quiet pride, " has a reputation
for training clerks well. I know. I've had the same kind
of offers myself, but every time I've turned one down I've
been gladder of it." He pushed his spectacles up on his
forehead and blew his nose.

" There have been firms risen faster, in my time.
Bayard, Gracie, Prime, Goodhue—but you won't find one
of them to-day that stands higher or solider than Chevalier.
They're the names that made America," said McVitty

with conviction. He went back to his desk and returned
with two thin ledgers. " Look," he said, showing one to
Ames. " That's the first book of the firm. It's a great
rarity. It's in Ferdinand Chevalier's own hand. Notice
the binding and the quality of the paper." He turned it
over, opened it lovingly, and read :

" Monday, February 15, 1782,
      " 2 lbs. rapee Snuff 6s.
      " 6¾ yds. flannel for drawers, £1 17s. 2d."

" That was this firm's opening transaction. It was a
small business even when I came." He opened the second
book. " You'll see here where my hand comes in : August
19, 1784. I'd been in the employ seven months at the
time. The entry's for 24 Tierces of rice. We'd had a
dispute the day before, and in the morning Mr. Ferdinand
found he'd been wrong, and he turned the books over to
me as a reward," Mr. McVitty said simply. " You'll
observe, if you go into the strong-room and get out the
books, that the firm began doing heavier business after
Mr. George took hold. Do you believe in ghosts ? " he
asked suddenly.

" I never saw one," young Ames said.

" Nor I. But it was uncanny the way to-night, when I
took that book down, I could almost hear Mr. Ferdinand
saying the way he used to, ' I only hope George has as
good a son to take over when he's my age, McVitty.' But
of course there were no children from his marriage, and
it's sad to think that Mr. George is reaching the age his
father mentioned." Mr. McVitty paused to let the wind
finish its wild voice over the mouth of the chimney. " I
thought I'd just tell you," he said, fixing his eyes earnestly
on young Ames's face. He saw the resentment in it.

" Who told you about Mr. Downey's offer ? "

" Nobody but you. I thought maybe you'd had one
from the way you've been worried. Mr. Bartlett, who's

Downey's chief clerk, picked me up at lunch yesterday,"
said Mr. McVitty. "And I can put two and two together."

"I suppose you'll try to tell me that Higgins & Downey
are rascals," young Ames said.

"They're a strong, ambitious store," said Mr. McVitty,
shaking his head. "But they're not merchants in the sense
of Chevalier's. That's nothing against them," he added.
"It's just the fact. You've got a talent for big operations,
Ames, and I'd hate to see you leave the shipping business,
for whatever extra in dollars has been offered to you." He
turned back to his desk, a little clumsily. "We ought to
line up the inventory. I've classified the lofts and merchandise, but there's an hour's work left and it's near nine
o'clock." He halted, one foot on a rung of the stool.
"What's that?"

Whatever it was, it was lost in the sudden rumble of
wind in the chimney. "It's blowing stronger," said Mr.
McVitty. "I thought I heard a bell."

"By God, I hope it's not a fire," young Ames said.

"Perhaps I imagined it," said Mr. McVitty.

But as soon as the wind left the chimney they could hear
the City Hall alarm bell tolling steadily; and, riding the
wind with it, young Ames thought he heard another bell.
Then it came clear.

"That's the South Church. On Exchange Place."

"What of it?" said Mr. McVitty.

"The fire must be close." Young Ames went to the
window, pulled the shutters back, threw up the sash, and
held it with his hand.

They heard the bells clear on the wind, and suddenly
the First Church in Wall Street chimed in. Mr. McVitty
held the lapels of his coat closed over his throat against the
cold. "Wait," he said, as young Ames started to let down
the heavy sash. "I can smell smoke."

Young Ames stiffened. The cold felt dry in his lungs.

"You're right. I've got to run." He had let the window
down now and was working into his coat. "I'm sorry to

leave you alone at it. But I'll be back as quick as I can."

"Never mind. Wrap up warm. It's terrible cold."
Rubbing his hands, Mr. McVitty still peered from the
window. Suddenly young Ames saw a ruddy glow reflected
in the old man's glasses.

"I saw it then," cried Mr. McVitty. "Right over
there. A long shoot of the fire. But it's gone now."

"That's where the Exchange is."

"Nonsense. The Exchange is fireproof. You know
that." Mr. McVitty's voice was tart. "That fire's in
Merchant Street. Take care of yourself. . . ." He turned,
but young Ames's feet were banging down the stairs.

8

Mr. McVitty saw the fire leap up and sink again before
he closed the shutters and came thoughtfully back to the
stove and put on an extra shovel of coal. "Fires!" he
said, sniffing. "They're a damned nuisance."

Alone, he would have a long night of work ahead of
him, and he soon became absorbed in his books. He
worked till midnight. The wind sounded incredibly
stronger; it was a continual roaring outside. He reared
back and started at his columns of figures and realised
that there was a red light flickering over his desk.

"Good gracious," he thought, glancing towards the
window. The shutters were outlined in red. When he
yanked them open, a wall of flame was rising over the
tops of the buildings behind Number 42, the buildings that
faced on Front Street. He blinked at them incredulously.
Then he rushed into Mr. Chevalier's office and looked
out on the waterfront. An engine stood on the corner of
Old Slip, but there were no firemen to work it. "I'm
mad," he thought, and put on his hat and scarf and coat,
and walked downstairs to see what was happening.

As soon as he came outdoors his hearing was engulfed

by the deep intermittent roaring he had thought was the wind. But it was fire that made it, fire like nothing McVitty had ever seen. The entire sky had turned red. Looking up South Street he saw the block on Coffee House Slip burning with such height that the sheets of flame torn off by the wind were tossed halfway across the river.

" Good God," Mr. McVitty said out aloud. " Where are the engines ? "

Remembering the one on the corner, he ran to see why it had been abandoned, but the cause was apparent immediately when he got close enough. The suction pipe was not long enough to reach the abnormally low level of water in the slip. With a feeling of panic, Mr. McVitty looked up Old Slip, along which trailed the lengths of useless hose, and saw a second deserted engine, and a third. It was incredible.

He stood there on the corner of Old Slip, watching the fire burn towards him down South Street. He could see flames rise high over the rooftree of Number 42. All of a sudden a building on the corner of William and Water blew up with a dull explosion ; the roof caved in, and from the glassless windows came brilliant white gusts of fire. He thought mechanically : " That's Tardy's brandy going off." He didn't know what he ought to do. There wasn't time to notify Mr. Chevalier. There was no chance of finding young Ames. He hoped the boy was all right. The fire was already burning towards Coenties Slip, and Chevalier & Post was surrounded by it, cut off, " doomed," he thought, and said, " Eh ? " realising at last that there were other human beings on the scene.

They were going in and out of buildings and piling goods in the middle of South Street. They were like little black ants toiling in the glare. Mr. McVitty watched them and saw one coming towards him. It was Wentz, the clerk of Pruyn & Company.

" Our back wall's burned through," he shouted. " It

will be into your house in a minute. I got out what I
could."

Wasted effort, thought McVitty. Already loafers were
scavenging the piles. What wasn't stolen would be burned
anyway. Red-hot embers and bits of wood and flaming
splinters had begun to shower South Street. Even the
shipping was in danger.

"Look!" said Wentz. "Our roof's going."

Mr. McVitty, in spite of the hot blasts, suddenly felt
cold.

"I must get the portfolio," he said. It contained close
to half a million dollars in notes, bills of exchange, and
bills receivable. Insurance couldn't cover its loss.

"You're a fool," Wentz yelled. "The place is doomed."

Mr. McVitty did not waste a glance on him, as he turned
and marched into Number 42.

The inside of the building was uncannily quiet; but
he seemed to hear the great roar of the fire still in his
ears. The counting-room was all ruddy from the glare;
the gaslight was lost in it. When he went to the windows
to close the shutters he saw the fire pouring in a fiery
deluge through the back alley. The window panes were
already getting hot in front of his nose. He closed the
shutter with a sudden tremor in his knobby fingers, and
looked round the counting-room as though to fix it in his
memory. It was a terrible thing. "But we're insured to
the hilt," he thought.

He got the portfolio under his arms and picked the two
ledgers he had shown Ames off his desk. He put on his
hat again and paused mechanically to turn down the gas.
But he stopped himself, thinking how Gibbs would have
ribbed him for it.

"Gibbs!" he said aloud.

Had Gibbs gone out? He didn't know. He certainly had
not seen him come in. He went to the foot of the upward
flight and shouted up into the stairwell, "Gibbs! Gibbs!"
but he got no answer. One couldn't be sure where Gibbs

was concerned. He might be drunk, or he might be asleep, or one might have led to the other. But McVitty couldn't go out of the building wondering about any clerk of his.

As he climbed up the stairs, he imagined he could hear the noise of conflagration beyond the wall in Pruyn's counting-house. He thought he smelled smoke. " Gibbs ! " he called. " Are you there, Gibbs ? "

Both rooms were empty, of course. He found a candle and lit it to make sure. Then he came back to the stairs, telling himself that this was just the kind of nuisance one would expect Gibbs to make. He could make trouble when he wasn't even round. He was always trying to lead you to wrong conclusions.

He didn't have the candle any more, for he had blown it out and put it back where it belonged. As he felt for the top tread, smoke rolled up in the darkness against his face.

Mr. McVitty coughed and clapped his handkerchief over his nose and mouth. But he could smell the smoke anyway, it made him choke, and he had to stop for coughing. He managed to get down the top flight all right, though, and started on the next ; and then halfway down that he had to stop again ; and his eyes smarted too badly for him to see anything beyond a red gloom that he made himself blunder down into until he couldn't get any more breath at all. And he tottered helplessly where he stood, clasping the portfolio and the two ledgers tight in both his bony arms.

9

From the time he had rushed out of the counting-house until Mr. Chevalier and Gibbs found him in Hanover Square, young Ames had been too steadily on the dead run to think. Number 11, wheeling out of the engine-house, with Rock Doyle bellowing to " Start her lively " ; as if it were a routine alarm, was one of the first to get to Merchant Street. The fire was in the store of Comstock & Adams, and had already spread through the five stories above. They knew at once that they were going to have their hands full, but not even the Chief had an idea of the catastrophe that faced the city. Number 11 was placed at the end of a line of engines that had started at Coffee House Slip ; but when they got water it was only a small and feeble stream with which they could barely get above the second story. The fire burned out through the roof ; and in ten minutes it had jumped the street six stories overhead and gone careering off towards Hanover Street. They began then to have an inkling of what they were up against. Engines from uptown that kept arriving tried to form a line from Old Slip, but could not reach water there. Coffee House Slip was the only spot along the East side where an engine could get down to water.

Foremen were told to park their engines and help merchants remove their stocks from the path of the fire. Most of this was carried into the Merchants Exchange, which was known to be fireproof. Number 11 continued to play its pipe in Merchant Street, where it could get at the fire, in an effort to keep it from spreading west towards Broad Street, but it gradually worked by them. It was working into the teeth of the wind. Then the water failed, and a runner told them that the line had been cut in Hanover Street and that the Exchange was threatened. They wheeled their engine out of the narrow street, with the wind blowing hot blasts against them, and saw the fire away beyond them racing down William Street. It was dividing on the high bulk of the Exchange and the interrupted line of hose was now soaking the sides of the building. The Exchange itself was on fire.

The flames seemed to be spreading in all directions, eating through party walls on one story or another, and

then gutting the centre of a building. Sometimes it seemed
to eat into the next building in a single bite of all five
stories ; and the two buildings would seem to lean on
each other for the few minutes left before their collapse.
The walls went down with a strange effect of silence, for
the roar of the fire, like the element itself, was all-
consuming.

When they ran out on to the greater width of Hanover
Street, between the burning buildings on each side, they
learned that the fire was burning all the way down to the
river in some places and as far north as Wall Street.
Engine 33 was still getting water at Coffee House Slip,
and there was some chance of turning it there. But there
was no hope of stopping it on the south short of Broad
Street, and the Corporation had sent for marines to blow
the buildings in its path at Coenties Slip. Number 11
company rolled their engine to Hanover Square and parked
it out of reach of the fire. And young Ames, staring round
him at the encircling fire, felt the cold for the first time,
cutting through his sweat-soaked clothes.

He had no idea that he had been working three hours.
He could only stare, his dazed mind trying to take in what
his eyes saw. The entire square was filled with merchandise
and here and there a few citizens with buckets were
keeping guard against the fires continually starting from
falling embers. The bells had stopped ringing. You
could see people's faces as plainly as by daylight, you saw
the gestures they made, but human voices were of
no account. Gibbs, finding young Ames there beside the
engine, gave up yelling into his ear and shook him by the
arm.

Mr. Chevalier was waiting for them at the south end of
the square, facing the fire with the same frozen stare in
his eyes that young Ames had seen on more than one face
that night. But it was easier to hear his voice through the
inferno than Gibbs's yelling.

"You've had a rough time of it, John."

Young Ames nodded.

" Have you been to 42 or seen McVitty since the fire started ? "

" No, sir. I left him when the alarm sounded. He was working at the inventory."

" We'd better go right down," Gibbs said. " The fire's way down South Street now."

" Forty-two won't burn in a hurry," said Mr. Chevalier. " I built it myself. There are none of these damned party walls. But we must make sure McVitty's got the portfolio out."

He walked between them, still talking in a matter-of-fact hardness of voice.

" They wouldn't let me through from Wall Street," he said. " I had to go round to Mill Street. The fire's just getting there. We've lost the stuff in Mrs. Cleghorn's stable loft."

Young Ames said : " Murphy's, Trott's, Wheeler's, and Finch's warehouses went. I suppose the three on Front and Barker's on Water Street have burned. The fire's there."

" The fire's not missed anything," said Mr. Chevalier, with the same cold containment.

South Street was now a line of burning counting-houses, and 42 was one of the very few that still had an undamaged front. Mr. Chevalier looked at the blazing windows of the upper stories and sucked in his breath.

" It's queer McVitty's not around," he said, and started for the door.

Gibbs put a hand on his shoulder. " Let me and Johnny look for him."

Mr. Chevalier shook off his hand.

" You two will have to look through the rooms for McVitty while I open the safe."

They were running up the stairs now. The counting-room was empty of everything but smoke. The fire had just eaten through the wall of the junior partner's office, but Mr. Chevalier's was a mass of flames. The strong-room door was open, and the two younger men stopped beside it while Mr. Chevalier coolly opened the safe.

"The portfolio's not here," he said. "McVitty must have taken it. We'd better get out."

Young Ames was looking behind the door. "His coat and hat are gone," he said.

It was Gibbs who noticed the gas.

"McVitty would never leave it burning," he said. "He'd turn it off in hell itself."

"Nonsense," said Mr. Chevalier. But Gibbs shook his head.

"I know McVitty. Listen a minute."

It was then they heard his feeble coughing.

10

He seemed a little out of his head, and Gibbs and young Ames had to walk him between them along South Street, waiting once for a wall to fall, and once running him past another, while Mr. Chevalier followed. Behind them they heard a series of dull muffled explosions and young Ames said it must be the marines blowing buildings down at Coenties Slip.

It was a strange sensation to get across Wall Street and find the fire behind them and to feel the full piercing of the cold. They had the luck to find a cab at Pine and Water Streets and Mr. Chevalier paid the driver the extra dollar he demanded without an argument. In twenty minutes they had Mr. McVitty in Laight Street, and were helping him upstairs to the Chevaliers' best guest bedroom. Mr. Chevalier went downstairs again to rout out the nearest doctor, and it was while he was out that Mr. McVitty started to come to his senses. He peered out of his inflamed eyes at Gibbs and young Ames without seeming to recognise them, and suddenly his hands made motions and he said in a rough whisper : " I've dropped the portfolio."

" No you haven't," Gibbs said quickly, laying it on his chest.

Mr. McVitty took hold of it carefully.

" That's Gibbs. Where am I ? "

" In Mr. Chevalier's house. He's gone to fetch his doctor."

" Then I'll wait till he comes back," Mr. McVitty said, with a slight quiver of his chin. " But would you mind just bringing me a little whisky ? Just a medicinal bit, with no water in it ? "

There was a rustle at their backs, and they turned to see Christine in a silk wrapper bringing in a tray.

" John," she said. " You're all right. Is it Mr. McVitty ? Is he hurt ? "

" Just smoke, I guess," Gibbs said. " He was pretty well choked but he's managed to ask for whisky and you've brought it."

He poured a drink and held McVitty up, while Christine spread a quilt over the old man's feet. She looked from one to the other and asked : " Is South Street burned ? "

Young Ames nodded and Gibbs said : " The whole business section is gone, or will be gone, by morning. They gave up trying to save any of it long ago. They're saving the rest of the city."

" Uncle's counting-house ? "

" Yes," said young Ames.

Her eyes found his.

" Uncle was insured," she said.

They turned towards the door. Mr. Chevalier had come back. He was standing there now, looking at all of them, the same frozen grimness on his face.

" I was insured," he said. " Like every one else. We'll have to face it, Kisty. Almost all the warehouses are going, with almost everything in them. By to-morrow morning there just won't be any insurance companies. And most of my cash is invested in insurance companies." He stopped. " Chevalier's will have to start again, very near from scratch, if it can start at all."

They were all startled as Mr. McVitty's figure stiffened on the bed and he started to sit up.

" Miss Chevalier, don't you worry," he said. " The firm's gone through two wars and the embargo, and it'll come through this fire just as well. Mr. Chevalier and I've been in this firm fifty years together, and we both know that's true."

Christine looked into the grey strained face, and, moved by a sudden impulse, came round the corner of the bed, leaned over, and kissed him. Lifting her head, she looked directly into young Ames's eyes.

Mr. Chevalier said : " It's going to be hard on you two youngsters."

" John and I'll manage," she said. " Won't we, John ? "

Her eyes were challenging him ; and as he looked round him, young Ames knew that in this room were the four people he cared for most in the world. And it was Mr. Chevalier and McVitty, and in a strange way Gibbs, who really were Chevalier's, and himself, if he wanted to stay. They would be, as Mr. Chevalier said, starting practically from scratch, without a counting-house, without a ware-house, with all their autumn shipments gone, and with commitments bigger than the firm had ever had. It would take quick thinking and gumption and long planning to pull them out. The salvaged goods might go to the South American market. An enterprising man might buy up a hundred thousand dollars' worth before any one caught on, for next to nothing. . . .

He looked up and met Christine's eyes, grinned suddenly, and nodded.

XI

AND CO.

AMBER, the Chevaliers' butler, had bought an extra from a howling newsboy and brought it straight into the dining-room. Mr. Chevalier's eyes grew bleak as he read, and there was a kind of greyness on his face when he looked at Christine and young Ames across the breakfast-table.

"The fire's under control," he said. "They've got it bounded by Wall Street, Broad, Coenties Slip and the River, of course. Thirteen acres, the paper says. Six hundred and fifty buildings, and they estimate the damage as over seventeen million dollars."

He looked older, tired, and worried.

Mr. McVitty, still rather shaky, was standing by the door, about to start out to hunt up space in which the firm might set up temporarily.

"You're to go slow, understand, McVitty? Get Gibbs and let him do your legwork. Have Pinky Finnegan or Gibbs or Cummings keep watch at Number 42 to handle inquiries."

"Where will I get hold of you?" asked McVitty.

"I'll be round between three and four, probably. I'll have to attend an emergency meeting of the Franklin Company. I'll need to visit the bank. And I want to see Mr. Prime." A wry smile twisted his mouth. "I imagine half of South Street will have the same idea before the day's over. I want to get there early. Prime was always inclined to be slow with his loans. John, here, will make the round of the warehouses and see what we have left, if anything."

"We've got one thing most others won't have," Mr. McVitty said with a kind of dauntlessness, "and that's the firm's name and reputation. That's one thing the fire didn't get."

It was time now for Mr. Chevalier and young Ames to get started. Mr. Chevalier stood up with an effort. His back was straight as ever, but it seemed hard for him to keep it that way.

" It's going to be a long pull," he said. " Practically all the money I had that wasn't in the firm was in the Franklin Company. I'm sorry for you two youngsters."

" Don't worry about us," Christine said quickly. She looked across the table at young Ames and then back at Mr. Chevalier. " John and I talked it over this morning, Uncle. It's going to make an awful load for you, putting the wedding through on Saturday. I mean," she went on, " we wouldn't mind waiting for a week or so and then we could be married much more quietly."

Mr. Chevalier drew a deep breath. For the first time that morning they saw some of the icy fire return to his eyes. He stood looking down his nose at them for a long moment before he held his arms back for the greatcoat Amber had brought in for him.

" You youngsters haven't lost your nerve—you're not trying to call it off, are you ? " he asked suddenly, and he seemed to enjoy the flush that rose in both faces. " Well, then, don't waste my time with any more such foolishness. Mrs. Chevalier has the plans all made ; and fire or no fire, I'll be God-damned if I'll alter a comma of them." He nodded sharply, clapped on his high grey hat, and marched out of the parlour with a swing of his capes. They heard his cane rap smartly as he went down the front steps.

Christine's eyes were wet, but she was laughing.

" That must be the first time Uncle ever swore before a woman," she said.

Amber said : " You mustn't mind that, Miss Kisty. He don't mean it that way." His eyes were reproachful, and as he went back into the dining-room his back conveyed a sense of injury.

Young Ames said : " It's time I got started. I've got

to tell Downey on my way downtown that I won't take his offer."

Christine lifted her face to be kissed.

"I'm so glad you decided that way, John. I wasn't going to tell you if you hadn't. But Uncle needs help so much, and he needs affection. He depends on it. He came into my room last night, after every one was in bed, to tell me that we might be very poor, all of us, if the firm failed, and I told him what you had decided, and do you know what he said?"

"No," said young Ames.

"He said I oughtn't to have thought twice about what you'd do. You weren't the kind to sell out on a friend. That's why he was willing for us to get married."

2

Higgins & Downey had opened for business, and Mr. Downey was in his office off the display room on the second floor.

"Hallo, Mr. Ames," he said. "Been down to the burned section?"

Young Ames shook his head. "Not since last night."

"It's a terrible thing to see. You know it's only a year ago since I moved up here from 107 Pearl. Lucky. I might be as bad off as Chevalier & Post if we'd stayed." He looked down at his quiet hands and grinned. "I suppose that's what brought you here. Well, I'm sorry for Chevalier's, but I'm damned glad to get you. I suppose they're going to fold. Every one knows he was all tied up in fire insurance, too."

Young Ames said: "That's why I'm staying with them, I'm afraid. They aren't going to fold, either."

Mr. Downey perked.

"My God," he said quietly. "You mean that?"

Young Ames said: "Yes."

" I see you do," Mr. Downey said crisply. " The funny thing is I still think you're smart ; but I think you're letting your feelings sway your judgment. You'll never get far if you do that, Ames. Your feelings, even good ones, won't ever pay you cash dividends." He looked down at his hands again. " You haven't seen the burned district in daylight. I suppose you're going down now. I'll tell you : I said I'd give you till New Year's to make up your mind. It still goes."

Young Ames grinned.

" Thanks, Mr. Downey," hesaid. " But there isn't a chance."

" Well," said Downey, " then I'll have to start hunting. Good luck."

3

Mr. Downey was right about the desolation of the burned district. It was a waste, and as young Ames first looked through the columns of smoke that rose everywhere among the burned stumps of buildings, he felt that he had been a fool to turn down Downey's offer at keeping the job open.

He hired two carters and their carts, and with his note-book in his hand began the round of the warehouses that Chevalier had leased or owned before the fire. All morning he met clerks and merchants hunting like himself for salvageable goods. Sometimes they worked together on the same pile of rubble. Many of the warehouses had been partly or wholly emptied, but most of this merchandise had been piled in the middle of the street. Much of it had been burned there, and a good deal had been looted before the militia took charge. Identifying what boxes were in recognisable state was a slow job. Young Ames hired a boy to bring him and the cartmen lunch and they ate on the kerb.

It was late in the afternoon, near four o'clock, when he finally closed his notebook and told the cartmen, who now numbered four : " You'll have to go on down Water Street. I'll meet you at the corner of Old Slip."

There was just room for a man to walk between the fallen walls in Gouverneur Lane. As he watched the cart-men start their somnolent horses, he remembered the snowy evening two years ago when he had waited there for Mr. Chevalier with a pair of geese for New Year's. A couple of geese, Gibbs had told him later that night, might well mark the beginning of his fortune. It seemed dubious now.

Young Ames's face was set grimly as he picked his way towards South Street between the slides of bricks. Before the fire Chevalier & Post had had five hundred thousand dollars' worth of merchandise in storage. Now all of it that was worth saving was piled in the four carts rolling slowly towards Old Slip. In his figuring it amounted to a bare seven thousand dollars' worth.

The shipping, against the gathering dusk, looked almost normal, but the city side of South Street was one long row of blackened, broken fronts. He could hear the gulls screaming high over the smoke. The wind that had been the main cause of the catastrophe had by twelve o'clock finally blown itself out and now the cold also was moderating. As he came closer to Number 42, he saw Mr. Chevalier facing the doorway. He was leaning on his cane and looking at someone inside.

4

Only the husk of the counting-house remained, for in their fall the huge roof timbers had carried all five floors with them into the cellar. The gathering sunset shone with a reminiscent fire through the sockets of the windows and a pair of pigeons pattered the charred wall-plate with puzzled feet.

By a freak of the fire, the flooring of the ground-floor hall and the stairs leading down to the cellar had been left almost intact. Just inside the front door, Mr. McVitty was sitting on an accountant's stool which had one charred and dangerous-looking leg while he directed the search that Gibbs and Pinky Finnegan were prosecuting in the jumble of burnt and broken timbers, joists, and furniture that filled the cellar.

" It'll be farther over," Mr. McVitty shouted. " Near the back wall. A little more, Gibbs."

He didn't hear young Ames come up, but Mr. Chevalier turned. There was a strained, set look in his eyes. He said abruptly, " Ames," as if he had remembered a face. Then his voice cleared and he said : " Hallo, John. You've done the warehouses ? " But he sounded tired, and the corners of his mouth were drawn.

Young Ames said, " Yes, sir," and saw that Mr. McVitty was looking at him also. He knew what they wanted to know, but it was hard to tell them. Then Pinky's yelp distracted them.

" Look here, look what I found ! "

He was holding up a slender rod to which a tangle of some sort was attached. Gibbs took it from him and said : " It's an umbrella."

" It's mine," said Mr. McVitty. " I left it hanging by the door."

" Then the safe didn't land far from it, I bet," said Pinky. " Just lift that beam a little, if you can, Mr. Gibbs, so I can get under." His tight little rump gave a wriggle as he squeezed underneath, and Mr. McVitty was impelled to shout with hoarse consternation : " You be careful there, Finnegan ! " But Pinky was not to be checked. They could hear his voice emerging hollowly : " It's like a cave down here, Mr. Gibbs."

His activity seemed to have raised some slight animation of spirits in Mr. Chevalier, and young Ames took that instant to make his report.

"I've got everything there was, sir. It's in four carts round on Old Slip now. I ought to tell the men where to deliver it."

"Number 7 Depeyster Street," Mr. McVitty said. "Cummings is there to receive it. He'll pay the men off."

Mr. Chevalier said: "It's Coster's warehouse. Mr. McVitty's made room in the loft for a temporary counting-room."

Young Ames nodded. He had leased the space himself for the firm, and was surprised that Mr. Chevalier, who usually carried every minutest detail of the firm's business in his head, should have forgotten the fact. He said: "I know. The wooden one near Water Street, isn't it?"

Mr. Chevalier said, "Yes." Young Ames could see his shoulders stiffen under the cape coat. "Did you make a tally of the stuff, John?"

"Yes." Young Ames hesitated. Mr. McVitty was waiting also, with a grey expectancy on his face. "It amounts to only about seven thousand dollars by my figures. We seem to have had the worst of the luck, though they say Ciller lost $200,000 worth of silk alone. All our warehouses went to the ground. A lot of others were only half burnt. Pruyn's been one of the lucky ones."

He stopped himself. Talking only made it worse. Mr. Chevalier was staring at Mr. McVitty. The same stillness was in their faces. In the silence young Ames heard a ship's watch hailing someone on the docks and then the slow tread of Gibbs coming up the cellar stairs. Mr. McVitty said: "Pruyn & Co. won't be sorry for us."

There was a slight glimmer in Mr. Chevalier's eyes.

"Pruyn's always hated me," he said. "He's always been trying to beat me out and never quite made it, though he's never boggled at any means, either."

Pinky's voice piped up like a goblin's in the cellar pit.

"Pruyn's had to buy out a fish store to find a place to open in," he said. "And my Uncle Mike Dolan says it stinks of herring something terrible. He says they dropped a barrel of pickled ones when they was clearing the store. He was there when it happened and he says it was an accident."

Nobody paid him any attention so he said : " I found the safe. It was beyond the umbrella."

He stopped with his head above the stairs watching his superiors. Their faces looked so serious in the gathering twilight against the blackened walls that he was surprised no one had reprimanded him. He had heard his Uncle Mike Dolan say it was going to be a bad thing for some people and there would be precious few 24 per cent dividends paid along South Street this winter ; but you didn't think of Chevalier & Post being among the ones. Even Mr. Ames looked kind of grim, and if he looked grim things must be pretty bad.

But it was Mr. Ames who broke the silence.

" Pinky," he said, " run round to Old Slip and tell the four cartmen you'll find there to take the stuff to 7 Depeyster. You'd better ride along with them and make sure they get there."

It made Pinky feel better. It was just as if Mr. Ames was taking hold of the situation. Before then everything had felt wrong. Everything had felt uncertain. And it made you uneasy, with neither Mr. Chevalier nor Mr. McVitty hopping on you for speaking out of turn. He said, " Yes, Mr. Ames," and shed dust as he galloped out.

" You keep your eye on Mr. Ames, Pink," his Uncle Mike Dolan once told him. " He's the smart one in that place, and if he wanted to become a demmycrat he could be the president of Tammany."

5

Mr. Chevalier said : " By the way, McVitty, what's Mr. Post been doing ? "

" He came into 7 Depeyster about two o'clock," said

McVitty. " I don't know where he'd been before that. I told him I was coming here to meet you, but he said there's no sense in mooning over the ashes."

Mr. Chevalier ignored the chief clerk's tone.

He said slowly, " I don't see how we're going to swing it. We've got seven thousand out of the burnt places, according to John, here. And there is fifteen hundred dollars' worth of cotton in Coster's and we have thirty-five hundred of assorted French and Swiss goods in Kane's. That's only twelve thousand dollars' worth of actual assets plus our cash balance in the bank—say fifteen thousand dollars." He spoke slowly. " I've been pretty well cleaned out, personally, McVitty. The Franklin's busted, like every other insurance company, and will only pay ten cents on the dollar. I saw Mr. Astor this morning, and he agreed to buy up my Thirteenth Street lot, though he can't give me much of a figure. But I've got to take it to keep my household running."

Mr. McVitty said : " We've got the portfolio," with a kind of diffidence.

" I know," said Mr. Chevalier. " If it wasn't for that we'd never even fold decently. But the notes there will barely cover our own notes outstanding, and a lot of bills receivable are to merchants in the same boat as we are. We can't press them, McVitty." He paused. " We've got these big Henderson shipments coming in, and the exclusive Bantry consignments. Our cash balance will hardly meet the customs bills on those shipments. By heaven, McVitty, I don't see where we're going to get cash to meet the staff payroll, let alone porterage and general expenses."

Mr. McVitty snorted.

" Never mind the payroll," he said. " If they can't wait for once they can quit and be damned to them."

Darkness was gathering around them in Number 42. The sun had set, and the sky above the roofless walls had a greenish shine of clear and unrelenting cold. Young

Ames waited a minute and then said carefully, " It seems to me it's a question of time. The cash balance will meet the customs bills on the Henderson consignment—that's due any day on the *Orpheus*. But the problem is the Bantry shipment, and how long we'll have to raise cash. By the way, sir, did you see Mr. Prime ? "

Mr. Chevalier nodded. " He couldn't give me a definite word yet. He said to come round in three days." His voice had a drag in it. It was almost as if he had difficulty in keeping up even a sense of interest. The prospect of failure was harder to face when you were in your seventies. McVitty had forgotten that, when he talked about bringing the firm through two wars and an embargo. A little wry smile that hardly showed in the dim light twisted Mr. Chevalier's mouth. There had been excitement to that, though, and close thinking : the same kind of excitement he could see in young Ames now. " Prime generally makes up his mind on the spot," he said, and left it for them to form their own conclusions.

Young Ames reached his immediately. " What if he does ? " he demanded. " You've left out a lot of assets that the fire couldn't touch."

" Have I, John ? " There was a note almost of affection in Mr. Chevalier's voice, but it was tired. " What did I leave out ? "

" The Chevalier name, for one thing," he said. " And then you've the two ships."

" I haven't forgotten them," Mr. Chevalier said. " The *Unity* lying empty at Pier 26, and the *Lily Dean* in Smith & Dimond's yard. I don't know how I'll meet the bills on her."

" Don't," said young Ames. " Sell her."

" Sell that tub ? "

They turned all at once to the doorway and saw Mr. Post, his figure stiff inside the black uncaped coat, standing there.

He said : " I've been waiting at our new counting-room,

but it's getting late so I came down here. I've been all through our figures, Chevalier. In spite of what our Mr. Ames has to say, the situation's obviously hopeless." He waited an instant. Then he said : "That's why I'm getting out."

"What do you mean, Post?" Mr. Chevalier looked up at the wooden face of his junior partner. "You can't get out now."

"Yes, I can. Our partnership was drawn up with the definite stipulation that Deming or I could withdraw any time after the first two years, taking out with us what we had put into the firm, with interest. You didn't protest when Deming resigned last year. Well, I'm resigning now."

Mr. McVitty cried : "But that's not the same, man!"

"I'm not interested in what is or is not the same. There's a balance in the bank to cover the ten thousand in cash I brought into the firm."

"You're a fool," said Mr. McVitty. "The firm's not bust yet. It will recover."

"How?" said Mr. Post coolly. "You won't be able to handle our big consignments. You needn't think you can get terms out of people like Henderson or Bantry. They aren't the kind who give terms. They mean bigger business than Chevalier's was prepared to handle in the first place. You haven't even got storage room." He uttered a short hard laugh.

It surprised them all ; no one ever remembered his showing amusement over anything before. Young Ames felt his hackles rise. "If that's what you thought, why didn't you say so?" he asked.

"I did. But the junior partner never had much to say in Chevalier & Post. Our cash was wanted, I expect, when we came in, but not our opinions. Well, it happens I've a good opening for my money now. I can get a partnership where I'll really have something to say in running the business."

Mr. Chevalier had maintained an almost frozen silence. But now he stepped suddenly in front of Gibbs and faced Mr. Post. For a moment young Ames thought he was going to lift his cane, but he planted the ferrule on the floor and leaned hard on it with both hands.

" There is nothing to keep you here, then, Mr. Post," he said in his old quick voice. " Not even regrets."

Mr. Post paused. Then he said, " I agree." He turned through the empty doorway. " By the way, Chevalier," he said from the sidewalk, " I've attached the funds at the bank."

Mr. Chevalier blocked the doorway. " Let him go," he said. " I think we'd better go ourselves too," he added quietly, " and I wish you'd come along with me to 7 Depeyster. What are you doing, Gibbs ? "

Gibbs was bending over to pick up something white. He said deliberately, " It's a handkerchief. It seems to me that Mr. Post must have dropped it. I'd better take it after him."

He turned towards Old Slip as they started north, and though he seemed to walk unhurriedly, the length of his stride was in the sound of his footsteps.

6

" Mr. Post," said Mr. Chevalier, " has put the finish on us, I'm afraid." He looked towards the stove that had been set up in the middle of the loft. " Can't we have a little more heat out of that, McVitty ? "

Mr. McVitty shook his head. The stovepipe ascended through a mere hole in the roof and Mr. McVitty would allow no one to open the draughts. In his opinion the mind of man could have devised no better method of burning up the rest of New York.

The temporary counting-room was the second story loft of a narrow wooden warehouse wedged between two larger brick buildings on the north side of Depeyster Street. One reached it by a rickety open flight of steps that went up the front of the building. There was, of course, no gas ; they had to use candles, and with the rest of the staff gone home the one now burning on Mr. McVitty's desk and the two on Mr. Chevalier's table together barely showed bales of upland cotton piled against the back wall, the long planks set up on high trestles to serve the clerks as desks, or the boxes Mr. McVitty had had ranged in a low partition to form an office for the partners.

Mr. Chevalier said : "Then let's go over and sit near the damned thing."

There were spots of colour in his cheeks and his nose showed its curve. He looked better than he had, and Mr. McVitty, who had a habit of hissing through his teeth sometimes, when he saw his way out of a tangle in the books, began now softly to hiss.

"You know," said Mr. Chevalier, appropriating the high stool Mr. McVitty had carried back from Number 42, "this makes me think a little of our early days, McVitty, when I had my desk right in the counting-room." He smiled briefly at his chief clerk. "That was quite a while ago, and in the meantime I seem to have become an old man." He drew a deep breath. "You know I never really liked Post," he said. Then he looked across at young Ames. "What were you going to say about the *Lily Dean*, John ? I never thought of her as an asset, and I've tried to sell her a couple of times, but every one knows she's a slow one."

Young Ames said : "You sent me up there when they hauled her out to get Dimond's estimate on recoppering her hull." He felt his excitement coming back. He had seen the big barque hauled up out of the water, inert and monstrous and somewhat pathetic, like a whale washed out on a beach. The clamour of the yard surrounded her like watching gulls—the steady hammer of caulking mallets, the yelled orders, the long rasp of saws from the pits. But Dimond, who had a reputation for being able to spot the weakness in a ship, said that the *Lily Dean* had a beautiful hull. " He said her frame was all live oak and that though Webb built her he must have taken the hull off one of Eckford's old models and that Eckford would never have made a barque of her, not with her tonnage. He said she was undersparred. He said he wouldn't guarantee a flier if he put the right sticks in her, but Eckford's ships could all move."

Mr. Chevalier smiled. He knew the lure of ships to any merchant.

" How does that mean cash for us, John, when we couldn't even pay for the job of altering her ? "

" I bet we could get Dimond to do it on spec," young Ames said. " We'd value her, then he'd take the coppering off what she brings, and we'd split the profits over and above the two figures. Then with the *Unity*—we haven't chartered her to any one, and we're not likely to get a charter for her in a hurry. Why couldn't we make her up a cargo of goods out of the fire and send them down to South America ? We'll buy up what we can ourselves first, and then offer the rest of her hold to any other merchants that want to get rid of their fire goods."

Mr. Chevalier said : " Yes, I agree with all that, John, and you can go see Dimond to-morrow—if he'll do it on spec. But where are we going to get cash ? I'm stripped."

Young Ames looked up at him. There was something odd about Mr. Chevalier perched on an accountant's stool. He grinned. " You said the insurance companies will only pay ten cents on the dollar. But that's fifty thousand. Post may have forgotten that. It's just about half a cargo, and that's what I figured for us to put on the *Unity*. I figure too that we'll be able to buy cheap enough to make it pay double. Those goods are all odds and ends, but they're better stuff for the most part than generally gets into the South American trade and they'll go better. We'll borrow on the insurance. Even Prime ought to be willing to lend on that. The main thing is for us to beat the starting gun on the others. To-morrow, with no room anywhere for storage, everybody ought to tumble over themselves to get a little cash in hand, but we've got the *Unity's* empty hold and we'll shove the stuff aboard her as fast as we buy it."

His face was flushed under the freckles, and Mr. Chevalier suddenly remembered his father picking out the flaws in his first schemes. Mr. Chevalier's father had always been a slow and careful operator, but young Ames was like himself.

" John," he said, " all you've said makes sense to me ; we ought to be able to swing it ; but we're still looking for the cash Post is relieving us of. As he has a right to do, of course," he added, and Mr. McVitty snorted, took snuff, and sneezed like a minute gun. " Good riddance," he said.

Young Ames tried to make his voice sound cool. " I've got a couple of thousand in cash," he said. " I think Mrs. Funk in Pittsburgh's in a position now to buy out my share in her business, say fifteen hundred dollars. It's worth more, but she'll have difficulty raising the cash. Say I put three thousand into Chevalier's. Maybe Mr. McVitty could put up some, and you'll have a little something out of the Thirteenth Street lot Mr. Astor's buying."

Mr. McVitty gave a start. He looked slightly embarrassed. " I've got a little put away," he admitted. " Maybe ten thousand, but the firm's welcome to it."

Mr. Chevalier continued to look at them both for a long moment before he spoke.

" Thanks," he said. " It's good to have friends. But I can't let you take the risk, John. You've got to think of Kisty."

Young Ames grinned.

" She'll stand it all right."

Mr. McVitty clicked his snuffbox. " If you're considering my sister, she's a very economical woman," he remarked.

Mr. Chevalier smiled. " I'm sure of it, McVitty." He went on with a slight halting in his words. " I must be getting old. This morning I was ready to quit. I saw very little hope. But John's put life in us, McVitty. He and Post," he added with a wry grin.

Young Ames started to say, " The main thing now's to move fast, sir . . ." But Mr. Chevalier raised his hand. " You don't give me a chance to finish, John. If you're going to put this much into the firm—it will amount to eight thousand dollars for you, John. If you do, it's only just that both of you have a word in the handling of the business. We'll incorporate, and you'll both hold limited partnerships, in the amount of your investment. That will be better for you if the new firm holds." His blue eyes looked at them in turn. " What do you say ? "

" I say we won't fold," said Mr. McVitty, and helped himself to snuff.

Mr. Chevalier said : " You've been a good friend, McVitty." He turned to young Ames : " How about it, John ? You're coming into my family anyway, and I've always planned to have you in the firm if I could get you."

Young Ames nodded. He found it hard to say anything. He was putting all his eggs in one basket, a pretty worn basket at that. But if he could make the eggs hatch he would be at the top of a lot higher heap than he would if he had taken Higgins & Downey's offer. Thinking of Downey, he wondered if he couldn't get him to pay them something on account as he would be the chief buyer anyway of the Henderson shipment. Maybe enough to cover the customs. They needed cash, they could shave the profits for a while. Damn it for being so late, he thought. He had a lot to do. And then he'd have to find someone to act as supercargo of the *Unity.* They'd want a good man, someone who had some interest in Chevalier's.

He looked up with a start, under the impression that Mr. Chevalier was talking to him ; but Mr. Chevalier was only saying to Mr. McVitty, " I wish we had a little of the old brandy here. Or any brandy, for that matter ! "

It was Gibbs, coming up the outside stairs and through the board door, who answered them. As young Ames saw him against the opening, with the snow falling beyond in the darkness and his hat and shoulders dusted with it, he knew who he'd get for the *Unity's* supercargo. Gibbs had always wanted to travel.

He had cut his right hand, and he carried a bottle under the other arm, and one of his eyes was puffy ; but there was none of the usual sardonic gleam on his face. He wore an air of complete and mellow satisfaction.

" It turned out it wasn't Post's handkerchief after all," he said, " and somehow or other he started calling me a liar. But he was all right, once he had apologised, so I got him a cab and sent him on to Pruyn's."

" Pruyn's ! " said Mr. McVitty.

Gibbs nodded and licked his barked knuckles.

" He's joining Pruyn & Company. At least that's what I thought he said."

" Then the firm damned well can't be allowed to fold. I'll sell my house and my horses before I'll let that happen now. I'll live in the Five Points," said Mr. Chevalier. " Howard, is that a bottle of brandy ? "

" It is," said Gibbs. " Do you want any of it ? "

" I do," said Mr. Chevalier. " I want to drink to the health and prosperity of Chevalier & Co. Damn it, McVitty, I suppose there isn't a glass here."

" No, there's not," Mr. McVitty said, obviously chagrined to be caught out in one want. But then his eye brightened. " The new inkwells came in," he said, " and that Finnegan's forgot to fill them."

" By George," said Mr. Chevalier, and he opened the bottle and went along the desk filling the inkwells. " Here's four of them. I give you Chevalier & Co."

Mr. McVitty echoed him. It was obvious that he couldn't get over it. He looked almost bashful. " & Co.," he repeated.

7

Dick, the Chevaliers' coloured coachman, drove the brougham round on the tick of time. He was wearing the maroon livery with the ivory satin facings, for it was the nineteenth of December, 1835, and at one o'clock in St. John's Chapel, Christine Chevalier had been married to John Ames by Bishop Onderdonck, and Dick, with Amber and the other servants, had been there to see it.

There was a portentous expectancy on his broad face, but he kept his eyes on the horses' ears, as a high-class coachman should. The greys were restive ; they kept lifting a little with their forefeet ; and Dick had to keep saying, " Hesh, you ! " softly at them. He knew the coachmen on all the other carriages that ranked the kerb were watching him with critical alertness ; he had the dignity of the family to maintain ; yet he couldn't help his eyes rolling round as the front door opened to an outpouring of voices. He couldn't help smiling.

For there were Mr. and Mrs. Chevalier, with the guests crowding the hall behind them and looking out the front windows. And here in her going-away clothes came Miss Christine with her hand on Mr. Ames's arm. And she certainly did look stylish, Dick thought, touching his hat with the thumb of his whip hand and hissing " Hesh ! " again at those greys. They seemed to have caught the frolic in their feet, and they danced a little as the springs swayed—that was Miss Christine getting in. The tall dark gentleman, Mr. Gibbs, who'd been best man, was standing so as to shield her from a prancing young lady who was throwing rice. Then the springs gave again, and that was Mr. Ames.

Dick brought the greys gently on to the bits. His gloved thumb that held the snapper of the long fawn-coloured whiplash became as delicately ready as a harpist's. Mr. Gibbs was leaning through the door and saying, " Good luck." And then there was Miss Christine's voice, just a little throaty, to thank him : " I think you were a perfect best man, Mr. Gibbs." And there was Mr. Ames, sounding a little uncertain : " Good-bye, Howard, and thanks." And then mercifully the door closed and Dick swung the greys out and sent them on a spanking trot down Laight Street.

He turned left on Greenwich, passing along the Park ; and the guests were still there, waiting and laughing and calling good-bye, and it was the perfect end of a wedding.

He waited till he was well out of sight before he answered the whistle in the speaking tube. He put his ear against it ; and it was Mr. Ames saying, " You're headed the wrong way, Dick. We want to go to Bleecker Street. To our own house."

Dick put his lips close and said, " Yessuh, Mr. Ames. I'se gwine turn hyere." Of course he was going wrong, but he'd thought it all out himself last night, lying awake in bed. If getting his business burned out hadn't stopped Mr. Chevalier giving Miss Christine a slam-bang wedding, Dick certainly wasn't going to let the guests guess the same fire was keeping the bridal couple from starting on a bridal tour. No, he'd start out as if he were heading for the steamboat pier on Cortlandt Street . . . but it was all right to turn now, left on Franklin, up Broadway and over on Bleecker.

8

They stood on the front step watching Dick wheel the greys and start back towards St. John's Park. Up in the next block they heard the clanging from a blacksmith's anvil. Christine said, " Poor Dick ! He doesn't really think he ought to leave me here ! "

The house, far up on Bleecker Street, was tiny ; and they felt very conspicuous there, while a small group of urchins watched them from a corner. Christine said : " Delia ought to be here." And young Ames lifted his hand to the knocker for the second time. His eyes met hers with a kind of panic, and he saw the hint of a dimple come into her cheek. She said gravely : " It must be a habit of the house."

The first time they had come to see it they had been kept waiting, with the same audience of urchins, while the agent tried to explain to himself why the front door key did not fit the lock. But now, all crimson with apologies, Delia opened the door, and Christine whispered, " Carry me over, John."

The gas was lighted in the hall, and candles shone on the mantel of the little parlour. A bright fire burned there, and the house smelled warm and clean ; and holding Christine in his arms he became conscious of her warmth, and it suddenly occurred to him with a kind of wonder that everything here was his.

She kissed him while he still held her, her lips quick and tender, and she said, as he set her down, " Don't look so surprised. It's not complimentary. Did you think I was made of fluff ? " She put her hand in his as they went into the parlour. " I'm not, you see. You needn't be afraid I'll break, or blow away."

In the dining-room, the table was set for their supper, with a bottle, decked out in a huge white ribbon, standing in the centre of it. The card bore Mr. Chevalier's stiff spidery handwriting and Christine bent over to read it : " To Kisty and John, for their wedding supper, with my love."

Young Ames saw her eyes grow moist.

" It's the Château Margaux," she said. " Oh, John, are you as happy as I am ? "

Before he could answer, the door from the kitchen stairs opened with violence. " Will you be wanting to eat yet ? " asked Delia, bursting practically upon them. " Or when will you then ? " she demanded, becoming suddenly confused.

" We'll have supper at six, Delia," Christine said quietly. " And please put out two claret glasses."

" Them with the small waists and the big feet on them ? " Delia asked in awe ; and with a kind of gulp she bolted back down to the kitchen.

They went back to the parlour and lingered there, and Christine asked him if he remembered this or that person at the wedding, and she asked about Gibbs. " He's kind. That was what I thought the first time I saw him, that he was very kind." She looked up, still holding his arm.

Young Ames had never thought of Gibbs as kind, but he saw now what she meant. It was Gibbs who had remembered that Ames's clothes had all been burnt out and who had shopped all Friday for him, somehow getting clothes that fitted, while Ames himself was on the run to Dimond, to Downey, and to Mr. Prime with Mr. Chevalier. They had got things rolling now. Perhaps Gibbs was kind. " He said he was going away," Christine said.

" He's going out on the *Unity* as supercargo. I shouldn't wonder if he stayed somewhere there. We could use an agency in Valparaiso. Gibbs would be good in a Latin country."

" You'll miss him," Christine said.

Young Ames said, " Yes." He was thinking of the first days, and she saw suddenly that this would be the moment for her to leave him. " I'm going upstairs, to take my things off. I won't be long," she said.

They had an instant of hesitancy, in which her smile became tremulous, and her eyes suddenly shy. Afterwards, when he was alone, he prowled the downstairs, fingering the wedding presents, and he surprised himself and gave Delia a fright by appearing in the kitchen. He tried to cover it by asking if everything was all right, like a proper householder ; and Delia gasped, " Yis," in a frightened way, just as a potful of soup boiled over and nearly quenched the fire entirely.

An acanthus tree grew in the back yard. Christine was planning to put a bench under it and plant flowers there next spring. But there was only raw dirt in which some scraggy grass grew tuftily, and in the midst of it, inexplicably, the imprint of a bare and adult human foot. It made him think of the picture of Robinson Crusoe on the beach ; and in a way he too was starting a new life from scratch, though his commitments were heavier than Crusoe's had been.

He wasn't afraid of the business. He knew what he was going to do. There you took things as they came and beat them if you could, or else you failed. And if you failed, you wrote it off, and made a new start somewhere else. But now . . .

He looked up at the back windows of the little house. Christine was beckoning to him to come in. She was waiting for him by the fire, with sherry ready on a small tray beside her. She had changed her dress to a house gown of a deep soft rose that set off the creamy warmth of her skin and her black hair. There was a kind of hush upon her, and her dark eyes looked up at his as if to ask for his approval.

THE   END